FAREWELL,
    MY SLIGHTLY
    TARNISHED
    HERO

Also by Edwin Corley

SIEGE
THE JESUS FACTOR

FAREWELL,
MY SLIGHTLY
TARNISHED
HERO

By Edwin Corley

DODD, MEAD & COMPANY
New York

ISBN: 0–396–06364–0
Library of Congress Catalog Card Number: 74–162616
Printed in the United States of America
by The Haddon Craftsmen, Inc., Scranton, Penna.

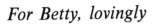

For Betty, lovingly

It's a funny thing—the past. Maybe there isn't really any past. Maybe it's all back there waiting for you to find it. . . .

—JOHN P. MARQUAND

PROLOGUE

SPRING in New York is often a grim and foggy time. Cold gray mists tumble in from the river, and distant hoot-owl noises fill the early morning air as oil-stained tugs cluster around the piers. Sometimes you get the feeling of being lost far away in space, of being cast adrift in the fog with the heavens blotted out and no buoy bell to warn you of the reef. Those are the bad days, the days when you tear April's calendar dates from the pad and leap ahead to May, half believing that this will bring the sunshine a little sooner. And, during the nights, you are filled with a dismal, disconsolate hopelessness.

Sometimes you find that you are not only adrift in space, but also in time. You begin to feel that your yesterdays never happened, and that tomorrow came a long time ago. But sanity is preserved by loss of memory.

I was not so lucky. I can remember some things that never happened.

Like so many other millions, I have seen the three films John Calvin Lewis completed. But I never met him. Johnny had been dead more than a year when I returned to the United States from my Air Force tour in Tokyo.

We had many mutual friends, however, although not at the same time. Those who were his friends in the mid fifties, at least some of them, are my friends now, and so I suppose it was logical that when Film Arts decided to make his life story, that I would be chosen to work on the screenplay. My fascination with the motion picture form and its personalities is no secret among publishers or producers.

Our preliminary story conferences were held in Hollywood, and finally I insisted on returning to New York City where I am usually able to keep some slight hold on reality. I holed up in the Great Northern Hotel, an affectation inherited from William Saroyan, who wrote *The Time of Your Life* there in six days, back in 1939. *The Johnny Lewis Story* took me somewhat longer, but eventually, in April of this year, it was finished, and now I can stretch contentedly beside the small, kidney-shaped pool of the Hollywood Hawaiian Hotel and wait for the first day of shooting.

To while away the time, I have been re-examining the events of the past spring, trying to separate out the things which I really remember from the things I could only have imagined. When writing an extended script like this, you immerse yourself completely into the life stream of another person, and it is only natural to lose a little of your own identity in the process . . . but I am afraid this facile explanation is not sufficient to account for the many things that I remember, but have no right to remember.

One might say easily, "You were dreaming." Perhaps. But how can dreams account for notebooks full of facts and dates and things that Johnny Lewis said, pages crammed with rich details that are tangibly, incredibly complete and detailed recollections of a friendship with a boy I never met? I have no answer. I am only bewildered and perhaps a little frightened and, above all, grateful that this experience was granted to me. I cannot attempt to explain it. But I can remember it for you.

NEW YORK

CHAPTER
ONE

These are memories. They never happened.

W HEN I saw Johnny Lewis standing outside
the Davega store on 42nd Street, looking at the camera display
in the window, I knew there was something subtly wrong. First,
let me tell you how he looked. He had no face. I mean, he had
a face, but it was blurred in my vision. It was as if I had caught
him in the blind spot of my eye. I had no doubt who he was,
but that was because I knew, not because I could see his face,
which was hazy and out of focus.

I knew that, although the time was now, it was also somehow
1952, and things were still hot in Korea, and Ike was going to
run and win. And as Johnny looked up at me shyly, through
his thick glasses, I saw a pose that has since become famous,

but that in 1952 had only been seen by his friends and the bartender at Downey's. Years later, when it was all over, a Hollywood columnist would fill her eulogy for Johnny Lewis with drivel about how much he looked like a little boy, peering up through those thick specs, and how naive and full of beautiful illusions he had been and how it was almost wonderful that he would never be robbed of them. Johnny would have been the first to spit in her eye and tell her what a pile of horse manure those sentiments were, but of course, he never got the chance.

So, seeing that characteristic pose of his for the first time, and when I did not feel the chill that should have come from viewing this ghost, this boy whose life had touched mine only after his death, I knew firmly and without reservation that I was asleep.

Ike would run and win, and Korea would fade into Suez and Vietnam, and Kennedy would be elected and assassinated, and Johnson and Nixon would take office and time would flow past us until it became spring of this year and I would be hard at work in my room on the ninth floor of the Great Northern, writing a screenplay about a boy who was dead, tragically and in youth. So I knew, as I stood on 42nd Street, that when I had gone to sleep this dismal April night, Johnny Lewis was a dead and famous personality of the past, not a living, disheveled boy staring into a Davega window looking at cameras he could not afford.

He walked in a slouch, both hands jammed in the pockets of his dirty khaki trousers. His shoes were scuffed and unshined. It was brisk enough for a coat, but he did not wear one. His hair was dark, with little flashes of gold, and the wind ruffled it as he moved.

I followed him into Bryant Park behind the Public Library.

As I crossed Sixth Avenue, I stepped in front of a taxi. It blared a raucous horn at me. I looked real enough to the driver. If the car struck me, would I die?

14

I didn't wait to find out.

When I reached the park, Johnny Lewis had disappeared.

I walked around for a few minutes, and then went away. To Somewhere. Someplace. I don't remember where.

Maybe I was turned off until I was needed again.

Then it was summer, still in 1952 (although it was also still a cold, blustery spring now and there was rain outside my ninth floor window of the Great Northern Hotel.) I wandered into a Blarney Stone Bar on Eighth Avenue. Johnny was there, in a corner, squinting up at the TV set and sipping at a beer.

The bar was air-conditioned and cool. Outside, heat shimmered up from the baking pavement.

I went over.

Johnny Lewis looked up. He spoke to me. His voice was husky, but high, and something in it made the hackles on my neck rise.

"You want a beer?" he asked.

I nodded. Johnny raised two fingers, and the bartender brought over a couple of glasses. The beer was cold, and tasted sharp and bitter.

Raising his glass, Johnny said, "Here's how."

I toasted with him.

"You know who I am," he said. He was not asking a question.

"Lewis," I said. "John Calvin Lewis. You're from Iowa."

He nodded as I spoke, chuckling to himself over each word. Then he took something from his pocket and pressed it, and there was a *click* and a silver flash and he held an open knife, grinding its point into the polished bar. The noise was hollow and sounded like beavers chewing up the wood.

"So who are *you?*" he asked softly.

"You never heard of me. Ed Corley. And if I told you where I'm from, you'd never believe me."

His face was white and strained.

"You'd be surprised," he said. "I *do* believe you. You're like something weird, do you know that?"

"Could be," I said.

"Excuse me," he said. He reached out with the knife and touched the back of my wrist with the point. He pressed and the skin stood out whitely around the blade. He twisted it slightly and there was a sharp sting and a ribbon of my blood trickled down my hand and spattered on the floor.

Johnny looked sick. He closed the knife and put it back in his pocket.

"I thought you'd go *pop*," he said. "Like a balloon. Pop. Disappear. Just like you did that day in the Park."

I took out my handkerchief and wrapped it around my wrist. He waited, gripping the bar with both hands.

Finally, I asked, "What day?"

"Couple months back. You put the tail on me down on 42nd Street. I shook you in Bryant Park. Then you disappeared. Not faded away or ducked in somewhere. Just, *pop!* I mean, for real. The air rushed in where you weren't anymore, and it sounded like a balloon popping."

Truthfully, I said, "I didn't know about that."

"Man," he said, "it was like real eerie."

"Do you want me to go away?"

He shook his head. I noticed a ring of sweat around his mouth, although it was cool there in the bar.

"I'm not sure what I want," he told me, "but I think I'd rather have you where I can see you."

"In that case," I said, "how about another beer?"

"Only if you're springing. I just went through my allowance for the day."

"Allowance?"

"I'm on a tight budget. No telling how long before something

16

starts coming in. So when I take off from the rooming house, I give myself two bucks and stash the rest in the closet down in my extra pair of shoes. I just went through the last of today's slice, so no movie and no more beer."

"You'll get another beer, anyway."

He grinned at me. "I figured I would."

We had another beer and I ordered sandwiches. The Blarney Stone whips up a pastrami on roll that beggars description. The mustard doesn't kid around.

Johnny gave me a hard time about the sandwich. "I spent my two bucks," he insisted, "and I don't deserve any sandwich. I don't really even have any right to this beer."

When the pastrami sandwich came, though, he ate it in about three bites. I could almost see his conscience booting him in the pants.

"What do you want?" he asked, blotting mustard from his chin with a paper napkin. "If you're queer for my body, I'd better warn you, I don't like fags."

"Don't worry," I said. "You're not my type. Besides, I like my wife better."

"So what's the bit? Are you writing a book or something?"

"You'd be surprised."

"How wrong can you be?" he shot back. "Nothing in this big old world can surprise me any more. I wouldn't be surprised if you told me you just arrived straight from hell. So what's with the watchbird act?"

I decided to give it to him straight. Or, at least, as straight as I had it myself.

"I'm writing a screenplay about your life," I said. "It's more than twenty years from now, and the kids are still crazy for you. So the studio wants to cash in on it."

"It's 1952," he said.

"Right *now* it's 1952," I said. "But for me, it's also a long time from now. It's like I'm dreaming all this. Maybe I am. Maybe they've got me locked up somewhere. Maybe I went crazy from reading too many old movie magazines about you."

He squinted at me through those foot-thick specs. "Do you mean you came back from the future?"

"No. I didn't come back. I'm still there. But I'm here, too. I can't explain it. It's like I was having a walking dream."

He looked at the blood stain on my handkerchief. "You don't bleed like a dream."

"I can't explain. I don't know the answer myself."

"So," he said, "your story is that you want to put the glom on me."

"Pardon?"

"Give me the eyeball. Follow me around. Dig up the real facts for your screenplay."

"For a while," I answered. "I don't know how or why it's possible, but since it *is,* I'd like to try."

Johnny draped himself over the edge of the bar and looked at me from the corners of his eyes.

"Twenty years," he said quietly.

"That's right."

"So I was real big then."

"Not was. You *will* be."

"Acting?"

"Yes."

"Movie acting?"

"Yes."

He rocked back and forth, hitting his thighs with sharp, slapping sounds.

"I knew it!" he cried. "I knew I'd make it! I always knew I would! That'll show those silly pukes!"

"Who?"

"Those movie bastards. I did extra work out on the Coast,

18

you know? Son of a bitch, an extra is nothing more than a movable prop. Three of you, get over there. Hey, Shorty, stop mugging the camera. Somebody get that kid with the glasses out of there. They're kicking reflections right in the lens." He spat. "Those bastards!"

I ordered more beer and we drank it slowly. Johnny rocked back and forth on his stool, laughing to himself.

"You know," he said suddenly, "I grew up on a farm. I mean, I worked with my hands, you know?" He shoved them in my face. They still wore calluses and looked hard as granite. "Well, I finally got out there to UCLA, and those *brothers,* those fraternity halfwits, they started hazing me. Plowboy, they called me. Plowboy of the Western World." He chuckled. "Boy, I mean to say I enlightened those bastards. Wham! Bam! Thank you ma'am! Right in their sneering kissers! I went through those delicate little boys like a ripsaw through a pine plank."

"So they kicked you out of school."

"*Invited* me out. Shit, I was going anyway. Who needs a law degree to *act?* And by then I knew that acting was all I ever wanted to do. So, in twenty years, I'm big, huh? By then, half of those pricks will have had their asses shot off in the army and the rest will be fat and bald and stuck with six kids. The Johnny Lewis Story. . . ." Now he was almost singing to himself. "The Jolson Story, The Babe Ruth Story, The Johnny Lewis Story, the Johnny Lewis. . . ."

He stopped. The bar had gone dead quiet. Or so it seemed. Actually, there was a lot of noise. The TV, the street sounds outside, the bartender rattling glasses, two drunks arguing. But it seemed quiet.

"There is something fishy about you," he said. "I don't know if it scares me or not."

"It sure in hell scares me."

"Look," he said, "let's shake this joint. What time is it? Quarter of one? Let's head down to the Village. Ever been to the Circle in the Square?" I shook my head. Johnny was caught up in some wild excitement now. "I hear Gerry Page is rehearsing a new show there. The stage manager's a good friend of mine. He'll slip us in. This wonderful dame, she's not pretty the way you say 'pretty,' but my God, she's *beautiful!* I tell you, she is somebody. She's doing *Summer and Smoke.* She was a seamstress or something and Joe Quintero dug her out of the woodwork. I bet you never heard of her."

"Don't bet too much," I said.

"Aha!" he exalted. "So she made it too? Great! Wonderful! Say, what the hell, let's get moving, huh?"

I stood up, wondering what it would be like to see the old Circle Theater, when it was still on Sheridan Square, but then the scene whipped away from me and vanished into the past where it belonged and, sure enough, I was in the Great Northern Hotel, asleep just seconds ago, but now fully awake with the night glare of the city outside my window and a strange, unexplained odor of stale beer in the air.

When Ned Barker, of Film Arts Studio, approached me to write the Johnny Lewis screenplay, he had already laid out the ground rules through my agent.

"Tell Corley this isn't the usual whitewash with 'Glorioski, Sandy, ain't people wonderful' crap. Baby, we're competing with television, and I want this to be a flick they *have* to show in theaters. Get the kids the hell in there with their three bucks. These days you've got to show them *screwing!* Try putting that on the boob tube. We're going to make a *movie* movie! That's the bit, Elvira, and lay it on the line with Corley. No fancy dialogue. Get their pants off in the first reel. The real stuff. Get inside Johnny. Rip his guts out. Find out what makes him tick and show him scuffling, get what I mean?"

My agent, who is a lady as well as a woman, smiled sweetly over her eggs benedict.

"Ned," she said softly, "knowing you as I do, I felt I might not be able to transmit your instructions with all the . . . shall we say, color? You have a forceful, delightful way of expressing yourself. So I have taken the liberty of recording your comments with my handy-dandy purse cassette recorder, which I am now shutting off. Rest assured, I will let Edwin hear the tape in its entirety."

"Elvira," breathed Ned Barker, "you are a wonder."

"That I am," she beamed. "Now, Ned, why don't you fuck off like a dear boy while I eat my lunch?"

John Calvin Lewis has been variously described as the "liveliest dead actor in the movies," the "Spook of Sunset Strip" and—in the funeral eulogy delivered by a Baptist minister in his home town of Centerville, Iowa, as "a star whose brightness will never fade. After all, God is directing the production."

Not since the hysteria surrounding the funeral of Rudolph Valentino had there been such mass excitement about the death of an actor. Johnny Lewis had only appeared in three motion pictures. Two were still unreleased, and represented some seven million dollars tied up in celluloid that might be suddenly worthless. There is a tradition in Hollywood that pictures featuring actors recently dead continue the process by dying themselves at the box office.

The studio had little choice. Johnny Lewis *had* to remain alive. Neatest trick of the week. Because I, and his friends, and indeed the whole world, all knew that Johnny had piled his Harley-Davidson motorcycle up against a concrete abutment near San Diego, and that there had been barely enough remaining to bury, let alone make an appearance on "What's My Line?"

Never underestimate a publicist. They pulled it off. If necrophilia ever becomes a major religion in this country, you can thank the flacks who set out to build the Johnny Lewis legend in those days following his death.

Rumors began to spread.

Johnny isn't dead! A buddy riding double with him had been thrown into the abutment and was so severely mutilated that he couldn't be told from Johnny. "Come back, Johnny!" wrote thousands of fans. "We know you're in hiding because your beautiful face was damaged. But it doesn't matter to us. We love you no matter what you look like. Don't hide, Johnny, don't be afraid."

One afternoon in Hollywood, trying to blot out the California smog with a parade of Navy Grogs from Don the Beachcomber, Ned Barker and I had a brief but violent argument about this manipulation of public grief.

"Don't shit yourself, Red," said the producer, sucking at his Grog through its ice-encased straw. "Public grief is the best kind. Don't think for a minute that those Kennedy funerals weren't put-up affairs. My God, when they put JFK under! Those guys playing 'Hail To The Chief' at half tempo. And that walk across the Potomac to Arlington. What was that if not laying on the schmaltz? You know, confidentially," and with this, Ned Barker leaned forward confidentially, managing to sweep his necktie across the plate of ramaki, "I was a little surprised that de Gaulle used the bridge. Personally, I thought he'd stroll across the water!" He leaned back and roared with laughter. Nearby, a smooching couple sat up in startled fright and earnestly began discussing Ronald Reagan. Ned Barker had obviously favored me with one of his favorite and more disgusting analogies, and I had to wait until he had stopped enjoying it himself for us to get back on the track of the story conference.

"Johnny Lewis was a good actor," I said, "and that's all. The kid wasn't a giant. He wasn't even what you and I call star quality. He had a big raw talent with limitations. The best thing that ever happened to him was that he died before the odds had a chance to catch up with him."

Ned wagged his big forefinger in my direction. "Oh, hell," he said, "don't you think I haven't heard that before? You wanna know what Bogart said about the kid?" I knew what Bogart had said, but agreed that I wouldn't mind Ned repeating it. He said, "Bogie gave a quote, 'Johnny had a great sense of timing. He went at just the right time. If he'd lived, he'd never have been able to top his publicity.' How about that?" Ned snorted through the straw at his Navy Grog. "Look who was talking! Bogie's grossed more since he died himself than *Gone With The Wind*. And who's to say that's wrong? You? What the hell have *you* done for the world? Wrote a half-baked novel about blacks taking over Manhattan? Told us the atom bomb doesn't exist? This one project, which you do not deserve and would not have a shot at were it not for my feeble-minded wife who owns fifty-one percent of the company, will let you speak to more people than Shakespeare ever suckered into a theater during the past four hundred years. But do you have gratitude? To me? Or to that poor kid who had to take a dive into a concrete wall to make it big? Like hell you do! With raw talents and limitations you greet me! I told Elly, what do you want with some fancy-schmancy New York writer? Aren't there enough good writers starving in Beverly Hills? But no, nothing would do but that we import Mr. Off Broadway himself to give *The Johnny Lewis Story* honesty and class. Honesty and class you wouldn't know if it came up and bit you on the fanny. Ah, drink your drink and don't talk no more."

I wanted to snap back, but he had hit me a low blow with his crack about Elly Barker, who had indeed forced me down her husband's unwilling throat. Elly had played the lead in an Off-Broadway Provincetown Playhouse production of my modern version of *Hedda Gabler,* and from that unprofitable experience had carried away some flattering but undeserved notions about my talent and integrity.

Ned must have seen the despair rummaging at the ordinarily placid features of my face, because his eyes softened and he reached over and slapped me on the shoulder.

"Go ahead, baby," he said, "drink your Navy Grog like a nice little writer. You're a good boy. I ain't mad at you. Drink up. It's on the budget."

I guess a month or two had passed back in 1952 when I found myself there again, in that New York which was apart from my lonely vigil in the Great Northern Hotel. The sun was high in the sky, but it was still morning and as I stepped out from the curb at 57th Street and Broadway, two things happened at once.

A bus bore down on me, air brakes hissing angrily, horn blaring—and a strong hand caught my elbow and pulled me back onto the sidewalk.

"Hey, you got to keep on your toes," said John Calvin Lewis. "Those mothers will run right over you."

I could feel my heart pounding. I nodded my thanks, and since it was expected of me, fell into step with Johnny as he stepped off down Broadway.

"Making the TV rounds," he explained. "There's a part on U.S. Steel, and another one on Kraft. I don't have a chance, because they don't like to cast except through agents, but what the hell? It's better than sitting on your ass waiting for something to drop down the chimney."

He handed me a cigarette. I lit it. We walked in silence for a while.

"You know," he said, as we crossed 53rd Street, "you caused one hell of a ruckus that time at the Blarney Stone. I don't dare go in there any more. They figure I'm hooked up with a counterfeiter."

Shocked, I said, "Counterfeiter? Why, in God's name?"

Johnny grinned. "*You* paid the tab."

"So?"

"So let's take a look at the money in your pockets."

I never carry my money in a wallet; only a wad in my left side trouser pocket. Puzzled, I hauled it out and handed it to Johnny. He examined the bills carefully.

"This one's all right," he said. "So is this." He held a third bill up to me. "But here's one that will get you in a peck of trouble."

"It looks like any other twenty to me," I said.

"Yeah? Listen to this: Series 1963A, Henry H. Fowler, Secretary of the Treasury. Where do you think you'll end up, old buddy, in 1952, spending money that wasn't even printed until 1963? See, these others are okay. Series 1950. John W. Snyder, Secretary of the Treasury. They're fine. But old Fowler will land us both in jail."

Despite myself, I found laughter spilling out.

"Okay, Johnny," I said. "Any more tabs I pick up, I'll check the money first. Honest Injun."

"It's not as funny as you think," he said grimly. "For one thing, I had a hell of a time explaining *you.*"

"Sorry about that."

"They thought *I* had passed the bill. It wasn't that no one saw you with me when you were there. It's just that after you were gone, no one could really remember you. It went all fuzzy for them. Like you weren't plugged into *their*

25

part of the world as strong as you are into mine."

"Johnny," I said, "I'll try to watch myself. The last thing I want is to cause you trouble."

"Fair enough. Hey, here we are!" We were at Broadway and 49th Street. "They package a new CBS show out of here called 'Private Eye.' "

As we rode up the elevator, he put troubled eyes on me again. "Look," he advised, "don't say anything, all right? It's okay for you to tag along and watch if you want, but don't screw me out of a part by spooking these guys. They're nervous enough as it is."

I promised to be careful, and we entered an office labeled "Phoenix TV Productions, Ltd." Inside, a long row of chairs ran along one wall, and a blonde, heavily-mascaraed girl sat behind a railing, alternately answering a telephone and perusing a copy of *Variety*.

"No, I'm sorry," she told the phone, "Mr. Wallace is not casting today. If you will send a picture and a resume, we would be happy to call you if anything should turn up. You're welcome." She turned, saw us, and her voice relaxed. "Hi ya, Johnny," she said huskily. "How's the boy?"

"Starving," Johnny said cheerfully. "I heard that Wallace needs a psycho for his next show."

"Psychos we've got coming out of the walls," she said. "But I think Sam has a grocery boy bit. He's out right now, grabbing a bite. But you can wait."

We sat. Johnny nodded toward the girl.

"She's a good one," he said. "Not like some of the trash you run into. But she's got no real say. All she can do is let me hang around. And these chairs aren't her fault, either."

It was hard not to notice the chairs. They were like upside-down saddles, with curved contours that might have been form-fitting for a pair of cantaloupes.

26

"You see these damned things all over town," Johnny said. "I think they're made especially for producers, and the scientists have spent millions researching their exact dimensions. They're designed so that in exactly eleven minutes, your ass starts to hurt. But I fool them! I sit on one cheek for a while, and then on the other. By God, I get my full twenty-two minutes before *I* have to leave!"

The office door opened and a small, furtive man slipped inside. He sidled up to the railing and spoke to the receptionist in a quiet voice.

"That's Sam Wallace," Johnny whispered. "He's afraid some *actor* might see him and ask for a part. Watch what happens when I do." He stood up, glancing around wryly at the seat of his pants. "I think," he said, "the only disadvantage to my system with these chairs is that my ass is starting to mould itself to fit them."

No one noticed me as I followed him up to the railing.

"Mr. Wallace?" said Johnny. "John Calvin Lewis. You remember me?"

"Lewis? Lewis?" the little man repeated frantically. "Yes, yes, of course. Sorry, we're not casting today. Leave your picture and. . . ."

"My resume?" Johnny growled. "Christ Almighty, you've got enough of them now to heat this place for a month. Don't give me that no casting crap, Sambo."

"See here, young man," Wallace said, "no actor calls me Sambo."

"Got your attention, Sambo, didn't it?" said Johnny. "That's my specialty, grabbing attention. Like, I hear you got a grocery boy bit. Let me have it, I'll get you attention. I'll knock their eyes out. I mean it."

Wallace shut his eyes. He appeared to be in pain. "Oh," he said in a different tone of voice. "It's *you*. Amazing, isn't it, how

27

I was able to forget your face over just a single week-end. Wish fulfillment, I guess. Come on in."

Johnny followed him to the inner office. He jerked his head after me. Feeling foolish, I tagged along. No one seemed to notice. Inside, Wallace shut the door and immediately threw himself down on a red leather couch.

With his eyes closed, he said, "Have a drink."

"No thanks," said Johnny. "You can't buy me off with a drink. I'd rather have the part."

"Look, Johnny," Sam Wallace said in a tired voice, "why do you make it so difficult for me? You know I owe that part to at least nine good, responsible actors around this town. Men who have worked for me in the past and who deserve a buck if I can throw it their way. Why don't you get in line if you really want to work in this business? It wouldn't take you long. Six months at the outside."

Johnny spat. On the floor. It was a juicy, glistening oyster. Wallace sighed and rolled over with his face turned into the sofa's back.

"You mean, be an extra for you?" Johnny grated. "So you can see how I move and walk? You mean, be a movable prop for assistant directors to piss on? You mean, stand around with my cap in hand and tugging at my forelock and addressing you as 'Marse Wallace'? Hell, Sambo, you've got two thousand like that outside your office every Monday morning. You never let one of them in here, or try to buy them off with a drink. Why are you fighting it? You see something special in me, and I know you do, and you know that *I* know that *you* know, so why don't you can the crap and let's do some business?"

Wallace sat up, his small eyes blazing.

"You punk!" he said. "You conceited, loud-mouthed punk! I'm trying to be kind to you and you spit in my eye. Get the hell out of here before I forget my age and put you over my knee."

"Okay," said Johnny. "See you again next week."

He started for the door. When his hand was on the knob, Wallace rolled back into the depths of the sofa and his voice was muffled.

"See Sharon and give her your measurements," he said. "Tell her to advance you enough dough to join AFTRA. You'll do for the grocery boy. Until I fire you."

"That'll be the day," said Johnny, grinning. He skipped out the door. I followed. He grabbed the receptionist from behind, cupping her breasts in his hands, and squeezed hard. She let out a yelp.

"I got the grocery boy," he said.

"That ain't all you got," she yelled back, and stamped his foot with her high heel. Johnny grunted and wilted back against the wall.

"Sharon," he mumbled, "I didn't know you cared."

"Actors!" she said.

Johnny's eyes glistened. He reached forward and stroked her hair.

"Honey," he said, "thank you, Thank, thank, thank you! I know you did it for me. That bastard wouldn't have given me the time of day if you hadn't been working on him."

"I've got some letters to type," she said. "Here's an advance. Join the union, and for heaven's sake, get your hair cut. Not too close. Get a razor trim. There's a guy over on Sixth Avenue who specializes in it."

"Baby," he said huskily, "let's go out tonight. We'll eat Chinese."

"Not on your life," she said. "Actors are nothing but trouble. Now get out of here. I've got letters to do."

She held up her cheek and he kissed it. Then, with a jaunty wave of his head toward me, he skipped out the door and into the barren hallway.

"Hot damn!" he said excitedly, "We did it!"

29

"You forgot your advance money," I reminded.

"Screw the advance money! I don't want any favors from Sambo. I pay my own way. I got the part. That's what counts. Who gives a shit about money?" The elevator came and we got in. He said, "We've got one more stop, to tell Aunt Em, then we celebrate."

"Aunt Em?"

"Don't you know anything? I thought you were the big-assed expert on Johnny Lewis. Aunt Em's my agent."

In my mind, I rummaged through the little I knew of Johnny's early New York days. He'd managed to find an agent, all right, as I recalled: a former dancer named Emily Woodford. That fitted. I hadn't known of the Aunt Em nickname, however. But that was unimportant. Or was it? I was beginning to feel that nothing about John Calvin Lewis was unimportant.

"Look," Johnny said patiently, "she reminded me of Judy Garland's Aunt Em in *The Wizard of Oz,* and what the hell? Every guy should have an Aunt Em, right?"

"Right," I said.

Emily Woodford had a tiny cubbyhole of an office on the third floor of a commercial building on 43rd Street, just off Sixth Avenue. Although there was a receptionist's desk, it obviously served only as an overflow for the piles of photographs and resumes that had exploded away from the agent's own desk.

Johnny walked in without knocking. Aunt Em looked up with nearsighted eyes that were too proud to use glasses and put herself unwittingly into position for a wet, smacking kiss on the cheek from Johnny.

"Wonderful news, Aunt Em," he said. "I got a part."

"Johnny Lewis," she said, "I'm in no mood this morning for your pranks."

"This is for real. I finally got Wallace to come through. It's only a bit, but it's mine."

She took a pencil out of her tousled hair. "When?"

"Week after next," Johnny said. "I don't know about the rehearsals yet."

"Did you sign anything?"

"Nope. Sambo wanted to give me an advance for AFTRA, but I didn't take it."

"Good," she said with satisfaction. "Wallace is a fair man, but don't let him think he's doing you any favors. I'll get over there and fix up the contract. Leave it all to Aunt Em."

"Don't I always?" Johnny said softly. He kissed her again and then we were walking down the two flights of dingy stairs.

"By Christ," he said emphatically, "I'm going to take her out of here. I really am. She's going to have a suite in Rockerfeller Plaza and flunkies all over the place. You just wait and see."

We walked west on 43rd and emerged into Times Square, surrounded by the Criterion and Paramount Theaters and, over across the divider, the Astor Hotel. I remained silent, and we strolled up Broadway. Johnny spread his arms wide and tightened them around his chest as if he were cuddling every theater marquee in sight.

"It's starting to happen!" he said wonderingly. "By God, it's really starting to happen!"

Johnny's early life has been carefully documented by the sob sisters and the fan magazines, so the Aunt Em of his New York days should have come as no great surprise to me. I know it seems too pat and obvious to be true, but the fact remains that Johnny spent most of his all too few years on this earth searching for an Aunt Em. Everywhere he went, he created one, or —finding one—tried to destroy her. In fact, there was only *one* Aunt Em: the one he carried in his secret heart, submerged deep beneath memory or words. Her name wasn't Em, it was Sarah, and she was the second mother Johnny lost.

"I was nine," Johnny told me one night after more than enough cheap Chianti. It was winter now, and the room was cold. "I never even saw my first mother. She died when I was less than a year old. As far as I was concerned, Aunt Sarah *was* my mother. Oh, the kids at school never let me forget that I was an orphan. They didn't know my father was still alive in California, and I was damned if I'd let them have the satisfaction of saying I was in worse shape than being orphaned . . . I was deserted. But what the hell, I didn't really care what they said. It rolled off my back like water off a duck. I had Aunt Sarah, by God, and as long as I knew that, I knew I had a mama and it didn't make a damned bit of difference what *they* thought."

I knew what was coming, and would have stopped him from telling it if I could. But there are times for silent listeners. This was one.

"Aunt Sarah always knew what I was up to," Johnny said. "You couldn't pull the wool over *her* eyes. If I got up on my high horse, she'd bring me down to earth with one look through those gold-rimmed specs of hers. Like this."

Then Johnny gave me a look down his nose and through his glasses, a look that has become world-famous, and now I knew where he had found that mannerism.

He smiled at me. "I remember one time when I found out that if you give a duck a piece of salt pork, it goes right through him in about ten seconds. So I got me some fishing line and tied a piece of pork to one end and fed it to a big drake. It passed on through, and I gave it to another duck, and then another, and before long I had the whole barnyard full of ducks all strung together like pearls on a string. You should have heard them quack. Aunt Sarah did, and she came out on the back porch and you know, she didn't say one word. Not one little word. She just looked at me, down through her gold-rimmed glasses, and sighed. I tell you, I felt about yea high. I had to get a knife and cut those blamed ducks apart. It ruined fifty yards of good fishing line that was hard to come by."

He held out his glass and I poured more Chianti into it. He held the glass to the light and sniffed at it as if it were a rare vintage instead of $1.75 a gallon Club 67 Brand.

"You know," he went on, "we used to have the best breakfasts. Aunt Sarah'd get up around five and get the big wood stove going with some kerosene to save time, and then she'd fry up home-made bacon. She'd of made biscuit dough the night before and left it out to rise. They'd go into the oven, and by the time I came in from washing my face at the pump, the eggs would drop into the hot bacon grease. God, I can still hear them sizzle. The kitchen was all warmed up by now, and then she'd yell out the window for my Uncle Ray to come in from whatever he was doing, and we'd all sit down at the big kitchen table, not the one in the dining room, and tear into that food like it was going out of style. This crap we get here in the city, it's not food! Aunt Sarah's home-churned butter would make Sealtest hang their heads in shame. And margarine? She wouldn't feed that to the hogs."

Johnny took a sip of his wine and looked out the dirty window, down at the clutter of West 81st Street, filled with heaps of cold gray slush.

He saw me looking too, and gave a slight nod.

"There was snow on the ground that morning," he said. "That's one of the reasons I hate snow. It got her all wet and muddy and cold, and didn't do one damned bit of good."

He sipped at his wine. "She got up at the crack of dawn, as usual, and I heard her moving around in the kitchen. It was cold, real cold, and I felt so comfortable in bed, I just didn't want to move. I wasn't sleeping, just lazy and stretching under the big feather down comforter. I heard her clinking a bottle and didn't think anything of it because she always got the fire started with kerosene even though Uncle Ray chewed her out about it. You have to remember that we didn't have newspapers

33

to throw away on fire starting. Anyway, I heard the bottle clink, and there was quiet for a moment, and then a big whooshing sound that was almost like an explosion. I mean, it wasn't loud, but you could feel the air move like it does when there's an explosion. I knew right away there was something bad wrong, even before she screamed, and I jumped out of bed and ran into the kitchen. She was backing away from the stove and she was all in flames. The kerosene jug was busted on the floor, and it was burning too. I could see the fire climbing up her dress, over her shoulders and twisting up through her hair, and her mouth was wide open and screaming. And I couldn't MOVE!"

Johnny smashed his hand down on the window sill with the glass of Chianti still in it. The wine splashed all over the window pane, and the glass broke in his hand. His palm began to bleed. I reached for it, but he jerked it away from me.

"I stood there like a jerk," he said. "All I could do was cry. Aunt Sarah was sagging toward the floor and I just watched her and bawled my empty head off. Uncle Ray must have heard the screams, because he landed on the back porch like he'd jumped down out of the sky, He didn't even bother to open the door. He just crashed through it like it wasn't there. He caught Aunt Sarah up in both arms, flames and all, and threw her out the door into a snow bank. He dove out after her and rolled her over and over until the fire went out, and by then she was all wet and muddy. He yelled at me, told me to stop bawling and to get a blanket. I ran in and tore the one off my bed, and he snatched it from me and wrapped her up in it. She was trying to talk now, and all she could say was 'I'm sorry. I'm sorry.' Uncle Ray got her into the car and told me to stay there, that he'd send somebody, and he took off down the road to Centerville, and as the car pulled away, I could still hear Aunt Sarah crying, 'I'm sorry. I'm sorry.' "

Johnny cradled his head in one hand, the one that was still

bleeding. The blood rolled down his cheek, mixing with his tears.

"I never saw her again," he said, his voice muffled. "She was so bad that they kept the coffin closed. She lasted three days, but the pneumonia got her. And it was all my fault. All my fault. I never loved her enough when she was still alive."

CHAPTER
TWO

ELVIRA DOBBS and I met for lunch at The Venus, a restaurant a few blocks away from the Great Northern. I arrived early and nodded at Jerry—owner, maitre d' and head bartender.

Building me a dry martini, Jerry asked, "How's the story coming?"

"Slow." I fished the lemon peel out of the glass and rubbed it around the rim. Jerry didn't take offense. He knows it is a nervous habit of mine, which has nothing to do with his skill in preparing drinks.

"I'm still not sure I understand what you're doing," Jerry said. It was empty in the bar, and he had a chance to talk. "Hasn't this boy, this Johnny Lewis, been dead ten years now?"

"Closer to fifteen."

36

Jerry shook his head. "Forgive me, Mr. Corley," he said, "but I cannot pretend to understand the show business."

"Welcome to the club."

"What I mean is, why this sudden interest in an actor dead all those years?"

"It happens. Things run in cycles. Take Bogart. He's bigger now than when he was alive. And I guess they hope they can pull off the same trick with Johnny. Except it makes me feel like a spook, digging back into the kid's past and, all the time, I know how it's going to come out. But there's a lot of money behind this project, and I learned a long time ago not to argue with the bank. Especially when baby needs new shoes."

The door opened and Dick Fowler came in. He is a big, bluff man who works as a copywriter at BBDO. We had met during my brief sojourn there a few years ago. He mashed my knuckles in a bruising handshake and ordered a double martini straight up.

"What's this I hear about you going straight?" Fowler asked. "You've quit the ad game?"

"As long as I can afford it," I told him. "My last two novels have paid the rent for a couple of years in advance, and I figured I'd never get a better chance to see if I could get out a few good books. But as for my going straight, you have been sadly misinformed. I have been tempted by the devils of Hollywood, and I have surrendered to the siren lure of their greenbacks."

"Sure," he said, lifting his glass. "Well, buddy, I wish you luck. I hear you're digging through about six tons of flack to get down to the truth about Johnny Lewis. It's about time somebody did."

"Peace," I said, clinking my glass against his.

"Seriously," he went on, "I've always wondered about that guy. Was he for real? Or was he just a product some sharp operator packaged to give the kids living, walking, filmed proof that it's all right to be lonely, misunderstood and unappreciated? I'd like to know the answer to that one, and if you put it on the screen, I'll spring *my* three bucks."

"I still don't know," I said. "I took a look at his first film, *Paradise Gate,* the other day and it affected me the same way it did when it first ran. I felt like someone had sneaked up in the dark and kicked me in the stomach. I identified with the kid so hard that when the lights came up and I found myself back in Preview Theater I felt as if I were lost. You have to remember, we were both the same age. And that's the magic of film. I'm a lot of years older now, but Johnny is still twenty-four, tortured, misunderstood. . . . And he always will be. All the rest of us are twenty years closer to old age, and maybe that's part of the reason for our interest in him. Maybe we're restless for those days when we could project ourselves into a Johnny Lewis and believe that, for the first time, the world was seeing us as we really were. Maybe *we* want to be twenty-four years old again, before the bald spot and the mortgage and the worries about paying the kids' college expenses. Twenty-four is an age when you still believe you can really *do* something about the world. Maybe we want to buy those years back, and John Calvin Lewis is the currency we have to use."

A woman's voice behind me said, "For the love of Mike, don't let Ned Barker hear you talking like that. He thinks he's making this movie for the under-twenty-five market."

It was my agent, Elvira Dobbs. I introduced her to Dick, and we had a few moments of polite, meaningless conversation and then we went off by ourselves to sit at a table half-hidden in an alcove. I ordered a sherry for her, and another martini for myself. Her eyes hardened.

"Your second?" she asked.

"Third."

"Is that such a good idea?"

"Relax, Elvira. I finished my pages for today. I'm written out. I got up at three this morning with a real case of the whips. Managed to write them away, and in the process, got fourteen good pages. So this drink is the payola I owe the little gnome who lives in my head and runs the typewriter."

Remorselessly, she said, "You sounded upset when you called me."

"I *was* upset when I called you. But I'm over it."

"You said you wanted off this assignment."

"That was at nine this morning. The crisis is past."

"What crisis?"

"Elvira, have you ever watched someone you love die in agony?"

It was a moment before she answered. "Not with my own eyes. But I know about it, Edwin. Oh, yes, I know about it."

"Well, when I called you at nine this morning, I had reached the point in Johnny's life where I was going to be forced to watch a woman burn to death. And I wouldn't be able to look away or cover my ears, because I had to memorize every detail so I could put it all down on paper."

"Johnny's Aunt Sarah?"

"Yes."

"Why should that affect you so strongly? You've written of death before."

"This isn't the same."

She said, "All writers are lunatics. That's why I'm in business. Somebody has to take care of you. Look, is it so terrible to be involved with what you're writing? All this says to me is that you're breaking through, that you're reaching some level of being with Johnny. You're becoming a little part of him. You ought to be glad about it."

"Elvira, I know things about him that I have no right to

know. Things I couldn't have read anywhere because they were never written down."

"Things like Johnny's feelings as he watched his Aunt Sarah burning to death?"

Elvira touched my hand. "Edwin," she said softly, "you're projecting the character out of your mind as you believe him to be. As new facts emerge, that image changes, but it is always still an image created and nurtured in your brain. Why be disturbed when you recognize yourself in that image? After all, part of it—perhaps the most important part—*is* you."

Finally, I said, "Oh hell, forget it, Elvira. I'm just all wound up in this Johnny Lewis thing, and I'm afraid it's going to get worse before it gets better."

"Consider it forgotten, then," she said. But there was still a question in her voice.

"Let's have another blast," I said, reaching for her glass. My hand glanced off my own drink and spilled it, over the edge of the table and onto my trousers. I pulled a crumpled handkerchief from my pocket and started blotting at the gin.

"Edwin!" Elvira said sharply. "What's that?"

Dumbly, I looked at the handkerchief. It was stained with rusty blots.

"Blood," I said with suddenly numb lips. "A friend of mine cut his hand. On a Chianti glass."

Later that day I sat in my room and watched dusk ooze over the city. My conversation with Elvira still disturbed me. I was uneasy about the way my life was joining that of John Calvin Lewis . . . or at least, with the fictional character who wore that name in my screenplay. As a writer who has spent too many hours staring unhappily at blank sheets of paper that refuse to fill with words, I knew that I should welcome this bridge between myself and my character. But why had my mind chosen to bewilder me with bloody handkerchiefs stained by a midnight nose bleed . . . or by what I thought I remembered?

My mouth was dry. I wanted a drink. There was nothing in the room, a precaution I always take when serious work is afoot. But room service was only as far away as my telephone.

I looked at it, thought of Elvira, and decided to fight the urge. She worried unnecessarily about my devotion to the bottle. Of course, history had given her good reason. She had seen the fatal attraction between liquor and writers more than once. A waking nightmare which she described to me one winter evening was the memory of six days spent with Brendan Behan during his last, prodigious binge. She felt that Behan had been on the edge of greatness, and had been cheated of both it and life by the two-faced genie in the bottle.

Well, if I couldn't drink, I would work.

My typewriter was on a small table beneath the window. I went over and looked down at the sheet of paper still in the roller, at the words I had writen that morning.

JOHNNY (As he rushes, alone, up Broadway)
It's starting to happen! By God, it's really starting to happen!

I was standing outside the Astor Drug Store. I went inside and saw Johnny sitting near the end of the soda fountain. He was eating a hamburger between gulps of a Coke.

"Hey!" he said. "Have a bite. And keep that funny money in your pocket. I'll spring. I just got paid and I'm holding pretty good today."

"Not now," I said. "How's it going? You making a good grocery boy?"

"Grocery boy? Hell, you're miles behind, man. That was three weeks ago. I was a smash. Five lousy lines and I stole the whole show. The letters are still coming in. Do you know what those TV pukes tried to do? They tried to tell *me* how to be a grocery boy. That pansy director who's never even seen dirt, unless he dropped his scarf on the dining room floor at '21' and someone stepped on it, he tried to tell me how a poor kid who has to be a grocery boy acts. La de da! What is it? Do I wear a sign that says, 'Here I am, fags, come and get me'? My God, they come out of the woodwork. The first day, that fairy held me after rehearsal to work on my scene privately, and the next thing I knew, he had his hand up my fly to the elbow."

"What did you do?"

"I pissed in his hand, what do you think I did? But what bothers me is I think he liked it. Anyway, then he starts working on my movement. He thinks I should move like in a ballet. For Christ's sake! A grocery boy ballet. So I played along with him, what the hell? I needed the job. But when we went on camera live, I did it my way. Man, you should have seen his face. I thought he'd rupture himself. He threw me right out of the studio. 'You little tease,' he told me, 'I'll make sure you never work in this town again!' Even scared me a little. But then the next day the mail started rolling in. And old Sambo Wallace called Aunt Em and pleaded for me to do a return bit this week. Big part. Practically the lead. I play a nutty kid who gets out of the psycho farm and moves in on two nice old ladies."

"Sounds rather like *Arsenic and Old Lace.*"

"Except this time, it's the old girls who get it in the neck. He strangles them both. And I've got this real bit I'm going to put in. When this creep is throttling the old one, the one who reminds him of his aunt, he's going to kiss her. That'll stand their hair up."

"Speaking of Aunts, how's Aunt Em?"

"Happy as a clam. She's like all agents, a little spooked that I talk back to those pukes, but she'll come around. I don't talk unless I know what I'm saying, and that's what makes the

42

difference. Did you know I was a star basketball player? Me, at five feet six? Honest injun, I was, and I won the big game of the year in the last five seconds of play because I did it *my* way and wouldn't even let the coach tell me what to do. He was okay, there wasn't anything wrong with him, but he only knew what was right for him and guys like him. He didn't know what would work for me. I had to do it my own way. It's the same with acting. Remember when we barged in on Wallace? You think he'd let anyone else get away with that shit? He hates my guts, but he noticed me. He *had* to notice me."

Johnny's voice stopped, as if he had run down. He looked over my shoulder and spoke: "Hey, look what the cat dragged in."

"Hello, Johnny," said a tall girl, her eyes invisible behind a huge pair of sungalsses.

"Maggie McBride," Johnny said. The girl did not seem to notice me. She sat down beside Johnny.

"I've been trying to reach you," she said. "Don't you answer your phone?"

"I haven't been home much," Johnny answered. "I've been hiding from the Fag Patrol."

"Har har de har," said Maggie. "Look, I couldn't care less about your sex life."

"That's good," he said, "because right now it's practically nonexistent."

"I bleed for you."

"Oh, that time of month? Buy your own Coke, then."

"I want coffee," she said, and the waiter brought it. She took off her sunglasses and stared at Johnny. "Are you, or are you not going to do the scene with me?"

"Why so hot under the collar? You've got a whole week. What's the rush?"

"The rush is, John Calvin Lewis, that you get only one

chance in your life to audition for The Workshop. Maybe it means nothing at all to you to work with the best directors in the whole damned world, now that you're so rich and famous in television. But it means a lot to me, and you promised to help me with this audition. If you aren't going to, tell me so I can get somebody else. I don't have much time."

"Simmer down," he said. "I told you I'd do the scene, didn't I? And I will. Let's get together tomorrow night at my place and we'll work it up. Okay?"

She relaxed. "Thank you, Johnny," she said softly. "I know it's not much to you, but it's important to me. Thank you."

"Hell, don't thank me," he said. "I can stand the exposure too." He paused and looked at her thoughtfully. "Hey, wouldn't it be funny if we auditioned and you flunked, but I got in?"

A television studio's control booth is a chaotic madhouse kept under bare control by the quiet voice of one man—the director. This one was named Tony Warden and it was obvious that he was not the one Johnny had mentioned. He was thoroughly masculine. His quiet voice, amidst the terrified cries of the disorganized technicians, network executives and agency representatives, somehow kept the studio from disintegrating.

The control booth was filled with monitors. One, in the center, was larger than the others because it was the one that showed what was going out over the air, and on it flickered a commerical for Happy Flakes, the new detergent that was "faster than soap." Out through the glass windows, I could see the studio floor, crowded with equipment and technicians, and beyond them, the single set of living room and kitchen which would house the drama. This, you'll remember, was the era of live television, and the hallmark of such productions was economy. Two sets were never built when one would do.

"Roll into film," Warden said. "Get ready to punch up film, get ready to punch up camera one."

I watched the monitors. The film chain was showing a series of numbers counting down from ten to two. Camera one was picking up a full shot of the living room. The actresses portraying the two old maid sisters were huddled near a prop radio.

"Punch up film," said Warden as the commercial faded out. A technician hit a button and now the big monitor in the center showed a filmed sequence that announced this was "The Happy Flakes Suspense Playhouse." "Get ready to punch up one, stand by on two. Get ready to roll audio."

I looked at the number two monitor. It showed a closeup of the two actresses.

"Punch up one," said Warden. A technician hit the switch and now the main monitor showed the long shot of the living room. "Roll audio." A reel of quarter-inch tape began to turn and we heard a broadcast seemingly coming from the radio in the set, warning that an inmate had escaped from a local sanitarium. "Ready to punch up two. Punch up two."

The scene shifted to the closeup. As the sisters pretended to listen to the radio, Warden said, "One, get in tight on that window." On camera one's monitor, I saw it moving for a closeup of the window between the faces of the two actresses. The "radio" droned on, and the performers reacted accordingly. "Ready to punch up one. Punch up one." The switch was thrown to bring on the closeup of the window and then, in a moment filled with as much fear and horror as I have ever seen on TV, a face rose slowly outside the window, eyes glazed with madness. It was Johnny. The camera pushed in for a tight closeup, and he smiled. It sent chills up the back of my neck. "Get ready to go to black. Go to black. Switch to network." The scene faded, and we saw a Happy Flakes commercial from another studio.

The teleplay was none too good; it was the usual two old ladies alone in a great big house being terrorized by a madman script. But Johnny brought a strange quality to the role, a sense that here was a kid who had started out fine but somehow drifted off the track, warped by some unseen flaw. The sequences played well and the half hour was soon over. As the teleplay drew to a close I could tell by occasional curses and mutterings among the technicians that Johnny was giving them a few problems. There were almost-missed shots, probably caused by his not being where he had been during rehearsal. Warden seemed undisturbed and corrected the camera positions with quiet instructions.

In the final seconds of the play, as we heard police battering down the front door and as one of the sisters lay dead, Johnny moved to the other and I sensed the tension as Warden said, "One, get in there and follow him. Hell, keep him in closeup! Where's the little bastard going now? My aching back, he's *kissing* her! Two, give me a medium shot. Ready to switch to two, switch to two. Ha! Got the bastard. One, get back for a long shot. You can't tell what that kid's going to do, keep the shot wide, anticipate his moves! Ready to switch to one. Switch to one. Where's he off to now? Follow him, follow him! He's heading for the kitchen. Three! Get the hell over fast, cover the kitchen. Audio, bring up the kitchen mike! Okay, he's in there. Ready to switch . . . goddamnit, switch to three!"

The two "policemen" arrived in the living room. They were supposed to discover a madman cackling over his victims. Instead, smeared with fake blood two actresses huddled on the floor trying not to laugh or move. The floor manager pointed frantically to the kitchen part of the set. Since there was nowhere else to go anyway, the actors rushed in, just in time to see Johnny raise a huge meat cleaver and, with a cry of "They wouldn't let me love them!" swing it in a murderous arc and

46

apparently cut off his own head. He went down in a heap and one of the actors forgot he was on the air and said, in awe, "My God!" and that was the closing line of the "Happy Flakes Suspense Playhouse" as Tony Warden said limply, "Fade to black."

As usual, Johnny was thrown out of the studio and warned never to come back. His only defender was Tony Warden, who insisted "the way the kid did it was better than the rehearsals."

We retired to Downey's and were soon surrounded by a group of young performers, most of whom had seen the drama on the bar TV set. They were full of praise and favorable comments on the play. But in spite of their obvious admiration for him, it was equally obvious that their voices were tinged with envy and petty remarks. Most attacked the script; whenever in doubt, attack the writer.

I wonder if you remember how it was in those halcyon days of live TV in the early fifties. Drama was the king, New York was Mecca, budgets were small and talent was everywhere. Today, a producer may squander two hundred thousand dollars on a single pilot episode. In 1952, that budget would have produced eight to ten shows. Rod Serling, Paddy Chayefsky and Reginald Rose were the writers of the moment. This was chamber theater, created in part by its very budget limitations. The spoken word was important, because nobody could afford a mountain or a flood. And the odd thing was, during those golden years, no one on the scene believed that one tenth of the medium's potential was being touched. "Wait until TV grows up," was the cry. "Then you'll see what can really be done!"

Alas, television never *did* grow up. Like Peter Pan, it shrank from maturity and, instead, weakened and withered, spawning an endless cycle of situation comedies and hackneyed Westerns and detective programs. So the promise made in 1952 was never met. TV, with all bets going for it, managed to run last in the field. Only rarely has it achieved its great potential, and very little of that in the past ten years.

But in Downey's, in late 1952, the boys and girls around Johnny were full of dreams and sure of the future. I sat quietly among them, sipping my drink, and wishing I did not know so much about the way things would be. For the first time in his life, Johnny was surounded by admirers and he was flushed and dazed with the impact.

Shortly after midnight, the first editions arrived. The four morning papers were unanimous in their praise for Johnny. The *Times:* ". . . as the psycho killer, newcomer John Calvin Lewis scores strongly. This is a young man to watch with care." The *Tribune:* "John Lewis made a terrifying journey into the world of madness, and proved that he is one of the season's finest young actors." The *News:* "Lewis is great. Remember, you saw it here!" The *Mirror:* "You will hear much about John Calvin Lewis before Hollywood steals him away from us. He is on his way up."

Until now, I had never seen Johnny drink more than a beer or two. And, once, too much red wine. But now, in Downey's, with the praise of the critics ringing in his ears, he turned to Scotch, and there were dozens of willing admirers fighting to pick up the tab. As he drank, he became profane and angry, until his voice echoed among the wooden booths.

"What would *you* do about a father who deserts you?" he yelled, sloshing whisky across his chest from a half-filled glass. "Hell, he could have figured out some way, couldn't he? Was it my fault my mother died? If he wanted to get rid of me that bad, why didn't he flush me down the toilet? He never loved me. He never loved anybody. What would you do if you ended up in Centerville, Iowa, with that goddamned town square and the Sears Roebuck, and the Farmer's Union? What the hell chance

48

did anyone have in that scene? And all the time, my father, goddamn his soul to hell and back, was living in *Burbank,* Burbank California, with sunshine and orange groves! Wouldn't you kill that man, if you could seek him out amidst the milk and honey? I would! By God, I will! I will take my accumulated riches and buy me a BB gun and shoot him in the eye with it, by Christ!"

His audience had become quiet. At first they thought he was joking, but then it became clear that he was all too earnest.

At this unfortunate moment, Emily Woodford arrived.

"Johnny, you bad boy," she said. "I've been looking all over for you. Goodness, you've been drinking. Well, it's to be understood, I suppose. But don't worry. All is forgiven, dear boy. Sam Wallace sends his apologies and begs that you overlook that little misunderstanding at the studio."

Still playing the nearsighted owl, Johnny looked up.

"Why," he said quietly. "It's Aunt Em. Good old Aunt Em."

"Johnny, let me take you home. I think the celebration has gone quite far enough."

"So," Johnny said, "you want to take me home?"

"You need your rest," she said. "And you're not used to drinking."

"Listen, ratface," Johnny said, smiling, "I will decide when to go home. *I* will. Not you. I am with my friends. Who the hell invited you here? Now that I've made it on my own you think you can climb aboard the golden wagon? Perhaps you hope you can escort me to your wallow and tuck me in among the old bones and leftover condoms and then slide your greasy snatch in under the covers to see how much of me you can gobble up before I wake? You ought to see yourself! You're old and you're ugly and you never meant anything to me. You're not my Aunt Em! You're nobody's Aunt Em. Who needs you? Go off and set fire to yourself. You're not *my* Aunt."

Before he could say more, Maggie McBride materialized from the shocked crowd and took his arm. I took the other, and we led him from that terribly silent place and out into the night, and all the time, he kept shouting over his shoulder, "You're not my aunt! You're not *my* aunt!"

We manhandled him into a taxi. As he thrashed in our grasp, Maggie told the driver, "Brooklyn Heights," and then the driver began to curse under his breath about deadbeats who wanted to go into the wilderness in the middle of the night and who probably wouldn't even give him a decent tip, and somehow that put the topper on the whole evening.

Staring out my hotel window, a cup of coffee cooling in my hand, I was beginning to have real doubt about ever being able to communicate one of the most essential parts of my story about John Calvin Lewis. The coffee was my own brew, Instant Yuban, heated to a boil with a small emersion unit I picked up for a couple of bucks at Walgreen's. During those terrible hours between midnight and dawn, when room service is either asleep or nonexistent, my jar of Yuban and the heating coil have done valiant service. But, as I sipped the tepid brew, tiny bug-like fears still crept around my hairline. Would I really be able to convince an audience that Johnny Lewis was a genuine and honest talent, and not just a wild nonconformist?

Again, I looked at the page in the typewriter:

DRIVER *(Muttering angrily)*
Brooklyn Heights? World travelers I get! Why not Alaska?
(Assorted half-heard curses)

Now, how, I asked myself, can words on paper convince anyone that John Calvin Lewis was a superb actor? Especially if Ned Barker chose to cast some pretty-boy rock singer in the leading role. All that would be left in that case would be the anger and the curses and the frightful spectacle that men of genius invariably make of themselves.

Maybe we could use testimonials. What if we had a little section in the film in which the greats of the profession spoke about Johnny's talent? It could be shot as a montage:

LAURENCE OLIVER: Stunning. In the work Johnny did, his range was limited by the script. But who can say what he might have achieved eventually?

FREDERIC MARCH: The boy was stupendous. He died too soon.

JOSÉ FERRER: He was so young. But he did it all, in television and on the stage, and then in films. His talent was gigantic. If he had been allowed to refine it, I think he would have been worth waiting for.

GERALDINE PAGE: Johnny was—oh, what shall I say? So gentle and yet so strong; so lost, and yet so full of purpose. So full of little interstices that you could roam around and around in and never see the same place twice.

ELIA KAZAN: I was planning to direct his next picture. It's too bad.

ARTHUR KENNEDY: He always said he was going to play Hamlet before he was thirty. It's too bad. I think he would have made a hell of a Hamlet."

SHELLY WINTERS: Johnny was like that candle of Edna St. Vincent Millay's poem. It wasn't meant to last. But it cast a lovely light.

GEORGE STEVENS: I almost directed *Texas.* If I had, I assure you Johnny wouldn't have been riding motorcycles.

HEDDA HOPPER: Poor, lost Johnny. I think he was all caught up in the myth of Marlon Brando and Montgomery Clift and all the rest. He saw the public faces of these stars and thought that was how *he* should act. He never saw them behind the scenes. I tried to tell him, but he was too young . . . too young.

WALTER KERR: I only saw Lewis act once. On the stage, that is. He was a frightening monster . . . the kind of monster that our theater could not exist without. It's too bad he gave up the stage. He would have been superb.

THE FANS: Please Johnny, say you're not dead! You can't be dead? We love you! There will never be another Johnny! Come back to us. Send us your picture.

I leaned back and looked at what I had written. Then I pulled the sheet out of the typewriter and tore it up. It sounded too much like a soap commercial.

I was riding in a taxi and when it stopped at a red light at the corners of Central Park West and 61st Street, the door opened and Johnny got in.

"Saw you through the window," he said. "Can you give me a lift? I'm late."

The taxi driver turned. His neck was red with anger. I looked at his hack license and saw his name was Morris Sandof.

"Do you know this guy?" he grumbled.

"It's all right," I said. "He's a friend."

"So where to already?"

"81st and West End Avenue," Johnny told him. "And let's go, huh? I'm way behind."

"Keep your shirt on, Junior," said Morris Sandof. "With your permission I will wait until the light turns green."

"What's the big rush?" I asked.

"Maggie wants to work on the scene for her Workshop audition. It's tonight, and we haven't done anything on it. But we'll get by. She's got her part down cold, and I'm a quick study."

"Am I invited?"

He squinted over at me. He was smiling, but it was a wry smile.

52

"Aren't you always around when something's happening to me? Sure, you're invited. I guess I could ask you how the audition's going to turn out. But I won't. I want to find out on my own."

The taxi stopped and I gave the driver a dollar bill. The date on it was all right. I had taken to carrying money that predated 1952. I even had, as a pocket piece, an uncirculated 1879 Morgan silver dollar, with the old classic version of Miss Liberty on the face, and the ferocious spread-winged eagle of the Great Seal on the back. Today, silver dollars are rarely seen: this particular one, never.

"Come on up," Johnny asked, peering at me through those glasses.

The old brownstone had originally been a one-family mansion, back in those late years of the last century when city living was still gracious and walls were built thick enough for privacy. Now it had been split up into four tiny floor-through apartments and privacy was as extinct as the horse and carriage. This was the age of the sofa-bed and the Castro convertible; the age of roommates who take turns walking the night streets, sipping beers in dingy bars and huddling in old movies so the lucky one can have privacy with his girl. Johnny was fortunate: he had a roommate on the road with *Mr. Roberts,* and was even luckier that his absent partner was still sending his share of the rent.

Johnny's door was unlocked. "I always keep it open," he said. "Someone might want to come in and wait for me. There's nothing here to steal. One night I found a bum asleep on the floor, but mostly nobody bothers me."

The apartment was empty of bums this afternoon. But Maggie McBride was there, inside the open bathroom door, washing out a pair of nylons. I saw at once that she was living in the apartment. It was not because of what she was doing. A bachelor apartment, no matter how well-cleaned, has a different feeling from one that is lived in by a woman. Johnny's apartment

53

had changed since my last visit, when we shared Chianti and memories.

Maggie came forward and gave Johnny a warm kiss. She more or less nodded at my presence, although she did not greet me. When she poured coffee, there was a cup for me, but no conversation. Yet she did not seem disturbed or puzzled by my presence, and when Johnny and I were in a conversation that excluded her she waited patiently. Like everyone else in Johnny's world, she was all but unaware of me.

"Maggie moved in here the day after that big bash down at Downey's," Johnny said. "Her folks got upset when she brought me home, so she packed up and moved out."

"Have you seen Aunt . . . Miss Woodford since then?"

"Sure," Johnny said, stretching and yawning. "Oh, sure. I took her a big bundle of flowers the next day and she cried all over me. She knew I was plastered. I don't get like that much. I'm just not used to the hard stuff. I guess I'd better stick to beer and wine."

"Do you really hate your father that much?"

"Hate my father? No, I don't hate my father. Hell, why should I? That was the booze talking. He did the best he could for me, I guess. Oh, I know what I said. Maggie gave me a playback. But it's like there are two Johnny Lewises. There's the one sitting here now, and he understands why certain things have to be. But the other one, the one who came out of that Scotch bottle, he's a grade A sonofabitch. You can't get off the hook with that one, no excuses allowed. I guess you could say he hates my father, but that's not the whole story. *He* hates the whole damned world, including himself. Mostly himself."

Maggie came over and curled up beside him on the sofa, nestling her head down on his shoulder. It made her look about ten years old.

"You know," Johnny went on softly, and if she was listening,

54

she gave no sign, "I've been doing a lot of thinking about you since that first day. It's your fault that a bunch of people have decided I'm going animal crackers. They suddenly discover, after you're gone, that I've been talking with myself. At least that's the way they put it down, because they can't remember you. But you know something funny? It hasn't hurt me one damned bit. It's like you've become my good luck charm. So I got to thinking, why bust my horns with this acting bit? With what you know, we could wipe out the stock market in two weeks. We could go to Ike and tell him exactly where and how to stop the war. We could set ourselves up in business, predicting . . . and stopping strikes or accidents or even polio epidemics."

I opened my mouth but he raised his hand and cut me off before I could speak. "Now don't get in a lather. I said we could, I didn't say we would. Where the hell's the fun in playing a sure hand? No, you've told me all I ever want you to tell me. Because of you, I know I'm going to make it. Big. I can't lose. That's all I ever want you to let me know. Don't give me advice, don't warn me about the rain storm so I'll carry an umbrella, don't remind me to check in with my phone service or I'll lose a part. Because if you do, if we start out with these small things, it'll grow and keep on growing until you tell me what I don't want to know."

He closed his eyes and slumped back against his girl. She brushed her lips against his ear. He smiled, but it was a sad, lost smile.

"You see," he said finally, "I figured it out. It took me a while, but I added it all up. Twenty years from now I'll be pushing forty. That's not old age, not these days. My career should be rolling along in high gear. So why would any studio be interested in doing a film about me? Hell, even Jolson had to be in retirement before they got around to that. So, that's the way I feel. You can watch. You can listen, you can write things down. But don't tell me anything more about myself. I don't want to hear. I'm going to hit the top, nothing can stop me, and that's all I want to know. Just don't tell me the real reason you're writing about me. Because I already know it."

As he and Maggie huddled together on the couch they looked like two lost children. His voice when it came was distant and full of wonder.

"You see," Johnny said, "I know that in twenty years I'll be dead."

CHAPTER
THREE

THE macabre motif of death that was such an important part of the legend of John Calvin Lewis has often been commented on, even exploited. Two months after his death, a friend who dabbled in the occult published a book that asserted she was in constant contact with Johnny in the "nether world." Her fantasy grew in scope, until at length, an entire series of magazines were published, detailing her ectoplasmic romance with Johnny's spirit.

Photographs were printed showing Johnny in one of his favorite poses—lying in an open coffin, pretending to be dead. And it was common knowledge that when you entered the living room of his bachelor house in Coldwater Canyon, the first thing that met your eyes was a dangling, ready-for-action hangman's noose.

57

Amateur psychoanalysts sprang up by the score, all spinning various explanations for Johnny's obvious "obsession with death." The supposed causes ranged from the familiar, "they'll be sorry when I'm dead," to a genuine self-hate and a will to die. It is a matter of record that on many occasions, Johnny explained his compulsive working habits by saying, "I've got to hurry. I don't have much time." Some dismiss it as the usual maudlin self-pity in which all young artists proclaim firmly that they will never live to see the shady side of thirty. Others see in the comments a disposition to suicide, a prediction that Johnny Lewis, with his fast sports car and his hot motorcycles would somehow manage to do away with himself one day.

To those who tried to fathom his behavior at the time the truth would have come as a mighty shock. Johnny Lewis was doomed to die. And he seemed to know it. The only thing he did not know was how pitifully short a time he had left. When he lay in a coffin, posing for a photograph that would become famous after his death, he knew it would be all too soon that the game became real. But that was just his way.

After that one late afternoon on 81st Street, when he pleaded with me never to speak to him of things that I knew, the subject was carefully avoided.

The Performers' Workshop is a labor of love on the part of directors, writers and actors who try to repay their own debt to the profession by contributing their time and talents to helping newcomers in the theater. It is not a school, as schools commonly go. Nor is it truly a workshop, in which projects are conceived and executed. Rather, you might call the Workshop a forum, in which a talent is tried and tempered in the fiery heat of adversity. For nowhere in the world are there fiercer, more unforgiving, critics of any flaw or imperfection. To stand before a gallery of your peers and unveil your very soul can be one of the most painful ways of maturing your ability. It does not work for everyone. Some fine, gifted performers are unable to accept the constant and unremitting attack on their work and their personality. One was John Calvin Lewis.

We arrived just after eight, and waited in a room for almost an hour. Although the audition had been scheduled for 8:15, it was obvious that earlier scenes must have run overtime.

The Workshop was located at that time in a small building near Tenth Avenue. Once a residence, it was surrounded by warehouses and trucking firms. Directly across the street was a Dodge Truck dealership, and the constant traffic filled the evening air with an obbligato of rumbling wheels.

Maggie was nervously pacing off the four walls of the room, muttering under her breath. Her hair was pulled back in a tight bun, and she wore black leotards under her checkered dress. Johnny slouched against a door jamb looking at nothing in particular and once, when she was not watching, he sneaked up on Maggie, tickled her ribs violently and hissed, "Boo!" She very nearly jumped out through the door.

"Don't," she said crossly. "Do you want me to wet my pants?"

"Be my guest," said Johnny. He giggled. "What are you so nervous about?"

"Oh, *Johnny!*"

The door opened and a young man wearing a black T-shirt and khaki pants leaned out.

"Will you follow me, please?"

Maggie jumped again, and then she looked at Johnny and he gave her a big smile. She stepped forward, adjusting her clothing, and Johnny and I followed her through the door and up a flight of stairs, into a small hallway.

"Go in quietly," said the young man, "and take a seat. Mr. Newman will be right with you."

We crept into the room. It was large, and almost filled with chairs. They were all shapes and sizes, obviously gathered from a dozen different sources. At the front of the room, there was a small arena, lighted by three harsh spotlights. In the second row, to one side, sat two men and a short, dumpy woman. One of the men looked up.

"Hello," he said. "You're?"

The woman referred to a clip board.

"Maggie McBride and John Lewis," she read.

"Come down here," said the man. Slowly, the two young people moved forward. Then they stood in the arena, blinking into the spotlights. "I'm Jerome Newman," said the man, "and this is Arnold Ross. And our secretary, Miss Schoonover. I understand you want to audition for the Workshop."

"Yes," began Maggie, and her voice cracked. She cleared her throat and began again. "Yes, I do. Mr. Lewis is helping me with the scene."

"Very well," said Newman. "Begin whenever you're ready."

"Thank you," said Maggie. "In this scene, I play the role of a girl who has just been told by her doctor that she's going to have a baby. She isn't married. So she goes back to her room, and waits for the boy to come home. As he enters, the scene begins."

It was the usual trite, self-pitying routine that so many young actors seem to love—full of long, suffering pauses, and carefully planned, inarticulate mumblings. Through the awful material, you could see that Maggie had a certain flair, but the total effect was not outstanding in any way. She was simply another attractive girl, reading words that did not really seem to spring from within her.

As for Johnny, I could not make up my mind. Where the rehearsals I had seen earlier in the day had made the character of the boy seem harsh and insensitive, that impression was not coming across here in the Workshop arena. His boy here was

60

hurt and bewildered, and the lines that had originally made him appear cruel and tough now worked for the opposite effect. Where, in the rehearsals, when he had driven the girl away, his action was to laugh roughly and start going through his address book for a new date for the night, now he looked after her departure with tears in his eyes, and although he reached for the book, he was never able to find it, because he was blinded by his own grief and self-hate.

There was a long silence after the scene was over. I could see the two directors conferring.

At 43, Jerome Newman had achieved greatness in both the theater and in film. Working with such relatively new playwrights as Arthur Miller, Tennessee Williams and William Inge, he had made a fast and yet lasting image for himself as a fiery, colorful director. And then, almost without shifting gears, he had gone to Hollywood where, in less than a year, he directed three films of note. Now he commuted back and forth between Wilshire Boulevard and Broadway, and seemed to thrive on it.

Arnold Ross, ten years older, had passed up a chance to join Harold Clurman in the Group Theatre, and had gone, instead, to Moscow, to spend two years working with disciples of Stanislavsky. Returning to this country just before the war, he had invaded Broadway with a striking series of Chekhov and Ibsen plays that revived the naturalistic theater of Belasco. Later, he was to adapt these techniques for more modern works. Now, in his early fifties, he had the pleasure of hearing constant references to a "Ross style of acting," and his participation in the Workshop kept the legend growing.

During the conference, Maggie and Johnny stood under the glaring spotlights. No one had asked them to sit, so they stood.

"Thank you, Miss McBride," Newman said finally. "We think you are a very talented girl. You could use a course in diction, and might I suggest the Speech Clinic at Columbia? Other than that, I am afraid there is no help this Workshop can give you. Thank you so much for auditioning."

The tears sprang to Maggie's eyes, and with an angry toss of her head, she started up the aisle, Johnny following her. Newman's voice leapt after them.

"One minute, Mr. Lewis. I just wanted to say that if you would like to attend our sessions, we would be happy to see you. Tuesday and Thursday afternoons."

Maggie dropped Johnny's hand and stared blindly into his face. Her voice had a crumpled sound.

"Oh, Johnny," she cried, "you didn't play the scene the way you rehearsed it!"

She whirled and ran out of the room. Johnny looked at me and shrugged.

"Silly broads," he said.

It is only in movies and bad novels that any single event changes the course of love. Although terribly hurt and disappointed by Johnny's triumph at the Studio, Maggie did not thereupon take flight. She went back to her parents' home for a day or two, but soon she was back, sharing the small apartment on 81st Street. It would take dozens of hurts and dozens of flights before one would become permanent.

With each bitter argument and each new "betrayal" by Johnny, the ultimate end came closer and closer, and I am sure that both of them saw it approaching. As Johnny's fame increased, he needed the girl less and less, and yet he could not bring himself to make the final break. He would have been kinder to do so, because his coldness and disinterest in her was far more painful than firm rejection would have been. But he was John Calvin Lewis, and he had his own way of doing things.

I have a vague recollection of attending many sessions of the Workshop with Johnny, but only one stands out in any detail. I recall that it was late September of 1953, and Johnny was planning to go away for a few weeks to crew Abner Thompson's *Trade Winds* on a cruise through the Virgin Islands. Johnny had never been aboard a sailing vessel in his life, but when he learned that Thompson was the principal investor in a new Broadway-bound play, *Tiger Row,* he read every book he could find on the subject, and poor Abner never had a chance.

The thrill of being accepted by the Workshop had long since worn off, and Johnny now attacked its methods with all of the venom he had previously reserved for his father. The attacks had been made in private, up until now, and no one at the studio that Thursday afternoon had any idea of what they were in store for. Johnny was sitting, as usual, in his favorite seat, to the rear and on the aisle, so he could jump up and get out whenever he felt like it. I sat beside him, and there was an unusually large turnout, because many performers were in town for the beginning of the theatrical season. Ben Gazzara was there, as were Janice Rule, Jack Palance and Geraldine Page. None of these actors belonged to the Workshop, but they were granted the courtesy of attending an occasional session as guests.

As a student scene wore on in the arena, Johnny leaned over and whispered to me.

"Look at these turds," he hissed, indicating a large group of young men and women sitting down close, apart from the older members of the audience. "You think they're watching that scene? Like hell! They're tearing it apart in their heads, and they can't wait until it's over so they can analyze it!"

"Shhh," said Ben Gazzara. Johnny waved a friendly hand at him and settled back.

The scene finished, and there was a confused buzz from the spectators.

"Comments?" said Newman.

A thin, lanky girl in a blue sailor's sweater and incredibly paint-spattered jeans, stood up.

"Uh," she said, "I, uh, felt there was no real contact between the husband and wife. Ummm, he was—uh—probably fired from his job today, so he was taking it out on her, but the two, they didn't relate, you know what I mean?"

"There was nothing in the dialogue about him being fired," said Newman.

"Well, no, of course not," said the girl. "It's behind the dialogue. Otherwise, I mean, why would he attack her?"

"Maybe he just doesn't like her," yelled Johnny.

A husky boy who had both hands in the pockets of a leather jacket stood up.

"I didn't believe anything they said," he growled. "It was all just words, you didn't see no people. I think the scene was over-rehearsed, and all the life went out of it."

He sat down. The girl half of the pair on stage burst into tears.

"What I want to know," said an intense, very thin boy, "is what was the man thinking, *before* he rang the doorbell? Was he planning to give this broad a lay? Maybe that's what's missing: this dialogue would have played better if he was giving her a poke while they said it."

"Oh, really!" chirped the girl in the sailor sweater. "You think everything is sex, sex, sex!"

"The way we saw it," said the boy who had played the husband, "was just that the husband was feeling guilty about a crack he made to her last night, and now when he tries to make up for it, she is cold to him and that rejection of his apology makes him even angrier."

64

"Shallow thinking," said the boy in the leather jacket. "That motivation doesn't even scratch the surface."

"Scratch my balls," muttered Johnny.

The girl in the sailor sweater whirled and screamed at him. Her mouth opened so wide that you could actually see her tonsils. She seemed to hiss. I was shocked at the hatred and venom in her reaction.

"Listen to John Calvin Lewis!" she spat. "The boy wonder! Why don't *you* come down here and show us how to do it? I know you feel safe and exclusive sitting up there on your ringside throne, but why don't you come down and sweat a little with us peasants?"

"Why not?" Johnny said softly. As he stood and inched his way into the aisle, then slouched down it to the arena, there was a murmured rustle in the audience. It was well-known that Johnny had refused to perform beyond his original audition for the Workshop. "Why the hell should I?" he asked me one evening. "I'm here to learn whatever I can, not to put on a show for those clowns. Some of them *ask* for it. Maybe they like to be torn to bits. But not me. I watch and keep my mouth shut."

He stepped out under the spotlights and touched the boy there on the shoulder. "Arne," he said, "you don't mind, huh? I have to show these vultures something."

"Any time," said the boy named Arne. "I've got a script in my coat pocket if you'll wait a minute."

"Don't bother," said Johnny. "I listened to the words. I know them."

Perhaps no one else in that room believed him, but I did. I had seen his amazing ability to learn a role in a single reading demonstrated before.

The scene began again, and played straight through with no apparent reaction from the small audience. While Johnny did not duplicate Arne's performance, his interpretation was not that different in outward essentials. Watching carefully, I could see many little touches of expression and reading which he had added to the role. Yet, without being able to explain why, I knew that this hackneyed little scene was reaching out to the audience to affect them with what was fast becoming Johnny's stock in trade: lost, helpless, *loneliness*. His character was fiercely lonely for his wife; miserable in the loss of her affection.

There was a scattering of applause as they finished.

Johnny stepped over to the edge of the playing area and stared down at the girl in the sailor sweater.

"How did that grab you?" he asked.

"I'm a fair person," she said. "I can admire the good things you brought to the role. Of course—"

"Save it," said Johnny. "If *you* like it, I'll have to start worrying about what I did wrong."

"John," said Jerome Newman, "that was an amazing demonstration of your ability to absorb and retain lines. But what else were you trying to prove?"

"You ought to be able to figure that out yourself," said Johnny. "Olivier himself couldn't be good in this junk, you know that. All these little exercises in relating to each other's needs! What the hell are we supposed to be, actors or psychiatrists? Who cares what the husband had for breakfast, or if he had a fight with his wife last night, or if his boss just tossed him out on his ear? The way I see it is if that kind of stuff was important, it would be in the script. Assuming the author knew what he was doing, all the information the audience needs ought to be in the dialogue and the stage directions. Never mind about digging into whether or not the character had a tough time getting toilet trained. Getting the words and the movements right, that's what matters. And this is all I did just now. I deliberately brought nothing to this part. I said the words and made the moves, just the way I saw Arne do them, and that's all."

But of course, he was wrong. I was not sure if he knew it or not, but Johnny had contributed dozens of deft touches to bring the character into reality. And, even then, Johnny moved almost like a dancer. His slim, youthful body seemed incapable of an ungraceful movement.

"So you're telling this group that they're wrong, and you alone are right?" Arnold Ross' voice was sharp and rose to almost crack at the end.

"No sir," said Johnny. "Look, I got a lot of respect for you and Mr. Newman. That's what I came here for. I figured, between the two of you, you probably know just about everything there is about acting. All I am saying is, that from what you pass along to us, you'd never guess it. If you say something to me about my acting, I'll listen, and I'll respect what you say. But why should I—or Arne, or anyone—set himself up so some wound-up chick like that one—" and his finger almost speared the girl in the sailor sweater "can get her jollies by crapping all over our work? What right has she to criticize? Look, you take this same crummy part and give it to three different actors. Give it to Montgomery Clift and Brando and Paul Muni, and I guarantee you, you will get back three absolutely different versions of the same thing. And all three may be right. So who is to say that just because their way of seeing reality is different from my way of seeing reality, that these creeps have a license to crap on what I did? You're the experts here. You know when we are doing something wrong with our voices or our movement, or with the way we see the role. You ought to tell us."

"The purpose of the Workshop is not to instruct," Ross said coldly. "It is to provide a forum for self-expression. We give the student a place where he can learn to discover himself. Criticism and self-analysis are valuable to the process."

"Forgive me, Mr. Ross," said Johnny, "but my answer to that is, bullshit! What you're talking about is what they're doing right now in those Chinese prison camps in North Korea. All their students are supposed to tear each other apart too, and snitch on one another, and stand up and confess. You may call it self-expression, but I call it brainwashing. And maybe that's not so far off, if you want the truth. You got the idea for this place when you were in Russia, didn't you?"

If Ross made an answer, it was lost in the shocked gasp of disapproval that came from the audience. Johnny looked around, shrugged, and strolled up the aisle. He scooped up his light jacket from the back of his chair and without another word or a look around, left the room. As I followed, I saw, from the corner of my eye, Ben Gazzara looking at the still closing door and saying in wonder, "I'll say this for him, he's a gutsy little sonofabitch."

Abner Thompson's *Trade Winds* was the nearest thing to an actual clipper ship I had ever seen. It was a trim, two-masted, seventy-foot schooner. Once a year, Thompson took a month off and, staffing all but a few of the most critical jobs abroad with landlubber friends, set sail for the Caribbean. Although a respected investments broker, Thompson led a double life. He was a prominent "angel," and it was well-known that he had seen black ink on five out of his last six shows. Now, the word was circulating that he would own a sizable chink of *Tiger Row*, the new play by Jean Billingham, the precocious young Southern novelist.

It was typical of Thompson's adventurous spirit that he would choose early October to sail through the Caribbean, flirting with the hurricane season. Johnny had wrangled passage through a designer friend, who had been engaged to do the costumes for *Tiger Row*. Unlike many investors, Abner Thompson usually got deeply involved in the production of plays in which he had invested. While not willing to take on the added responsibility of actually producing a play, he was often consulted on decisions. It was universally agreed that there was not a man in all Manhattan with Abner's determination to get the most mileage out of a dollar. Not a miser, he still demanded and got full value.

Thus, I am sure that my presence aboard the *Trade Winds* must have given his bookkeeper a few tense moments. I toiled not, neither did I spin. I recall that I ate well, and drank well, and had a delightful cruise . . . all the more delightful in that six days aboard the *Trade Winds* cost me less elapsed time than one full evening.

We ran on the auxiliary engine until the Ambrose lightship faded behind us. Then Abner's crew of professional seamen hoisted sail. The white canvas crackled stiffly as the following wind puffed it out, and the ship dug her head in and seemed to lurch forward. It was an impressive performance and none was more impressed than Johnny, who huddled alongside the wheelhouse in a blue nylon jacket that was too light for the chill October evening.

"Look at that," he marveled. "You wouldn't think this big old tub would move along that fast. Look at that water go by. You know, this reminds me of the time I went out to Burbank to visit my father."

"You never told me you had visited your father," I said.

"Didn't I? Must have forgot it. It wasn't much, anyway. He wouldn't let me stay. But I was out there for two weeks, and one Sunday, we went down to Malibu and one of my father's friends took us out for a sail. He had a little dinky boat, not a big one like this, and it heeled over in the water every time we came about. But that thing *moved*. Just like this one. You wouldn't guess there was that much power in just the wind. That was a good Sunday. I was eleven years old. I was still having nightmares about Aunt Sarah, and I remember I had one when I was sleeping out on my father's sofa, where he put me because he had only a single bedroom. I was sitting up screaming, and he came out and hugged me and said I was just having a bad dream, and everything was all right."

Johnny's voice trailed off and he leaned forward into the icy spray for a moment. The next words were torn from his mouth by the wind.

"He was lying. Everything wasn't all right. The next week, he sent me back to Centerville. And the farm."

The ship's bell clanged several times, and we got up and went below, to the small lounge that would double as dining room and general meeting place. The room was crowded, and standing at one end, I saw Thompson, a tall, muscular man in his fifties.

"Everybody here?" he asked. "I want to introduce all of you people to my First Mate. This is Larry Heller. I'm carried on the log as Captain, but Larry really runs the ship. He'll get around to all of you individually and assign you regular duties. Nothing you can't handle. After all, this is a pleasure cruise. But there's work you can do and still have fun, and I know you'll all do your best not to get in the way of the professional crewmen. Larry?"

The First Mate waved a casual hand our way. He seemed to be in his late twenties, with a shock of gray-flecked hair that made him look years older than his boyish face.

"Running a pretty good swell tonight," he said. "Wouldn't advise anyone going on deck after dark unless you absolutely have to. Then, you wear a life jacket, and hang on to something when you move around. Don't go over the side, for Christ's sake. That water's cold. Even with a jacket, you wouldn't last ten minutes. Don't let the ocean fool you. She's good to you if you know how to handle her. But drop your guard for a second and she'll deep-six you."

"Now," said Abner Thompson, "since the sun has been over

the yardarm for some time now . . . Cookie, break out the rum!"

Cookie was actually Abner's pert blonde wife, Chris, for Christine, and the rum was really your choice of martinis, Scotch or bourbon, but the nautical urge was upon us all, and even Johnny got in his share of "Avast there, ye lubbers," aimed at the casual acquaintances who might or might not become friends by the end of the trip.

Although there had been no obvious pairing off, the mix of men and women worked out almost evenly. In addition to Abner's Chris, Jean Billingham was aboard, as were several other women whom Johnny immediately set out to meet. With Johnny and Abner, there were two young men who later turned out to be actors; a man of Abner's age who, we soon learned, was Richard Robeson, director of *Tiger Row,* and several others with whom we would become acquainted in due time.

There is sometimes a doll-like quality about actresses that makes you afraid to breath on them, lest their hair should puff away and their china-like complexions shatter into tiny shards of fragile glass. Two of the girls aboard had that quality . . . eyes too wide, with the whites showing all around the pupil, and with artificial lashes that could slice open your cheek if you happened to get too close during an emphatic flutter. Their diction often seems to be deliberately breathless, as if it were not enough to merely form the words and speak them, but that it is then necessary to puff them across the room toward the listener, to keep them from floating off in the wrong direction. I have always adored these delicate creatures, and have waited, mostly in vain, for the facade to crack away and reveal the true person beneath.

Johnny had slipped into the pack and cut out two of these lovelies, and had them in a corner all to himself. They were both taller than he, even without heels, and I don't know what he could have told them, but the depth of their adoration for him spilled from their eyes in quantities only exceeded by the amount of calculating jealousy each turned upon the other, mixed with little nibbling, not-quite-catty remarks.

"Hi, buddy," said Johnny. "Meet Sally and Gretel."

"Gretchen," said one of the dolls. She was the blonde. Sally had flaming red hair. Both had heavily-painted lips and hairdos that must have taken their dresser all morning to prepare. It was too bad, I observed smugly to myself, that one stroll around deck in a strong breeze, and their crowning glory would be reduced to the tousled casualness of us mortal folks. Which shows how little *I* knew. There was a hairdresser on board, singing for his supper by keeping the girls spectacular.

"Sally and Gretchen are roommates," said Johnny.

"Only on the *Trade Winds,*" Sally hastened to explain. "I just flew in from the Coast to audition for dear Richard. And when he invited me to cancel my television appearances and come along on this marvelous cruise, why I just leaped!"

"How wonderful," purred Gretchen, "that 'What's My Line' was able to find another contestant on such short notice. I haven't accepted any television assignments, myself. I feel it's so much wiser to wait until the medium has become a little more . . . mature. Don't you think?"

"Knock it off, both of you," said Johnny. "I know for a fact that you're both scuffling for a walkon in *Tiger Row,* so don't bust yourselves up trying to impress me. I love you for what you are. And what you are," he leered, "is 38–24–36."

"Oh, Johnny," giggled Sally, "you've been peeking."

"Not yet," he said, "but is that an invitation?"

"Baby," said Gretchen, "you just bet it is. Excuse me." And off she huffed, leaving Johnny doubled up with silent laughter. Then, to Sally's despairing surprise, he tickled her ribs once and slid off into the crowd, calling over his shoulder, "See you later. Don't take any wooden C cups."

72

Later, sipping a Scotch and soda that was mostly soda, he nodded over toward the two girls who were both stalking the director, Richard Robeson.

"You gotta lay off those kind," he said, clinking the ice against his teeth. "They're the real tigers in the forest. Get hung up on one of them and it's goodbye, Charlie. They cut off your balls and fry them for breakfast. But it's fun to play tag with them, because I know how dangerous it can be, and that flips me."

"Aren't you being hard on them, Johnny? I know they're neither one candidates for Miss I.Q., but they're both good looking, probably very nice girls."

"Those very nice girls," said Johnny, "would let Robeson screw them in Macy's window at high noon if they thought it would land them the part in *Tiger Row*. That isn't what frosts me, though," he went on quickly. "Hell, I might drop my pants for him myself if I had to. What pisses me is, they do it for the *wrong reason*. They don't want the part because it might give them a chance to do good work, or learn something, or break through some rough technique block. They don't even know what good work is. To them, the whole thing begins and ends that moment when he says, 'Okay, you got the part.' That's what they want. The score. The hit. From there on, it's all downhill. They don't really want to do the part. They want to get it. Once they've got it, it's not a score anymore, and they have to head out and look for another score. And they're the same way with men. If they can get me to go absolutely, stark raving mad over them, then they have scored on me, and it's time to move on for fresh territory. So I give it right back to them. I don't give a shit. And they know it. That drives them nuts, and they'll do anything in the world for me, hoping that eventually I'll lose my cool and flip over them, so they can know they beat me. But they never do, and that's why I can do absolutely anything in the world I want to with them, and they'll let me get away with it. Because they're still hoping to score."

Obviously, my slight disapproval at this attitude got through to him, because his face clouded.

"You think I'm snowing you? Boy, sometimes I think those guys at Film Arts got the wrong bird to watch me. How can you see what I am if you don't understand? I tell you, those aren't girls. They're walking, talking, IBM machines wrapped up in mink and some peculiar drive that won't let them rest until they've castrated every guy in the world. They'll do anything to get a shot at you. Watch this."

He went over and dragged Sally out of a small crowd of men and maneuvered her into a corner so her back was to everyone else in the room, and only he and I could see what he was about to do.

"Sally," he whispered. "I got a bet. My bet is that, under that cashmere sweater, you are wearing nothing, absolutely nothing, except those magnificent boobs."

She giggled and flushed.

"As a matter of fact," she whispered back, "I'm not. You see, I don't need any uplift."

"Just what I said," Johnny said calmly. "Now, what I want, Sally, is for you to show me your tit."

She smiled weakly. "You're funny," she decided finally. "I like a guy with a sense of humor."

"Let's see your tit. Just pull down the neck of your sweater."

"I couldn't do that," she protested.

"Nobody else can see," he promised. "I just want to take a look."

"Here? In public?"

"That's the way I get my jollies. Come on. Let's see it."

She glanced over her shoulder, and then, as I almost choked

74

on my bourbon, moved forward toward Johnny, making sure
to block out the rest of the room from what she was doing.

"All right," she whispered, "since it means so much to you.
But just this once."

She bent forward and I saw Johnny glance down, and his face
was split by a smile.

"Thanks, honey," he said, as she straightened. Her sweater
was wrinkled where she had stretched it, and she pulled at the
wrinkles as she went back to join the other group.

"Sonofabitch," Johnny whistled softly. "You know what, old
buddy? She actually had lipstick on the nipple!"

Elvira and I had coffee and Danish in a mirror-and-chrome
lunchroom on Sixth Avenue. My phone had snarled into my ear
at 8:30 and it was her, inviting me to join her.

"You look like hell," she said sweetly.

"Worked late," I mumbled. "Didn't sleep good. More coffee,
please." I am unable to speak or to coordinate my hands too
well for an hour or so after I get up. Some people leap out of
the sack, full of energy and alert of mind. I envy them. I start
slow and build. I would have made a hell of a cave man. Some
morning, the tyrannosaurus would have swallowed me up
whole and been starting on dessert before I would have been
able to comprehend that something was nibbling on my toes.

"Hitting the sauce?"

"Elvira! You wrong me."

"Just checking. I still remember those four martinis at The
Venus." This was the closest she had ever come to reminding
me of my remarks that long, martini-filled afternoon. I was just
as glad. I didn't feel any too heroic, taking on a nice little dame
like Elvira.

"Elvira, dear heart, believe me as I swear on this copy of the
New York News: I am not hung. This is the way I always am

75

in the morning. You don't know the agony my poor wife went through before we agreed not to notice the other was alive before noon. And, dearly as I love you, I would be much more talkative along about eleven instead of the crack of nine."

"Sorry," she said. "I've got to catch a plane down to Philadelphia. I do have other clients, you know. And right now, one of them has a play in bad trouble. But I wanted to see you before I left."

"So see. It's not my fault I look this way before I shave."

She opened her purse and took out her little tape recorder. Elvira has embraced progress with a hearty will. She owns a Sony Videotape machine and has trained the maid to tape programs from TV that she would otherwise have to miss. And her office is bugged more thoroughly than CIA headquarters. The little purse recorder set her back at least two hundred dollars, and came from Kedelski in Switzerland. "When your stock in trade is your word and whom you give it to," she once told me, "it pays to make sure that everybody heard the same thing." She never plays tricks with her gadgets. She gives fair warning that they are eavesdropping. Just as she did on the recording she had me listen to there in the lunchroom. I had to keep the volume down, but we could both hear clearly enough, so good was the frequency response of the little unit.

First I heard a phone ringing, and then Elvira's voice: "H'llo?" It did my heart good to hear her mumble, to prove to whoever was listening that it wasn't only me who started the day a hundred and eighty degrees out of phase.

"Elvira?" said a man's voice, distorted by the telephone speaker. "This is Ned. Ned Barker."

"Ned Barker! Where are you? What's wrong?"

"Where the hell do you think I am? I'm in Beverly Hills."

"Are you aware that it's three-thirty in the morning here?" I heard the anger in her voice even on the tape.

"Sorry, Elvira. It's just a little after midnight here. . .well, twelve-thirty. I keep forgetting about that damned time difference."

"Never mind, Ned. I suppose it's important. Incidentally, I'm recording this conversation."

"Don't you always? And you're fucking-A it's important."

"I think you just violated a couple of Federal laws, Ned."

"Sorry, Elvira. I'm all wound up. It's that red-headed genius of yours."

"What's he done now?"

"It's what he hasn't done. I thought I'd have a first draft by now."

"You were promised a first draft by the end of April. That's next week."

"But how's it coming? Nobody tells me nothing. I have to rely on a crystal ball to convince the bank that I'm not building a casino with their dough."

"I've given you reports. Twice a week. I think the script is coming along very well. In due time we can all sit down together and I think you will be pleased. In the meantime, you are only running up phone bills and your blood pressure."

"For two thou a week, I think I'm entitled to something more than promises."

"You're getting something more than promises, Ned. And you are starting to make me angry. You and I have had a fruitful and profitable relationship over the years. I have never mislead you or allowed you to be taken. We all agreed that Edwin was the writer for your project, and all of us signed the contract in good faith."

"I'll tell the world we did," he said. "That's why I'm so upset. I've been trying to get your boy for the last three nights. He never answers. What the hell is he doing? Drinking Costello's dry on my money, that's what! Why is he always out when I call? And lying about it, that's what bugs me! The desk clerk says he's in, but he won't answer the phone. I let it ring 43 times last night."

"Maybe he puts the phone in a bureau drawer."

"I don't care if he shoves it up his ass! Is it asking too much that I should be allowed to talk with him, to see how he's enjoying my two grand a week? And maybe even get some kind of hint as to what the hell he is doing with my script?"

"I don't see why you shouldn't talk to him. I don't understand your not being able to reach him. As for the script, we agreed that there was to be no interference with the first draft. That is why you are not going to see one word until the entire film is written. But I see his output, every day. He sends it over by messenger, and my girl types the stencils. I can promise you, Ned, it's good material, and you're going to be very happy."

"All right, I believe you already. But will you please ask him to call me? I want to go over a few points with him, if that won't rupture his artistic muse too severely."

"I'll pass the message along, Ned. Is that all?"

"That's all. Still love me?"

"Of course I do. Good night, Ned."

"Good night, sweet lady."

There was a click of phone receiver being replaced and the tape went dead. I took a deep swig at my coffee. It was getting cold.

"Well," I said, "Ned was right. I was down the hall."

"I see," Elvira said slowly. "There is a—shall we say, friend —in a nearby room, a fast scoot down the hall, and another louse of a husband gets his free kicks while mama stays home and listens to the kids yell."

"Did I say that's what it is?"

"Will you say that's what it's not?"

I looked down into my coffee and saw my face reflected. My

nose was foreshortened, and looked big and red. I was probably blushing. It was almost funny, Elvira getting hot and bothered because she had caught another of her "boys" straying off the straight and narrow. It would bother her for a while, and then she'd forgive, if not forget. And I knew I could count on her not to turn it into a gossip item.

"You'll call Ned today?" she asked.

"Promise. How about right now."

"You wouldn't. It's six-thirty in the morning there."

"Serves him right."

I would call Ned, and I would hope that neither he or Elvira would do much more checking up on me. It was one thing for them to think I was down the hall with a girl. But I found myself wondering how they would feel to discover that, somehow, I was back in 1953, having a ball of a cruise with John Calvin Lewis as the good ship *Trade Winds* sailed quietly through the blue Caribbean.

CHAPTER
FOUR

T HE *Trade Winds* made port on an early Sunday morning at Charlotte Amalie, capital of St. Thomas in the U. S. Virgin Islands. The harbor is a beautiful one, and as we slipped quietly in, still under sail, we were swallowed up by steep, green arms of land jutting out on both sides of the channel.

Two of our passengers were impatient to land so they could get the hell off the schooner. Sally, undaunted by Johnny's frequent sniping, had made a tremendous pass at Abner at the same moment as Chris was entering the lounge with a pitcher of steaming hot coffee. Most of it went down Sally's front, and for the last two days of the St. Thomas leg, her cleavage was salved with vaseline and packed with cotton. Chris apologized sweetly for the accident and suggested that the next time Sally made goo-goo eyes at Abner she might wake up going over the side with an anchor on her leg. Abner said nothing. Although he had not encouraged Sally's raid, he had not resisted it too actively either.

The other deserter was the hairdresser, who called himself Pierre. I learned later that his real name was Irving, and that he was from the Bronx. Pierre-Irving was quite upset at Abner for not including at least one other gay boy. And what was worse, for a while he thought Abner *had,* in the person of John Calvin Lewis.

"I don't know what it is in me that draws them," Johnny said. "I don't tease them on, the way I do the Sallies. Hell, I think I'm sorry for them. I know this, I never saw a happy fag. So why can't they leave me alone? This guy, Pierre, I knew he was up to no good when he started patting me on the heinie while I was heaving my guts out into the Atlantic. Being seasick is bad enough: who needs Lucky Pierre groping around? So I told him to blow, without thinking, and naturally he jumped on the word and said, 'Sweetie, that's what I do *best!*' My wise crack cost me two days of that nut leaping out from behind things and inviting me down to the sail locker. Finally, I told him that I was going to kick his ass off if he didn't leave me alone, and that tickled him pink. 'I just love rough trade,' he said."

"How did you finally get rid of him?"

"It was easy. One night, I took him up on his offer. I said for him to meet me in the sail locker in an hour, when it was good and dark. He showed up, hot and ready to go. When he came in, I whispered for him to get undressed, and man, he just about ripped those cute sailor clothes off. Then I asked, 'Ready?' and he gasped, 'Ready, sweetie!' and that's when I turned the light on. I tell you, he almost shit. There we were, Sally and Gretchen and me, drinking champagne, and there he was, buck naked,

81

with a big stiff dong and an open jar of vaseline in his hand. He looked at the girls for a long time, and you could see the idea that he'd been had working its way slowly through his head, until he finally got it and busted out crying. He ran out on deck with his clothes flapping behind. I guess he got dressed before anyone saw him. Anyway, he never bothered me again."

And now the hairdresser was joining Sally in debarking at St. Thomas, to fly over to San Juan on the shuttle run, and catch a DC-6 up to New York where the weather was colder, but where hearts might be warmer. I felt sorry for both of them.

In 1953, the mass tourist boom had not yet swept away all the gentle charm of this little island, and the waterfront was still dotted with working boats, on which dark-skinned men sweated, dragging yellowtail and tuna out of the Caribbean.

We split up in various directions, promising to rejoin the yawl in time for a dawn departure for St. Croix, and somehow Johnny paired off with Jean Billingham. This was surprising because during the trip down, the feisty little writer had been cordial to Johnny, and that was all. She had spent a lot of time with Robeson, discussing *Tiger Row,* and more time by herself, making changes on the script. Now, on the jetty, she suddenly detached herself from Abner's group and announced that she and Johnny were going to see the sights. Robeson started to make a kick, but Abner shut him up with a hard look.

We rented a jeep that had a purple awning over it, and bounced up the road to Bluebeard's Castle for something to eat before we did the tourist bit. Johnny drove, skillfully—but on the wrong side of the road. A truckload of jeering Negroes almost shoved us off the mountain, and finally Johnny figured out that in St. Thomas, you drive on the left.

Sitting on the patio of Bluebeard's Castle, looking down over the rusty smoothbore cannon, you could see Old Fort Christian, now the police barracks, and beyond it, the translucent blue-green of the harbor.

"I just must have a banana daquiri," said Jean Billingham. "I think that is the only reason I joined this odyssey. Abner told me the banana daquiris here are like ambrosia."

"Okay by me," Johnny said. I had the same, and Abner hadn't lied. The blend of rum and skillfully crushed bananas made a deceptively gentle-tasting drink. With it, we had conch chowder, which did not make as big a hit. "Just like Manhattan clam chowder," Johnny decided.

"You're a strange boy," Jean said. "What are you doing mixed up with this crowd?"

"I'm an actor," he said. "I want a part in *Tiger Row.* I had a chance to come along, I jumped at it."

"I must say, you're keeping your motives a deep, dark secret. I don't believe Richard even knows you're aboard. And Abner certainly doesn't know you're an actor. In fact, to almost everyone on the *Trade Winds,* you're a young man of mystery."

Johnny grinned.

"That's part of my plan," he confided. "Now, you take those other two, Rosencranz and Guildenstern."

"Brian Catton and Roy Jackson?"

"Yeah, them two. My God, the way they prance around trying to get attention, I expect them to do the dueling scene from *Hamlet* any minute. I know they're both friends of Robeson's, but even so, everything they do is just what you'd expect. I mean, if they can't surprise *me* how do you think they're going to surprise an audience?"

"Perhaps it isn't necessary to surprise an audience."

"Not every minute, no. But those folks out there don't pay five-ninety to have you soothe them to sleep. They want something exciting to happen every now and then to remind them they're alive. And that's what theater is all about. It's sure death to give people what they *expect.*"

Jean laughed. Her tawny hair was cut very short, and it made her look almost like Johnny's younger brother. She was older than he by some ten years, but being an attractive woman with no excess weight, it did not show.

"Why, you're a little monster," she said with delight. "That's wonderful. For a long time, I thought I was the only monster in the world, and even now, it's damn seldom I run into another one."

Solemnly, they shook hands. The check came, and Johnny picked it up and handed it to her. She laughed and paid it, and we piled back into the jeep.

"You drive well," she said as we wound our way up the tortured road to the top of the mountain.

"Learned on the farm," Johnny said. "By the time you're ten, you get to drive everything. Tractors, cars, trucks. Hearses."

Jean looked at him strangely. "Why did you say that?" she asked.

"I don't know," Johnny mumbled. "It just came out."

"I've got this thing about bulls," Johnny had told me, one day as we walked through Central Park. "There was that film Robert Rossen made with Mel Ferrer. *The Brave Bulls?* Well, up until I saw that movie, I never knew why I was so hung up on bulls. Then I knew. And buddy-boy, when I get the loot, I am going to go to Mexico and hire the best damn matador down there to teach me how to fight a bull. Up to now, the only thing I ever did with a bull was to ride him."

"Ride a bull?"

"It was back in Centerville."

The County Fair was in town, and Johnny had just turned eighteen and had hurried down to his local draft board. Maybe he could get drafted and get sent to the West Coast.

After stumbling through the eye test, Johnny was surprised to hear the doctor say, "All right, let's do it once more. This time with your glasses."

84

"I don't wear glasses," Johnny said.

"Come on, boy," said the doctor, "don't waste my time. Put on your glasses so I can tell what your corrected vision is."

"I said, I don't wear glasses."

"All right," said the doctor. "Suppose you tell me how you managed to get through high school without glasses? You're blind as a bat without them. That right eye isn't any better than 20/80, or I miss my guess. Glasses or not, boy, you're 4F."

"Now, wait a minute," said Johnny. "I didn't know I needed glasses. I guess I figured everybody couldn't see the blackboard any better than I could. So I listened real hard. But if you say I need glasses, I'll get glasses. I'll have them by tomorrow, I promise you."

"Wouldn't do you no good anyway," mumbled the doctor. "Can't send you off to the army with those kind of eyes."

"I've seen soldiers wearing glasses."

"Maybe. But I bet you they could see better than 20/80 without them. No; sorry, son. No point in wasting both our time. But you get those glasses anyway, you hear? You're a menace to yourself without them."

That afternoon, Johnny signed up to ride the Brahman bull at the Fair.

"It wasn't the $25 prize for staying on him thirty seconds," Johnny told me. "I was so shook up by that doctor, I *had* to do something big, or I would have dug a hole and crawled into it. My motorcycle was laid up with a busted carb, and besides, that wouldn't have worked. I had to take on something new."

Pound for pound, a Brahman bull is the most treacherous and dangerous creature you will find in the world. In many rural areas, riding the Brahman bull is the high spot of the action at a traveling rodeo or county fair. And so it was in Centerville.

The potential rider is lowered onto the bull's broad but slippery back as the animal is contained in a wooden chute. Tied around the bull like a bellyband is a rope, and the rider must hold onto that with one hand, and keep the other hand in the air at all times. Then the two are released into the fenced-in arena.

"I had a beat-up straw hat to wave in the air," Johnny said, "and thirty seconds didn't seem like a long time. When I slipped my legs down around that big black mother, I wrapped them around his ribs to help me hang on, and the first thing he tried to do was mash me against the sides of the chute. Then they slid the front gate open, and he leaped out like he was on springs. It seemed like we were up in the air a hundred feet, and all the time he was twisting and squirming, trying to slip me off. He hit the ground with all four legs stiff, and it almost broke my back. That's when I lost my balance, and I never really got it back. I thought I bounced around on that bastard's back for at least half an hour, until he finally got me started to slipping off to one side, and I couldn't pull myself up again, and finally I had to drop my hat and grab hold of his neck with both hands to keep from falling. Then he twisted his head around and tried to bite me, and I had to let go, and I dumped, right between his four legs. He jumped off me, and turned around, and I could tell from the way that he was coming at me that I was going to get stomped, good and proper. But they had a wrangler dressed up like a clown, and he drew the bull off by waving a cloth at him. When the bull caught up with him, he just jumped into a rubber barrel, and let the bull butt it across the ground, while the other guys were pulling me out. I thought sure I'd busted my shoulder, but it was just sprained. They showed me the stopwatch. I'd stayed on the bull just a little less than nine seconds."

That Saturday, Johnny went down and had his eyes fitted for glasses.

Overlooking Magen's Bay on the far side of St. Thomas is a view area, and a stone bench with letters carved into it that read, "Drake's Seat." The legend is that Sir Francis Drake sat here and, staring at the water below, plotted out his world conquests.

It's a good story. Maybe it's even true. At any rate, the seat was once again being used for plotting, as Jean Billingham and John Calvin Lewis sat there, close together, and conspired against the unknowing Richard Robeson.

"You don't have to worry about Brian or Roy," Jean told him. "I know for a fact that Richard doesn't want either of them. It wasn't his idea, bringing them along. Abner has something else up his sleeve for them, some movie project, I think. As a matter of fact, Richard was a little put out at this whole idea. He likes to take his own vacations, where and when he wants them. But the script changes had to be made anyway, and he couldn't really spit in Abner's eye. What I mean is, by not being a squirch about business, you may have made a better impression on our director than you would have otherwise."

Her almost instant partisanship would have surprised me more, had I not seen so much evidence of Johnny's irrestible likeability in action before. And Jean was getting both barrels. He spoke softly to her, swore less than usual, and when the jeep pulled up near Drake's Seat, he actually helped her out of it. This, for Johnny, was courtliness at its height. The view from this place is one of the finest in the Caribbean. Off to the left, you can see Outer Brass Island, and over the rich green water, in the distance, the clouds seem to be almost at eye level. This spot was deliberately constructed for romance, and I could tell that Johnny was using every advantage it gave him.

Below, the water was so flat and glistening that I had an impulse, which I resisted, to throw my new pocket piece, the

1879 silver dollar, skipping across the waves.

Jean Billingham was in her early thirties then. She is now in her late forties and confined to a sanitarium in upstate New York. The public believes she is there for incurable alcoholism, but it is common knowledge in publishing circles that she must be restrained from hurting herself. A strong undertone of suicide was apparent in her last book, published the summer after Johnny's death, and she has not written a publishable word since. Like the brightly-painted ceramic sparrows you buy in Mexico, once Jean's delicate image was shattered it was impossible to ever glue it together again without leaving visible marks of the broken edges.

To see these early stages of their friendship, Johnny carefully showing the image he sensed she wanted to see; she, giving perhaps a little too much of herself, as she so often did; the knowledge of what was to come later made me feel even more like an intruder. I remembered my promise to Johnny, and for a second, felt like violating it by telling him he was setting forces into motion that would eventually destroy them both; that this sunny afternoon with them sitting close together on Drake's Seat would brew more harm and despair than either could survive. But of course, I said nothing.

"Now," she said, "you may have read an earlier draft, but the changes I've made make a tremendous difference. The part of the boy in the cave has been expanded. It fits you like it had been written for you."

"Wasn't it?" asked Johnny. It was impossible to tell if he was joking.

"No," said Jean. "Not for you specifically. But it was written for someone who could be what I call, The Youth. And I think you could be just what I had in mind. I've never seen you act, so I'll have to assume you're professional. But I like the way you look, and the way you think. The rest can't be that difficult."

"Thank you," said Johnny. His eyes took her in, alertness hiding behind quiet smile and the shy glance. I knew he was having difficulty fitting Jean Billingham into any of his usual niches. She was certainly no Aunt Em, nor was she a Sally or Gretchen. Her interest in him did not seem to be sexual and there was nothing to be gained by tricking him. Since coming to New York, Johnny had met few who helped him principally because their hearts were good, so it is understandable he did not recognize such an individual when she came right up and sat on Drake's Seat with him.

"How did you get into this writing business?" he asked, probing.

"Would you like the official biography, or the truth?"

"The truth."

"I was the ugliest girl at Sarah Lawrence. I had to do something with my time, so I wrote a book about my home town. Cedartown, Georgia. You'd think there was nothing interesting about Cedartown, but by the time I got through with it, there wasn't anyone left in town who would talk to me except for Ezra E. Browne, and he was the local drunk. Since I was twenty and by then had learned that if I cut my hair off I looked like a cute little boy, the subject matter of my book shocked the literary world considerably. This was before the war, remember, and people weren't used to men writing like that, let alone little girls. The book sold like crazy. How could it help but sell? It wasn't a very good book, but the money I got from it saved me from having to go back to Cedartown and grovel in the town square. The funny part was, I got all my facts about sex straight out of Kraft-Ebbing; the parts that were published in Latin."

"I read your book," said Johnny. "You called it, let me see, *March To The Sea.*"

"It wasn't bad at all," Jean said. "The people were real enough, all right. But you have to remember that when I left home I was sixteen, going on seventeen, and I didn't really know that old Banker Morris liked to be whipped, but I knew that if anyone did, he was most likely the one. I just took the case histories out of the book and fitted them to the faces I remembered from home. I changed the names, of course, but I bet I hit close to the mark a couple of times. Otherwise, why would everyone have gotten so mad?"

Johnny giggled. He was genuinely amused.

"Since then," Jean went on, "I've sort of specialized in Southern decadence. When Tennessee Williams came along, I actually felt like he was violating my copyrights. Of course, he's twice the writer I am, but he's limited by not being willing to work in the novel form. The temporal sense of the theater tricks him into saying things he would never say if he knew they were going to be set in 12-point Garamond and issued in an edition of twenty thousand copies. There's something so permanent-feeling about a book, it makes you think twice before you let that final draft out of your hands."

"One of these days, I'm going to write a book," Johnny said. "Just to get it out of here—" and he pressed his chest hard. "Sometimes I think that if I felt one ounce more of sorrow and pain, I'd just crumble down to dust. I go along, forgetting about it, and get to thinking it's gone, and then it up and chews a big gash out of me again as strong as ever."

"I sensed that about you," she said. "I don't know if you have truly suffered anything really terrible, or if your threshold is set so that whatever has happened to you seems terrible. In the last analysis it doesn't make any difference, because the effect on you is the same. And that's why I wanted to spend today with you, away from Sally and Gretchen and your friend Pierre."

"Hey," said Johnny, "he's no friend of *mine.*"

"I know," she said. "I was joking with you. But I really did want to see you as I knew you must be when you aren't reacting to that other world of theater and stage-struck girls. Out here on the island, we can be alone and perhaps discover each other. I hoped to discover my Youth, and I think I have. Now, what were *you* after?"

"Well," said Johnny, "I'd be lying if I said I didn't hope you might help me get a shot at the play."

"I'm glad you told me the truth," she said. "I don't blame you for it. I never knew what it was to be young and struggling, but I can imagine, and I don't blame you for using any tool you can get your hands on. And I will help you. Richard detests writers having opinions about casting, I've been warned about that. But I can get around him. It probably won't take that much manuevering, not if you are as good as I think you are. So now we both have what we came after."

"Not everything," Johnny said. He leaned forward and kissed her. It was not a quick motion; his lips almost touched hers, then stopped and hesitated for a moment, until her eyes met his and did not look away, but closed slowly in submission. He did not move either of his hands from the stone bench, and as they swayed, it was Jean who had to reach up a hand to steady them both.

"God, you're so young," she whispered.

Tiger Row went into rehearsal in mid-November of 1953, with John Calvin Lewis in the role of the Boy in the cave. The play was allegorical, although the plot and dialogue were naturalistic enough. I have always felt that Jean Billingham, in this, her only play, touched genuine mainsprings of dramatic greatness. My original exposure to it was in the hallowed pages of *Theatre Arts,* the great monthly magazine which brought not only all the theatrical news to those of us too far away to get the theater section of *The Times,* but which published a current, still-on-Broadway play each and every issue. It was like having a little bit of Shubert Alley transplanted to Florida, and

I looked forward to its arrival by air mail (which cost me more than the subscription itself) every month. Thus, I first saw photographs of Johnny Lewis while I was still stationed at Patrick Air Force Base, since the magazine always included several pictures from the play along with the script. In fact, I knew a director who, in preparing a production of *Light Up The Sky* for a local amateur group, took those photos to be gospel. Under each picture was a caption, taken from the text of the play, and in his direction, he insisted that the cast be lined up to match each and every photo when the dialogue had progressed to that point.

I was much taken with *Tiger Row,* I recall, and would have enjoyed seeing it. I did "see" it, as I always do with playscripts, casting it in my mind's eye and virtually hearing the actors as I read the lines. But nothing in my imaginary performance could have touched the reality. Then I put the magazine away and awaited the next one impatiently.

When I finally got around to calling Ned Barker, he was out at Columbia Ranch, shooting, and Elly answered the phone. I had not seen her since our mutual disaster Off-Broadway with *Hedda,* since she had been in Europe during my final negotiations with Ned and my trip to the Coast.

"Hello, stranger!" she boomed at me across three thousand miles. "I suppose you know it's 6:00 A.M. out here."

"I'm afraid I do," I said. "My idea was to pay Ned back for calling all of us here in the middle of the night. Sorry you got caught in the trap."

"Been up for hours," she said cheerily. "One of the kids has the projectile whoops, and I've been mopping up curdled milk since midnight. The maid will be here in another hour, and then I'll flake out."

"Well, I heard Ned wanted to talk with me and hasn't been

having much luck. My room is so noisy I use ear plugs, and probably couldn't hear the phone." With the last, I crossed my fingers and hoped the management of the Great Northern would never learn of my cruel lie. "Why don't you tell him I called, and that if he calls me during the daytime, I'm bound to hear the phone over the gentle rattle of my Hermes 2000."

"Ned? Call in the daytime? You have to be kidding. You know he never thinks of phoning anybody in the East until after midnight their time. It's his schtick. That way he keeps reminding all you peasants that the real clock is kept in Hollywood and that you're perpetually three hours behind the times."

"Well, I ought to get to him or he to me. He has Elvira a little itchy, and that's not good for any of us."

"*I* know what he's after," Elly Barker said. "In case you were misled by my matronly ways with my miserable brat, I am still co-producer of *The Johnny Lewis Story.*"

"So shoot."

"You won't like it."

"It's your money. You've got a right to know how it's being spent. I'm hard at work and living clean, that's the truth. I'm getting more good pages a day than I ever expected. The second draft will be a snap, with all the good stuff that's going into the first. You'll be a month ahead of schedule, I promise you."

"Stop kvetching," she said. "I've got faith, Elvira has faith, and I think even poor Ned almost has faith. I'm banking on the end of the month, and that's it. No, what has us a little worried is the direction you're taking."

"What do you mean, the direction I'm taking? How the hell do you know the direction I'm taking? You *don't* know, not until I finish the first draft. That was the deal. I don't want any interference until I've had my say. I have enough faith in my approach to think you'll like it. But if I check in with you every twenty pages, we'll all get off the track and nobody'll be happy.

That's why we put in the no peeking clause."

She sighed over long distance. "Ed, do you think my sainted husband would turn loose of two thousand bucks a week without marking the bills?"

"I hope that doesn't mean what I think it does."

"Be your age. Ned has a spy in Elvira's office. We get the pages the day after she does."

"That double-dealing sonofabitch! Does he have my phone bugged, too?"

"Actually, darling, it was *my* idea. I made poor Ned swear not to come to any decision before the entire script was done, but this way he at least knows from day to day where his money is going."

"I suppose you've got some guy sneaking in every night with a Minox camera to microfilm the evidence."

"You're funny. I thought you'd be more upset, actually. No, Ed, these days anyone with access to a Xerox machine can run off documents for a dime a page. Remember that William Manchester book about Kennedy's assassination? How do you think the unedited manuscript got out of *Look* and all the way to Formosa for that bootleg printing? Some office boy and his handy dandy copier."

I looked at my watch. We'd been on this call for ten minutes. If I didn't cut it off soon, my phone bill would be larger than my weekly stipend.

"All this is lovely, Elly. And you're right, I'm not too upset to find out you've been flimflamming me. Obviously you're holding Ned in check, or he would already have descended on me screaming vengeance. My no-peek idea was to avoid prejudgment of my approach. As long as Ned stays out of my hair, I don't really care that he's sneaking the pages. I wouldn't let Elvira know, though. She's not as weak-willed as I am."

"You're not weak-willed; just realistic. Like the man says, 'when rape is inevitable'—"

"—Relax and enjoy it? Yuk yuk. Okay, Elly, what's bothering you two? You said something about the direction I'm taking."

"It worries us, hon."

"Isn't that too bad? If you hadn't sneaked a peek, you wouldn't be worried."

"Maybe worried is too strong a word. Questioning, is what I ought to say. It seems like you're going pretty deep into certain things that we can never film. For one thing, his *language.* You have Johnny saying things to poor Emily Woodford that would make the mike cable melt. We can't film something like that. We'd all go to jail."

"I refer you to a couple of lectures by Ned in which he spoke with great admiration about the fornication scenes in *I Am Curious, Yellow.*"

"But that film wasn't *profane.*"

"Look, Elly, I'm not insisting that every word Johnny used stay in. They're there now to give the scene its right flavor. If we can get the same effect with a couple of 'Gee Whiz's' and 'darn it's,' why we will."

"Don't patronize me. You know as well as I do some of those scenes would collapse if we weakened the language. Never mind that point; we'll work it out in the second draft. Our other question was, aren't you putting in a lot of fictional stuff? Johnny's life has been very well documented. You have reams of material to work with. So why all this imaginary stuff?"

"Those scenes actually happened. Perhaps not precisely the way I wrote them, but believe me, they're basically true."

"How could you know about them? Look, I'm not complaining about the content of the scenes. Some of them play beautifully. But we don't want to end up with a million lawsuits for invasion of privacy. Most of those people are still alive, and suppose they turn up yelling cop?"

"The best defense is the truth, Elly. And, painful as it some-

95

times is, that is exactly what I'm writing. Not because I'm so honest, but because it's easier than thinking up lies."

"Oh, really," she snapped, and now real anger had crept into her voice, "talking with you is like trying to pin down a press agent. You forget that we're paying your salary. You're accountable to us."

"Look again, Elly," I said, getting a little mad myself. "Nobody's paying any salary. You agreed to pay a certain sum in exchange for a first draft on your lousy film. You also agreed to stay the hell out of my hair while I was writing it—an agreement you violated at the very first opportunity. This conversation is exactly what I wanted to avoid when I stipulated that I take this first shot at the script without interference. I know there will be problems later. But that's where I want to keep them—*later*, when the basic work is done and we can talk without getting emotional."

I would have said more, but she cut in on me sharply.

"I can't talk any more," she said. "The monster's whoopsing all over the kitchen again. You'll hear from us later."

"Sure I will," I said, but I was already talking into a dead phone.

Rehearsals for beautiful plays are invariably held in the most dismal surroundings available, and *Tiger Row* was no exception. There are a klatch of drafty, depressingly bare, musty rooms on second and third floors in the theatrical district, which rent out for three dollars an hour and are laughingly referred to as "rehearsal halls." Here, especially in November, actors gather in little groups like sheep, huddling to keep warm, and speak their speeches trippingly on the tongue with frosty white breaths punctuating every word. The coffee, when it arrives at all, is almost always lukewarm, and the pastry is stale. No self-respecting plumber would work under such miserable conditions, yet every year hundreds of the highest-paid performers in the world subject themselves willingly to these surroundings, and would feel uneasy if things were any different.

The basic cast of *Tiger Row* was a small one. There was Elijah, the Holy Roller preacher, who kept his sixteen-year-old brother imprisoned in a cave to "guard the boy against the angel of death." Johnny, of course, was the boy, and as Elijah, Bert Klen had returned to the stage after a six-year stretch in Hollywood. Klen, who had spent his Hollywood career being cast as the perennial "older brother" had deliberately chosen a vicious parody of the same role for his return to Broadway. Then there was Elijah's wife, Judith, played by Nora Gibney. Nora, then in her late thirties, had been a solid, although never star-touched, citizen of the Broadway scene for most of her life. The fourth and only remaining major role, that of Sister Sukey, a traveling gospel singer, was taken by Georgia Marshall, a tall, handsome Negro girl who had actually traveled the gospel route herself. The other parts, of townspeople and lawmen, were so small that they were not to be brought into the rehearsals until the final week.

Richard Robeson was directing, and had chosen as stage manager the television director, Tony Warden, who had been at the console during Johnny's last role on *Private Eye*. Tony's appearance at the rehearsal hall raised a few eyebrows until word spread that the TV series had been canceled. Periodic unemployment is a frequent visitor to those in show business, and this common bond soon made Tony one of the gang, despite the illegitimacy of his television background.

Until you have attended a first readthrough of a play by its newly-assigned cast, you have never really understood the definition of the word, Faith. *Webster's New Collegiate Dictionary* defines that word as "complete confidence, especially in someone or something open to question or suspicion." And if anyone had reason to question or be suspicious of the abilities of a group of people, that anyone would be the director of a cast during its initial readthrough.

Having achieved his position by dint of repeated auditions, pleas, application of personal pressure, bribery or perhaps demonstration of sheer talent, the recently hired actor seems to take delight in doing his best during a first reading to convince the director, the producer, and especially the author, that hiring him for the part was the biggest mistake in the theater since David Merrick decided to make a musical out of *Breakfast at Tiffany's.* But faith, gentle faith, strengthens the director's resolve. He knows that the muttered, grumbled, hopelessly disinterested reading his actors are blundering their way through is merely another theatrical tradition, just as is the prohibition against whistling in a dressing room. He has faith that having thus wasted the first two hours of paid rehearsal time, his cast will get down to business and put a little muscle into the job.

Jean Billingham, however, was unaware of this tradition, and sat in the back of the hall, suffering the agonies of the damned. When the last act dragged to its mumbling close, she buried her face in both hands and began to wail like an Indian widow who has just cut off all her fingers.

"We're ruined," she said. "The critics will set fire to the theater. If we don't cancel now, the city will lock us up for maintaining a public nuisance."

Robeson sat down beside her and lit up a long, black cigar.

"I thought it went rather well," he said smugly.

"Rather well!" She stared at him as if he had just announced his candidacy for the office of president. "I'm in the company of a madman. Rather well! Perhaps you also plan to star Sonny Tufts as Hamlet? Rather well! And as for you," she shouted at Johnny, who was passing by with a paper cup of coffee in his hand, "you told me you could *act.* They ought to bust you out of Actors Equity." He grinned, said nothing, and toasted his coffee in her direction.

"Relax, Jean," said Robeson, relenting. "A first readthrough is always like this. Actors think it's bad form to give a performance at the first reading. After they have their coffee, we'll get down to the real work."

She stiffened, anger working on her gamin little face.

"You mean you let me sit back here and go through the worst ten years of my life and you *knew,* all along? You bastard!" Johnny, passing by again, laughed. "And that goes for you, too, John Calvin Lewis!" She plumped herself down with sharp-pointed elbows jammed onto her knees and, for several minutes, growled under her breath, punctuating the inaudible portions with a sharply uttered, "bastards!"

The next reading went much better, and before long, the anger left her, and Jean was leaning forward anxiously to hear lines that had been born in her mind springing to life in the dingy room. Johnny had openly discarded his script at this point, to the amusement of Tony Warden and the chagrin of his fellow actors. Having gone along with the tradition of the listless first reading, he now went all-out. I think it was his finest performance. Although lines would be changed and movement added, Johnny was never again as good as he was that chilly afternoon in the drafty dinginess of the rehearsal hall.

Nor was I the only one to notice this about him. Later, during the out-of-town tryout, Bert Klen was to tell him, "Look kid, you're fine in the part. Everyone's going to like you. But you're not great, you know what I mean? You were great on the second readthrough that first day of rehearsal. From there, you went downhill until you leveled off."

"I know," Johnny said. "I can't seem to hold onto it. I get it once, and then it's repeating myself and some of the fun goes out of it."

"Don't knock a good thing," said Klen. "My guess is you're a natural for films. You only have to do it once for the camera. Once they get you on film, that's it. One of the troubles we have in films is with the actor who can't get up for the first take. He has to go five, six, ten times before he gets the mood right. But if you can hold yourself down during rehearsals and go for broke when they roll the camera, you can't miss. None of this six nights and two matinees a week jazz. Do it once, do it right, and let the whole world see you. Take my advice, kid, don't ever look down on the movies. The only thing wrong with them is some of the people who run the operation. If you're lucky, the movies can be awfully good to you."

But there, on the first rehearsal day, no one knew that Johnny would never again achieve the magic he wrought there in that miserable room. And so, when the second readthrough finished, the air was one of jubilation and great confidence in the play.

"Jeannie, you're wonderful," bellowed Robeson. "Damnit, you even had me crying during that last scene. Where does a dame learn to write like you do?"

"Blame it on Johnny if you're sniveling," she said. "I just wrote the words."

"Damn fine job, kid," Bert Klen mumbled. This was before he was to come to love Johnny, and all he could think of now was that it was beginning to look like he had left Hollywood only to be upstaged in his own starring play by a punk kid fresh out of high school.

Nora Gibney, on the other hand, knew that her best hope for a long run was a brilliant cast around her, and her congratulations to Johnny were warm and lengthy. "I just know we're going to adore working together," she said.

Georgia Marshall said nothing, but her dark, black eyes were filled with warm approval as she looked Johnny up and down as if he were a new ensemble being exhibited for her opinion.

100

Tony Warden forgot his semi-menial position as stage manager and pounded Johnny warmly on the shoulder. "Hot damn!" said Warden, "I knew you had it, ever since that crummy TV show, I knew you were going to deliver."

Johnny's reaction to this earned praise was quiet and modest. He pushed his thick horn-rimmed glasses down on his nose and looked over their tops with a tight, fixed smile on his lips. Robeson dismissed the cast, after reminding them the call was for ten the next morning, and Johnny gathered up his belongings and started for the door. He walked past me with a blank stare that denied me recognition. I caught up with him on the stairs, and it took my hand on his shoulder to stop him.

"Johnny!"

"What? Who?" He looked at me almost in fright.

"Johnny, what's wrong?"

He shook his head. A different light came into his eyes. He reached up and centered his glasses against his face. He sighed deeply and shuddered.

"That was a bad one," he said numbly. "Come on. I gotta have a drink."

We went downstairs and out onto wind-blown Sixth Avenue. Just down the block was a Martin's Bar, and we headed into it and sat on the high, plastic-seated stools.

"Scotch," mumbled Johnny. "A double. Straight." It came, and as I had a beer, Johnny tossed the double down with one backward thrust of his head. Actually, it was closer to an ounce and a half, but still a sizeable drink taken straight.

"That's better," he wheezed, tears spilling down his cheeks. "I'll take another one," he choked. "This time with soda."

The bartender looked at him suspiciously.

"Are you sure you're eighteen?" he asked. "Let me see your draft card."

"Sure thing, sport," Johnny said quietly, tossing his wallet up onto the bar. "There's my age, right there," and his voice hardened, "right near where it says 4-F!"

"Okay," said the bartender. "No offense. But the Liquor Authority makes it rough on us for underage sales. No offense."

"No offense," agreed Johnny. He breathed a deep sigh, and sucked on his teeth, making a squeaking sound. "Sorry I shook you up," he said to me. "Something happens when I really get inside a part. I don't know how to explain it, but coming out of that rehearsal hall, I wasn't me, Johnny Lewis, I was Bud Younger, and my nutty brother had just hung himself and they'd let me out of a cave for the first time in ten years. I didn't know who anybody was, and it was like all of a sudden I found myself in the wrong world." He grinned suddenly. "You must know what that feels like."

I nodded and sipped my beer. His Scotch and soda came and he stirred it carefully.

"We never talked about how I approach my acting," he said. "It's something you ought to know about, if you are going to understand what you write about me. You see, while it's true that I think the words and the movement the playwright wrote are the important things to concentrate on, I never told anybody the rest of the truth. I think Jerry Newman guessed it, after that mess I made at the Workshop. I told him all I was doing was saying the words and making the moves, but he's a shrewdie. He *knew,* even after only ten minutes of seeing the character, that I was being swallowed up in the role. And if that can happen in ten minutes with a piece of garbage for a script, imagine what Jeannie's play and two weeks of reading it have done for me. I go out and walk the streets at night, and when I come home, I don't know where I've been. Half the time I'm not me at all, I'm Bud Younger. You ask Johnny Lewis a question, and Bud Younger answers."

Then the mood was gone, and the laughing, kidding Johnny was there in Martin's Bar with me.

"Hey," he chuckled, "I haven't seen you since you cut out on St. Thomas. Too bad you didn't stay around. Once we got rid of Sally and Lucky Pierre, we really had a swinging cruise. And let me tell you, buddy boy, there is something to be said in favor of older women. That Billingham, she knows how to twist and pull that thing, and turn you every way but loose. You know, she's the first babe I ever had that I didn't end up feeling sick and dirty afterwards. You don't think I'm falling for her, do you? My God, I couldn't be. She's an old woman. She's thirty-two!"

Before I could answer, he clapped his hand over my mouth and said, "Never mind. I forgot. Ask you no questions and you'll tell me no truths. I don't need any spooks telling me what's what. I am John Calvin Lewis and I am going to be a big movie star. And you are my friendly neighborhood shadow, watching my stumbling way to the grave and making notes on your sleeve. Thank you for coming back to learn the truth about me," he whispered. "I owe the world whatever it is you can steal from me. You can have my talent, my thoughts, my words, my youth, even my life. Now I belong to the ages, right?"

I couldn't answer. He leaned forward and his breath was hot against my chin as he hissed:

"Jesus, how I hate you!"

CHAPTER
FIVE

THE night before *Tiger Row* was to go down to Princeton for a weekend of tryouts at the McCarter Theater, Johnny and Maggie McBride were walking together along Macdougal Street in Greenwich Village. I joined them as they reached the Provincetown Playhouse, where a sign announced a repertory season of Gilbert and Sullivan under the direction of John Francis.

The evening was chill, and the streets were almost empty. At this pre-beatnik time, beards were not yet in full fashion, and had some young man appeared in a Beatle haircut, he would have been jeered from the scene. The girls, including Maggie, had a great fondness for black leotards, but they had not yet adopted the long, lank, straight hair that was to characterize the Village of the 70s.

104

Maggie and Johnny were avoiding conversation. Once, he stopped and looked at some ceramic earrings in a window and he asked if she would like them. She shook her head, and they walked on.

At the corner of Minetta Lane, the doors of the Minetta Tavern invited them in out of the cold, and they accepted silently. Johnny jerked his head for me to follow.

Inside, the air was warm and cheery, and in the dimness of the room, Maggie became very soft and beautiful as we were ushered into the rear dining area. We sat at a corner table, under framed photos of celebrities in the theatrical and boxing worlds. I had a martini, Johnny a Gibson, and Maggie ordered a Scotch Mist.

Having a few dollars to spend had made no difference to Johnny's appearance. Tonight, he wore blue jeans, a white T-shirt and a heavy leather jacket with a natural wool collar. It even smelled like sheep.

"Friend of mine once said," he mused, "a Gibson is like life."

"How's that?" I asked.

"This," he sipped, "the drink, that's illusion. And this—the onion," and as he said onion, he bit into it, "that's reality."

"How's the play coming?"

"Not bad. Robeson's taught me a lot. Little things, that don't interfere with the way I think, but help me bring them out enough so an audience can tell what the hell I'm trying to do. He's a good man. So is that Warden."

"And Miss Billingham?"

"She hasn't been around for a couple of weeks. She says that hearing her own words over and over again is starting to make her sick. I think she's just scared she'll get involved, and that's the last thing she wants. I still see her every now and then. She may be all screwed up, but I honestly think that little redneck is one of the world's greatest dames."

"Coming from you, that's impressive."

"Johnny," said Maggie, "can I have another Scotch?"

"Sure, hon," he said, and waved for a waiter. He ordered all around and as he spoke, I looked deep into the girl's shadowed face. There was sadness there, and fright, and a set look of determination. When the waiter was gone, she reached over and lay her hand on Johnny's arm.

"I'm going to miss you," she said.

"Well, hell," he said, "come along, then. There's plenty of room. I'll have Tony get you a room at the Princeton Inn."

"No, I can't," she said.

"Suit yourself," he said, dismissing the brief whisper of intimacy that had begun to grow between them. He turned back to me. "Jeannie's going to come down to Princeton for the tryouts. Robeson wouldn't let her out of it. Said there would certainly be rewrites and she had to be there for them. Abner and Chris'll be down, too. Just like old home week on the *Trade Winds.*"

The drinks came and we sipped them as the waiter dealt out menus. Maggie ordered shrimps marinara. Johnny wanted an order of osso buco, but settled for veal parmigiana when told they were out of the veal knuckles. I ordered my favorite linguine with white clam sauce, and of course we all had the magnificent Minetta Salad. Even now, Minetta's prices are embarrassingly low for such delightful fare; in 1953, they were scandalous. Without a word, Maggie got up and went to the ladies' room.

Munching on the crisp Italian bread, Johnny mumbled, "Bud Younger doesn't understand food like this. It's too fancy for him."

"You're still involved in the character?"

"More than ever. Last night, Maggie showed up. She's living at home again. But she turned up with a bottle of wine, and we

106

played music on WQXR. It was warm and lazy and she got a little friendly, nothing she hasn't done fifty times before, but this time something happened. Our friend Bud took over, and he bashed her in the mouth and knocked her clean out of bed. 'You are a vessel of sin,' he yelled at her, 'a whore of Babylon, lusting after the filthy pleasures of the flesh.' Poor Maggie. She just sat in the corner and cried."

"Bud did this? You mean, you did."

"I mean, Bud did! I had no more to say about what happened than Maggie did. Hell, I could hear the words coming out of my mouth, and they were no more me than they were planned. I didn't plan to say them, and I couldn't stop saying them, and you know what, old buddy? Those weren't even words that Bud says in the play. They're words his *brother* says. I think maybe Jeannie has written the wrong ending on this play. I think it is too late for Bud, that he's never going to get out of that cave. Give him five years after the curtain falls, and I bet you he'll be the spitting image of his brother."

"Sounds a little rough on the girl."

"You think I don't know that? She's a dope to mess with me anyway, though. I'm bad for her. She's pretty and smart and all that, but she ought to get out of the business. She'll never make it as an actress."

He was right, but the cruelty of his calm remark brought a flash of resentment to me.

"Naturally, that's all that matters, right, Johnny?"

He grinned over at me and shook his head sadly. "Don't get involved with your subject matter, old buddy," he warned. "You're supposed to watch."

Maggie returned, the food came and we ate in silence. She sipped the red wine Johnny had asked for with the meal, and looked at him over the bell-shaped glass. Johnny ignored her preoccupation and, with frequent sloshing gestures of his wine glass, launched into an account of his brief stay at UCLA.

"Boy, was I corny," he laughed. "A hick, right off the farm. Everybody convinced me to go out for pre-law, and how was I to argue with my father? He was picking up the tab, and as far as he was concerned, actors were all bums. Did I ever tell you what *he* did? He was a car salesman. Was? Still is. He works for a guy who has a Ford dealership in Burbank. Naturally, this is a man who would know all about actors! It takes one bum to know another bum. Anyway, I signed up for pre-law, with a dramatics minor. I'd seen some of the stuff the Theater Arts Department put on there, in Royce Hall. Now that was some barn of a theater! You could just about hold a football game in it. They had all the lighting equipment ever built, and good sets and everything, but hoo, boy, did the acting stink. On ice. I knew I could do better, if I just got a chance. But even there, the competition was rough. There were all those guys living it up on the GI Bill, and naturally all of them went out for dramatics because being good native Californians, they were all going to crash the movie business. So was I, but I was *really* going to do it. Anyway, I looked the situation over and it was just like everything else. It wasn't what you knew, but who you knew. And I didn't have any too good an image there anyway. I was right off the farm, you remember, and I looked it. Not sleek and—" as he patted his T-shirt, "dapper like I am today. Plowboy, they called me. The Plowboy of the Western World. But I met this girl, she was going to try out for *Othello*. I think I'd of ended up as the Third Spear Carrier, but I took that instructor aside and showed him a letter I'd written all filled with dates and places and even some of the names they'd used at various motels. Poor clown, he looked like someone had kicked him in the balls. I felt so sorry that I gave him some good advice, that the next time he wanted to screw around with some underage student, to pick one who didn't gossip so damned much with her other boy friends. Well, I got the part. Iago, the one I wanted. And that poor instructor practically got fired over that. The head of the department wanted to know what the hell he thought he was doing, giving the second lead to a punk like me? But it was too late then."

"Were you good?" Maggie asked.

"Good? I was putrid!" He put on a deep midwestern accent, " 'Look to your wife, observe her well with Cassio. Wear your eye, thus, not jealous nor secure.' Can't you just hear it? The critics practically ate me alive. And I don't blame them. 'In Venice, they do let heaven see the pranks they dare not show their husbands; their best conscience is, not to leave't undone, but keep't unknown.' Good Christ! It must have sounded like I was calling the hogs!"

Maggie smiled and held her wine glass in both hands. The expression on her face was softer now.

"Well, hell," said Johnny, "it was mostly my own fault. Sure, I was as green as grass, but not so green that I didn't know, going in, that I'd never be able to beat old man Shakespeare. Not at that age. One of these days I will, though. One of these days, when I'm still young enough for it to make the character real, I'm going to do *Hamlet*. I'll do what John Barrymore did, I'll get the best damned voice coach in the world to rebuild my throat for me. I'll never make that mistake again, going in when I don't have the equipment to do the job."

He slopped the last of the wine into his glass and drank deeply.

"Anyway," he went on, "those fraternity brothers really made my life miserable from then on. They didn't like me anyway. I was a carpetbagger from Centerville, Iowa, stealing their dear old daddies' tax money to get my education. It didn't matter none to them that my father was a California resident. They had a grudge on for me from the very beginning, and this

Othello disaster really set me up for the kill. They started calling me Olivier. I was only a pledge, anyway, and that's the lowest form of fraternity living creatures. But I took it. I ate shit and came up smiling and asked for more. But they didn't have sense enough to know when to quit. One of them had a gadget that was new then, a tape recorder, and those bastards planted it in my room when I was rehearsing a scene. It was that great balcony speech in Brian Hooker's translation of *Cyranno,* and I was reading all three parts, including Roxanne. And the next morning when I sat down to breakfast, they played the recording through the radio. I tried to take it like a joke, but the more I went along, the more they needled me, and finally one of them got to going, 'sooooie' like he was calling a hog, every time I read one of Roxanne's lines. So I let him have it right in the kisser with a plate of ham and eggs. I'd of made him eat the plate, too, but they all grabbed me from behind and hustled me under a cold shower. You can guess what happened next. A pledge had clobbered a full time brother! They acted like they were doing me a favor by giving me time to pack my clothes. In fact, I forgot a raincoat, and it's probably still hanging there in the hall closet. I never went back there, or to UCLA either."

"You should have finished your education," Maggie said.

"For what? I haven't got time to waste on school. I've got to make it right away."

"You sound like you're going to die," she said, and then caught herself with a startled gasp.

"How do you know I'm not?" he said.

"Don't talk like that, Johnny," she said. "You have a very long and happy life ahead of you. And, well, education is important."

"So go get educated," he said. "I'm too busy."

"That's what I wanted to tell you," she said. "I'm not going to be able to see you again. At least, not for a long time."

"What?"

"I'm going back to school."

"That's right, you're taking speech at Columbia."

She shook her head. "No, starting next month I'll be going to the University of Pennsylvania. I think it's obvious I'd better plan on doing something with my life other than acting."

"But Pennsylvania? What's wrong with NYU?"

"You're what's wrong!"

"I'm what's wrong!"

"If you're just a subway ride away, I don't think I would have the strength to stop seeing you. So I'm going away. That's what I wanted to tell you last night. When you—"

"Damnit," he yelled, "I told you that was a scene from the play. That I got so wrapped up in the character—"

"You don't have to explain," she said. "But I think if you hadn't hit me last night, you would have today or tomorrow, or sometime soon. You want to get rid of me, Johnny, you know you do. There's nothing for us together. You're going to be a big star one day, and by then I guess I'll be a schoolteacher somewhere, and I'll be able to tell my students, 'I knew Mr. Lewis when he was not much older than you.' That's all there is left, so please don't pretend it's important any more."

Johnny got up and slung his heavy leather jacket over one shoulder while he fumbled in a trouser pocket.

"Hell," he said, "I'm not making it important. I was just thinking, you could have said all this an hour ago."

"Why then?"

"Because," he said, tossing the money down on the table, "then I would have saved ten bucks."

She burst into tears and an old woman at a nearby table looked up, startled, as Johnny rushed out of the tavern.

111

It is a pleasant drive down to Princeton, especially in autumn. Although it was the week after Thanksgiving, some of the trees were still bright with red and golden leaves. The company were traveling together in a rented bus, all except for Abner and his wife Chris, who were driving a 1952 Lincoln. By the time we had gotten through the Holland Tunnel, they were already a mile ahead of us, and no one had seen the black sedan since.

Johnny sat with Jean Billingham in the first row of seats. I was across the aisle, behind the driver. Johnny had insisted on taking the window, and he sat now with his forehead pressed against the vibrating glass.

"Nice of you to join us peasants," he told her. "Don't you like to ride in big, black Lincolns?"

She grinned and hit him on the arm with one small fist. He winced in imaginary pain and pretended to collapse.

"Pick on someone your own size," he gasped.

I seem to spend so many of my memories of those days gone by noticing how much things today have changed, and not for the better. But it's true that in 1953, the roads leading out of the city had more trees lining them, and fewer housing developments. The air was clearer and smelled with a leaf-scented freshness, untainted by massive air pollution. The fears of nuclear destruction or racial revolution might have touched your thoughts once in a while, but they had not yet become a national psychosis. And on that November morning in 1953, I found myself wishing I could go back and remain there permanently. I cursed the me who, years younger, had lived those golden days in youthful blindness, indifferent to the riches that surrounded me.

"This is motorcycle weather," Johnny mumbled.

"What's motorcycle weather?" Jean asked.

"A brisk, snappy day like this," he said. "You've got to dress

112

up warm, because that wind'll cut right through you. It gets through the zipper on your jacket, and if you don't wear long gauntlets, it'll go up both sleeves and freeze your arms off. But once you get your hands and your ears covered up so they don't get frostbite, there's a different feel to riding on a day like this. The air is so crisp, the exhaust just pops against it and echoes off the pavement behind you. Man, that's something else. I wish I had my bike here. I bet I'd of beat that Lincoln on a road like this."

"Where is your machine?"

"Back in Centerville, in my Uncle Ray's barn, up on blocks. I left it there when I went out to California. I packed it up good, though, in gunk. She shouldn't rust out or anything."

"You seem to love her."

Johnny grinned. "Yeah," he said. "Isn't that funny? To figure a machine's a *she,* I mean. But if you ever rode a motorcycle, you'd understand. They're so tempermental, they can't be anything else *but* she's. Takes a long time to warm one up, but when they're hot, whewie!"

Jean Billingham looked down the highway ahead. A smile kept picking at the edge of her mouth, and I could see her blush all the way across the aisle.

"Know what I mean?" Johnny whispered, teasing her. The smile finally won out, and lit her face with its impish curl.

"Do I ever," she said. "But don't talk dirty, little boy. This bus is full of loudmouths."

"You just know it is," said Johnny. "And every one of them's talking about you and me."

"How about you, Johnny?"

"How about me what?"

"Have you been talking about me to anybody?"

He looked over her shoulder, at me.

"No," he said finally. "Not to anybody."

113

Tryout audiences can go either way. They can approach the stage with a resentment at being used, or they can enter with rich anticipation of being the first to enjoy a production that poor Broadway must stand in line for later.

The turnout for *Tiger Row* was in the latter classification. The lobby buzzed with anticipation as the faculty members, students and a sizeable number of visitors from New York, all attempted to fill their lungs deep enough with tobacco smoke to tide them over the cigaretteless wastes of the first act. Such an audience is a joy to encounter. From the moment the curtain goes up, they are with the players and the play. To disappoint such an audience is like promising a child Christmas, and then on the magic morning, yelling, "April Fool!" But to come through on your promise, to deliver the enchantment and delight—then, the partnership between audience and play is complete. It is such rare moments that keep both audience and producer coming back to each new play.

The first performance of Jean Billingham's play reached toward its promise, faltered briefly in the second act, rallied and surged toward the climax and what amounted to a standing ovation from the delighted audience. Taking his final, solo curtain call, Bert Klen bent to the inevitable, and called Johnny out to share the stage with him. Even after the great curtain had been closed firmly for the last time, the audience seemed unwilling to leave. Instead of streaming up the aisles, its members trickled out two and three at a time, talking excitedly and glancing over their shoulders at the shrouded stage.

Because of the small cast, Johnny had a dressing room to himself. He and Jean Billingham were toasting paper cups of champagne when I entered. Johnny handed me one, and as I sipped, Richard Robeson burst in, chomping on an unlit cigar.

"Here you are," he said to Jean. "On your horse, little lady.

We've got to get moving. There's something rotten in the second act. Good job, Johnny," he went on without pause. "Rehearsal at 10:00 A.M. to put in the new scene."

"What new scene?" said Jean.

"The new scene you and I are going to write tonight," said Robeson. "Hi ho, on your feet."

One hand high in the air holding the paper cup of champagne, the other wrapped in the director's firm grasp, Jean Billingham was hustled from the dressing room, looking back with a surprised grimace on her face.

"Well," said Johnny, pouring some more wine into my cup, "there goes what was going to be a swell evening."

"Where's my favorite caveman?" said a deep voice. It was Georgia Marshall, still in her evangelistic white robes from the play. She, too, held a bottle of champagne. Johnny looked around and smiled broadly.

"Then again," he said under his breath, "who knows?"

"There you are," she said. "Look what Georgia's got. Oh," she said then, "somebody beat me here."

"The author," said Johnny. "But she's gone, and so is her champagne. Thank God you got here with reinforcements."

"Let me bless your cup with this bubbly," said the big Negro girl. She upended the bottle and poured.

"Hey," Johnny protested, "my cup runneth over."

Georgia sat down on the floor and started crooning to the bottle of champagne.

"Baby," she said, "it has been a long, hard winter. If this play doesn't pan out, it's back on the gospel trail for little old Georgia. But thanks to you, Johnny Lewis, you beautiful boy, this play is going to signify! That audience was the prettiest thing I ever saw. Do you know, they're still out front? They don't want to leave. We're going to have to turn the lights out on them."

115

"Hey," said Johnny, "that's great." He didn't sound as though he meant it. Georgia cocked her head at him.

"Here, here," she said, "why that miserable face, like you just took castor oil? You mad at me for coming in?" She started to get up, and he pushed her back down again.

"Hell, no, Georgia," he said. "I just had a thing on with Jean, but she got drafted to write a new scene for the second act."

"So little Johnny's left all high and dry? Didn't bring none of that wolf pack of gals that follow you around down from New York? How could you be so short-sighted, don't you know never to hang everything around just *one* woman? I ought to cut out too, teach you a lesson. But I'll tell you what, if it wouldn't embarrass you too greatly to be seen around town with a big black cat like me, why Georgia would be delighted to ease your loneliness."

"Are you sure *you* wouldn't mind?" he countered.

"Me? Are you kidding, John Calvin Lewis? Can't you *tell* I got the hots for you? I just never figured on any chance like this to scratch the itch. But if you don't let the color thing bother you, it sure in hell ain't going to fuzzle *me.*"

"I rented a car this afternoon," Johnny said. "I hear there's a real swinging spot out on the Trenton highway. Let's go get some fried chicken."

"*And* watermelon," she said. Her big, work-scarred hand reached out for his. As he pulled her up, I could see that she was trembling.

"Get out of that bed sheet," he said. "I'll get the car and pick you up at the stage door in ten minutes."

"All right, Johnny," she said in a small voice. Much of her accent had suddenly vanished. She closed the door behind her, and Johnny looked over at me.

"Change my luck," he said. He gulped down the rest of the champagne. Then he crumpled the cup and threw it at his reflection in the mirror.

116

He put on his heavy leather jacket. Tony Warden had grimaced painfully when Johnny turned up at the bus dressed as if he were out for a spin on his cycle, but had said nothing.

"Let's go," he said. It was just assumed that I would be going with them. We waited in the car for a few minutes, and then the stage door opened and Georgia came out. She had changed to black slacks and a heavy pullover sweater. The rented Chevy purred through the night, and in minutes, Johnny parked it in the lot behind a neon-lighted road spot called The Blue Ridge Inn. Our feet crunched on the gravel, and when Johnny opened the door the noise burst out at us like a roar of greeting. Inside, as Johnny shucked out of his leather jacket and revealed the garish flannel shirt underneath, a man in a dark blue suit and carrying a clip of papers rushed up.

"Do you have a reservation, sir?" he asked breathlessly.

"Me? No, I don't have a reservation. Miss Georgia, do *you* have a reservation?"

"Reservation?" she said, in a cold, dead voice. "What's a reservation?"

"Look," said Johnny, "it's almost midnight. You've got plenty of tables. What's with this reservation bit?"

"Ah," said the headwaiter, "even so, our policy is not to serve gentlemen without coats and ties—"

Johnny looked over his shoulder. At a nearby table, three college-age men were eating French fries and drinking beer. Only one had on a jacket; the others wore sweaters.

"What are those boys wearing?" Johnny asked softly. "Dinner jackets?"

"Or ladies in—ah—pants—" the headwaiter went on desperately.

"Come on, Johnny," said Georgia. "I've heard this song before. Let's get out of here."

"Like hell we'll get out of here," said Johnny. His shoulder hunched, and I sensed that he was about to throw a punch.

117

Before he could move, a third man had pressed his way between them. He was in his early thirties, with a shaggy blonde mustache and an even shaggier plaid sport jacket.

"Well, well," he said, "Frank, your humble joint is honored tonight. Do you know who these folks are? Actors from that new play over in Princeton I saw tonight," he told Johnny, "and may I congratulate both of you? Come along and join me at my table," he said, brushing past the headwaiter. "Relax, Frank," he said over his shoulder.

"In that case," Frank began.

"Screw it," said Johnny. "I saw a Howard Johnson's back there. Let's settle for a hamburger."

"I insist," said the Shaggy Mustache. "I claim the right to buy both of you a drink in exchange for the great pleasure you gave me this evening."

"You paid for your ticket," Johnny said, but he let us be towed along by the other man.

"I beg your pardon, sir," said the man. "You certainly didn't mean to suggest that *I* pay for a ticket? I write for one of the nearby newspapers."

"Oh," said Johnny. "A freebie."

"Free as the breeze," said the man. "I am Lester Brooks, of the *Philadelphia Bulletin*. You are Georgia Marshall, and you, sir, are John Calvin Lewis. Here we are."

Brooks gestured for a waiter, and before long we were all sipping long, tall drinks, and Brooks was holding forth on his opinion of the play.

"Superlative," he said. "Fine script and performances. Lovely set. I have rarely spent a more enjoyable evening in the theater."

"Thank you," said Georgia, loosening up a little.

"Oh, you're very welcome, Miss Marshall," he said. "And may I apologize for Frank? I assure you, he doesn't ordinarily embarrass black patrons."

118

"Then why did he pick on us?" asked Johnny.

"My dear John Calvin," said the critic, "you, of all people, should know why. You look like you have just returned from a gang rumble. Miss Marshall is presentable enough, but in your company even she takes on a certain effect of—disrepute, if you will forgive me. Poor Frank feared that you were the forerunners of an invasion of boppers from Trenton."

"Tough luck for him," Johnny muttered.

"I am impressed with your abilities," said Brooks. "What are your plans after this play?"

"I hadn't thought that far," said Johnny. "I guess there will be time enough for that later." Then, noticing a strange look on his host's face, "What the hell are you staring at?"

"My dear John Calvin—" Brooks began.

"Don't you dear me," said Johnny. "What the hell is eating you?"

"You don't really believe that *Tiger Row* will run?" Brooks said.

"Why won't it run?" Johnny asked. "You liked it. The audience liked it. Everybody agrees we've got a good play."

"Oh, yes, indeed you have. But, Mr. Lewis, there is a world of difference between a good play and a successful play. I thought you knew that. Why, the very quality of your play is what will destroy it. Caviar for the general, and all that. I am willing to predict that the critics will fall on you like wolves at the feast. You will close by Saturday night."

"Boy, talking with you is a barrel of fun," Johnny said.

"Shall I be more polite?" Brooks asked. "I can avoid speaking the truth, if you wish. But that won't change it, or keep it from happening."

"Mr. Brooks," said Georgia, "what you're saying is just your own opinion, is it not?"

"My very own," he said. "But I am seldom wrong."

"How nice for you," she said.

"To hell with you," said Johnny. "If you're so smart, go out and do your own play. We've got something good going here, and I'm not going to let some bastard like you wreck a nice evening just because you're sore about being stuck in Philadelphia instead of the *New York Times.* Come on, Georgia."

They got up and Brooks raised his glass after them.

"Thank you for joining me," he said. "I apologize for being the bearer of evil tidings, and wish you both luck. I really do."

"Shove it," said Johnny. He took his jacket off the rack and barged out, letting the swinging door almost hit the girl behind him. We got back into the car and, instead of starting it, he pounded both hands on the wheel until he accidentally hit the horn and set it blaring. "Goddamn that guy," he said. "Why did we have to go in there? He spoiled everything. Like hell we'll close in a week. With *Tiger Row?* It's the best damned play I ever read. Screw him. Let's go somewhere else."

"It's late, Johnny," Georgia said. "And it'll be the same at the next place. You'll just get in a fight and wind up in trouble."

Johnny straightened his shoulders and inserted the key in the ignition forcefully as he reached a decision. The car started and he switched on the lights. He ground the gears into first, and screeched out of the parking lot and headed back toward Princeton. We drove in silence for a while.

"Honey," Georgia said at last, "I'm sorry it turned out bad for you."

"Forget it," he said. "I wasn't hungry anyway."

"I mean about the play."

"Don't tell me you're starting to believe that nut?"

"He could be right."

"Don't even think things like that. We've got a hit play. I know it. That joker is just chewing sour grapes. What does a fag like that know?"

"Still, Johnny, what he said—"

120

Johnny slammed on the brakes and swooped the car into a half-hidden side road. He coasted in for a short distance and then stopped the car and killed the lights.

"Johnny," Georgia said, "what are we stopping for?"

"What do you think?" he asked.

"Boy, are you sure you know what you're doing?" she whispered.

"I'm sure," he said. They were two shadows that merged into one.

"Ooooh," she gasped. "That hurts." There was a rustle of cloth, and she said, "No, don't let go. Hold the other one, too."

"I'll do better than that," Johnny said, and lowered his head.

Lester Brooks was right again. *Tiger Row* lasted exactly six Broadway performances. The critics tarred it with the brush of pretension, of avant-garde introspection, and called it "obscure," "bewildering" and "totally inept." These comments bewildered cast and audiences alike, but there is rarely any second chance when you have lost five out of the seven daily critics, and that was the box score that December afternoon the day after opening.

Johnny and Jean Billingham were having lunch at Patsy and Carl's Theatre Bar on 45th Street. I had just wandered in, after finding myself on the street outside, and shortly thereafter, Tony Warden came in, carrying copies of the *New York Post* and the *Journal American*. John McClain on the *Journal* hated the play. Vernon Rice, on the *Post* saw merit in it, deplored its flaws, and then wrote, "but the evening is made worthwhile by the debut of John Calvin Lewis as the Boy in the Cave. Not since Marlon Brando tickled our fancies as Marchbanks in *Candida* have we seen such an auspicious beginning to what must certainly be a notable career. Well done, Mr. Lewis!"

"Oh, Johnny, that's wonderful!" said Jean. She really was

thrilled for him, despite her own sense of failure, but Johnny missed the importance of her reaction.

"What the hell good does that do?" he cried.

"You did very well," said Tony Warden. "Six out of seven of the dailies had good things to say about you."

"So what? Am I supposed to play the part to an empty theater? Why are they doing this to me?"

"You're not the only one they're doing it to," Tony said, with a glance at Jean. "Anyway, you won't have to worry about the empty theaters. The closing notice is up."

"Already? They don't even wait for the body to get cold!"

"I repeat," said Warden, "don't let it get you down. The play may not make it, but these are money notices for you. Who's your agent?"

"Why do you ask?" Johnny said suspiciously.

"Because my bet is the phone is ringing off the hook. Remember, television is my back yard. Right now every director in town is trying to line you up for a spot. I know I would, if I had a show."

"Well," Johnny said carefully, "right now I'm sort of in between agents. I was using Emily Woodford."

"She's a good one," Warden said.

"For radio and TV, maybe," said Johnny. "But she doesn't have anything going for her in movies or theater. Who do you think I ought to have?"

"Hell, if you want the best rep you can get, there's only one guy I'd swear by."

"What's his name?"

"Jerry Conklin, over at MCA."

"Would he talk to me?"

"After these notices? Anybody in town would talk to you."

"Johnny," said Jean Billingham, who had been listening quietly, "you never told me you and Aunt Em busted up."

122

"She's *not* Aunt Em," Johnny said tightly. "Not any more. And since when do I have to tell you everything?"

"Oh-ho, little monster," she said, getting up. "We're coming of age, are we? Well, don't sharpen your baby teeth on me. I invented the game, remember? Tony, I'd better go see Richard. Is he at the theater?"

"Was a while ago," Tony said. "Wait, I'll go with you."

Johnny shrugged his shoulders. "Sorry, Jean," he mumbled. "I'm just jumpy today."

"Sure," she said, touching his hand. She straightened, tossed her short hair in a defiant gesture and set out for the exit with a big smile for everyone she knew.

"Whew," said Johnny, "I was afraid they'd hang around another ten minutes and really put me in the soup."

Accepting a stein of beer, I asked, "What do you mean by that?"

"You'll see," Johnny mumbled into his own beer. "Hey, what do you think of that guy, Warden?"

"He's a good director," I said. No need to mention that in the coming years, Warden would win two Academy Awards, or that Ned Barker was now trying to get him to direct *The Johnny Lewis Story.*

"Maybe Bert Klen was right," Johnny said. "The thought of going back to that theater tonight turns my guts. If this was a movie, all of it would be on film now, and I could go on to something else. Not to mention the money. Did I tell you what I'm getting in *Tiger Row?* Equity scale! I end up with a lousy hundred bucks a week."

"Plus a handful of the best notices in town. I'd say you did pretty well for your side of the deal. Think of Abner Thompson. If he hasn't lost a hundred thousand, he's lucky."

"So what's a hundred thousand to him? That's like ten bucks to you and me. I feel for him, but I can't quite make the reach."

He gulped at his beer again, looked up and said, "Here comes trouble."

I looked around. Emily Woodford was entering. Behind the bar, Patsy greeted her with a big smile. She spoke quietly to him, and he waved in our direction. The agent nodded her thanks and came back to join us.

"I hope this is a good lunch," she said. "I had to get in a temporary girl from Brown's Steno to answer the phone. It's going crazy. I think you're going to be a very busy young man for the next few months."

"That's what I wanted to talk to you about," Johnny said, and it was then that I knew with a sinking certainty that he and "Aunt Em" had not yet called it quits, that he had only made his decision to leave her after reading the notices, and that he had been pumping Tony Warden for a replacement, knowing that she was due to arrive in minutes. As she was taking off one of her gloves and saying, "What do you mean, dear?" I got up and went to the bar, where Patsy served me a beer with a vacant nod. Out of sheer meanness I gave him a Kennedy half-dollar. He rang it up without noticing, but someone found it later, because during the late 50s and early 60s, one of the waiters used it as a pocket piece and finally it was mounted over the bar and shown to people during slow evenings as "this funny counterfeit half."

I could see Johnny and Emily Woodford talking earnestly. She had stopped removing her gloves, and her coat was still over her shoulders. Once, she reached a hand out to touch his and he pulled away. She spoke at length, and he kept shaking his head, and finally he just turned his chair completely around and showed her his back. She stopped speaking and sat silently for a moment then got up and, reaching into her purse for a small package, tossed it onto the table. She stood up straight and walked out of the bar without looking to either side.

124

Johnny sat in his chair for another few moments, then got up and stretched and joined me at the bar.

"I didn't think she'd take it so hard," he said. "But that's the way it goes. I don't have time to fool around just for sentiment. Sentiment is for slobs. Drink up. We've got to go see a man."

Carl came over with the small package.

"You left this," he said.

Johnny tore open the paper. Inside was small 35 mm. camera. It was an Argus C-3 with a leather case. There was a card. Johnny opened it.

"CURTAIN GOING UP," read the card. "Let's look forward to a long run together."

"Goddamn it," said Johnny. "Goddamn it all to hell and gone."

"What?"

"I completely forgot," he said. "Today's my birthday. I'm twenty-one. That means I can vote. And sign contracts legally."

He crumpled the card in his hand.

"If sentiment is just for slobs, Johnny," I asked, "where did that tear come from?"

As it happened, Jerry Conklin was no longer at MCA. He had left a few weeks earlier to set up his own talent shop and was now operating out of a suite in Rockefeller Center. As we rode up in the high speed elevator, I noticed that Johnny was almost dressed for the occasion. Although he wore no tie, the shirt was white, the sport jacket moderately conservative, and wonder of wonders, he carried a topcoat.

"This is it," he said, outside a door that read, "Conklin Associates." We went in, and there were the usual form-fitting chairs and a fresh-from-the-mold receptionist with the standard blonde hairdo and the pearl-rimmed glasses. Who was calling? John Calvin Lewis was calling, and no, he did not have an appointment, and oh, she would see if Mr. Conklin was in.

Was he ever in! He bounded out of his office, seized Johnny by the hand with one fist, pounded his shoulder with the other.

"Glad to see you," he yelled. "Come on in. Forgive the mess. We just moved in."

The "mess" was wall-to-wall carpeting, expensive Danish furniture and a long bar with three TV sets, all tuned to different channels. Conklin's desk was as big as a billiard table, and just as bare.

"My congratulations," said Conklin, still yelling. "You really wowed them. You set this town on its ear."

"Did you see the opening?" Johnny asked.

"No, can't say that I did. But I read the papers. Too bad about the play, but it's just as well for you. If it ran, it'd only tie you up. Cut down on your other work."

"That's why I came over," said Johnny. "I need an agent."

"An agent?" Conklin said, suddenly soft spoken. "You've got an agent, haven't you? Emily Woodford?"

"Not any more," said Johnny. "Not since about an hour ago."

"How about your contract?"

"We never had a contract."

"Not even a verbal one?"

"We both agreed that if it didn't work, either one of us could bail out."

Conklin whistled softly. "I don't know," he said. "That doesn't sound like the Emily Woodford *I* know. Either you don't know what your deal with her was, or maybe the old gal went soft on you. I'd have to know more before you and I came to any understanding. But one understanding we might as well have right now, kid. I am not an agent. Get that? Never call me an agent."

"Then what are you?"

126

"Personal Representative. And don't laugh, kid. You'll find out there's a hell of a big difference between the two. One of the big differences is my fee. Agents take ten percent. I take fifteen. And I earn it. If you come in with me, it's like I took you to raise. I'll dress you, I'll choose your barber for you, I'll okay your girl friends, and by God, if it comes to that, I'll even tell you what brand of rubbers to use."

"Never use them," Johnny said dryly. "Like taking a shower in a raincoat."

"You'll use them now," Conklin said. "More kids your age ruin their careers by knocking up some chick and getting tied down. Later on, when you've made it big, it costs a fortune to get rid of them."

"I suppose you'll tell me when to take a crap, too."

"Every day, in the morning. Keeps you toned up. I like you, kid. You aren't scared of me. That's good. What's Emily's number?"

"Trafalgar 9–7909."

Conklin punched a button on his desk. "Martha? Get me TR 9–7909. I'll talk to anybody." Then, back to Johnny: "Ten to one, the old bat still has you wrapped up, at least partially. I'll see what I can work out with her. Money talks."

"I don't have any money."

"You will have, kid. You will have." A buzzer rang, and he picked up the phone. "Hello? Emily? Jerry Conklin. Yeah? What do you mean, that's what you figured. Oh. Oh. Why, that little bastard. Yeah, he's right here. Well, look, maybe you and I can work out something. Nothing at all? That doesn't sound like you, are you getting old? How about a little bit toward the office expenses? Well, at least, let's work out something on the calls that you must be getting today. Can I pick up the ones you've already got, and have your girl forward the rest? You know I'll be fair if anything comes out of them. Yeah. Yeah.

Yeah. Okay, but I think you're losing your touch. Goodbye, Emily." He hung up the phone and looked at Johnny with cold respect. "Why you little prick," he said. "You really took that old lady for a ride. She sends you her regards, and hopes you rot in hell."

"So we're in trouble?"

"Trouble? Not a bit. She says there's no contract, verbal or otherwise, and that you're as free as the proverbial breeze. What's more, she's going to forward all of the queries that have been coming in since last night so I can take action on them. Without fee, I might add. She says she won't touch a cent of anything you have anything to do with. Because, she says, whatever it is you have, it might be catching."

He pressed the buzzer again, said, "Martha, come in and bring your book," then leaned back in his leather chair and plunked both feet on the desk. "Just so you don't get any more funny ideas," he told Johnny, "I am not Miss Woodford. I'm meaner and crookeder than anyone you ever met, so don't figure on playing any games with *me*. We're going to have such a contract, you and me, that it'd be easier to change your name and move to South America than to try and break it. But that ain't all. Despite the law, a contract is no stronger than the word of the people who sign it. So if you ever screw me, kid, I won't wait to haul you into court. I'll pick up this telephone, and around three of my ex-wrestler friends will bust a couple of ribs for you and maybe gouge out an eye so you shouldn't look pretty any more."

"After that," said Johnny, "you still expect me to sign with you?"

"Absolutely," said Conklin. "I can be mean and rough for you. Or against you. If I'm for you, we'll both make a pot of money. I'm not greedy. I don't kill the golden goose, or even rupture it. Fifteen percent is plenty for me. And that leaves

128

eighty-five for you, eighty-five that you'd never get a whiff of without someone like me opening doors for you."

"I suppose you kick them open," Johnny said.

"That's the spirit," Conklin said, yelling again. "I like a boy with guts. Martha! Where the hell are you?"

The receptionist poked her head in the door. "I had trouble sharpening a pencil," she said.

Conklin sighed. "Crazy broad," he said. "Take a letter of agreement, between Conklin Associates, et cetera, et cetera, and—"

"John Calvin Lewis," Johnny supplied.

"You got that? Exclusive representation starting as of now, and until regular contracts are drawn up. The usual terms and so forth. Get that typed up right now. Then I want you to send a messenger over to Emily Woodford's office. Look it up in the book. She's got some queries on Johnny. I want to get on them this afternoon."

"Yes sir," said the girl, starting for the door.

"Come back here. I'm not through yet. Get a dozen long stemmed roses, send them over by another messenger. Take a hundred bucks out of petty cash and enclose it with my card. No, wait a minute. She'd just send it back. Forget it. Just pick up the queries. I got a better idea."

As the receptionist left, he turned to Johnny. "Doesn't Emily still handle that broken-down pug who turned actor?"

"Sailor Willis? I think so. I've seen him there a couple of times."

Conklin buzzed Martha, said, "Get me Tom Dunkerton over at NBC. I'll hold." To Johnny, "Watch this and maybe you'll learn something. Hello? Tom? How's it going? Yeah? Well, that's what I'm calling you about. Yes, yes, I know you've been waiting to hear and that you've got a schedule, but—will you stop talking and listen? Maxie Rosenbloom is out. I can't get him. I know I said I could, but I just found out I can't. Hey, hey, don't panic. Have I ever let you down, baby? I did a little checking, and found out that Sailor Willis is available. What the hell do you mean, who's Sailor Willis? He's merely great, a funnier prize-fighter type you never saw. Look, Tommy, he's not even my client. That's right, why would I lead you wrong when there's not a nickel in it for me? Emily Woodford. Yeah, call her direct. No, don't mention my name. I don't want anyone owing me favors. Any time, Tommy. Best to the wife. Oh. Okay, to the new girl friend then. Yeah. See you."

He hung up the phone and beamed at Johnny. "First," he said, "I really couldn't get Maxie, so Tom would have had to go somewhere else anyway. Second, I don't want anybody owing me no favors, and I don't like owing them myself. Now I am off the hook on account of you and Emily. Finally, even though I said keep quiet, Tommy is sooner or later going to shoot off his big mouth and my stock as a good guy goes up another notch. Any questions?"

Silently, Johnny shook his head.

"Okay. Now, how much longer do you think that dog'll run?"

"*Tiger Row?* We close Saturday."

"Good. I could get you out of it, but since it's that soon, why bother? Now, I don't want you to talk business to anyone, understand? Anyone wants to know anything about your availability, or your price, or anything except the time of day, you send them to me." He wrote something on a card, handed it to Johnny. "This is my number. It's unlisted, so don't lose it. Any time, day or night, either I'm there or my service will pick up. Let me know where to get back to you and stay there. During the day, I'll either be here, or Martha will know how to get me. Clear?"

Johnny nodded, and just then the receptionist came in with

130

a sheaf of papers. Conklin signed three of them, shoved them across the desk. "Better read it, kid," he advised. Johnny laughed and signed.

"I've got my own ex-wrestler buddies," he said.

Conklin laughed and got up to shake Johnny's hand. "I like your style, kid," he said. "We're going places together. Leave your number with Martha. . . . Oh, no phone? Well get one. Right away. Call in the number. Need any dough?"

"No thanks," said Johnny. "By the way," he added as we walked toward the door, "do you know Tony Warden?"

"The director? Sure. His series was canceled, wasn't it?"

"That's the one," said Johnny. "If we get an offer from Kraft or U.S. Steel, I don't go without Tony as director. Okay?"

Conklin stopped short and looked down at Johnny. "Why your high-handed little sonofabitch," he said. "You really mean that, don't you."

"I really mean that," said Johnny.

Conklin shook his head slowly. "Okay," he said, "I think I can swing it. But only because everyone knows he's a damned good man."

"And don't let anyone know I'm the one who's insisting."

"How the hell do I manage that?" Conklin began. "It's bound to get out and. . . . Oh, I get it. You learn fast."

"Glad to see you," said Johnny. His voice was an exact mimic of the greeting Conklin had given us as we entered. The big man dissolved into laughter and waved us out of his office.

We left the east entrance, and across the street, by the outdoor skating rink, the big Christmas tree was already high in the air, gaily decked out with a rainbow of brightly colored balloons. Christmas carols wafted up from the loudspeakers in the rink. We walked over to the railing and looked down at the skaters sliding by below. Johnny turned and tilted his head to stare up at the towering mass of the Center.

"And I was going to put her in there with a suite of offices and an army of flunkies," he said softly.

I didn't need to ask who "she" was.

I was hard at work in my room at the Great Northern, cursing my Hermes typewriter and its triple-damned French keyboard. The machine actually belongs to my sister-in-law, and was loaned to me for my trip. My own Olympia, while in all respects a superb machine, weighs a ton. The Hermes is also a fine machine, except that on this particular model, the % is where the " should be, and vice versa, so my characters often end up saying, %Hello,% instead of "Hello."

The phone rang, and I said, %Hello?%

"Edwin, this is Elvira."

"Good morning. How was Philadelphia?"

"Dreadful. The City of Brotherly Love didn't have any affection left over for my poor client's play."

"Sorry to hear that. But you can't win them all."

"This week I'm not winning any of them, Edwin. You and I have got more troubles than that poor boy in Philadelphia."

"I was afraid of that," I said.

"I understand you talked with Elly yesterday."

"Not on purpose. I called Ned, just as I promised to. He was out on location, so Elly and I shot the breeze."

"The breeze isn't all you shot," Elvira said coldly. "I think you also neatly shot yourself out of this assignment."

"What gives you that idea?"

"You and I are commanded to appear before the powers that be at lunch today."

"The powers? You mean Ned and Elly are in town?"

"Got in on the red-eye flight this morning. I didn't talk to them personally, but I have it on good authority that smoke came out of the telephone."

"What can I say?" I told her. "Elly and I had a little disagreement, but I didn't think it was all that serious."

"It's serious. I wish I could talk to you before, but maybe we can meet a few minutes early."

"Okay. Where?"

"Hedin's. Know where it is?"

"58th, just east of Madison."

"12:15, at the bar."

"I'll be there."

"If I'm a little late," she warned, "don't decide that just because it's a bar, you have to drink it dry."

"Elvira, love, I'm off martinis for life."

"You can have two. No more."

"Good lord!" I said, "we must really be in trouble."

"We are," she said, and hung up.

I replaced my own phone in its cradle and sat back. Suddenly the typewriter seemed distant, and the words on the yellow paper were stiff and meaningless. The carefully-nurtured mood had been destroyed by the phone call. I looked at my watch. It was just 10:30, and I'd been working since before six, when I had waked drenched with sweat. It occurred to me that I had not even made any coffee, and that if I were going to drink martinis and fight with the Barkers all afternoon it might be wise to lay down a foundation. Lunch, if it came at all, would arrive too late to make any difference.

I walked up to the park and strolled across Central Park South, looking down at the swans swimming in the lake. The hazy weather was nothing to write home about, although high overhead the sun was making a feeble attempt to burn off the mists. The odds were that the mists would win.

Stopping at one of the Oo-la carts that sell exotic European snacks, I bought a cup of tea, since the girl running it said she didn't have coffee. I gave her a coin and she looked at it strangely.

"Are you sure you want to use this?" she said. "You don't see them very often."

"Sorry," I said, retrieving it and giving her a crumpled bill instead. I had almost spent my silver dollar.

The tea finished, I wandered over to Hedin's, past the display of wines nested in ice, and up to the bar.

It was unlikely that I would do any more writing today. Perhaps, on this particular project, not any day. So I took Elvira at her word and ordered an extra dry Lamplighter martini on the rocks with a twist of lemon. I drink them that way because I am a slow sipper and a straight-up martini almost always becomes too warm to endure by the time I can finish it. When the drink came, I fished the lemon peel out with a swizzle stick and rubbed it around the rim of the glass. Since this bartender was unaware of my little nervous habit and also knew that he had prepared the drink exactly right, he was entitled to a free glare.

I was three sips into the martini when Elvira arrived.

"Scotch," she said. "On the rocks. Double."

This didn't faze the bartender, but it shook me up a little. Elvira was behaving most unElvira-like. The drink came and she practically upended it, waved for another.

"You have this thing," she told me, "of seeing how many of your friends you can turn into enemies. You know the only reason you got this job was through Elly."

"How could I ever forget?" I said. "Between you and Ned, it's all I seem to hear."

"So why go out of your way to upset *her?* You've already got poor Ned climbing trees. Why not play it smart and hang onto your last remaining ally? She says you called her at six in the morning."

"Sorry about that," I said. "I forgot about the time difference."

"I bet you did."

"Ned does it to us. I was just paying him back a little. How was I to know Elly would answer?"

"Be that as it may. Then you have to read her off like she is some suburban housewife instead of merely your very own producer."

"Co-producer," I said. "Did she give you any details about the famous read-off?"

"Only that you absolutely refused to cooperate, that you took an unreasonable stance on that high horse of yours and refused to come down."

"She lies."

"Elly? Lies? I don't believe it."

"Maybe not deliberately. I think she probably thinks I was being unreasonable. But the truth is, I only held out for what we all agreed was the best way to attack this project. I wasn't going to mention this, but since I seem to be the dog in the manger, I'd like to have a little company. The reason she and Ned are here today is because they're unhappy about the way the script's going."

She took a deep dive into her second Scotch and came up for air.

"Nonsense," she said. "They're mad at you, for your damned contrary Irish attitude."

"No, Elvira. They've been reading the script. They think Johnny has a dirty mouth."

"So do I, if you must know. But how do *they* know? What do you mean, reading the script?"

"Somebody in your office has been xeroxing the manuscript and mailing it out to them."

"Ned wouldn't dare."

"He would, and has. And that's the bone of contention here.

They don't like all of this unpublished stuff I've been digging up about Johnny. They say they're afraid of lawsuits from the survivors. They want me to tone him down a little, and listen to their suggestions perhaps. I don't know what all they do want."

"And the reason they've reached this decision is that they've been getting secret peeks at the script?"

"Exactly."

"And I suppose that when you found this out, you just pulled at your forelock and said, well it didn't matter anyway, that'd you hoped you could trust them to stay out of your way until the first draft was done."

"Something like that."

"Now here they are in New York. It doesn't sound like they took your advice. That Barker man! It's one thing if he's managed to sneak a spy into my office. But if he corrupted one of the girls already working there, I'll kill him."

"Here's your chance," I said. "They're coming in now."

Ned and Elly strolled over, all smiles and California tan. Ned stuck out his hand to me and I did my level best to crush it, but only managed a bare draw. Elly hugged Elvira, then she smooched over me.

"Shall we have a drink at the bar?" boomed Ned.

"Too public," Elvira said. "I've got a table. Let's go. Edwin, pay the man."

"Have it put on the lunch bill," said Ned. "Our treat. Don't get to the city often enough."

"I've learned through sad experience," she said, "that if you have the bar tab transferred, that's the last the bartender sees of his tip. The table waiters eat it. So pay the man here."

The tab was $6.40 of which the better half seemed to be taxes. Ned put down a ten. "Keep the change," he said.

"Well," said Elly, "how good it is to see you, Ed. You've put on weight."

"I've lost hair," I said. "Keeps the balance about even."

She went ha-ha and as we reached the table, Elvira motioned for me to let them have the inside plush seats, while we sat out in the aisle.

We ordered drinks, and made small talk until they came. Elly couldn't seem to meet my eye, while Ned seemed to want to talk about anything in the world except the script. This seemed odd at first, considering they had come all this way to make some kind of pronouncement about it, but Elvira was calling the shots so I waited for her to make her move.

She did, halfway through the double Scotch, her third in less than an hour.

"I understand you're dissatisfied with the way the script is going," she said.

"Not dissatisfied, exactly," Ned hedged.

"Then what exactly?"

"Ed seems to be fictionalizing Johnny a lot more than we had in mind," Elly said. "He's got stuff in there that there's no way in the world to prove."

"Pardon me all to hell," I said. "I thought this was a movie, not a case history. And let's see you try to prove those scenes didn't happen."

"Now, now," Elvira said sweetly. "We agreed that Ned and Elly should have their say. After all, they hired us."

"That's so sensible, Elvira," said Elly. "We knew *you'd* be reasonable."

"Now what would you suggest we do?" Elvira asked.

"Oh, nothing much," said Ned. "We want to make sure we're not off on the wrong track. I thought we might all get together with a few people who knew Johnny well, and just— well, sift through this new material. It never hurts to go to the source, you know."

"You haven't mentioned," said Elvira, "how you come to know about this new material, as you put it."

137

"Oh," said Elly.

"Well," Ned said, "I imagined *he*—" (*He* was me and from now on I would have about as much acknowledgment as a tennis net between the Barkers and Elvira.) "—would have told you all about it. It was just a little precaution, Elvira, I hope you don't mind. It's just that there was so much money involved—"

"—That you hired one of my girls to spy on my client."

"We didn't hire anyone," Elly said hotly. "We wouldn't do *that*. We sent in one of our own people. She's doing temporary typing for you."

"Many thanks," said Elvira. "That's all I really wanted to know from you. Now I don't have to suspect any of my old crew. Edwin, shall we go?"

"Hey, wait a minute," said Ned. "Where do you think you're going?"

"Somewhere to have lunch in peace," said Elvira. "And, of course, Edwin must get back to work on his manuscript, if it is to be delivered on time."

"Edwin," said Elly, "isn't working on any manuscript, at least not until we get some things cleared up."

"Like letting some of Johnny's old friends check out what's been written to see if they agree with the way they've been interpreted?"

"Well, what's wrong with that?" Ned asked. "We don't want lawsuits."

"That's your problem," said my gutsy little agent. "We committed to deliver a powerful, theatrical, and above all, honest, script to you by the end of this month. We will keep our part of the bargain, even though you have already violated yours. I hope that you persist in this clumsy attempt to precensor the script. Then I'll have grounds for a whopping damage suit against both you and Fine Arts. I do so hope you enjoy your visit to New York. Try and see the new musical at the Winter Garden. Mary Martin's so wonderful. Coming, Edwin?"

And out onto the street she steamed, with me in hot pursuit. I remembered my briefcase, but my rain hat is probably still there.

CHAPTER
SIX

I FOUND myself walking along Central Park West. It was spring, and the sun was warm and softly golden in my eyes. The numbers on the license plates read 1954, and the cars looked strangely round and squat.

A motorcycle roared up beside me at the crosswalk and a leather-encased figure leaned over and yelled, "Get on."

I scrambled up behind Johnny. I had some trouble getting down the rear pegs as he balanced the machine with both legs stretched out on either side of the grumbling cylinders. It was a big blue Harley-Davidson, and it looked brand new.

"Hold on, now," he warned, releasing the hand clutch. With a snarling rumble, the Harley hurled itself forward. I clutched at the hand-rails on the buddy seat as Johnny guided it along the street, deftly toe-shifting into second gear. He was small

140

enough so I could see over his huddled shoulders and the sight of the oncoming traffic was none too pleasant as he slipped from lane to lane by shifting his weight from one side to the other, not turning the handlebars at all.

"Where are we going?" I yelled in his ear. He shouted something back over his shoulder, but I couldn't hear it over the sound of the cycle, so I just tightened my grip on the rails and hoped we would not hit a patch of oil. At Columbus Circle, he turned west on a side street, and soon we were bouncing south down the cobblestones under the West Side Highway. To the right was the waterfront, on the left the buildings of the city rose, a brick and concrete barrier as the cycle's exhaust purred against the concrete abutments. Eventually, he turned left, and we passed the Christopher Street Post Office and the Hudson Tubes entrance. Soon we were speeding through Sheridan Square, past Jack Delaney's restaurant and near it, The Circle in the Square. Beneath the theatre was Louis' Bar, gone now these many years, I thought glumly with my present middle-aged spread bouncing on that 1954 street in Greenwich Village. Johnny turned the cycle into tiny Cornelia Street, and parked it outside Number 21. It was a dingy-brown building of five stories and as we entered, the reek of stale urine hit us.

"The bums get in here and piss on the wall," he said. We climbed two flights of stairs and he kicked open a door. Inside, a young woman looked up from her book, threw him a kiss in greeting. She nodded absently at me and then wrapped her long sweater-sheathed arms around Johnny as he bent over to kiss her.

"Dee Dee Aldiss," he told me. "Actually, it's Deborah Delilah. She's a photographer. Those are her pictures up at the Circle in the Square. Right now she's doing the new show over at Tom Hill's Originals Only. I have appointed Dee Dee my official photographer."

141

Once he mentioned her name, any further introduction was superfluous. I knew her name and her work well. In later years she would have abandoned photography for the richer pastures of TV commercial production, in company with such other photographic names as Bert Stern and Howard Zeiff. But in the mid-fifties, her detailed photographic biography of Johnny would bring her fame.

"Jerry Conklin called," Dee Dee told him. "He wants to know if you'll do that U.S. Steel in June."

"The one with Eddie Albert?" She nodded. "Do you think I should? The play'll be settled down by then. It might be fun to work with Eddie."

She shrugged. "Do you need the money?"

"Are you kidding?" he said. "I'm running out of things to buy already. Every time I turn around, Jerry's got another check for something or other. Did I tell you how much he hung up Billy Rose for the play? Five hundred a week. Rose screamed like a wounded buffalo. But he paid it. No, what the hell, I don't need any more television for a while. I don't want to get pegged as one of those New York TV actors. Jerry's working on a test with Warner's. And believe it or not, this play is hard work. Tony's sweating my ass off climbing up and down that goddamned tree."

He turned to me. "Tony Warden's directing *The Tree House.* We go to Philadelphia next week. But then, you already knew that, didn't you?"

"Listen," said Johnny, to Dee Dee. "The reason I dropped by was to see if you wanted to come down with the show."

"I don't think so," she said. "I'm right in the middle of the Originals Only thing. And Stella Holt, up at the Greenwich Mews, wants me to do their new play. Besides, you'll be busy."

"What the hell," he said. "I wasn't inviting you down to *sleep* with me."

142

"Maybe that's why it's not worth the trouble," she said. "No, you go ahead and plow your way through all those nineteen-year-old Philadelphia girls. The change'll do you good. You must be getting tired of ballet dancers and little brunettes from the Bronx."

"What's that got to do with anything?" he said defensively. "I like to have a lot of girls around. It doesn't mean anything. They're for screwing or to run out for coffee. You can't *talk* with them."

"If it's talk you want," Dee Dee said, "there's always Jean Billingham. She'll be there for the opening, won't she?"

"Could be," said Johnny. He looked into her eyes for a long moment, and then they both burst out laughing. "Damn it, Dee Dee," he said. "You're jealous. Admit it. You're green eyed, spitting mad jealous."

"Admitted," she said. "I'll get over it. But not in Philadelphia. It's not enough I've turned into your goddamned social secretary, taking your phone calls, I have to go down and watch those juvenile delinquents climbing all over you? Why don't you get an answering service?"

He hugged her and nibbled at her ear. "Because answering services don't give me all the services I can get someplace else."

"Well, no more services today," she said. She pushed him away and got up. "I've got about a million prints to make up as soon as it gets dark. God! One of these days I'll have a real darkroom instead of a kitchen table and blankets on the window. If I ever have that, I'll die happy."

"Well, if that's the way you're going to be," Johnny said.

"That's the way I'm going to be. Besides, you little bastard, you didn't come here to screw. You came here to torment me, and I'm fed up with your jokes. Did it ever occur to you that if you had a phone service, Jean Billingham wouldn't have called *me* to leave a message for you that she will see you in

Philadelphia? Out! Out, and let me get my negatives orga-
nized."

"I'm going, I'm going," he said, pretending to cower. At the
door, he said in a normal voice: "Dinner tonight?"

"Gee, hon, I can't," she said. "Honestly. I've got all this
damned work."

"Okay," he said. "Be seeing you."

"Sure," Dee Dee said.

Two small Italian boys were bouncing up and down on the
motorcycle when we came out of the building. They leaped off
and prepared to run, then saw that Johnny was not upset, and
began pestering him for a ride.

"Not today, kids," he said. "Next time." He stood up on the
starter kicker and the Harley rumbled in the narrow street. I
crawled on and away we went, down to where West 4th Street
crosses Sixth Avenue, and then up the Avenue with the Empire
State Building looming in the sky ahead. We rode past it, past
Byrant Park at 42nd Street, past Radio City, and at 59th Street,
headed into Central Park.

"Hang on," he yelled. "Here we go."

He wound the Harley up. The wind began to whip at my
clothing and my hair slapped hard against my temples. When
the motorcycle's roar filled the world around us, he shifted into
a final gear, and the sound settled down to a low-pitched pur-
ring. We caught up with a pack of cars, and without changing
speed Johnny slipped the Harley down the centerline between
them, took the lead, and left them behind. In minutes, we were
sweeping around the curved hill near the city reservoir, turning
the northern-most corner at the top of the park, and once again
heading south, toward the heart of the city. At 72nd Street,
Johnny slowed the machine and we left the park. My ears
throbbed from the wind and my hands were white from gripping the hand rails.

144

"Figured out," he said, "that if you double up your speed, you can still make all the lights. I went around three times last week without ever once seeing a red one."

"How about police cars?" I asked. "Ever see any of them?"

"Just lucky, I guess," he said. He parked the Harley near a fire plug, and we went into his building. As usual, the apartment door was unlocked. This time, though, there was no Maggie McBride. Instead, the face that looked up as we entered was that of Georgia Marshall.

Perhaps Spring is not really Philadelphia's rainy season. Perhaps some mysterious fate dogs my tracks whenever I decide to go to Philadelphia in May and the word gets passed saying, "He's there again. Rain on him." If that is the case, I truly apologize to the soggy citizens of Philadelphia for the misfortune I invariably bring them. In any event, our visit to that beautiful city in May of 1954 was no different than any other springtime pilgrimage in my experience: the heavens opened and the streets ran two inches deep in water.

Where the original schedule had called for a simple runthrough on the new stage, the cast had been thrown into consternation by an announcement calling everyone in the company together at ten on a Saturday morning. And in the theater, darkened except for glaring rehearsal lights, the general confusion was compounded by a stage manager who kept promising to tell "something big" as soon as the director arrived. A little later, he was beckoned backstage, and reappeared in a moment.

"Ladies and gentlemen," he said, "I don't believe any introduction is necessary. Meet your new director."

Into a shocked silence, Arnold Ross walked out on stage. Even I was surprised, for I had forgotten that the famous director had been brought in to replace Tony Warden.

"Mr. Rose has asked me to inform you," said Arnold Ross, "that Mr. Warden has asked for his release, and that henceforth

I shall be in charge of this production. This is a decision that has not been arrived at lightly. The producers have decided that, as it is, *The Tree House* is not ready to open. Therefore, our Philadelphia opening has been postponed for a week, and our New York debut indefinitely."

"Balls!" said Johnny, starting up the aisle.

"Mister Lewis!" Arnold Ross did not raise his voice, but it cut through the tense theater air sharply. "Where are you going?"

"To see Billy Rose," Johnny said. "We made a deal. If he's changing the rules, I'm getting out of the game."

"Sit down," said Ross. "Like the rest of the company, you are under contract. And that contract does not, I am sure, give you director approval. You should be thankful that Mr. Rose honors both sides of a contract. Otherwise, you would leave my theater for good. But since we must both work together, I suggest that we get on with it. A week is short enough for all that we must do."

Slowly, Johnny sat down. The other actors huddled together, whispering quietly.

"We will be rehearsing here, on the stage and in the set," Ross went on. "I must warn you there will be considerable change in the script, so if you were planning any heavy social activity in the next week, I advise you to forget it. Mister Harper and Miss Norse, where are you, please?" The two performers raised their hands. "Will you please stop by Mr. Rose's office at once? Your roles have been written out of the play, and the producers will settle your contracts with you or your agent. Would you go now, please? And thank you for your work until now." Stunned, the two actors got up and left the theater.

"There will be other changes," Ross warned. "Several of you may not find your roles as large or rewarding as before. I am sorry. But if we do not save this play, no one will be employed.

146

Working together, I am confident that *The Tree House* will not only survive, but will be successful. Now, if you will all report to our stage manager, he will give out your schedules. I must insist on punctuality. I must insist on your being well up on your lines before each rehearsal. I must insist that there be no arguing, no quibbling. This is not a workshop: we are in the professional theatre working against a deadline. I am the director. That's all."

He turned and left the stage. The stage manager came down to the apron, a sheaf of papers in his hand. "Okay, kids," he said, "line up."

Veteran Broadway actor, Martin Marks, stood up. "Don't," he said coldly, "ever address this cast as 'kids.' Arnold Ross may be Lord High Director, but you are merely the stage manager."

"Oh, Christ," said the stage manager, "this is going to be one of those weeks."

How prophetic he was! The week of rebuilding *The Tree House* in Philadelphia still lingers in the memories of its cast as one of the most painful of their careers. But they all admit readily that during this time of turmoil and eighteen-hour days, a strange thing happened. A play that had been pleasant and competent, and that they had foolishly convinced themselves was ready for Broadway, turned itself inside out and became something at once entirely different, and yet the same. All of the potentially ironic overtones of this social comedy about the events surrounding the son of a Newport first family who builds a $400,000 tree house in his front yard, while his parents are on their annual tour of the Rivera, blossomed into genuine satire. A vicious martinet, Ross yet had the gift of bringing life to every scene, to lines that seemed to have no meaning until he had taunted and goaded the actor into digging into them so deeply that no secret nuance could escape. As the week wore

147

on, and the rain continued to flood the streets, the initial shock and gloom departed the Shubert Theatre, and while each and every cast member shared an abiding hatred of their new director, curses and allusions to his ancestry took on a tinge of respect for his creative abilities. "If it had to be that we would fall into the clutches of a despotic bastard," Martin Marks said one night, "thank God that he's at least a talented one."

Meanwhile, Johnny had been involved in several long phone conversations with Jerry Conklin. "Jer doesn't want me to quit the show," Johnny told me, as we sat in the William Penn bar, sipping Schmidt's Beer. "The word is out that it'll be the best thing all year. It ought to get a shot at all the awards, since the season's almost gone and it'll be so fresh in everyone's minds. But how can I stay in after what they did to us? They fired Tony Warden without asking one of us what we had to say. I know this isn't supposed to be a democracy. You can't vote your way into a good production. But in spite of what they say, I don't like this play the way I used to. Maybe it will be more successful because of what Ross had done to it. But it isn't what I set out to do. Remember how I used to get so involved with the character that I took him home with me after the rehearsal? Well, all that's gone now. I may be coming across like I mean what I'm doing, but this really is just technique. I can even hear myself when I'm reading a line. I never used to listen. I don't like myself this way."

He turned the beer glass slowly in his hands. "Still," he said, "I can't bail out just yet. For one thing, that goddamned understudy couldn't find his ass with both hands. They need a nut like me to make this part come off. If they opened with the wrong guy, it'd kill the play. But once they've opened and got their notices, that's another ball game. Hell, I told Rose to replace me. He wouldn't. He'll let me quit if I really want to, but he won't let me off the hook on what I'll do to the show if I do. Still, I know a couple of guys who could do this part. Two in particular. Brando is one; he could do this part standing on his head. But Rose has his eye on him for something else. And there's a new guy I've seen on the rounds, Paul Newman. Now he's got something going too. But if Rose won't put somebody like this in before the opening, then I've *got* to open. They got me by the balls."

"And lovely balls they are," said Jean Billingham, slipping into the booth beside him.

"Gad, woman," said Johnny, "but you are becoming crude."

"Frustration," she said. "Once you develop a taste for monsters, nice little boys won't set you off any more. Sorry I'm late," she said more seriously. "Crisis at the publisher. He discovered four pages of Carson McCullers in my latest chapter."

"You're kidding," Johnny said.

"No," she said, accepting the beer that came as a result of Johnny's hand wave, "as a matter of fact, he's right. You see, sometimes I find a scene that I like and so I type it out in manuscript. It's almost like I were writing it myself, that way, and the mood, the feeling, gets in my head better. Trouble is, in this case, I was in a hurry to get down here and the goddamned scene itself got into the final typescript. Thank God some sharp copy reader spotted it. If it had ever gotten into galleys, I'd have been cooked. Once it's in type, a copy somehow always manages to get out of the shop." She sloshed down a huge swallow of beer. "How did the rehearsal go? Ross still chewing everyone's tail off?"

"And rubbing salt into the hole. What pisses me is that he's usually right. If he was wrong more often, it'd make it easier to hate him."

"Why is it so necessary for you to hate him?"

"Jeannie," he said quietly, "I must hate men like him. No one

149

has the right to be so sure, so self-sufficient, so frigging confident!"

"You're pretty confident yourself," she observed.

"That's different," he said. "Maybe I've got inside information. Maybe I know that if I weren't confident, if I didn't come on strong, I would never make it in the time I've got. I need confidence. But what the hell does Ross need? He's already got it made. What's he pushing so hard for? He's already there."

"Oh, Johnny, Johnny," the little woman said sadly, "how little you really know. I keep thinking you are as tough as me, because I love you and no longer see you as the little boy you are, and then you say something like that. Don't you know that no one *ever* has it made? No one ever gets to the top because there isn't any top. Everyone has demons, eating their talent and their lives, and the miracle always is that we get any good work accomplished at all. The monsters like you and me, and yes, like Arnold Ross, we somehow manage to beat the game for a little while and come up lucky. But sooner or later the house percentage will wear us down, and those sneaky little zeroes and double zeroes will eat us alive. Arnold Ross in the afternoon of his life is no more immune from the demons than you are, Johnny. Good heavens, listen to *me!* You'd think I liked the man."

"Wouldn't surprise me if you do," Johnny said. "I'm discovering that you are able to find the good in everyone, and if there is any good in our Mr. Ross, I'm sure you've ferreted it out. But let's drop it, huh? It's almost midnight, and I'm tired, for once. I've got to get to bed. We've got a 9:00 A.M. call again. I feel for those kids who aren't quick studies. They gave us six new pages of script today. No sweat for me, but I'm tired all of a sudden. I think I'm. . . ."

Whatever it was, he never finished. John Calvin Lewis sat in a padded booth in the bar of the William Penn Hotel and slept.

150

Unlike the early success and ultimate failure of *Tiger Row*, *The Tree House* did not achieve false fame out of town. It played to dismal houses for its two weeks in Philadelphia, to audiences who did not laugh when they should and who shambled out of the Shubert into the chilly rain without a backward glance at the miserable actors, caught naked on the stage when the applause ran out suddenly in the middle of the second curtain call. The reviews were merciless, the cast despondent. All of the gloom of the early days of what the cast called "hell week" returned, and the only smile seen in the Shubert was on the face of Arnold Ross.

Suddenly, as the apparent disaster moved closer and closer to its Armageddon, he abandoned his sarcasm and dour mien, and became a man of rare wit; a raconteur, filled to the brim with delightful stories of the Lunts and Kit Cornell, and the young Orson Welles defying City Hall. Not an actor was able to leave the theater without fulsome words of praise ringing in his ears from this oddly-formed genius from the lower East side. When, one particularly discouraging afternoon, a deputation from the cast went to him after a matinee before less than a hundred soggy souls and pleaded for some miracle to save the show, he looked at them with genuine bewilderment.

"You don't *want* them to like it," he said. "This is not a Philadelphia show. This is a New York show. If they liked it in Philadelphia, I would be worried. In Philadelphia, who knows from Newport? They think it's a naval base in Virginia. Billy made a mistake bringing this show down here. We should have spent our time with previews in New York. But our tour is up Saturday night, and we can go back to the city. A week of previews will put some backbone in you.

And that reminds me, did you ever hear the story about Alexander Woolcott and the bobby soxer who surprised Alex in his bedroom early one Christmas morning? Well . . ."

"Demons," Johnny muttered. No one knew what he meant.

Johnny was alone in not despairing. "I wish it would close," he told me. "Right here, and never be heard of again. But I think Ross is right. I can tell the show is okay. It's the audience. The advertising we had before Ross changed the play is tricking them. They come in here expecting one thing and get another. I don't blame them for being mad. I don't like the show any more myself, but if you accept his point of view, it's just about perfect right now."

"You two getting along any better?"

"Not particularly. It's my fault too. He wants to bury the hatchet. But I don't want to understand him. If I do, I may end up forgiving him for what he has done to this play. He's probably made it into a hit, but I still don't want to forgive him for it. I just want to get it all over."

"Does Jerry agree?"

"No, but the truth is he can't give me much in the way of arguments to keep me in after the opening. If I'm good, I get the notices and that's all he needs. Running week after week wouldn't really do either of us much good."

"What do you plan next?"

"Who knows. The screen test fell through. They're cutting back at Warner's. Seems there's this thing called television. Anyway, I wouldn't want one of those big studio contracts. Not the seven year ones. I've got too much to do, to get locked in for that much time. I'm not worried. I'll get there. I know. A little bird told me."

Saturday night did come, and the curtain closed for the last time in Philadelphia on *The Tree House*. The audience was a little warmer, probably due to a transfusion of fresh blood down

152

from New York to view the body before it was laid out for the formal wake in New York. The big-towners were agreeably surprised by the play, and managed to breathe some of their own enthusiasm into the try-out audience. The curtain call was respectable, if not exactly an ovation. Backstage, the performers were whisking off their makeup, using a variety of individual blends. Cold cream is effective, but expensive. Baby oil is cheaper, but messy. Three of the girls in minor roles shared a large can of Crisco, and it took off the Max Factor grease paint as well as anything. Officially, the cast were on their own time now, and not due to report in again until Monday, at the Cort Theatre in New York. And, from my own observation of the out-of-town tryout, I knew pretty well what the pattern would be.

During the initial days of rehearsal, relations between performers of both sexes are cordial, each searching out the other in a friendly but dispassionate way. Friendships, of a sort, are struck up, and continue until a week or so before the play is due to go on the road. Then, glances become more intense. Conversations are more intimate; jokes more risque. By the time the train leaves for Philadelphia, a rough pairing-off has been achieved. Oh, not all in the company participate. Some refuse because they have their own private lives that follow them even to the City of Brotherly Love; some because they have no desire to play silly games; some simply because they got a bad shuffle in the opposite numbers available and came up empty. But the first week on the road would be one of experimentation for most of those out there. Johnny was direct enough about it. "If that bastard Ross hadn't worked us all to death, we'd have all switched off practically every night until we all settled down with one setup that felt good to both of us. But Ross left us so little time and energy that instead of screwing all night we just slept together."

153

Barring arguments or illness, the temporary arrangement was usually maintained until the end of the tryout period, with the understanding, of course, that in the event of a visit from a back-home spouse, legal or otherwise, all bets were off. Now, on the last night before the trek back to civilization, it was orgy time. Tomorrow, within the limits of their individual moralities, the company would revert to normal behavior. But the last night on the road is a night to howl, and no one from Billy Rose down to the lowliest walk-on extra expected anything different.

Even Arnold Ross surprised everyone by turning up at the first rump party with Miss Schoonover from the Workshop on his arm. Mrs. Ross was nowhere to be seen, so no one mentioned her. As for Miss Schoonover, after three strong snifters of Créme de menthe, she began to tell queer jokes, of which she had a seemingly inexhaustible supply. The fun went out of that soon enough, and after having stayed long enough to leave decently, Ross wheeled her out the door. A few minutes later, with democratic protocol out of the way, the rejects and undesirables were left behind to enjoy each other's dubious company while the more favored retired to gentler pursuits elsewhere. In this evening's case, that happened to be the suite shared by Martin Marks and a young lady whom no one had spoken with before, but who had attended each and every performance of *the Tree House.* No one chilled the atmosphere by bringing up Martin's gray-haired little wife, presumably huddled at that very moment in their large co-op apartment in Kew Gardens with their four cats and Martin's press book. The young lady's first name was Kay, and if she had a last one none of us ever heard it. That is too bad in a way, since Kay was going to cause a hell of a lot of trouble by turning up in New York on opening night, and she should get more credit than I am able to give her.

It was well after two in the morning, and everyone was lined up playing The Game. Charades have always left me cold, but in the hands of talented professional actors, The Game is usually interesting, if not always family, entertainment. Martin Marks had just finished acting out "Sir Patrick Spens" for his team, and had actually conveyed that not-too-visual name to them. The stage manager, at the party on sufferance anyway, had disgraced himself by writing "Old Shep" as his choice of subjects, only to discover that no one in the room except me had ever heard of that old Kentucky ballad, and I didn't count. Now it was Kay's turn, and Johnny had written the charade. She read it and went white for a minute, then began to giggle and held up the game for a few minutes while a soothing Scotch was fetched to revive her.

She held up one finger, and her team mates cried, "First word?" and she nodded. She pointed at herself and they yelled, "I", "me," "mine," and finally got, "my." Then Kay held up three fingers. "Third word," yelled the team. She flurried around, letting them know it was a two-letter word, that the first letter was "i" by pointing at her eye, the second "s" by pointing at her ample behind. "Ass," yelled one happy soul, connected it with the "eye" and came up with "is." Kay indicated the last word, and clued her team by tapping on the floor. "Wood," cried one, "floor," another, and after several false answers, one got, "hard." Now the line read, "My —is hard." For the final clue, Kay simply strolled over to the wall, pretended to zip down a fly and in that classic scene from *Bicycle Thief,* to urinate on the wall. "Prick," someone yelled, and then Johnny read the whole line, "My prick is hard." There was a spurt of laughter and then an embarrassed silence as we all looked at Johnny, who lounged against Jean Billingham, smiling his tight smile and looking up over his invisible glasses. Kay filled the gap by sidling over in the obvious "sneak" walk of cartoons, then reached out and grasped his crotch. Her face

155

reddened, but she kept her hand there while she said, "Good heavens, it *is!*"

That was as far as she got. Jean Billingham fetched her as neat an uppercut as I have ever seen a girl throw. This was no female slap, but an honest-to-goodness jawbreaker. It seemed to start down around Jean's ankle, and it finished up against Kay's chin with a solid clunk that knocked the girl a couple of inches into the air. She went down in a heap, out cold, without even a whimper. Johnny kept smiling, but he reached for Jean, and that was his mistake. She jabbed her heel down on his instep and as he yelled and bent over to grab his foot, she brought her knee up in his groin. He reeled back against the wall, white with pain, and as his mouth worked to suck in air, Jean smiled sweetly and unzipped his fly.

"Good heavens," she said in mock surprise, "it isn't hard *now.*" And that was the end of the orgy.

With the New York previews, confidence returned to the cast. Once a few ragged spots had been smoothed out, the play began to draw the audience response everyone hoped for, and by opening night on May 29, 1954, the performance had been frozen without changes for two days. Curtain time was at eight, for the convenience of the critics on the morning papers, and by seven-thirty, the theatre had started to fill. When I arrived shortly after eight, the house was packed. The curtain rose at 8:15, which is early for a so-called 8:00 P.M. curtain. The set by Jo Mielziner was greeted with applause, and then Martin Marks made his first entrance as the mayor of Newport, and the play was off and running.

Johnny scored heavily that night. No one who ever saw him in his film work would have recognized him in this role. Although he despised it, as he had told me so many times, he brought a comic timing and delivery to the part that would have excited envy from a Barrymore. In the role of a teen-aged boy who takes on the combined forces of authority and morality by constructing a split-level tree-house, he won laughter with almost every line. *The Tree House* played with one intermission, and during it the comment heard throughout the lobby was, "Who's the boy?" "What's he done before?" "I've never seen anyone like him." The play came in a close second, and from the delighted comments on it, it was obvious that if the second act held up, as I knew it would, there was a new hit in town.

The final curtain came down with a thunderous tumult of applause. There were nine calls in all, and during two Johnny was called forward by the audience to take a solo bow. I pushed my way backstage and managed to elbow my way into the traffic jam that was Johnny's dressing room. He was talking to several men, two of whom I recognized as reporters. The critics had already taken off for their cubbyholes at a dead run, but these were newsmen with a less pressing deadline.

"That's it," Johnny was saying. "Any more details you want, you'll have to get from Mr. Rose. All I can tell you is that I have handed in my notice and that I'll be replaced as soon as they can get someone in."

"But you can't walk out on a hit on opening night," one of the reporters said.

"Just watch me," Johnny said.

"Johnny doesn't feel the play is up to his artistic potential," said a female voice.

"Keep out of this, Kay," he said. Sure enough, it was the dear girl from Philadelphia.

"But I'm on your side, baby," she told him. "You don't need this crummy play. They need you."

"The lady's right," said the reporter. "If you leave, you might cut months off the run of the show."

"Tough luck for them," said Johnny. "I didn't want to open

157

in the first place. I did them that much of a favor. I don't know what else you can expect me to do. I haven't got time to screw around with crap like this. They busted their word to me. This isn't the play I signed to do. I don't want to hurt anybody. I opened, didn't I? But that's all."

"I think you're wonderful," said Kay. "You don't owe them a thing."

"I wish the hell you'd shut up," he told her. Then, to the reporters. "Sorry. That's all. I want to get dressed. No, no, no more." He forced them out of the room by walking forward with both arms outstretched, and then slammed the door in their faces. With a sigh, he threw himself down on the army cot that stretched across one end of the tiny room, serving as a couch. "Damn it all to hell," he said, "nobody understands."

"I understand," said Kay. "What do you get out of staying in the show now that you're such a hit? You can get anything you want. You don't need Billy Rose."

"Will you for Christ's sake shut up before I belt you one?" he said. He bent over the sink and rinsed his face in cold water. I handed him a towel and he dried off. "Am I doing right?" he asked me suddenly. I looked away, and he cursed again and threw his costume jacket across the room. It bounced off the wall and landed in an overflowing waste basket. He slipped into a pullover knit shirt and threw on a blue nylon jacket. "Come on," he said. Kay and I followed him out into the pushing, yelling, laughing crowd. In the alley below the stage door, Martin Marks caught up with us.

"Johnny," he hollered, "wait a minute. How about coming over to 21 with us—" then he saw Kay, and stopped. "Oh," he said. "It's you."

"Don't worry, Martin," she said, laughing. "I didn't come up to cause you any trouble. What do I want with an old fart who can't get it up any more? Mamma and the four cats are safe from me."

His face distorted, and saying something that sounded like, "Why you bitch," Marks went after her. Johnny jumped in to intercept him, and Marks turned with a shout of gleeful rage, happy to have someone to fight. His fist arced through the night air, and as Johnny ducked under it I suddenly realized that I was well within range. The ham-like fist seemed to go into slow motion as it began to fill my field of vision, and then there was a solid, painless crunching sensation and a thousand stars blazed in the night. I felt myself lurch backward and there was a whirling in my head, and as they say in court, everything went black.

My pillow was covered with blood and I choked out great gouts of it as I staggered into my bathroom in the Great Northern. I spat out a mouthful into the sink, and grabbed a wad of tissues and held them against my nose. The cold water was running, and I threw little splashes of it up on my face with my free hand.

Eventually, the bleeding stopped. I scrubbed away at the clots on my lip and chin and manfully resisted the clogging urge to blow my nose. I felt its bridge gingerly. It moved ever so slightly and made crunching sounds. My cheeks were already starting to swell. I looked at my watch. Six-thirty in the morning. Some hour to call the house doctor. I decided to tough it through for a while longer, and made up some coffee with my handy dandy emersion heater. It helped, and feeling better, I came to the conclusion that I would probably be able to get to a doctor's office on my own. While I was arriving at this decision, I must have fallen asleep in my chair, because it was well after eight when next I looked at my watch, and the sun was streaming into the room.

I called Elvira. She recognized my voice and started to tell me something about Ned Barker, but I cut her off.

"Who's your doctor?" I asked.

"Doctor? Who needs a doctor? What for?"

"*I* need a doctor," I said. "I think I busted my nose."

She gasped, and became all efficiency. I could hear her on another phone, getting through to someone, and meanwhile telling me to be calm and not to worry. Soon she came back with a name and an address not far away, over on East 63rd Street.

"It's before office hours," she said, "but he's expecting you. Take a cab."

"Many thanks," I told her. "And stop worrying. It's nothing serious."

"Who's worrying?" she said.

"Who, indeed? When I got to the doctor's address half an hour later, there she was, waiting on the sidewalk.

"You look pale," she said. "Hold on to my arm."

"Good heavens," I said. "I'm not bleeding to death. I just banged my nose on the corner of the bed or something. I woke up with a nosebleed and the bones hurt."

"You could've fooled me," the doctor said when he finished examining my tender beak. "With those two shiners I would be willing to swear in a court of law that you've been in a fight. But don't worry: they'll fade in a day or so. As for the nose, nothing serious. Just don't work it around with your fingers. You'll feel like blowing it, but try not to. Might start the bleeding again. And try to stay out of fights."

"Bar room brawls," Elvira sniffed.

"The hell with you both," I growled. "I hit my nose against the corner of my bed while I was having a dream, and that's my story."

"Fine," said the doctor cheerfully. "Stick to it. Elvira will forward my bill."

We had breakfast, after a fashion, at a nearby Rikers coffee shop. I didn't feel much like chewing, so contented myself with half a doughnut and two cups of coffee.

160

"I called you last night," Elvira said, "but you were out. Fighting, I see now."

"Be that as it may," I told her. "I have nine more pages for you. In fact, although you will never believe it, I practically have the little bastard on his way to Hollywood. In view of that, what's a little fight between friends?"

"You mean you've kept on working? Even after what they said?"

"Hell yes," I said. "This is my story, too. I think it's a good one. If the Barkers want to sneak out of their contract, I can think of at least two producers who would be mighty interested to see what we've got. Come to think of it, maybe I'll pass that word along to Ned-baby."

"That won't be necessary," Elvira said. "Ned and Elly and I had a long talk last evening. I wouldn't answer their calls on the phone, so they came by in person. Full of apologies, I might add. They have reached the conclusion that their—if you will —over-zealous conduct *did* violate the letter, if not the spirit, of the contract. I rather suspect they spent the afternoon with a good lawyer and he told them to forget it. Anyway, the deal is still on. You finish the first draft, and any changes necessary can be agreed on and incorporated into the second draft. Happy?"

I nodded. "Hell," I said, "I don't blame them too much. That's a lot of dough for a pig in a poke. Well, tell them not to worry. It's coming along great and we'll make that May One deadline with no trouble at all."

"All right," she said, "but you watch yourself. What if someone had hit you with a bottle? You could wind up in the hospital. My advice is, if you find yourself in a tough situation, run!"

"My sentiments exactly," I said. And silently called down a few curses on Martin Marks and his lousy aim.

Centerville, Iowa, is a handsome midwestern town of some 7,000 population named, perhaps, after the huge courthouse square that forms the very center of Centerville. The stores front on four sides of what is touted as being the largest courthouse square in the country, and the rest of the town radiates away from there.

Johnny walked through the square, stalked by Dee Dee with one Leica clicking away and two more flapping around her neck as she worked. I joined them as she posed him against the courthouse.

"Dee Dee's got this assignment from *Life*," he explained. "Home town boy makes good and comes back, you know the bit. I got a lot of publicity out of quitting the play, and I guess they figure it might be smart to have something in the bin in case I get any luckier."

"Johnny, get up on the steps," Dee Dee said. "I want a shot of you jumping off them."

I stayed back out of camera range as he climbed the steps and complied with her request that he leap from them like a little boy. He did it three times before she was satisfied.

"We got in yesterday," he said. "Drove all the way straight through. You know, that Dee Dee is some driver. She's got this little MG, straight from the factory. But she really knows how to handle it. Might get myself a sports job myself. Didn't realize how much fun they are.

At Dee Dee's request, he struck another pose in front of the courthouse. A crowd was starting to gather. Two were boys Johnny's age, and they came forward. "Hey, there," said one, "it's John Calvin." "Darned if it ain't," said the other. "Hi, Johnny. You come back to stay?"

"Ed and Petey!" yelled Johnny. He seemed genuinely pleased. He wrapped his arms around both their shoulders and pulled them close. Dee Dee was getting it all with the Leica. "Yeah, yeah, just for a spell."

162

"We saw you on television," volunteered Petey. "When we found out you was to be on that there U. S. Steel show, Mr. Evans he lent a big TV to the school and everyone that didn't have a set at home came in and watched. You were real good."

"Why, thank you," Johnny said. "Coming from you, that means a lot. It really does." To me, he said, "Petey was the leader of the loyal opposition to my one and only stage appearance here in Centerville. When we did the high school play it got in the way of my basketball practice. Petey thought that was disloyal to the team, and decided to make me see the light. Hey, Petey, remember when you and the guys tried to give me that GI shower?"

"Aw, shucks," said Ed, "I don't know what you want to bring that up for now. That was a long time ago."

"I don't mind," Petey said. "I was wrong, and if I ain't never admitted it before, I'm admitting it now. I just got riled that we might lose that last game of the season on account of Johnny and his damned play practice. Besides, I sucked hind tit on that deal anyway, excuse me, ma'am."

Dee Dee forgave him by jamming the Leica in his face for a closeup shot.

"The boys on the team sent word for me to come right over to the gym after dress rehearsal," said Johnny. "Not to even take off my makeup. You see, they were planning to scrub it off with GI brushes. But I fooled them. They were all waiting just inside the double doors when I arrived. Remember that, Petey?"

"Do I ever! There we were, all riled up and ready to scrub off a little hide when in comes Johnny. Riding his motorcycle. Right up the steps and in through the door. Bruce Higgens, he actually threw his shoulder plumb out of joint getting out of the way. Remember that, Ed? And none of us could lay a hand on him. He rode that machine around and around, and the more we chased him the funnier it got, until we plumb lost heart and yelled that it was okay, that we weren't mad no more. So Johnny stopped there in the middle of the court and looked me up and down and says, says he, 'Petey, let's you and me go for a ride.' Well, shoot, I couldn't back down in front of all the fellers, so I got on and off we went, down the steps, and onto the lawn. You know them big pines, with about two feet between their trunks? Well, Johnny, he set sail straight for them and I couldn't see how there was any chance at all for us to get between them, so I rolled off and took about six inches of hide off my rump. Johnny, he didn't look back at all, he just went straight like an arrow, right through that little bitty hole. I know for a fact that both handlebars scraped the trees, because the next day I found rubber marks on the bark. Boy, those were the days."

"Yes," said Johnny, "those were the days."

"Been out to the farm yet, Johnny?" Ed asked.

"Not yet. We're going out later."

"Well, say hello to your Uncle Ray for me," the boy said. "I helped him out last summer and he was real good to me."

"Okay," said Johnny. "We've got to go now. See you around."

We all piled into Dee Dee's red MG. Johnny sat up on the top of the seat with his feet on the transmission hump.

"Head out that street there," he told her. In a few minutes, the frame houses of the town had given way to rolling farm land. Topping a hill, we came on a small general store. "In here," he said. Dee Dee swooped the little MG into the parking lot with a crunch of gravel. We scrambled out and went up on the cluttered porch, our feet clumping against the wood. We were surrounded by galvanized wash tubs and hoes and spades. A bell on the door tinkled as we entered. "Hey," yelled Johnny, "Mister Thomas, are you at home?"

There was no answer, and as we looked around, Johnny

talked. "This is the closest store to the farm. A lot of our things, we'd get here. Some of the things Mr. Thomas carries, you can't even get in town. Here, let me show you."

He took us through a door into another room. It was filled with new oil stoves and pump handles, and over in one corner, on sawhorses, a dusty coffin. Johnny lifted the lid. The inside was lined with green velvet.

"Mr. Thomas always keeps one of these in stock," Johnny said. "A lot of these farm people, they like to take care of their own folks. So instead of going to a funeral home, they come by here. Looks peaceful, doesn't it?"

He stepped on a convenient box, and swung himself into the coffin. "Real soft and comfortable," he said, lying back and crossing both hands on his chest. His eyes flickered, closed, and he was very still. There was dead silence in the room. I could hear my heart beating in my ears. I don't know how long we would have stood there if just then the door hadn't opened, and in came a tall man in his sixties, wearing blue bib overalls.

"Saw your car from over in the barn," he said. "What can I get for you all?" He saw Johnny in the coffin, and his eyes squinted. "Who's that? What are you doing in that there coffin? Sit up so I can see who you are."

"Can't sit up," said Johnny. "I'm dead."

"Johnny Lewis, is that you? Damnation, it *is* you. I might have known. So you come home, eh?"

"Dee Dee," said Johnny, "take a picture of this before I get out."

"Oh, no," she said. "Not like that."

"You," he said to me, "take the camera. Shoot a couple of me like this. Dee Dee, give it to him." She did. I looked at the lens. The aperture was set for outdoors at f-16. I opened it up to f-2.8, pointed the Leica at the macabre scene, lined up the two images in the rangefinder and squeezed off three exposures.

165

Then I handed the camera back to Dee Dee. She accepted it without comment. Johnny crawled out of the coffin. It was only then that I realized that I had just taken the picture that would run on the cover of *Life* the week after Johnny's death.

The farm was much as I'd imagined it. The house was big and weathered, and beautiful in its simplicity. Johnny's Uncle Ray had married again, and "Miss Mary," as Johnny called her, carefully avoiding any references to aunt, was a tall, handsome woman of around forty-five. She was a local girl, a childless widow, and she and Uncle Ray seemed to enjoy the passionless relationship that obviously existed between them. They were both glad to see Johnny again. We sat on the front porch and Miss Mary served iced tea in tall glasses with flowers on the sides.

"Mary pestered me near to death to get a TV," Johnny's uncle said. "But now I'm right glad she did. It sure is strange to look at your own flesh and blood up there on that thing. Especially when you undertake to show us one of those maniacs that goes around killing people."

"It's only playacting," Miss Mary said. "We're all right proud of you, John Calvin. Why, just the other day, there were two newspaper people here all the way from Chicago, asking questions about you and taking pictures. From what they said, you made some fuss up there in New York. Quit your job, or something? Anyway, they wanted your baby pictures and all, but lucky we had already received your letter, so I told them, no, no sir, those pictures was already spoken for by *Life* magazine. That didn't faze them one bit, they tried to give me money for a loan of them, but I said, sorry. Finally they gave up and went away."

"You did right, Miss Mary," Johnny said. "Dee Dee here has been assigned to shoot pictures of you all and the farm, and I'd appreciate it if you didn't let anyone else on the property."

"If you say so," Miss Mary said. "But goodness me, I didn't know there were lady photographers."

"There aren't," Dee Dee said with a wink but it whistled right over their heads.

"I'd better get back to the field," said Uncle Ray. "Still got a couple of hours to do over on the back pasture."

"I'll give you a hand," said Johnny.

"No you don't," said his uncle. "Already got Bib Conrad's young'un helping me. You stay here and enjoy yourself. I'll be back before sundown."

"As for this girl," said Dee Dee, "I think a cold shower is the ticket. I'm carrying ten pounds of dust."

"Afraid we don't have a shower," said Miss Mary. "But I'll be glad to fill the tub for you."

"Wonderful," said Dee Dee. She and Miss Mary went inside, Uncle Ray vanished around the edge of the porch, and Johnny and I were alone. He examined me through his sun glasses.

"Your nose is crooked," he said.

"I'm lucky to have a nose at all," I said. "Small thanks to Mr. Marks."

"Remember that first day in the bar?" he asked. "When I nicked you with my knife? You knew then that you could get hurt here. Why didn't you watch yourself?"

"I *was* watching myself," I said. "My mistake was in not watching Marks. How did it all turn out?"

"He thought he'd hit me. You were gone, but there was plenty of blood around, so Kay started throwing up. Last I saw, Marks was holding her head. Next morning, I got a call from Billy Rose's office. They didn't want to see me again. That was fine by me. Sorry you had to get a bloody nose in the process, though."

167

"It wasn't fatal," I said. "I see you and Dee Dee are still getting along."

"Mostly business," he said. "She's starting to learn that I belong to no one. She either has to harden her heart, or go around with it busted all the time. So she's hardening it up."

"And Jean Billingham?"

"Not a word. Someone saw her out front at one of the previews, but she didn't come back."

"You haven't called her?"

"Nope. Been too busy. Jer has been working my everloving ass off. I did two Studio Ones and a Kraft in three weeks, turned down around two hundred play readings, and did a terrible recording of *This Is My Beloved* for Atlantic. It's been a full two months. Things are slow right now; they always are in July, Jer tells me. So when *Life* offered to pay our expenses, to get this home town bit, he figured it was a smart move. There's no guarantee they'll use any of it, but it's better than a sharp stick in the eye. And it's a break for Dee Dee. Meanwhile, we're sweating out the right movie offer. Warner's got hot again, but it's just a contract deal; no actual property in mind. Screw that. We're not hurting. Something'll come along by September."

He got up, stretched lazily. "Come on. Let's see if we can get some quail."

Johnny led the way into the front room and took down two shotguns from a rack near the door. We broke them to be sure they were unloaded, and filled our pockets with red Remington shells. Miss Mary came in as we were preparing to leave.

"Don't come back without enough for everybody," she said, smiling.

"Count on me," he said. He slung a cloth newspaper-boy's bag over his shoulder.

A hundred yards from the house, we stopped and loaded up. I tried the balance of my gun. It felt heavy in my unaccustomed hands. Johnny threw his weapon up against his cheek, squinted down the barrel. "Pow," he said.

We left the wagon path and moved cautiously through the knee-high broom straw. As prickly burs attached themselves to my legs, I became aware that I was poorly dressed for a hunting expedition. My loafers began to fill up with bits of straw.

"Too bad it's not winter," Johnny said. "One New Year's Day I took nine rabbits out of this one field. Big, fat ones. We ate rabbit for a week."

"For someone who complains about the farm as much as you do," I said, "you seem to have enough fond memories of it."

He looked at me sharply. Just then came a whirring sound and a covey of quail leaped from the grass almost at our feet.

"You go left," Johnny yelled, and raised his gun to fire at the birds flying to the right. I tried to lead my birds, couldn't catch up with them, fired and felt the savage kick of the shotgun just as I heard Johnny's go off behind me. I missed completely; not even a floating feather.

"Two of mine went down," Johnny said. "Over there."

We scuffed through the broom straw and quickly found the still-warm little carcass of one of his birds. It took a few minutes to locate the other. It was wounded in a wing and both legs, and inching along the ground trying to find a hiding place. Johnny picked it up, smiled sadly and said, "Poor little bastard, it just wasn't your day." He pinched the quail's neck hard and it shuddered and died in his hand. He tucked the two birds into the cloth bag.

"Keep your eyes open," he said. "Bet there's another covey around here somewhere. I'll keep the right. You go left again."

A few yards further and he won his bet. Another covey leaped into the air and streaked for freedom. This time I managed to bring one down, and once again Johnny brought down two. We found them all, and then went for half an hour before flushing another batch. By late afternoon, we had a dozen, and were out of shells.

"Before we go back," said Johnny, "come on over here with me."

We climbed a split-rail fence, crossed a narrow dirt road, and went up a hill on the other side. As we reached its crest, we found a low stone fence, and inside it, a small cemetery.

"Nobody much uses this one any more," he said. "There's no upkeep, you have to do it yourself. Over here." We walked down along the fence. Near its corner, Johnny climbed over and I followed. He stood before two low tombstones. One read, "Monica Lewis. Born 1910, Died 1934. Rest in Peace." The other had a large word almost filling the stone: LIFE. And at its base, in smaller letters, "Sarah Lewis, born 1906, died 1940," and Raymond Lewis, born 1899, died . . ." and no date yet.

"My mother and Aunt Sarah," he said. "I used to come over and sit here. It isn't that I believe they're here, but this is the only place where there is anything at all of them. I think I'd like to be buried here myself. Maybe I'll put it in my will."

We sat there, silent. I knew that he would put his request in his will, and knew also that it would eventually be ignored on the grounds that a shrine to such an idol as he could not be erected in a quiet little country cemetery ten miles out of town, with no upkeep or security against vandalism.

"It isn't dying I mind," he said after a while. "It's that I know, whenever it happens, I'll leave so much undone that I wanted to do. I want to see and taste everything in the world. There are so many beautiful girls I could love. That's what I'll miss most of all, I think. I know you will never believe this, but I do want to love someone."

Everyone was out on the porch waiting when we got back. Dee Dee ran down the road toward us, her hair all tied up in a towel.

170

"Where the hell have you been?" she shouted. "I was getting ready to send out the state guard. You've got to call Jerry Conklin. In five minutes! He has a conference call set up so you can talk to him and to California at the same time. Good Lord, I've been going out of my skull. What's in the bag?"

As she pried open the cloth edges, Johnny said, "Quail," just as she screamed.

Johnny handed the bag to Miss Mary who weighed it with a professional hand and nodded and went inside. The phone, an old-fashioned upright, was standing on a table near the front door. He picked it up and jiggled the hook.

"Hello," he said, "this is Johnny Lewis. Will you give me long distance. Oh? You are long distance? Well, are you holding a conference call for me?" He nodded to me, and by putting my head in close to his, I could hear the voice on the other end.

"Yes sir," it said. "Between you and a Mr. Jerry Conklin in New York City, and a Mr. Jerome Newman in Hollywood, California. Shall I connect you?"

"Go right ahead," said Johnny. There were strange clickings and beeps and then Jerry's voice saying, "Hello, hello? Johnny?"

"I'm on," said Johnny. "What's this about Jerome Newman? He's in Hollywood?"

Before Jerry could answer, a female voice came on the line saying, "Argos Studios," and our operator said, "A conference call from New York City and Centerville, Iowa for Mr. Newman." "I'm on," said Newman's voice before his secretary could answer. "Conklin, are you there?"

"We're *all* here," said Jerry. "Johnny, Newman has to have an answer today, that's why I didn't talk with you first. Can you hear us both?"

"Like a bell. Go ahead, Mr. Newman, what's this all about?"

"Johnny," said Newman, "I want you to come to Hollywood. Right away."

"What for? A test?"

"It's not a test," cut in Jerry, "he wants—"

"I'll tell it," Newman said. "Johnny, I've been hired to direct the new version of *Paradise Gate*. You may remember, Robert Taylor did it in 1938."

"I remember," Johnny said. "It wasn't a bad flick. Why are they doing it over?"

"Because Charles Holbrook, who wrote the book back in the thirties, just won the Nobel Prize for literature. At the very least, all of his novels are going to be reissued, and the studio wants to cash in."

"What do you want me for?"

"The son."

"That's not the Taylor part?"

"No, no. The son got lost in the first version. But the part is vital and it has been built up in the new script. It's not really the lead. There are no leads in this picture. But it's one of the four important roles and I need a young, exciting actor to pull it off. That's you."

"I thought you'd be mad at me after what I did to your buddy."

"*The Tree House?* No, I agreed with you. When Arnold got through with the play, it was successful all right. But it wasn't the play you all started out with. I would have rather seen him take that and make it successful. Look, kid, my neck is out on a limb a mile long because I want to give this part to an unknown. They want Montgomery Clift. But they can't touch him, not after *From Here To Eternity*. Besides, this is *my* film. I want New York people, and I'm going to get them."

"Who else besides me?"

"Nobody's signed yet. Either Julie Harris or Maggie Atwell for the sister. Helen Hayes for Momma, if we can get her. I've already got Bert Klen as the Uncle. That's why I'm in such a hurry. I want to get that key scene, the one between you and your uncle on film, to show these bastards that I know what I'm doing, that I'm not just a New York stage director who got lucky."

"Then it *is* a test," said Johnny.

"Not so far as you're concerned. I'll sign you for the film. Twelve hundred a week, ten-week guarantee."

"Fifteen hundred," said Jerry.

"Fifteen," Newman agreed. "If I get kicked off the picture, they still have to use you. Or at least, pay you. What do you say, kid? Can you get out here right away?"

"What's right away?" Johnny asked.

"Tonight. Tomorrow at the latest."

"You'll have the contracts waiting?" said Jerry Conklin.

"Christ, yes! Get off my back, Conklin. You know my word's good."

"Good as gold," said Jerry. "It's your studio I'm worried about."

"The contracts will be over at your Hollywood office an hour from now," Newman said. "How about it, kid? Are you on your way?"

Johnny lowered the phone for a moment. His eyes looked at me, glittering with triumph and excitement. I could hear both Jerry and Newman yelling from both sides of the continent, then Johnny put the receiver up to his mouth again and said, "Yeah, Mr. Newman. You can depend on it. I'm on my way."

HOLLYWOOD

CHAPTER SEVEN

I COULD still hear Conklin and Newman yelling from opposite sides of the continent with me, good old Johnny Lewis, in the middle again. My hand started to shake as I hung up. I looked around. Everyone was watching me. My Uncle Ray. Dee Dee. Miss Mary. And the big red-haired man named Corley. No one paid much attention to him. I was the one they all watched.

"That was my agent," I said. "They want me to go out to Hollywood. Jerry Newman asked me to do a movie with him."

"Oh, Johnny!" said Dee Dee. "That's wonderful." I noticed that she was getting it all down for posterity with her Leica. Corley stepped back to get out of camera range.

Miss Mary asked, "When do you have to leave, John Calvin?"

177

"In the morning. I'll have to check on flights out of Des Moines."

"I'll take care of that," said Dee Dee.

"Well," said Uncle Ray. "I guess that's mighty fine news. Hollywood. That'll put you near your father."

"Yeah," I said, feeling suddenly tight and cold inside. "I guess it will."

I went out onto the porch and sat down in the swing that hung from two chains bolted to a beam above. I was tired, and I could still smell the gunpowder from the shotgun shells that had exploded alongside my cheek.

Hollywood. I was really going back. Everything Corley had told me was coming true. It was hard to believe.

He came out and sat near me on the steps. I almost didn't notice him. That was always the way, when he was around. I barely noticed him, and other people didn't at all. By now I had gotten used to behaving as if he wasn't there. He was just a spook in the corner. If you blinked your eye, he would vanish.

What if I asked him—?

Shit, no! You don't ask that question. You have to think you're going to hit a hundred. Quick and fast, that's the way I want it to be, with no buildup and no screwing around. One, two, three, you're out.

So it was back to Hollywood. Back to those bastards who pushed me around like I was a goddamned prop, which is all an extra is anyway, I guess. But this time would be different. This time, *I'd* be the one doing the pushing. I wondered what my father's face would look like when he picked up the *L.A. Times* and saw my picture and read that I was coming back to Hollywood to star in a motion picture! Then I realized what a sap I was being. I wouldn't see his face, and even if I did he'd claim it didn't make any difference to him what happened to me. Nothing I ever did would make any difference to him.

178

I turned to the spook, Corley, and said, "What did my father think?"

He looked puzzled and answered, "About what?"

"About me going back out there. About me being a movie star."

Carefully, he said, "I honestly don't know. I think he was pleased. That's the way I remember it, anyway."

"Pleased. What the hell does that mean?"

He spread his hands. "It's all I know, Johnny."

Well, hell. Anyway, it would make an impression on the kids at Schwab's! They know this isn't the kind of thing that happens every day; it isn't often that Jerry Newman picks an unknown to star in a major feature. And not with a bunch of dogs, either. With Julie Harris, by God! Or, at least, with Maggie Atwell. Maggie had more picture experience than Julie. But might that work against her? Newman said he wanted New York people in this one.

I heard a click. It was Dee Dee, still stalking me with her camera. I was glad she had been here to get it all. And with me going to Hollywood, the chances were much better that *Life* would actually use the pictures.

"Listen," I said, "what are you going to do now?"

"Go back to New York, I guess," she said.

"Why don't you come out there with me?"

"I'd like to. But I can't just drop everything in New York."

"Why not? What's so great about the Greenwich Mews? I bet they pay you a big fifty bucks to shoot a whole show."

"It isn't just the money," she said. But I could tell she was weakening. "And there's the MG," she went on. "What on earth could we do with it? I can't drive all the way to California. Besides, he wants you out there right away."

"Store it in the barn," I said. "With my motorcycle. They make a nice couple."

"Oh, you nut," she said, laughing. "Still," she said, thinking, "I bet *Life* would extend the assignment. This puts a better finish on the story."

"Then you'll come?"

"Yes," she said, deciding. "I'll come. There's a flight out of Des Moines at noon. It gets in at two-thirty, California time. I've already booked you on it. I shouldn't have any trouble getting on too. And I wired Newman to expect you, so someone from his office will probably be at the airport."

"My God," I said. "I thought I was bringing along a photographer and she turns out to be the best assistant director in the state of Iowa."

"Thanks for nothing, chum," she said. "Listen, if we're going to be in Des Moines at noon, we'll have to get out of here at the crack of dawn. So how's about you and me walking around the farm a little now so I can get some shots? I don't have very much on this end, and I think they'll want it."

"Okay," I said. "Come on out to the barn and we'll play in the hay."

"We'll take pictures in the hay," she said.

"Great," I said. "That'll prove I'm not a fag."

"You," she said, "are incorrigible." But she was smiling.

My motorcycle was up on blocks in one corner of the barn. I stripped off the tarp and got on the scuffed leather seat. I remembered the hours, winding down the country roads, with muffler bypass out and the engine in full song. That was riding! With the wind smashing into my face and the telephone poles going by in a brown blur and the Dunlop tires throwing me away from the asphalt at seventy miles an hour. I remembered the only spill the two of us took, the only real spill, that is; you don't count wheelies that go wrong or tumbles you take hill climbing. It was on the old coal mine road, when I came around a curve and there, stretched clear across the whole road was a fallen tree. There wasn't time to react, or anyplace to go even if I had, and I had barely started to jam on both hand and foot brakes when the front wheel hit and we both somersaulted through the air in what felt like a slow motion dive. Luck was with us both that day. I landed off the road on a grassy slope that let me slide along, soaking up the impact and not even ripping off any skin to speak of. The bike landed on its handlebars, and toppled over with the engine racing so hard I was afraid it would tear the cylinder heads off. I scrambled over and tried to twist the throttle grip, but it was jammed, so I yanked both spark plug wires and she coughed into silence. The damage was so slight I fixed it myself. One foot peg was bent, and all I had to do was peel off the rubber, stick a pipe over the peg, and straighten it out.

And now I sat on her in a musty barn, with Dee Dee clicking away, and the bike's engine hadn't turned over for more than two years. I thought of cranking her up, but remembered I had drained the tank and lines, and the carb would be dry as a bone. In a moment of strangely precise foreknowledge, I knew all at once that I would never ride this bike again, that I had gone too far away from her and would never be able to get all the way back ever again. It was saddening, and must have shown on my face, because Dee Dee burped off four or five shots and then came over and put both hands on my cheeks.

"It made a beautiful picture," she said, "but I hate to see you so unhappy."

"Unhappy?" I said. "Who's unhappy? Come on, let's get some stuff outside before you lose the light."

"It's a beautiful place," she said, as we walked around the farm in the yellow light of the setting sun. "I'm glad we came here. I like being where you were a little boy."

"Don't get sloppy," I said. "It's a farm like any other farm. There must be millions of them. One is no different from the other. I'll be glad to get back to civilization. If you can call California civilization."

"Oh, Johnny," she said, "you don't *mean* that."

"Don't I? Dee Dee, you can take my word for one thing and count on it. I am never coming back here. Never, never again. Not unless I'm dead."

She looked at me sharply, and I wondered why what I had said seemed to upset her so much. By now, the sun was sitting on the horizon, and she had me lean against the windmill and rattled off another sequence of pictures. Then it was dark, and those were the last photographs she made at the farm.

I had never flown first class before, but since it was Newman's money, we splurged. One of the stewardesses was an old bat, but the other was around my age and I was in luck, because she had seen me on TV. So, while she pretended not to give me any more attention than the other passengers in the big DC-6, you would have had to be blind to miss what was really going on. Too bad for me, Dee Dee was anything but blind. I was in the middle of my second drink when she leaned over, covering my thighs briefly with her magazine and gave me a pinch on the inside of the leg that felt like I had been bitten by a horse. I let out a little yip and sloshed some of my Scotch into the aisle. Dee Dee settled back behind her copy of *Popular Photography,* a big shit-eating grin on her face. Naturally, she knew I would figure out something, and I did, when she had to get up eventually and go to the john. The stewardess and I headed for the small lounge in the rear of the plane like we had both been ejected from the mouth of a cannon, and I found out fast that her name was Marsha Wyss, and that she would be laying over in LA for two days at the Hollywood Roosevelt. I promised to call that evening, and was back in my seat by the time Dee Dee returned. She looked at me suspiciously, but had nothing to say,

182

and so the big plane droned through the sky and eventually landed at Los Angeles International.

Newman himself was there, waiting. He raised an eyebrow at Dee Dee as she scurried around, getting everything on film, then greeted her warmly when I introduced her properly.

"A plug in *Life* won't do us any harm," he said. "Right now, kid, we need all the help we can get. Here, give me your luggage stubs. Ken!" Ken, who was a heavyset guy around thirty, almost snapped to attention. I learned later that he was Newman's unit manager, the guy in charge of practically everything that has to do with the logistics of keeping a film outfit rolling. "Ken will pick up your bags and join us later," Newman said. "Come on, my car is out here."

It was a bright blue Cadillac with the top down. He and I got in the front, and Dee Dee crawled in back. "Jesus," she said, "look at the palm trees."

"Palmettos," said Newman. He slipped the car in gear and off we went. "We're due at a three o'clock meeting at the studio," he said. "We may be a little late, but it won't matter. Have you read the book?"

"What book?"

"*Paradise Gate.*"

"No. Was I supposed to?"

"I want you to. We're going to stick pretty close to the way the author wrote it. There's a lot of background in it that we'll never put on film, but it'll do you good to know."

"Okay," I said. "I'll get a copy. I couldn't have found one in Centerville, anyway. The book store there runs more to Mickey Spillaine."

"Don't bother. I've got an extra copy at the studio. You can have it."

We drove along the freeway in comparative silence for a while. Unless you have had the experience of hurtling along

183

those sunken strips of concrete at sixty-five, bumper to bumper, you will never understand how fully dependent you can be on another person. Because if any car in the ten-car pack ahead of us should have a flat tire, or jam on his brakes for any reason, a multiple pileup would be inevitable. At our speed, Newman would be unable to stop before he nosed into the car ahead, and that went for the car behind *us*, too.

"Where is the studio?" Dee Dee asked.

"On Santa Monica," he said. "Out past Goldwyn on the way to Beverly Hills. It runs between Santa Monica and Sunset."

"Hot spit," she said. "The way you toss those magic names around. Beverly Hills! Sunset Boulevard! It's enough to make a city girl like me go all giggly."

To my surprise, Newman burst into deep-from-the-gut laughter and turned around to look at her. I yelled and made a grab for the wheel as the car almost dived into the next, fully occupied, lane. Newman put his attention back on driving, although he kept chuckling to himself.

"When do we start shooting?" I asked.

"The scene, or the picture itself?"

"Both."

"Today's Wednesday. I'd like to do the scene between you and Bert Klen on Friday. That'll give me the weekend to cut together an interlock."

"So the picture depends on how the scene turns out."

"Not the picture. Argos is going to do it come hell or high water. But the scene will determine whether or not I stay on as director."

"You mean they might fire you?"

"Fire me? Hell no. But if they won't let me do it my way, I'll have to quit."

"I don't see why they wouldn't let you do it the way you want. After all, they must want a Jerry Newman picture, otherwise why did they pick you to direct?"

"Why did Arnold Ross keep you in *The Tree House,* and then make you do everything against your own instincts? He hoped that even doing things you didn't agree with, you would still be better than anyone else he might bring in. It's the same out here. They want a Jerry Newman picture all right, only they want me to do it their way. My other three pictures, you'd be surprised at how much I actually did go along with them. Many times they were right, and I was wrong. But not this one. This story cries for the kind of talent I can only find on the New York stage. I'll except Bert Klen, although in his heart, I believe Bert never left New York either."

He shifted deftly into the right lane, and soon we were gliding up a ramp and off the freeway onto Highland Avenue. Behind us were the Hollywood hills, and high up on them, spelled out in shiny white letters, the name, "Hollywood."

"Ever been out here, Dee Dee?" he asked.

"Nope," she said. "This is my first time."

"You'll like it," he promised. "Things are a lot different since the war, of course. Now there is a lot of industry, aircraft and oil mostly. Hollywood Boulevard is more like the main drag in Centerville, Iowa than anything else, believe it or not."

"Centerville has *four* main drags," I said. "One of the real reasons why I can't stand the place."

"What do you mean?" she asked him, ignoring me.

"Just that glorious, glamorous Hollywood Boulevard is mostly small shops and movie theatres," he said. "Oh, sure, Grauman's Chinese is a little fancier than the Centerville Ritz, but you can get the same popcorn. And the stores have the same fashions, close at the same six p.m., and every sidewalk in sight is rolled up and tucked away safely for the night at ten o'clock."

"Mr. Newman," she said, "you are destroying my one remaining dream. And here I was, all atwitter that my first sight would be that of Cary Grant smiling cruelly before he swept me up in his arms and hustled me off to Bel Air."

185

"Your first sight," said Newman, "will probably be a billboard advertising Forest Lawn. Death isn't a dirty word out here. People seem to delight in preparing for it. Pre-need counseling, they call it. When someone arrives out here, the two things he does first are to throw away his neckties, and start paying for a plot in the Hall of Memory."

Newman was so distracted he almost missed the turn off Highland onto Santa Monica.

"That's Sam Goldwyn's place over there," he said, pointing to the left at a walled-in complex of buildings. "Argos is down another eight blocks. See? The water tower with the big clock on it?"

"Does that thing work?" I asked. "Every time I've been here, it never seems to be moving."

"It works," Newman said grimly. "B. J. only starts it when a picture has gone over schedule. Then it goes until the shooting's finished. The whole damned city gets a chance to see how far behind the director is. It's a regular laugh riot. My last one went two days over, and it really started getting to me. I got up in the middle of the night and drove down, and that goddamned thing was up there, still ticking away."

"Who is B.J.?" Dee Dee asked.

"B.J. Fleming," Newman said. "A slimy little kike from Soho."

"Kike?" she said coldly.

"Relax," Newman told her. "Shall I show you my missing foreskin? When one kike calls another kike a kike, he is really a kike! It took me ten years to lose my old world drawl, and then I come out here and find out that there's a person in the world who speaks Yiddish with an English accent! I almost started going to Berlitz, until it dawned on me that I despised the little bastard for what he was, and not what he sounded like. So I saved three hundred bucks on speech lessons and passed them along to my analyst."

By now we were at the two heavy metal gates that barred the entrance to Argos Studios. Newman nosed the Caddié up onto the driveway, and the gates swung open. He waved at the guard, who touched his cap, and drove into the courtyard within. A baroque office building towered over the parking lot, and behind it I could see poles and ropes suspending what appeared to be huge ship sails.

Dee Dee noticed the canvas too, and asked, "What's all that for?"

"That's the back lot," Newman said. "There's a Welsh village there that they put up for B.J.'s latest attack on British political life. They can stretch the canvas over the whole set and block out the sky, so they can shoot night scenes in the daytime."

"Why not wait until night?" Dee Dee asked.

"Overtime, my dear," he answered. "The most hated word in a producer's vocabulary. Come on, through here. The meeting is in B.J.'s office."

I took a good look at him as we went in. It shocked me to see the great Jerome Newman visibly preening himself, checking his flowered sport shirt to be sure it was tucked neatly into his belt, and brushing his thinning hair back with one nervous hand. As a male secretary opened the door to Fleming's office for us, I tried to guess what I would find within. A potbellied little man stretched out on a built-in desk lounge, perhaps; smoking rare Turkish tobacco through a hookah. The reality was a letdown. B.J. Fleming was a slim, almost dapper man in his middle thirties, conservatively dressed in a double-breasted blue suit. His desk was a simple metal one, such as I have seen in a million receptionist's alcoves. It was piled high with scripts, and as for smoking, he seemed to be doing quite well with what appeared to be a Robert Burns Cigarillo.

"Ah, Newman," he said in clipped English tones, "you're late. But no matter. I know you had a plane to meet. Is this the boy? Lewis? You, son, I'm speaking to you. Are you Johnny Lewis?"

I felt an urge to tell him no, I'm Captain Ahab, but I took pity on Newman, who was actually dancing from one foot to the other as if he had to go to the bathroom and just nodded. Fleming stuck out his hand. It was cool and not sweaty at all. "Welcome aboard," he said. "I've heard many good things about you. I think Jerome may be right, for once, and that you are perhaps more suited to this role than Monty Clift, whom I opted for. I know of your Broadway work, and understand that you have been doing . . . ah . . . television."

He spoke it like a dirty word. "Be assured, Mr. Lewis, that the motion picture industry does things a little differently. Who's that?" he said suddenly, of Dee Dee and her Leica.

"Ah, Miss Aldiss," said Newman. "Of *Life* magazine."

"Free lance," Dee Dee said sweetly.

"She's taking *pictures,*" Fleming said.

"Smile," said Dee Dee.

"Has Publicity issued credentials?" Fleming demanded. He looked hard into Newman's face, and when he got no answer, whirled on Dee Dee. "Young woman," he said sternly, "Give me that film."

"What?" she said.

"The film, the film, he said. "Take it out of the camera. I do not allow photographs to be taken in this office."

"That's tough titty, fellow," she said. "Nobody told me. And nobody touches my film."

"You're trespassing," he shouted. "Marcel! Send in a guard. Off the lot! I want her off the lot this instant!"

"Simmer down, buddy boy," I said. "This young lady is with me. If she goes off the lot, I go too."

"Johnny," anguished Newman. "Don't be hasty. Please, B.J., I apologize. Miss Aldiss is not to blame. It's all my fault."

188

"I'm well aware of that," Fleming said coldly.

"I didn't think," said Newman. "I'll have Publicity issue credentials as soon as we finish here. After all, B.J., it is *Life* magazine."

"Very well," said Fleming, sitting down. "A bad beginning, Mr. Lewis. Let us hope the future improves on today."

"How can it miss?" I said. "Come on, Dee Dee. We'll wait in the car while Mr. Newman gets his ducks in a row."

Marcel examined us with suspicion as we strolled out through the anteroom. I flicked imaginary sweat off my eyebrow at him as I passed.

The afternoon sun was hot on the leather seat covers. We decided against burning ourselves on them and retired to a shady bench near a papier-mâché statue of Lord Byron.

"Hooray for Hollywood," said Dee Dee.

Marsha Wyss got right to the point.

"I want you to eat me," she said.

We had drunk our way through martinis before dinner at the Villa Capri, through afterdinner margueritas at the Brown Derby, through two hours of gut-wrenching dancing and boozing at various joints on the Sunset Strip, and now we were in her small, crowded room at the Roosevelt.

There had been no invitation, no small talk about it. I paid off the cab, asked what room she was in, got the sixth floor number, gave her five minutes to get up there, then took the elevator to six and tapped on her door.

"Who?" she said from behind the fireproof metal panels.

"The iceman," I said. The door opened and I slipped inside. One lamp was on, covered by a hand towel. The towel was pink, and so the room was filled with a soft, gentle glow. I turned to look at Marsha, and she was as I had expected, naked. Her breasts were small, but tipped with enormous red nipples, and the dark black triangle between her thighs gave the lie to her bleached blonde hair. She didn't fool around, reached out immediately and caught my prick in her hand and began to massage it through the cloth of my trousers. Softly, she repeated her request.

"Sorry, baby," I said. "I save that for my special friends."

"Your *boy* friends?" she said. "Oh, you don't have to tell me. I see you actors all the time. I wasn't always on the Chicago run, you know. I used to go into New York. I know all about you actors. Why do you think I let you come up here? I know what you like to do."

"Sweetheart," I said, "what I'd like to do right now is fuck you. If you're not interested, why that's all right too. I can smuggle this hard-on out of here and use it somewhere else."

"In that girl on the plane?" Marsha said. "You can have *her* any time. But how often can you have *this?*" She guided my hand into her, and she was wet and slippery, and burning hot to my touch. She drew herself up on her toes and hissed softly and impaled herself on my three fingers. I could hear her wetness squishing out. "That's good," she said, gritting the words out between clenched teeth. Her eyes were squinted almost closed, but she still managed to undo my belt and zip down my pants. They fell around my ankles and I stepped out of them. Her fingers fumbled at the buttons of my shirt and finally I reached up with my free hand and undid them. One popped off and rolled under the bed. Meanwhile, she shucked off my jockey shorts and in another minute I was just as naked as she, and we hurled ourselves onto the bed. I could feel the little nugget of her clitoris under my forefinger, and rolled it back and forth under the thin membrane of skin until she began to shudder and whisper frantically, over and over, "Don't stop! Don't stop!" and then there was a great widening of her vagina and as my fingers thrust in, I felt a coldness against the straining

190

walls, and heard a series of belching sounds as she expelled air against my moving hand. Excited beyond control, I threw her legs back until she was bent double, rested them against my shoulders and fumbled my prick against her streaming thighs. Her hand guided me and I plunged inside her until our groins met with a solid impact. I could feel her muscles massaging me deep within her, and her fingernails clawed at my buttocks. As I hurled myself down on her, her legs strained against my shoulders in convulsive movements and she began to beat her hands against my behind with sharp slapping sounds. I could feel her vagina sucking at me again and I kissed her and felt her tongue come into my mouth and slide down the back of my mouth. "Coming!" she gasped, "Come with me, darling! Now! Now!" I tightened my buttocks in anticipation of the climax, but instead experienced only a distant, *drifting* sensation, as if I were somehow cut off from my own flesh and knew, with fuming anger, that my orgasm had escaped me and that I was merely servicing this screaming, writhing woman with nothing in it for myself.

"Shit!" I said, and rolled off her and lay on the side of the bed, my organ still erect and glistening with her juices. Her rasping breathing subsided and the blindness left her eyes as she sat up slowly and looked at my nakedness.

"You didn't make it," she said accusingly. "I knew you wouldn't. I told you I know what you like. Don't worry, Johnny, I'll make you come. Just do what I say." And she turned herself around in the bed and as she lowered her pouting mouth over my prick said, "I'll eat you and you eat me."

"Like hell I will," I gasped, but then I lurched up with incredibly delicious sensation flooding through me, and as her black triangle appeared over my face, I *did*.

The scene between Bert Klen and me was a short one, in stage terms, and so I was surprised to learn how difficult the Hollywood production team regarded it as. There were less than three sides of dialogue—only a page and a half of script —for the two of us. The action took place between Fred King, my role, and Uncle Charlie, played by Bert Klen. In the scene, Fred discovers his beloved Uncle Charlie raiding the family safe where money for a land purchase has been placed overnight. In the scene, I was to confront Uncle Charlie with his theft and, after berating him for his treachery to my father, allow him to escape. End of scene.

Bert was glad to see me again, and we talked excitedly of the short-lived *Tiger Row,* and what a great picture it would eventually make. He asked after Jean Billingham, and seemed surprised that I knew little about where she was or what she was doing. The conversation was a little strained on my part because of the presence of Dee Dee, who had been granted her credentials by the mysterious Publicity Department. As Bert and I talked, she circled us with a constantly clicking Leica.

Dee Dee and I were ensconced in separate, although neighboring, suites at the Regency, a Hollywood residence-hotel which caters to show and advertising people. I knew she had expected a visit from me the previous night, but when Marsha Wyss and I parted company in her hotel hallway it was well after three and it was all I could do to get a cab and make it home to my suite. I spent the rest of the night on the sofa, half-passed out, and only after a freezing shower and two cans of cold beer was able to face the world and Dee Dee. She was properly suspicious, and restricted her comments to requests for poses.

"Just shows, kid," said Bert, "what a frigging small world this is. There I was, just passing along a little help to a nice kid in his first Broadway show, and bang! Here we are teamed up in the next Academy Award picture for Jerry Newman."

"I doubt it," I said. "I think Newman craps his pants every time Fleming walks by. I don't think they give Oscars for soiled underwear."

Bert laughed roughly. "I've seen that," he said. "But don't let it throw you. Jerry rolls over for B.J. on everything except the picture. Believe it or not, our Mr. Newman is a very gentle, nonaggressive person. So when B.J. shoves a cigar in his eye and shouts about starting the overtime clock, it throws a panic into Jerry. But you'll see. Just let B.J. or anyone else try to screw up Jerry's picture, and it'll be like letting a tiger out of the cage. Jerry eats people alive if they get between him and what he thinks ought to be on that film."

"I hope so," I said. "Because everything seems to be riding on what you and I do tomorrow with this scene. And to tell the truth, I don't much like the way it's going so far. I think you and me, we're just talking back and forth at each other."

"I have the same feeling," he admitted. "But I can't lick it. I think the scene plays, but I'm damned if I can feel it's really the climax of the picture. And according to Jerry, it *is*. He sees it too, and he's just as worried as we are. It'll be bigger on the screen, of course. But I don't know if that's the whole answer. I'm going to think about it tonight. You ought to do the same."

"Maybe we ought to rehearse some more. It might come."

"No," he said. "This has nothing to do with interpretation. There's a piece missing. Let's hope we can find it by tomorrow. See you then, kid."

Newman was deep in discussion with Ernie Glenn, his cameraman. He merely nodded at Dee Dee and me as we left, and called out, "Don't worry about a thing, Johnny. It'll work in front of the camera."

193

That morning we had found a studio car assigned to me, a new Chevy hardtop. I would have preferred a convertible, but the price was right.

"Where to now?" asked Dee Dee. Her attitude was still cool.

"Burbank," I said. "No use putting it off."

"Your father?"

"The same."

We found him on the floor of the Ford agency hard at work trying to convince a customer to order air conditioning for his convertible. And by God, he did! He got the signature, then told his boss he was taking off for a while and came over.

"John Calvin," he said, thrusting out his hand. I took it, feeling stupid, and heard Dee Dee's Leica click. "Isn't that something? My boy, a big name movie star."

"I'm not a movie star," I said. And almost, but not quite added, "And I'm not your boy." But I didn't. He drew me outside. "Come on," he said, "this calls for a drink. There's this place across the street. Are you old enough? Not that it matters, I know the bartender—"

"I'm twenty-one," I said harshly. "In case you forgot."

"Twenty-one! My God, how the years fly by. You look just wonderful, boy. Did I tell you that I saw you on TV? I meant to write a card, but maybe I forgot."

"Maybe you did," I said. We crossed the street and entered the Kit Kat Lounge. It smelled of stale beer and cheap whiskey. I laid a private bet that the friendly bartender had one set of premium bottles, and a lot of bulk hooch for refilling them. I felt embarrassed for Dee Dee, that I had brought her here, because I could tell as sure as sunrise, I was going to have a fight with my father. The only question was when, and over what. I hated myself for it, but I knew I was going to provoke him, and there was no way to stop it. I began by refusing to let him buy me a drink. "This is my treat," I said. "Then I can say, I walked right up and bought my old man a drink." The drinks came, Scotch for both of us and a Ranier beer for Dee Dee.

"Well," he said, "here's to your success."

"No," I said, "let's drink to yours."

"Mine?" he said, puzzled.

"Why," I said, "when you let it drop that your very own son is now a prominent movie star, that ought to bring you extra customers, shouldn't it? Maybe they'll even ask for your autograph. The least they can do for you is buy a car."

"No," he said seriously. "I'd never do that, even if it would help. What's yours is yours, boy."

"Including my name?" I asked sharply.

"That too," he said, puzzled. "Oh, I gave it to you. But it's yours now."

"Many thanks," I said. "That's all you ever *did* give me."

"John Calvin," he said, "I hope we're not going to fight."

"No," I said, "you only fight when you care enough about something. I don't care any more, so there's nothing to fight about."

"That's not fair," he said. Dee Dee had moved further away down the bar and was trying to avoid listening to us. "I did the best I could. Sarah and I talked it over, after your mother died, and decided the best thing was for you to go to Centerville. Then, when Sarah died, all your ties were there and it seemed cruel to take you away to start over somewhere else."

"You're so considerate," I said. "Did it ever occur to you to ask me what I thought?"

"You were only nine, John," he said. "How could you know what was best for you? Please, son, I'm happy to see you again, and proud of your success. Can't we just leave it at that?"

"Hell no, we can't leave it at that!" I cried. "Leave it at that with me stuck away on a farm, with no mother, and no father because father was too goddamned busy sitting on his sun-tanned ass in Burbank to worry about his son and what might be happening to *him?* You didn't even send me a Christmas card, one year! Christmas came and went, and the only way I could tell you knew I was alive was when Uncle Ray told me you'd sent a five dollar bill for me and what did I want to do with it?"

"That must have been the year I was sick, John. Try to understand a little what *I* was going through at that time."

"I'm not interested in understanding. It doesn't matter any more."

"I loved you, son. It was just that I had difficulty recovering from the loss of your mother. I even thought of remarrying so I could bring you out here, but it never worked out. I know I never showed it, son, but I wanted to be a good father to you. It just wasn't in me, I guess."

"Well, it's too late now. That's what I came out here to tell you. There's no second grab at the brass ring in this game. It is over, over, over. Okay?"

He didn't answer, but just lowered his head and I could tell he was about to cry. I wanted to reach over and squeeze his shoulder and tell him I didn't mean those things, that a madness drove me to say them and that I loved him. I wanted to, but I didn't.

Back at the Regency, I found a handful of telephone messages waiting at the desk. Two were from Marsha Wyss. Several were from newspapers and one said, "Call Hedda Hopper," with her number. Hedda Hopper! Hot damn! It was really happening. I almost broke an arm reaching for the phone, but when her number started ringing I began to think, wait a minute, there's something wrong here. I never made it before by playing the other guy's game. It's always been *my* way, one hundred per cent. I could blow everything by being what they

196

want and expect me to be. Someone lifted the receiver, and this must have been her private number, because I recognized Hedda's voice from the many times I had heard her radio program. "Hello?" she said. Then, "Hello?" again. I hung up.

In my room I showered and changed into slacks and a sport shirt, debating about calling Marsha. This would be her last night in town; she had a 9:00 A.M. flight back to Chicago in the morning. Our bed adventures disturbed me, though, and I wasn't so sure that I was in any hurry to repeat them. That freaky kind of sex had never been a regular part of my life, and it looked like with her, it was standard. It bothered me that for the first time, when sober at least, I had been unable to get it off in the normal way. No, I decided, let Marsha find new pleasures with someone else. In tourist-filled Hollywood, that wouldn't be too hard.

I picked up the phone and had the desk connect me with Dee Dee's room. After a while, she answered and when she recognized my voice, said, "It figures. I started wondering what to do with myself, so I said, I'll get in the shower. That'll make him call. And sure enough!"

"Get dressed," I said. "I'll buy you a malted at Schwab's Drug Store."

"Schwab's? That's way to hell and gone out toward Beverly Hills."

"You're too used to New York," I said. "Out here everybody lives on wheels. You have to get over that feeling that your territory is bounded by Sixth Avenue on one side and Seventh on the other. Out here you deal in *miles,* not blocks."

She grumbled a little, then agreed to meet me in the lobby in five minutes. I checked my pockets, saw I still had a wad of bills that looked like a roll of toilet paper. I wasn't used to having money; it made me uneasy, like I should rush out and buy something with it. Well, one thing I could do was buy a

Coke for some of my old friends in Schwab's. That at least would be satisfaction, seeing the same faces that had shared those lousy days after I got thrown out of the fraternity and decided to get into the movies. We sat around hours at a time, dissecting current pictures and plotting what we would do when we finally got our chance at doing things right. And now I had my chance, and they would all know about it from the papers. I'd play it cool, with an offhanded mention of Julie Harris or Helen Hayes as my co-stars. I needed something to take the bad taste of Burbank out of my mouth; a malted at Schwab's might be just the thing.

We parked in back and went in, past the cosmetic and makeup counter, around by the magazine rack. The soda fountain was almost full, and while most of the faces were unfamiliar, I saw two guys who had been extras with me in that Korean War film just before I went to New York. I gave them a sloppy salute, and they returned it, but didn't come over like I expected. We ordered two chocolate malts, and Dee Dee wanted a sandwich, but I talked her out of it. "We'll eat somewhere else," I said. "Where we can get a drink." Then I went over to the two guys. One was called Cowboy and the other went by the nickname of Buddy. It occurred to me that I never had learned their real names. "How goes it," I said. "Good to see someone I know."

"Slow, man, slow," said Cowboy. "Couldn't swing something for us in the Newman picture, could you?"

"Gee, I don't know," I said. "Nothing's set yet. Come right down to it, I might not even be in it myself."

"Sure, I understand," Cowboy said. "Well, write if you get work." He jerked his head toward the door and Buddy, who had not said anything, looked me up and down slowly, turned on his heel and went out with his friend. I stood there feeling silly for a minute, then went back to the counter.

198

"The natives don't seem too friendly," Dee Dee said.

"What the hell did I do?" I asked. "All I was trying to do was say hello."

"Maybe they thought you came around to gloat," she said. "Did you?"

"They were jealous," I said, throwing some change on the counter. "Come on, let's get out of here. It's all wrong. It's not like I remembered it at all. My God, how could I have been so wrong? I sat in that lousy apartment in New York and remembered beautiful things about this town that never existed. Talk about kidding yourself, I hold the world's championship! That's not the way it was, not ever. Hell, we were all ready to cut each other's throat for a twenty-buck walkon. If we did each other favors, it was only because we knew damned well we might need one ourselves tomorrow. And I took that and blew it up in my mind until we had the great brotherhood of unemployed actors, all for one and one for all!"

I nosed the Chevy out into traffic and headed back toward Hollywood. The neons along the Strip were all blazing now, and down below, on the right, the glare of the city extended all the way to the invisible Pacific.

"I think you make too much out of it all, Johnny," she said, lighting a cigarette. "Actors are by nature loners. Shouldn't I, of all people, know? When you gather together it's only a temporary thing, like a flock of sheep huddling together to keep warm. As soon as the sun comes up, you all hit out for your own goal. How can you expect the ones who were left behind, the ones that were forgotten, to welcome you back as you trot past on your way to your own personal mink-lined corral?"

"Sheep don't have corrals," I said. But she had made me smile, and some of the gloom fell out of the car right there on Sunset Boulevard.

"Sirrah," she said, "you promised me food."

199

"Food it'll be," I said. "I want you to meet a sweet guy, Patsy D'Amore. He runs the Villa Capri. By Christ, he'll be glad to see me." And I crossed my fingers, hoping he wouldn't mention I had been in there last night with Marsha. When we entered, I asked the maitre d' where Patsy was and he said, "Flat on his back with the Asian Flu, Mr. Lewis. He wanted to come in anyway, but we decided the customers would be safer if he stayed home. You shouldn't be served a Flu bug with your antipasto." We laughed, and he sat us in a dark corner and we ordered two very dry martinis.

"I didn't know you drank these," Dee Dee said when the cocktails came, icy cold and glistening.

"I'm growing up," I said, "and my tastes are maturing."

"Like your taste in women?"

"Ouch," I winced. "She was just a passing fancy. A thing of chance, a brief encounter on the field of love."

"Love," sniffed Dee Dee. "What would you know about it?"

"I've wondered that myself," I said. I guess my truthful reply made her think twice about riding me, because she dropped the subject and we enjoyed huge cherrystone clams and the Capri's famous fettucini. Our talk was bright and bantering and completely impersonal and it was only over the coffee that we became serious again.

"You're really worried about that scene tomorrow, aren't you?" she asked.

"You hit it," I said. "There's something missing. The dialogue seems to be complete, but when it's all over there's a big hole that still hasn't been filled in."

"Maybe the rest of it comes later in the script."

"No dice. If we don't pull this off, there won't be any rest of the script. Not for me, anyway. Fleming'll lash Newman and me both to that frigging clock of his and shoot darts at us. I can't get hold of it, though. Fred is all busted up to find out that

200

Uncle Charlie, whom he loved, has been robbing the family blind. And because he loves him, he lets him get away. It seems complete, but it isn't."

"What do you mean, loves him?"

"Loves who?"

"You said Fred loves his Uncle Charlie. Just now."

The violinists chose this moment to come over. "Welcome back," said the leader. "And congratulations."

"Thanks," I said, handing them a bill. "Play 'Long Ago and Far Away,' huh?"

"Sure thing, Mr. Lewis," said the leader, unoffended. They strolled off to the strains of "Gypsy Eyes."

"You just told me Fred loves Uncle Charlie," Dee Dee persisted.

"Well, of course he loves Uncle Charlie," I said. "Why the hell not? A guy's supposed to love his uncle. What's so strange about that?"

"Just that I didn't see anything in today's rehearsal that even suggested there was anything stronger than family respect between the two."

I looked at her. She looked back and smiled as I began to hop up and down.

"Dee Dee," I yelled, "you're a goddamned genius! Of course! That's what's missing. I knew I was supposed to love him, and it motivated my letting him go—but the love doesn't play with the words and action we've got! That's all we have to do, put the love the boy feels back in and then the scene means something."

"I think you're right," she said.

"Sure I'm right. And you spotted it. You know, there is more to you than meets the eye. If you're not careful, I might just marry you."

"If you're not careful," she said levelly, "I might just take you up on that."

I was at the studio and in makeup before eight the next morning. Movie-making starts early, and that's why, except for special occasions, you will rarely see a movie actor out after midnight. Those that you do usually don't remain movie actors too long. Nothing shows up quite so much on film as too much dissipation. Of course, some actors seem to benefit from it. I don't know anything about Joseph Cotten's personal life, but his is a face that speaks of late hours and a weary awareness of all the world's problems. Bert Klen has another of those faces. I *know* how Bert got his. For one thing, he has a Catholic wife left over from his early Broadway days who not only does not believe in divorce within the church, but refuses to accept a civil one either. With four kids already, Bert doesn't dare dip his wick at home for fear of a fifth, and spends every waking moment checking over his shoulder for private detectives. That, plus a fondness for good brandy, had given his face what the critics call "character." I could see him, through the open door to his dressing room, across the hall from mine. Bert owns one of the world's most believable hairpieces, and at this moment the hairdresser was attaching it to Bert's skull with spirit gum.

"Hey, Bert!" I yelled. "Don't tell Newman, but I've got the scene licked."

"Thank God someone has," he yelled back. "I wore out two call girls talking with them about that frigging Charlie. They finally decided he was my boy friend and all my talk about a film character was so much crap. Two hundred bucks for script counseling, that's what Ken's going to find on my expense account. What did you come up with?"

"I don't think I ought to tell you," I said. "It'll only work if it looks one hundred per cent spontaneous. Remember, you once told me that with film all you have to do is get it right once? That's what I'd like to shoot for. You just follow my lead and react the way you *feel*. And get to the cameraman before and make sure that he keeps rolling, no matter what happens. Okay?"

"Hell yes, I'll try anything. But what if *I* blow it? Not knowing what you're going to do, I may just go up on my lines."

"I doubt that," I hollered. "What can we lose? There's plenty of film in the camera. We can always do it again."

"I'm with you, kid," he bellowed. "Hey, watch that goddamned eyebrow pencil!"

"Sorry, Mr. Klen," said the makeup man.

The set was like a half-finished doll's house. Fleming was obviously saving money, and had not built a foot more of the scene than the camera would see. There were two rude wooden walls, with no ceiling. Lights were mounted in rows on top of each wall and held there by metal clamps. The camera was on a small dolly, facing into the cabin interior, and a long microphone boom stretched over the maze of small floor lighting units and into the playing area. I arrived a few minutes after Bert, and found him in earnest discussion with the cameraman, Ernie Glenn. "I don't know," Glenn was saying. "Mr. Newman blocked this scene in three shots, and now you want to do it in one, with no rehearsal? That sounds dangerous. We haven't rehearsed camera moves or focus changes, for that matter."

"Come on, Ernie," said Bert. "We'll do the whole thing from the long shot position. What I want you to do is put on a zoom and go in for a closeup whenever Newman indicates one. You can mark zone focus areas on the floor with chalk. We'll stay inside of them."

"Well, it can be done," Ernie said. "You'll have to get Mr. Newman's okay. And I can't guarantee the closeup lighting'll be the best in the world."

"It'll be fine, Ernie," Bert said. "You're the best man in the business."

Newman was a harder sale, and both of us had to work on him. "What the hell?" he shouted. "I gave you a whole half day of rehearsal for one lousy five minute scene, we blocked everything right down to when you breathe, and now you want to throw all that out the window and for Christ's sake, *wing it?*"

"Look, Jerry," said Bert, "what's to lose? We can always shoot it the other way. But when the kid came to me with this idea—"

"Aha!" yelled Newman, whirling on me. "So this is *your* idea! Your second day in Hollywood and now you're taking over the direction of my picture! No, Goddamnit, no! I've got enough problems, I don't need this too."

"If we don't do something," I said, holding my voice down, "this isn't going to *be* your picture, or mine either. Now there's something wrong with that scene, and I think I know what it is."

"He's right, Jerry," said Bert. "I'm worried about it, too. And I think you'd be just as worried if you weren't so busy resenting Johnny's interfering."

"I'm not resenting anything," said Newman. "You've got an idea? Fine. Tell it to me. I'll listen. I never once refused to listen to an actor, did I?"

"I can't tell it to you," I said. "It'll sound crazy. I want you to see it."

"Okay," he said, "Let's have a rehearsal. Show it to me."

"I can't do that, either. If it works at all, it'll only work once. We've got to get it on film that one time, because I don't think we'll ever be able to duplicate it again. At least not all of it."

"Jesus jumping Christ," Newman said. "From a nutty kid like this, I can understand such arrogance. But from you? Bert Klen, the pro? I should have my head sent out for examination.

204

I'm going to let you do it. B.J. will probably start his god-damned clock before the film even begins, but I am going to ignore my better judgment and give you this one shot. Ken? Where the hell are you?"

"Over here, Mr. Newman. Mr. Klen just turned in a two hundred dollar chit for script consultation. What am I supposed to do with it?"

"Wipe your ass with it. Turn it in to Fleming. How the hell do I know? Look, we're changing the schedule. The first shot is going to be the whole scene, straight through in a master, with a zoom. Tell the boom man there's going to be no rehearsal, to keep that mike at least two feet above their heads at all times. I'll stand by the assistant cameraman and tell him when I want to go in for closeups. Absolute quiet on the set, nobody moves until I say *cut*. Got it?"

Ken, who had survived dozens of eccentric regimes, got it. He set off at a trot, yelling, "This is going to be a sound take. Lock up the doors. Crew in position. Boom man, you'll have to fish for this one. But keep the mike up at least two feet, because they're working a zoom and you'll never know when it's in wide angle. Okay, hit the lights."

The gaffer threw a master switch. 40,000 watts of intensely white light burned down on the set. The test was being made in the new Eastman Color Negative and needed less light than Technicolor, but it was still considerably brighter than the television lighting I was used to.

Bert and I stood in the center of the set and read a few lines to give the sound mixer a voice level. The assistant cameraman darted out and held a light meter up against my cheek. "F–3.2," he said to himself, and dashed back to his position.

"The edge of that table," said Ernie, "is your closest mark. "Any closer than that and I can't hold focus."

"Right," said Bert. We both nodded.

"Okay," said Ken. "Stand by. Three bells, please."

The sound recordist pressed a button three times, and three bells sounded. A red light started to flash near the door. I knew there was another one outside, also flashing, warning everyone not to try and open the door while the take was in progress.

"Roll sound," said Ken. The recordist started his reels of 35 mm. magnetic film rolling, waited a minute, then called "Speed."

"Roll camera," said Ken. The camera operator flicked a switch. "Sticks," said Ken. The assistant cameraman stepped out in front of the lens, held up the black slate with its striped clap sticks, called out, "Production nine–oh–four, scene one, take one, sound one." He hit the two sticks together to make a common starting point on both picture and sound track, stepped back to his position at the camera and waited.

"All right, everybody," said Newman, "we're rolling. Settle down. Johnny, back up just a little more, we'll make this a clean entrance. Ready? Action."

With that one word, *Action*, I felt all my tenseness and apprehension vanish. Now I was doing what I knew best. I wasn't John Calvin Lewis, I was Fred King, and that man was my Uncle Charlie, and I had come to ask him to go hunting with me. But what was he doing in my father's safe, taking out the bundles of money that were supposed to be spent tomorrow for two sections of bottom land and full water rights? "Uncle Charlie?" I said, and he looked up, furtive and frightened, and I stepped in close and the scene began.

Most of it played much as before, with Bert pleading with me not to reveal his theft to the family, excusing himself for bad stock market hunches—and with me shouting curses at him for betraying his own brother. This was the tricky part. So far I had stuck to the script. I hoped the camera was still rolling and that no one would ask, "What's so different about this?" before I got to the key moment.

It came, and where I was supposed to tell him, "You wanted money. Take it." and open the door and let him walk slowly out of our lives, I started to put in the changes I had worked out. Instead of what had been planned, I made a dive for the pile of money, moving as slowly as I could so the surprised cameraman could follow me. I picked them up, all the time advancing on Bert, who—had he not been the fine actor he was —would surely have broken from character.

"Uncle Charlie," I stammered, "Charlie . . . Charlie. . . ." and I began stuffing the money down his shirt. "You wanted money," I choked, tears rolling down my cheeks, "well—" and then one of the packets broke and the bills scattered down his chest like old leaves. "Take it," I said, hugging him, "take it. Take it. . . ." and reached up and drew his face down to mine. Still crying, I kissed him full on the cheek.

Bert leaped back with a shout and I knew with joy even that was still in character although it wasn't in the script, and he slapped me hard across the face as I knew he would. He started to say something then, started to say, "Johnny . . ." but caught the warning in my eyes and had the sense to realize that we were still in the scene, and so he just clutched the money to his stomach and backed slowly out the door into the phony sunset. I put my hand up to rub my burning cheek, and bent slowly over the table, crying into the scattered bills that remained.

"Jesus H. Christ," said Newman. "Cut!"

207

CHAPTER
EIGHT

FLEMING hit the screening room ceiling. His cigar bounced on the plush rug and started burning a hole in it.

"Men kissing!" he screamed. "It's not sufficient that I permit you to waste good money on a test, you have to make one take only, one measly take, and then dismiss the crew? And what does that one take contain, may I ask? Men *kissing!* Are you trying to make me fire you, Newman? Do you know how much money you wasted? There's nothing, not a foot, that we can use, even if we do continue with the present cast. Please tell me what you thought you were doing?"

Newman was relaxed with both of his feet up on the back of the chair in front. His attitude was completely different from that first afternoon in Fleming's office.

208

"You couldn't *do* that scene again," he said calmly. "Camera and sound both said okay for quality, and a good thing too, because no matter what we tried, it would never be quite what Johnny and Bert did the first thing Friday morning. Come on, B.J. You spent enough time on a studio floor to know you could never duplicate the intensity of that scene with another take."

"I grant you that," said Fleming. "What I'm suggesting is that you wouldn't *want* to duplicate it."

"Do you find the scene offensive?"

"Absolutely."

"Louella doesn't agree with you."

Fleming began to choke. *"Louella?"* he gasped. "Are you trying to tell me you let Louella Parsons see this test?"

"Let's say," said Newman, "that she found out about it, insisted on a private screening Sunday afternoon, and that as far as she is concerned, Johnny is another Brando. With, if you like, overtones of Monty Clift."

"You know my standing rule," Fleming shouted. "No screenings for the press before I've seen the film."

"This wasn't just the press," smiled Newman. "This was Louella. And I tried to reach you. You were at the Springs hiding behind your private phone. I pleaded with Marcel to disturb you. Ask him." Fleming's head sank slowly as the studio head began to see how he had been outmaneuvered. "Anyway," Newman went on, "Louella knew you'd be spiffed, so she graciously sent me a carbon of tomorrow's column. Let me read you a bit. 'Jerry Newman was kind enough to allow me a private sneak preview of B.J. Fleming's great new discovery, John Calvin Lewis. And let me tell you, it was quite an experience. There will be several million broken hearts when girls all over the country realize they can't all take Johnny home and mother him, and if the scene I witnessed from *Paradise Gate* is any indication, that won't be too far in the future.

Johnny was testing with veteran actor Bert Klen, who will play one of the four leads, and I predict that this test will actually end up being used in the feature film. The intense pathos and agony displayed by young Johnny comes over so powerfully that I am not ashamed to state I was in tears as the scene finished. I won't spoil the picture for you by telling you the climax, but it is one people will be talking about for a long time.' Of course," Bert went on, "this is only the first piece. Her secretary is working out a Sunday magazine spread with pictures for the Hearst papers. Assuming, naturally, that you go along with the casting and the scene."

"You rotter," said Fleming. "I've been had."

"That you have," grinned Newman. "But doesn't it feel good to have Louella in on the play?"

"Newman," said Fleming, "have a cigar. You think you have tricked me. I can tell. But you haven't. I make pictures so I can sell them. I can't sell them unless people are willing to watch them. I personally find this scene offensive in the extreme. But if Louella Parsons does not find it offensive, then I am willing to assume that the American public will not find it offensive. After all, Louella has proven that she can touch the mainsprings of public opinion. So I capitulate with no hidden grudges, no ill will. I was wrong, and freely admit it. The picture is yours to do, with whatever cast you engage. I want to discuss budgets with you, and that is all. No rushes need clear through me. And I am increasing your budget herewith by another five hundred thousand."

"I don't need it," said Newman.

"So give it back if you don't use it," said Fleming. "But don't skimp. You said you want Helen Hayes? Go get her. Go get anybody you want. Perhaps you wonder at this total capitulation. Rest assured, I have not lost my mind. No, nor my business sense neither. But you have just shown me that even B. J.

Fleming can miss a bet, and when he does, B. J. Fleming pays off. Just do me a favor, Jerome. No more men kissing, huh?"

"Agreed," said Newman.

Newman, Ken and I got up and left the screening room. Out in the hall, Newman threw back his head and let out a war whoop.

"Yeeee-owww!" he yelled. "Johnny, you little sonofabitch, you pulled it off. I tell you, boy, you made yourself a friend today. I know what I want to do with this picture, and in spite of that it took your solid gold *chutzpah* to ring the bell. Boy, I love you, but I am going to work your loving ass off. And between the two of us, we will probably win every award in sight, screw all the great heads in Southern California, and make a lot of money on the side. Yeee-owwww!"

The screening room door opened. "Quiet," hissed Marcel, "Mr. Fleming is trying to sleep."

Back in 1951, after I bailed out of UCLA, I worked in two pictures. Both were relatively low-budget jobs, with about one star apiece. The one with Red Skelton, I only spent two days at the studio, and maybe the assistant director was a pretty good guy, because that job wasn't absolutely miserable the way the second one was. That one featured an ex-dancer trying to make out as a rugged hero, and John Wayne he was not. The assistant director on that bomb was a real prick and he treated the bit players and extras like dirt. He dropped broad hints that a small contribution might give us a better chance to be called for the next job. I took a piece of toilet paper, loaded it up with an appropriate gift, and sealed it in an envelope. I wrote his name on it and left it for him at the gate. That night he called me up and cursed at me for five minutes, then switched and invited me over to have a drink. I told him to go to hell on both counts.

But now, in 1954, things were very different. Ken Fresnol started out by calling me "Mister," until I told him I couldn't stand that formal crap. He worried about whether I had transportation, and whether or not I knew the best places to eat, and once, by God, he actually offered to fix me up with a starlet he knew who, said he, required daily servicing. I found that having money in my pocket and time to spend it made all the difference. To me, at least. Dee Dee backed off at regular intervals and read me the riot act about my casual girl friends. But I knew that under it all she had a letch for me that needed scratching bad, and I hated myself for taking full advantage of it by crawling back to her whenever things went bad with one of the chicks who always latched onto me at Googie's or Arturo's. More and more often I was finding myself unable to go all the way, unless the girls and I were able to pull off a Marsha routine, and what upset me even more than that was the way I started reacting to the fags who camped it up on the set or at the Stage Delicatessen after work. I began to wonder how it might really be to make it with one of them, and then would hurry home to the Regency and try to make out with Dee Dee. Sometimes I did, sometimes we just lay in each other's arms and talked, and that helped too.

"Stop worrying about the picture," she said to me one night. "It'll be all right. And so will you. It isn't good for you to stay up all night stewing over it. Jerry's a good director, and he'll come up with something that's right for both of you."

She ought to know, I reflected bitterly. Dee Dee and Jerry were seeing each other more often than I really liked. My reaction wasn't jealousy, exactly, but a kind of distant anger at having something I liked taken away from me. I knew it was bastardly of me to deny her the total commitment she obviously needed, and yet be angry when she gave up on me and looked for it somewhere else. But the feeling that something was being

212

stolen from me still lingered, and somewhere there in the first weeks of shooting, I made up my mind to do something about it.

But meanwhile, I was caught up in the miracle of being a motion picture star. Oh, there was a certain amount of laying back, waiting to see how things worked out. But now I found myself moving in circles that included the names I had worshipped on the screen all my conscious life. I remember one night at a party at Jimmy Stewart's. God knows what the reason was or how I ever managed to get invited, because Stewart is quite unHollywoodish about empty gestures. Anyway, Gary Cooper was there, and I started telling him how great he was in *Along Came Jones*. Then I asked how could he satirize not only the kind of pictures he was best at, but satirize himself too? And Coop came back at me with, "Well, Johnny, just because this is a serious world and a serious business doesn't mean that we all have to take it so blamed *seriously.*" And I didn't know whether he was putting me on or not, but either way it just broke me up. I mean, I guess he had feet of clay all right, but looking at them didn't turn me off the way it did when I met certain sex goddesses and found out their heads were absolutely empty and their shaven crotches had less passion than a peeled avocado. Thanks to Jerome Newman, I was accepted as a young man with star potential, and gradually as the publicity mill of the studio began to grind, that message started to dissipate out to the rest of the world.

"Johnny," Ken said one morning, "I know you don't like interviews. But they've arranged for Hedda Hopper to talk with you for a few minutes at lunch. *She's* coming to *you*. That took some doing. So be nice to her, will you?"

My first reaction was, why not? But as the morning's shooting wore on, and as Newman and I had trouble agreeing on the way an unimportant scene should be played, and as the takes soared from one to twenty, I felt the old hot anger coming over me and I started asking myself, why the hell should I be nice to some old dame who wanted to look me over and report to her faceless millions of readers? I wasn't mad at *her*, just at a system that didn't seem to give a damn what I thought, but that shoved me into any position that suited them. So when Ken called, "Lunch," I stayed in my ragged nineteenth century jeans and strolled into the studio dining room a few feet behind Newman, who headed like a bee for flowers to the table where I could see Hedda waiting quietly, a friendly smile greeting us all. That made me madder than ever, and the closer I got the blanker my mind became. I felt a tickle in my throat, and without really knowing why, I stopped at the wall near the table, examined a large photograph of Robert Taylor and then, without really planning it, cleared my throat and spat right in Robert's eye. It splattered against the photo, hung there for a moment, and started to slide down over his cheek. I bent over and said, "Excuse me, Miss Hopper," picked up her napkin and wiped the picture clean. When I turned around again she was on her feet and there were little sharp daggers coming out of her eyes. I was honestly a little surprised, because in a strange way I felt that what I had done was *funny*, but Miss Hopper obviously didn't agree. She whirled on Newman and let him have it with both barrels.

"This interview," she gritted out, "was a favor to *you*, Jerome, because I owed you one. But after this, I think you owe *me* a couple. If your New York aborigine ever comes down from the trees, let me know and maybe I'll talk with him if you provide an interpreter and a keeper. Meanwhile, as far as I'm concerned, Louella can have him." And with that she gave a saucy flirt of her behind and marched out of the studio commissary leaving behind one slightly panic-stricken director.

"What the fuck did you think you were doing?" said Newman.

"I don't owe the world anything except a good performance," I told him. "This wasn't my idea. I thought I was being funny. So I was wrong."

"You've got to apologize to her," said Ken. "She can ruin you."

"I say again," I said, "all I owe anyone is a good performance. If that lady wants to understand me and write about me, she has to take me the way I am. I am not a trained seal. If you want someone to balance medicine balls on their nose, you better get another boy."

"I don't believe in you," said Newman. "I won't be convinced that you actually exist. Do you really think that a punk kid like you means anything to the world without the publicity and exposure a studio and reporters like Hopper can give you? Without that, you're just another face in the 'with a cast of thousands!' You ought to learn about the game before you start changing the rules."

"Maybe we're not in the same game," I said. "As for being a punk kid, how far would you be in this picture without the changes I made in your rules?"

"What the hell's that got to do with it?" he asked sharply. "One has to do with your valid instincts as an actor. The other has to do with the dollars and cents of merchandising a star to the public. Don't you know that movie stars are sold by the pound, like sausages? Oh, the sausage has to have something appealing about it to begin with, but with six hundred brands on the market, how do you think you register the name of any one of them?"

"Shakespeare never had a press agent," I said.

"Stop kidding yourself," he said. "You're already on the winning end of a million-to-one parley. In spite of that, if you work hard to screw things up, you may blow it yet. So don't set up problems you don't need."

I could hear everything he was saying, and I understood

everything he was saying, and I even agreed with everything he was saying. So how do I explain my giving him a hard stare through my glasses and mumbling, "Why don't you take care of your end and I'll take care of mine?"

All during this time I was vaguely aware that the spook, Corley, was hanging around taking everything down. It didn't really bother me. Not at first, anyway. I knew he was bad news, but I didn't dwell on it. I was like the cancer patient who thinks everything will be okay if he can just gain a little weight. It wasn't that I didn't know what death was. Around the farm, you learn that at a young age. The chickens we killed and fried didn't turn up the next morning cackling and pecking at the feed I scattered from an old water bucket. When old Siegfried, the mule, broke a leg and got a load of buckshot from a sixteen-gauge shotgun in the head for his stupidity, he never again greeted the dawn with a whinnying snort of disgust. And no matter how many prayers I offered up during those two days alone in a cold, empty house, Aunt Sarah would never come back from that frantic ride to the hospital.

But it didn't seem to matter. I could greet Corley with a casual wave of my hand, and spill my guts to him, and kid myself that everything was going to come out all right in the end. How's that for nuttiness? The very fact that he was *here* had to tell me there wasn't any happy ending in his goddamned film script. Yet I accepted this knowledge calmly, as if it related only to some two-dimensional shadow on a movie screen, where the music would throb up to a final sigh, and THE END would dissolve in over the scene, and then the projectionist would rewind the film and the movie would start all over again.

One night I was down on the Strip, in Arturo's, and Corley turned up again. The big deal with Arturo's, unlike most of the under-age joints, was that you could always slip Artie a jug and he would see that your Coke was spiked with vodka whenever you gave him the nod. I liked to go there, because a bunch of kids had sort of adopted me, and they let me in on their problems, what with parents and the cops always ticketing their motorcycles. More often than not, one of them picked up the tab, so I knew it wasn't just my money that brought them to my table. Besides, I felt comfortable talking to them. I could loosen up on the things that really bugged me. And it was nice to reach out for the bongos and have them tossed your way without a second thought, because the kids honestly liked the way you could play them.

I was pounding away on a mambo when Corley joined me at the bandstand and sat there, one hand tapping along in rhythm with my beat.

"How's it going?" he asked.

"Pretty good. How's by you? What's happening up there?"

"It's raining," he said. "April in New York isn't all it's cracked up to be."

"So go West, old man. Go West."

"I will," he said. "In a couple of weeks, when the script is finished."

"Ding 'em good," I said. "Pry every last motherdollar out of those bastards."

"I'll do all right," he said. "Of course, things have changed. It's all Poverty Row now."

"You're shitting me. Hollywood'll go on forever. It's too mean to die."

"It won't die," he said. "But believe me, Johnny, the days of the big studios are numbered. Do you know what they did in 1971?"

"Elected Shirley Temple President?"

He laughed. "That's only half a joke. She did run for Congress. No, the studios auctioned off their prop rooms. Somebody paid an arm and a leg for Judy Garland's red shoes from *The Wizard of Oz*. MGM sold off its back lot for a housing project. It's a different world, Johnny."

"I don't think I'd like it," I said. He didn't answer, and I knew I had come close to the private, unspoken barrier between us.

After a while, he asked, "How's the picture going?"

"Good, I think. Fleming stuck to his word. He's staying out of the way. And Newman has us four days ahead of schedule. Naturally, you already know that we didn't get Helen Hayes *or* Julie Harris. But Bert Klen is going to knock off an Oscar for this. Hell, maybe I will. It's a great picture." I paused. "Isn't it?"

"Yes," he said slowly.

"You know," I said, tapping the bongos, "this movie-making is a gas. I mean, you get up with the chickens and most of the time you just sit around waiting for something to happen. Then you have to stand in a certain place for the shot, and maybe all you have to do for the camera is look over your shoulder and say, 'Huh?' and from all those little bits and pieces, the director puts together a huge jigsaw puzzle that turns out to be a finished movie. Man, that's where I think I'd like to end up . . . directing. That's where the action is."

"Some critics call film a director's medium," Corley said.

"They're right. It belongs to the directors. And the writers. There's no long-term future in acting. Oh, a couple of guys like Cooper and Fonda manage to last. But the smart ones move on. I had a couple of drinks with Brando the other night. You wouldn't believe it, what a nice guy he is. He told me that he's going to break out one of these days and start directing. He's got a big western in mind. He'd probably star in it, but he'd be behind the camera, too. Anyway, he told me that he thinks he's starting to repeat himself as an actor, and now they want him to do some costume piece called *The Egyptian*. It's a big secret, but I think he's going to cut out on that one. He dropped some hints about going back to New York and getting real sick. Anyway, while we were at it, he gave me the motorcycle lecture, and that's when we parted company, because I think it's a real crock when you consider that he just finished *The Wild One* and did a lot of his own riding in it. Hell, it isn't the motorcycle that's unsafe, it's the rider. And I'm one of the best riders around these parts. Everybody with balls rides. Clark Gable, for Christ's sake, is riding. And he's a real hot shoe, too."

"I remember something about that," Corley said.

"Well, if The King can fork a bike, I guess Johnny Lewis can."

He looked down at the floor. "I guess so."

"Hey," I said, "remember those pictures Dee Dee took on the farm? Well, *Life* bought them and they're going to put out a four-page spread on me next week. I showed B.J. an advance proof and he nearly creamed his jeans. I haven't been giving interviews, you know, and that frosts them. They think they have to sell me like soap. I told Fleming that after the *Life* piece runs, I may give a few. I just wanted Dee Dee to get first crack at it. It's the least I could do for her. That girl is a wonder. She sticks by me through hot and cold, and I bust her heart at least twice a week. You know, she's been seeing Newman a lot lately, and instead of being happy for her—this shows you what a prick I am—I'm *mad!* He's a sweet, gentle man and he'd do her good, but it gripes me to have something taken away, and I can sense a wall coming up between us because of it. To make things worse, I don't even love her, and doubt I ever could. I don't think I can love anyone, anymore. And maybe I'm better off that way. Anyone who would fall in love with an actor ought to have her head examined. Jean Billingham was right. We're monsters."

"Where is Jean these days?" he asked.

"Who knows? I ought to get in touch, but I never get around to it. She is one swell little dame. But she had no call taking off on me just because of some little piece of ass. Hell, she doesn't own me. Nobody does. Still, I miss her every now and then. Maybe Conklin can track her down. Jer can dig her out of the bushes if anyone can."

I got bored with the bongos and tossed them back to the kid who owned them. "Come on," I said, standing up. "This place is starting to give me the jitters. My car's out back."

"No bike?"

"Not yet. I've got an order in for a Harley, but they didn't have it in my color. It ought to be in next week. Meanwhile, I've got this studio car on loan. It's right over there."

We got in and I headed down the hill, toward Hollywood. Dee Dee was out with Newman, so there was no point in going to the Regency. I turned up Highland and parked at the entrance to the Hollywood Bowl.

"Come on," I said. "I know a way to get in. Behind that tree —see the gap in the fence? I used to sneak in here when I was poor and unknown, so I ought to be able to work it now that I'm rich and famous."

He laughed. "Are you?"

"Rich? Or famous? A little of both, I guess. Jer negotiated a new contract with Fleming. It commits me to do two pictures by the end of next year. Plus this one, of course. I'm guaranteed thirty weeks at two thousand, and there's an escalator clause that'll get me up to twenty-five hundred a week by the end of 1955. 1956, I have the whole year off, to do a Broadway play. Maybe I'll go to Europe. I'd like to talk with some of the theater guys over there. Bertolt Brecht, for one. He's in East Germany

220

now, you know. And Edward Gordon Craig is living in Italy. Not to mention Olivier in England. There's so much you can learn, once you get to the point where people will talk to you. Fleming shit his pants at that year-off clause. But by then we both ought to be able to afford it. Anyway, he's got me under his thumb already. At least he thinks he has."

We were inside now, and sitting on the curved seats, looking far down to the curved shell of a stage.

"How's that? Under his thumb?"

"Well, what they do is buy you a house. Hell, *you* know, they pay for it and take the payments out of your salary. So, zonk, all of a sudden you're a hundred grand in debt. It's painless getting in, but the only way you can get out is to keep reporting to the studio, and just about the time you start to get free and clear, you need a bigger house or something and the whole thing starts over. So Fleming convinced me that the Regency isn't the place for an up and coming movie star, that I need a place with more privacy and so on. The truth is, I do. I'm already starting to attract some cool glances from the management because of the guests I bring home. So we found this great pad up in the canyon, it's like weird. The bedroom is up on the second floor, and when you get up there, you can pull the stairs up after you. It's only four rooms, and the sonofabitch cost sixty thousand bucks. So I'm hooked, for a while at least. I don't think it's likely I'll get married and have kids and need more space, so I ought to be out from under by the time I want to take off for Europe. Not that it won't be a hard fight. The girls in this town, they're no more swingers than the girls in Centerville. Holding hands in the movies is all right with them, but if you want something more basic, you'd better have an engagement ring in your other hand. That's the decent girls, that is. Thank God there are still a lot of *in*decent ones around. Anyway, once Fleming gets the house deal set, which ought to be in a couple of weeks, I'm going to see if I can get Dee Dee to move in with me. If I handle it right, that ought to wash her up with Newman."

"That's a cruel way to do it," he said.

I hit his arm with the flat of my hand. "Listen, mister," I said, "who the hell are *you* to be talking about cruel? You're back here picking my bones to fatten up your own bank account, and I don't notice any tears in your eyes. If you want to moralize, do it on your own time. I didn't invite you here, and it wouldn't exactly break my heart if I never saw you again. If you're going to watch, *watch!* But keep your goddamned mouth off me!"

We sat in silence for a while, looking down at the Bowl and listening to the cars swishing by on the freeway. Then we got up and I went back to the Regency. I don't know where *he* went.

The *Life* issue and my new Harley arrived on the same day. Both created quite a stir. Dee Dee's photographs made me look very young and intense, and although they didn't use the coffin shot, they did use the one of me sitting on the old cycle in the barn, looking as if all the woes of the world were piled up on my shoulders. The text accused me of imitating Brando, but Marlon himself was the first to laugh that off. He phoned me on the set and said, "Don't let them get to you, Johnny. If you're more than one layer deep, they never find out about it until you're dead. Ignore them. I never copied anyone, and you're not copying, either."

As for the Harley, when I came out for a breath of air between takes, I found Newman and Fleming standing there, looking at it.

"This machine," said Fleming. "Do you mean to say it's yours, Johnny?"

"Paid in full," I said. "In cash."

"But isn't it dangerous?"

"A little. But so is living in California."

"I didn't ask for insolence," he told me. "The Studio has a large investment in you. You have an obligation not to endanger yourself."

"Don't worry," I said. "My obligation to my own neck comes first. Believe it or not, this is a very sensible means of transportation. I've been riding since I was fourteen, and I've never been hurt yet."

"You weren't riding in Southern California," Newman said grimly. I laughed at him and punched his shoulder, and the tension eased up somewhat. Fleming went back inside shaking his head, and Newman and I returned to the set.

"Are you going to reshoot the test scene?" I asked.

"I'm not sure," he said. "Do you think we could pull it off again?"

"The same way?" He nodded, and I shook my head. "Nope. Not a chance. Even if I could make it work again, Bert couldn't. No one, not even a great actor like Bert, could act surprise the way it really happened that first time."

"That's the way I figured it," Newman said. "I think we can break up a couple of the bad zooms and some of the sloppy sound by shooting some cover closeups. But the main part of the scene, we'll leave just as it is."

"Okay by me."

"Come on over in the corner," he suggested. "There's something else I want to talk to you about."

We strolled over, through the maze of light stands and equipment, to a secluded part of the studio. Newman, when we got there, scuffed his feet and looked embarrassed.

"Look, kid," he said, "I don't know how you're going to take this, but I figure I owe it to you, so here goes. Dee Dee and me, we've been seeing a lot of each other, and as far as I'm con-

223

cerned, she's the sweetest girl to come down the pike. So, if she'll have me, I'm going to ask her to marry me. That's it."

I looked at him in startled surprise and burst out laughing.

"What the hell's so funny?" he yelled.

"You and Dee Dee?" I choked. "That's wonderful. Honest, Jerry, I couldn't be happier. It's just such a surprise, that's why I'm laughing. Who would have thought it? And you coming to me about it, with your hat in hand like I was Big Daddy! Go in peace, my son, my blessings on you."

"I'm serious, Johnny," he said.

"So am I," I told him. And at that very moment, I was.

The shooting resumed, and as the long afternoon wore on, I started seeing her in his arms and lost concentration on the job and the work went badly. Finally at 4:30 Newman threw in the sponge and told me to go home and work on the script, that he'd fill out the day with closeups on Bert and Maggie Atwell.

I went up to the business office and talked to Fleming's business manager.

"How soon can I get into that house?" I asked. He started to give me some stuff about escrow and all kinds of legal terms, but I cut him off with, "Is there any real reason why I can't move in tonight?" It turned out there wasn't, so I thanked him and borrowed his phone to call the Regency.

"Dee Dee? I've got something important to talk to you about. What? I don't care if you've got a date with the Pope himself. Cancel it. I'll pick you up in an hour. You're about to be the happiest girl in California."

I put the phone down, and the money flunkey smirked at me. "Someone about to be married?" he purred.

"Wrong," I said. "Someone is about *not* to be married." And I went out of there fast, leaving a bewildered pout on his soft, fat face.

224

"Johnny, it's beautiful," Dee Dee said. "And you never mentioned it, not once."

"I wanted it to be a surprise," I told her. "I move in tonight. And so do you."

She looked at me sadly. "Oh, dear," she said, "you know I can't do that."

"Why can't you?" I asked, not giving her an inch.

"It's just that things are different now," she said, sliding down on the sofa. I sat beside her. "You're becoming so well known, and then there's—"

"Newman?"

"Well, yes, him too. Oh, Johnny, why couldn't you have asked me a month ago?"

"Because I couldn't," I said. "But I'm asking you now."

I pulled her over to me and our lips met. Hers were tight and unresponsive, but only for a moment, and they they softened and opened and I felt her breath catch in her throat as I thrust my tongue in. Her arms tightened around my shoulders and then she used her elbows to push me away and gasped, "No, no, Johnny! No! This isn't right. It isn't fair!"

I pulled her against me again and this time her response was instant and as we kissed I reached both hands in between us and cupped them around her full breasts. She stiffened in a taut spasm of excitement and her own tongue explored my mouth as her hand groped for my crotch. I squeezed both nipples through her light bra and pinched them suddenly, a technique that always drove her mad with lust. Throwing her head back, she cried, "Ahhhhhh!" and then began to shake it from side to side, whispering, "Please don't, Johnny. This isn't fair. Please don't." But as she pleaded with me to stop, her hand found my aroused maleness and clutched it tightly as if her body had a will of its own, beyond the mind's control.

I pushed her back against the sofa arm and slipped one hand

225

up along her thigh and under her panties. Her crotch was already wet and hot and my fingers slipped in easily and as I massaged her there, she lifted her head and looked at me coldly with one brief rational stare that might have been hatred before the rising urges of her body took control again and swept her into a gasping cry of passion that shut out all else. Then we tore at each other's clothes and threw them into a jumbled heap on the floor and I was in her and her feet beat against my buttocks as her fingernails clawed at my back. In less than half a minute I felt myself ejaculate, a cold, distant mechanical thing with no sense of the blinding orgasm I usually had with her, and almost as suddenly, my prick began to soften and shrink. "More," she pleaded, "I'm almost there, darling, don't stop now."

Withdrawing, I raised her legs until her knees pressed against her breasts and said, "Don't worry. I won't leave you like this." And holding her breasts in both hands I bent my head down between her thighs.

"Johnny!" she cried, "what are you . . . Oooooh! That's . . . no one ever did—that. . . ."

Her body lurched with the spasm and her hands clawed at my hair and it seemed to go on for hours until her passion slowly subsided and her legs relaxed. I drew myself up part way and lay my head on her breasts. She stroked my ear and my perspiring neck and pecked little bird-like kisses against my hands and wrists.

"Oh, sweetheart," she said, softly, "that was so good. It's the first time anyone ever did it to me. I've heard about it, but no one ever said how *good* it could be. I went right out of the room, then. And look what I've done to your back! You're all scratches! Oh sweetheart, I love you. No, don't say anything. I don't want you to say anything you don't mean. This is enough, lying here with you like this. Just rest, dearest, go to sleep for a while. I'll hold you, I'll watch over you, I won't let anyone hurt you. . . . Just sleep, Johnny. . . ."

When I woke, she had covered me with a blanket and was nowhere in sight. I sat up and felt a sinking sense of loss, then I heard the shower running upstairs. I wrapped the blanket around me and went upstairs. She was in the glass-walled shower, soaping her hair. I dropped the blanket and slipped in behind her, pressing up against her behind and holding both breasts again. She dropped the soap with a little shriek as I bent her over and entered her from the rear. She whispered, "No, Johnny! You'll slip and break your neck." But I ignored her little cries and plunged against her wet curves vainly seeking that fulfillment that had once come so easily and that was now fleeing away from me faster than the mind could follow. I ravished her there in the shower stall, with the water beating down on our bodies and even when she reached her climax and called out to me I was unable to join her. A savage longing swept through me, and as we uncoupled, I caught her head in both dripping hands and, wordlessly, pushed her down to her knees. She looked at what I was offering with an empty expression, turned her eyes up toward me in despair, then leaned forward woodenly and began to do what I wanted. I remember calling out obscenities as the orgasm came and pulling her face against me until it was all over and she collapsed against the tiled wall, retching.

"Dee Dee," I said, "I'm sorry. I'm sorry."

She tried to stand, almost lost her balance, then stood there with the water streaming down her long, beautiful body.

"Oh, Johnny," she cried, "what's happening to you?"

Jerome Newman never spoke another word to me outside the line of duty. He gave me my instructions in cold, precise sentences that left no leeway for discussion or personalities. One day, determined to drive him beyond the position he had adopted, I sat in my dressing room all morning, refusing to listen to the pleas made by Ken for me to report to the set. "Jesus, kid," he said, "Fleming's going to get a chance to start his goddamned clock if you keep this up. Give us a break, huh?"

Newman refused to budge. Eventually Maggie Atwell came in and gave me a large piece of her mind and shamed me into returning to the floor. Newman accepted my presence with calm detachment and work went on as if it had never been interrupted.

Luckily the key scenes had already been committed to film, because from the day Dee Dee moved in with me until the final day of shooting, Newman never once pushed me to do anything other than what I wanted. I expected him to ride me, but instead he ignored my presence as much as a director can ignore the presence of one of his four stars. And what made it worse was that I knew how much I had wronged him, wronged poor Dee Dee, and was continuing to wrong them both with each passing hour. But I was powerless to halt my wild vengeance against them for deserting me, for leaving me alone. My life with Dee Dee soon degenerated into a series of frantic sexual encounters. I found it harder every time to reach a climax and with every try Dee Dee became more frightened. Her work suffered, too. She almost never took out her cameras any more, and didn't come to the studio at all. One night when I came home I found her lying naked on the bed, crying, and there was a half-empty bottle of sleeping pills on the floor, near a pool of vomit where she had puked up the poison. I called a doctor and he gave out with the usual crap about an accidental overdose and gave her a stimulant, but when he left, I noticed he had taken the bottle with him. I gave her hell and she went along with the doc, insisting she had lost track of what she was doing, but from then on she started sleeping on the couch downstairs and only coming into the sprawling second-floor bed when I called her.

The days wore on, and finally one afternoon at 5:30, when Ken called, "That's a wrap," *Paradise Gate* was finished. Both Bert Klen and Maggie Atwell threw champagne parties in their dressing rooms and I wandered in and had a glass in both places. The top men on the crew all stopped in and had one for the road, and a couple of starlets from the next stage carried off poor old Bert in a haze of alcoholic glory, and then Maggie and I found ourselves alone in the mirror-lined room.

"Have another drink," she said. You have to remember that, although Maggie was playing a spinster of forty, she was actually in her late twenties, and in close proximity, the age added by makeup vanished and became only a peculiar kind of attractiveness. It worked on me, and as I handed her another glass of champagne, I leaned over and gave her a healthy kiss on the mouth. She responded politely enough, in fact a little more than mere politeness would demand. But when I drew back, her eyes were cool and intent.

"I've been meaning to have a talk with you," she said. "It looks like this is it."

"Talk away," I said. "We should have seen more of each other before this."

"I was in the business," she said, "when I was four years old. I ended up on Broadway because I felt that there I could do the honest kind of work I needed for my soul and drag in the kind of dough I needed for my bank account. If Jerry Newman had not camped outside my dressing room door, I tell you truly I would not be shacked up today in Hollywood, U.S.A. I regard Newman as one of the great men of our world, and that's why it burns me up to see a punk kid like you raking him over the coals. In case you don't know it, Jerry went out on a terribly long limb for you. He practically mortgaged his ass to B.J. to get you on this picture. When we started out, I thought *Paradise Gate* had a good shot at being one of the great pictures of the '50s.

229

"Well, you fixed that, John Calvin Lewis. You took the heart out of that man. He's been going through the motions for the last two weeks, and you know better than I whose fault that is. So all of a sudden we don't have a contender for the Oscar any more. In fact, if we weren't all living off the creative energy and planning that Jerry put into this picture before he threw in the sponge, it would be doubtful that this monstrosity would even get released. Luckily enough, it's still a good picture. No longer a great picture, but still a good one. With no thanks to you, John Calvin. Now, I find you terribly appealing physically. If you had come up to me on the street, a perfect stranger, and say, 'Let's go screw,' I would have probably beaten you to the bedroom. But now that I know you, you little viper, I wouldn't give you the right time of day. So enjoy that kiss you just got. That is the last giftie you'll ever get from Maggie Atwell, I kid you not. And shove, junior. I want to take this makeup off."

So I found myself out in the hall, a full glass in my hand. I shrugged my shoulders in case anyone was watching and slugged it down. There wasn't anyplace to put the glass, so I sailed it off into the set. It crashed into the little mining shack and splintered into a thousand shards of naked glass.

Outside, the sun was already sitting on top of the commissary. My Harley was parked down the row, just outside the men's room, and I started for it. Only started, because someone stepped out in front of me and his shadow stretched down the cement walk and blocked out the sun from my eyes. It was Newman.

"All right, Johnny," he said. "The picture is over. Come on, let's you and me even up old scores."

"Cool it, old man," I said. "I don't want to fight with you."

"Tough shit," said he. "Either fight or run."

"Move over, Newman. You're drunk."

"That I am," he yelled, and let go a rolling roundhouse swing that would have taken my nose off had it connected. But he was slow, and telegraphed, and I didn't even hit him, just shoved off the punch with a forearm and let him lunge past me and skid along the sidewalk on his face. He got up with raking red marks on his cheek and made another pass at me. This time the anger flared up and I gave him a sharp jab in the gut and he doubled over making *Huhhh!* sounds and threw up on his shoes. When he got his breath back he shook one finger at me accusingly and said, "Two out of three doesn't count," and came at me again. This time I was really mad and met him with two hard licks to the face and one of them loosened some teeth, because I felt them give. He went down in a heap and puked some more and by now the anger was so high in me that I stepped over and gave him a shot in the ribs with my toe. He screamed, a high, unexpected sound, and the door burst open behind me and out came Dee Dee. She had her camera, and had obviously come down to shoot the final festivities. She took a long look at Newman on the ground, and at me crouching over him, and then unleashed a sweeping slash with the Leica, held bolo-like by one end of the leather strap. It caught me against one temple and a terrible brightness flashed through my brain along with the sound of a solid *clunk,* and I felt the ground whirling out from underneath my feet. I hit hard, and that was a second earthquake that left me weak and sick to my own stomach. Dee Dee was screaming at me, and her words came from a far distance and it took a lot of effort to understand them, but finally they came through and I heard her loud and clear.

"Stay away from us," she shouted. "Take your sickness and peddle it on the Strip, you miserable sickening *queer!*"

231

CHAPTER
NINE

WHEN shooting has been finished on a picture, the job is only half over. The miles and miles of film must be edited down to a usable length, then arranged for the best effect on the screen. Music is composed and scored to fit the various scenes, and eventually all the pictures and the sound tracks and the music are blended together into the composite result you see on your theater screen. The process takes several weeks at the best; several months more often than not.

On the basis of first reports on *Paradise Gate*, there were feelers about my going into 20th Century's *The Egyptian*, which had lost Brando as I expected. But Fleming hit them with a preposterous financial demand for the loan-out, and I wasn't any too happy about taking a part that Marlon didn't like, so the deal fell through and eventually Edmund Purdom did the job. "For one thing," a Sunset Strip bit player said cruelly, "he's exactly Marlon's size, so they don't have to recut the costumes." By now I was giving out as many interviews as they set up for me, and got a charge out of stringing the reporters along with conflicting opinions. In the morning, I'd tell one that I would never make another film, and in the afternoon I'd tell another one that I was considering doing *Hamlet* for MGM. Fleming fumed and chomped at the bit, but it was all publicity for the film and outside of threatening me with suspension, he lapped it up and counted his clippings.

It was September now, and every weekend I'd wind up the Harley and zip down to Tijuana for the Sunday afternoon bull fights. With any luck, I'd do the 130 miles in under three hours and because I could cut in and out of traffic, even the tieup near the border didn't slow me down too much.

With Dee Dee gone, there was usually a new chick living in the little house every week but it wasn't really very good any more. I found that only by getting out on the bike and roaring up through the back country behind the Hollywood Hills could I strip off the tension that my lousy sex life built up. Week days were taken up with a string of interviews, with a dentist twice a week who was rebuilding my teeth with caps, and occasionally with dating one of the everpresent starlets who clustered around publicity like flies around honey. Weekends, though, were mine, and occasionally I'd ride with Keenan Wynn and, once, with Gable. But the fights were the big thing. I'd get there early and shoot the breeze with the other afficionados. Eventually someone recognized me, and I was invited down to meet the matadors. They were slight, slender men, with hawk-like faces, and sharp, intense eyes. Their gaze pierced right through me, and it wasn't until the third or fourth visit that I was really accepted. That was when I began staying over and making the drive back to Hollywood in the dawn hours of Monday. I

233

bought a cape and began practicing with it, and at night I'd go out on the Strip and duel taxicabs with it. The idea was to see how close I could stand to the cab as it went by, and play the headlights like horns.

I don't know how long this period of inactivity and boredom lasted. Too long, finally, and I barged into Felming's office and demanded another picture. *Paradise Gate* wouldn't premier until mid-December, and that was months away. If he was waiting for reactions from it before slating something else, I'd be withered up from activity. Fleming listened patiently, took the cigarillo out of his mouth and said, "If you'd read the papers instead of trying to shock them, you might have seen this item." His finger tapped a section of Sheilah Graham's column. I took it and read:

"Johnny Lewis is being touted around town as the likely contender for the lead in Jed Roberts' *Chicken Run,* an examination of the teen-aged drag strip problem. One could almost call this type casting, since young Lewis is reputed to have a heavy foot on the throttle in real life. Roberts will produce and direct for B.J. Fleming's Argos Company, and the cameras are scheduled to start turning in mid-October."

"It's news to me," I said. "First I ever heard of it. Nobody asked me a thing. I don't know how she got it."

"She got it because I told her about it," he said. "We English stick together, so I let Sheilah have a jump on Louella and Hedda. As for no one asking you, when have we been able to find you to ask anything? You spend more time in Mexico than you do at home. Now, let me give you a few pointers about Jed Roberts. He has made more films than you've seen. He doesn't want you in this picture. He heard about the trouble you had with Newman, and so far as Jed's concerned, he needs you like a hole in the head. But I am still chief of this Studio and viewed in that light, Jed saw reason. But he'll put up with none of your tricks. All business, that's Jed Roberts, and any time you decide that you're smarter than he is, he has my authority to swat you down. Now, one other thing. Until all shooting is finished on *Chicken Run,* you are not to ride that machine of yours. I can't afford lost shooting days because you're all bruised up and can't work. Put it in storage until the picture's done."

"What the hell's all this?" I yelled. "This isn't a slave camp. On the set, I'll do what you want. But my time is my own, and if I want to ride a bike, you can't stop me."

"Wrong," he said. "If you doubt my word, ask your Mr. Conklin. Believe me: I own you, Johnny. Don't fight it. I'm not being unreasonable. It's for your own good. None of us want to see you get hurt."

"Well, I say it's a crummy thing to do. How am I supposed to get down to Mexico?"

"If you insist on going," he said, "I suggest you drive a car like everyone else. Just be sure it's not one of the hot rods from the film."

"Thanks for nothing," I said, and stomped out of his office. I paused in the other room to try and get my anger under control. Marcel was away from his desk, and sitting in one of the chairs was a tall, dark-haired girl with an oddly familiar face. I went over and leaned on the desk.

"Hi," I said, putting on all the old charm. "I know I should recognize you, but I just can't hook up a name with the face."

"I recognize you," she said. "In this town you'd have to be blind not to know Johnny Lewis."

"Many thanks," I bowed. "But that still doesn't solve *my* problem."

"I used to make movies," she said. "A long time ago."

"What are you giving me? You can't be more than eighteen now. What do you mean, a long time ago?"

Before she could answer, Fleming came out. "Ah," he said,

"I see you've met. Good, Johnny, Miss Cooper is your co-star. We're very fortunate that she has decided to . . . ah, come out of retirement."

And *then* I knew her. Who could forget Diana Cooper, the bright-eyed child star who took up Shirley Temple's outgrown crown and wore it through the war years in a series of comedies and musicals that ended in 1946 when she found herself in the awkward, preteen age? I used to marvel at her, dancing with Fred Astaire and singing along with Sinatra in those great musicals they don't make any more. I bent over and took her hand, gave it a mock kiss.

"Miss Cooper," I said. "Welcome aboard." I shot a glance at Fleming, and he was blushing. But, then, so was Diana, and her hand trembled as she took it away. I felt a lurching sensation and an indescribable sweetness seemed to tingle through me as I looked down at her gamin face, framed in her dark hair, and seemingly full of big blue eyes and a quiet smile.

"You know," I said, "I think I'm falling in love with you."

Since I had to drive a car, I decided to make it a real gasser. I shopped around on sports car row, and finally decided on a Porsche Spyder, bright red. It looked a little like a Volkswagen, but the similarity ended with looks. The Porsche could go from zero to sixty in less than a block, leaving burning rubber all the way. When I skidded it onto the lot, Fleming happened to be standing near the gate talking with one of the designers, and I saw him shake his head and wince. But having ordered me off the Harley, he didn't have the gall to tell me what kind of car to buy, so I amused myself by racing the motor under his window a couple of times a day. Meanwhile, I got hold of Diana's address and the day the Porsche was delivered, I barreled it out to Beverly Hills and found the house without any trouble. The driveway was empty, so I shot into it and gave the horn a couple of blasts. The door opened, but it wasn't Diana at all. A heavy-set woman with gray hair stood there, blinking out into the sunlight. "Yes?" she said.

"Hi," I said. "I'm Johnny Lewis. Is Diana home?"

"I recognize you, Mr. Lewis," she said. "I'm Diana's mother."

"Pleased to meet you, Mrs. Cooper," I said.

"Mrs. Eisenberg," she said. "Cooper is my daughter's stage name. Her real name is Sharon. But I'm sure you must have known that."

"To be honest," I said, "it never entered my mind."

"My daughter is not home," she said. "But please come in. Do you like tea? We'll have a glass together and talk."

"Why not?" I followed her into the house. It was an ornate, two-story version of a Spanish villa, the stucco dyed a violent pink. "Nice place," I said.

"Laurell Drive is one of the older streets," Mrs. Eisenberg said. "See? Over there at number 1200? That is the home of Mr. Samuel Goldwyn. And down there, just around the corner on North Rodeo Drive, that was the last home of Lupe Velez. I am sure you must have heard of her."

"Yes ma'am," I said, wondering if she was going to give me the grand tour of Movie Star homes.

"We have lived in this house since Mr. Eisenberg passed away," she said, closing the door behind us. "Before the war, Mr. Leslie Howard rented it briefly, but it was actually built for a gentleman active in the securities market."

"Amazing," I said. She looked at me sharply. Diana's mother was no fool, I decided, and warned myself not to try to zing her. I wanted the old bat to like me. So I got out my glasses, the untinted ones and slipped them on and did the shy owl bit. "I have weak eyes," I said. "Since childhood. Without these,

I'm a white cane case. But I can't wear them on camera, naturally."

"Sharon's features were always perfect," she said, almost to herself. "We never had a tooth capped, never had a blemish removed. She was a beautiful little girl. Those awful people who accused Papa and me of exploiting her were all fools. Sharon brought so much beauty to the world, it would have been a crime to suppress it."

"She sure was a pretty little girl," I said. "And she's a mighty beautiful young lady today. I'm pleased as punch to be in the same picture with her."

"She doesn't have to work, you know," said Mrs. Eisenberg. "The money she earned has all been invested. Sharon receives more than thirty thousand a year just from interest—never mind the principal, which she will receive when she is 21. There's no need for her to go back to work at all. And in such a cruel, violent motion picture. Why do they make such pictures? Nothing at all like the lovely movies she did with Gene Kelly and Fred Astaire. Dancing and singing and comedy, those are the things you should put in pictures. Not this thing about juvenile delinquents and children who hate their parents. What is the world coming to?"

She handed me a tall glass of hot tea. We both sat down in the huge kitchen and sipped at it. "Mr. Goldwyn, sometimes when he is home early, he will drop in and have a glass of tea and talk with me, and he is bewildered by the things that are happening to the industry. Those films he did about small towns, my Sharon was in two of them, you know, those were the kind of pictures he and I understand. Where does all the hate and all the violence come from? Isn't there enough trouble in the world, why should people pay to see it on the screen? Drink your tea, Mr. Lewis. Is that your own name, Lewis? It wouldn't be Lewisohn by chance?"

"No ma'am," I said, burning my tongue on the scalding tea. "It's Lewis on my father's side, Hubbard on my mother's. Both families have lived in Iowa since Civil War days."

"Iowa," she said. "Sharon went to Des Moines one time, to promote a film. There was so much snow, nothing could move. The premiere was a failure." She glared at me as if I had personally dumped the snow in the streets.

"Yes ma'am," I said. "It snows a lot up that way. If the studio planned a premiere in January, they made a big mistake."

"We never went back," she said. "That was in 1945, I remember. The gross was down almost fourteen thousand dollars for the run. All because of the snow."

"That's too bad," I mumbled.

"Sharon worked very hard, Mr. Lewis," she said. "She appeared in literally dozens of those awful Hal Roach children's comedies before she emerged into her own right. It's so different today. A boy like you, he makes one picture, it is not even released, and suddenly he is a star. Does that seem fair to you, Mr. Lewis? My Sharon had to serve a long apprenticeship, for that same stardom that you leap into, straight from Iowa. Oh, the world has changed, and not for the better."

"Well, today there's television," I said. "That's where I did a lot of work before they brought me out here."

"Television!" she said. "I will not allow one in this house. Competing with the industry by showing pictures for *free!* What kind of business is that? Monkey business! And yet some of the studios are stupid enough to sell their old pictures to television. They give the enemy his weapons and then act surprised when the box office falls off. Producers! They should first run a tailor shop like my Jake did, then they'd learn about sending customers up the street."

I finished the tea and got up. If I didn't split this scene in a hurry I was going to give the old bat what for, and that would foul things up between Diana and me for sure. "Thank you for the tea, Mrs. Eisenberg," I said. "I enjoyed talking with you. Would you please tell Diana—Sharon—that I dropped by?"

She looked up at me as if I had just dropped in from Mars.

"Oh, Sharon," she said. "Didn't I mention it? That's why I wanted to talk with you. Except on the set, for business, I want that you should never see Sharon again."

"Mama's old-fashioned," Diana told me, as we sat at the lookout point, up on Mulholland, looking way down on the lights of Los Angeles.

"Mama's appointed herself in charge of defending the film industry against carpetbaggers like me," I said. "Do you know it's my fault you got snowed out in Des Moines?" She laughed, but not loudly, and I went on: "Seriously, honey, she's mad at me because I made it big in one picture while you had to put in a tour with Hal Roach. Well, is that my fault? Things work differently today. Hells bells, Diana, *you're* going to make it big in *Chicken Run,* too, and I bet your old lady won't kick then."

"Oh, Johnny," she said, "you really don't understand, do you? Mama doesn't disapprove of you because you made it fast. She's upset because you're not Jewish."

"What!" I yelled. "What the hell for?"

"Why not?" she asked. "Even today, lots of parents get upset when their Christian daughter brings home a Jewish fellow. Why shouldn't it work the other way around?"

"No reason," I said. "Except I never thought much about religion, one way or the other. I don't see why it should make a difference between people."

"It does, though. And if there are children, it becomes even more important."

"Children? Who the hell said anything about children? We

240

drove up here so I could ask if you'd come to a party at my place. Who brought up the subject of marriage and kids?"

"Your party starts at midnight," Diana said. "Knowing mama, if I went to a boy's place at midnight, I'd better come home with a wedding ring."

"Good lord, there will be twenty other people there. What does she think I'm running, an orgy? I just wanted to celebrate starting on the picture tomorrow. I planned the whole thing for you. What will it be like if you don't show up?"

"Johnny, I'm sorry. If only you'd mentioned it to me before tonight."

"I wanted it to be a surprise."

"Well, it was. Please forgive me. I just can't. Mama would be impossible. You don't know how old-fashioned she is."

"I'm starting to learn," I said, switching on the engine and swinging the Porsche out onto the street. We drove in silence, listening to Mantovani on the car radio. Diana reached over and touched my arm. I let her hand rest there for a little, then shrugged it off reaching for the gear shift. She sat stiffly against the door, until I turned off Sunset Boulevard into Beverly Drive, then left into Laurel.

"Stop here," she said. "I'll walk the rest of the way."

"Don't want Mama to see me?" I said harshly.

"Oh, Johnny," she said, flinging the door open and stepping out, "why do you have to make it so hard?" She slammed it and ran up the drive. I threw the Porsche into reverse, snarled around into North Rodeo Drive and let my exhaust backfire against the last home of Lupe Velez. I got back on Beverly Drive, headed north, up into the Santa Monica Mountains. My house was up Coldwater Canyon Drive almost all the way back to Mulholland. The car clock had gone on the fritz already, but my watch said it was 10:40, and it was a good bet that folks were already starting to arrive. A string of cars parked along the edge of the drive confirmed that hunch. Most of the kids made it a point to get to parties early, to scoff up whatever food might be available. Not too infrequently, this would be their only real meal of the day. I'd had the party catered by the Stage Delicatessen for that very reason. I knew what a gut ache from hunger was like, and it wasn't anything I liked to remember.

The Bogen hi-fi was blasting away when I went in. Two young actors, whose names completely escaped me, were Indian wrestling on the floor. "Hi, Johnny," said one. "The door was open, so we came in." "Hope you don't mind," said the other.

"Man, that's why I leave it unlocked," I said. I could hear noise coming from the kitchen. I went in, and there were two more guys and four girls, all rummaging through the fridge. "You're out of luck," I said. "There's peanut butter in the cabinet, but you'd have to scoop it with a spoon. I never eat here."

"Just looking," said one of the girls. She was the usual starlet, but near her was a woman I'd seen discussing horoscopes on Channel 3. As I groped for her name, she stuck out her hand and said, "Hi, Johnny, I'm Sandra Vidor."

"Oh, yeah," I said. "The horoscope lady."

"The same." She had long, lank black hair that fell to her waist, and a deep-cut black gown that looked like a shroud. She wore white lipstick and if there was any beauty under the blue and green makeup, it was well-hidden. "I brought you a housewarming present," she said, and held out a long cardboard box. I tore it open and found a ready-made hangman's noose.

"Hey," I said, "this is just what I needed. Especially if B.J. shows up. Listen, kids, I'm sorry, but you just got here a little early. The Stage is sending up some chow, but there's plenty of ice and the booze is out in the living room by the hi-fi."

"Never mind," said Sandra. "It's you we came to enjoy." She

looked straight at me when she said this and her sharp, pink tongue twitched along her startlingly white teeth. I went out into the living room, and with some help from a couple of the guys, hung the noose so it would be the first thing you saw when coming in the door. The rope swayed gently in the flow of air from the room air conditioner.

Lights flashed in the window, and the man from the Stage arrived with baskets of sandwiches. The girls helped him arrange them on the long table in the dining alcove and almost simultaneously three more cars arrived and the party was in full blast. Each time someone new entered, there was a big thing about the noose, and one white-duck clad fairy had to be physically restrained from getting up on a chair and trying it on for size. Sandra latched onto me and seemed unable to keep her hands off me. They held my arms, stroked my neck, lingered on my knee when we sat, touched her own white lips and then brushed mine. Whoever brought her never complained, so maybe he was glad to be rid of her. Shortly after midnight, someone got out the bongos and we had a session or two, playing them along with the hi-fi, and then we started to dance. Naturally, Sandra grabbed onto me, and as we waltzed to the tunes of Dave Brubeck, she started asking questions like, "Do you believe in astrology?" and "Don't you think that madness is a requisite for the truly creative artist?" I told her that I didn't think either idea was too hot, and managed to get away from her for long enough to have a drink.

Corley, the spook, had turned up again. I stood in a corner with him and had a drink.

"Glad you could make it," I said. "You're hitting all the high points, huh?"

"It looks like it," he said. "So this is your house. I tried to get a look at it last month. March, that was."

"March of your time? Or mine?"

"My time. Sorry. Anyway, the present owner—present owner in *my* time—has been pestered to death by your fans. He gets out a shotgun every now and then and threatens to reduce the population by a few dozen curiosity seekers. Or maybe it was that I hit him on a bad day. Anyway, I never got inside."

"Well, welcome to the pool," I said. "You told me I'd make it, and I did. Am I supposed to thank you? Or maybe you could bring back a tape recorder and I'd record a speech especially for you and your goddamned movie. That ought to get it off the ground, huh? An exclusive interview with John Calvin Lewis, taped from beyond the grave." Corley looked away, and I gave him a shot on the shoulder. He felt solid enough. "Hey," I said, "what's with the gloom? It's my life, isn't it? And it would have been the same with or without you. Or would it? Keep your chin up, old buddy. Without the push you gave me, I might still be sitting in those lousy casting offices in New York wearing out my ass with those form-fitting chairs. You know, a lot of the things I've done, I did just to impress you. Isn't that a weirdie? Some of the stuff I pulled led me here, to Coldwater Canyon and this whole bit of being a movie star. Cheer up. Without you, I might still be Joe Nobody from Centerville, Iowa."

"I know," he said. Obviously, he didn't like the idea.

"So have a drink. Take a hangover back with you, anyway."

But she came over and grabbed my hand. "I want to dance," she said. I let her drag me out into the middle of the room and just when she had plastered herself to me like a black drape, the doorbell rang. I had only time to pull away slightly before somebody opened the door and there stood Diana, looking at me through the loop of the hangman's noose. The hi-fi was at full blast, and Sandra was still attached to me intimately, and the bongos were clattering away. Diana stared at me through the smoke and spoke above the noise.

"I—slipped away for a while," she said. "Mama's asleep. But

I shouldn't have come. I'll see you at the studio in the morning. Good night, Johnny."

And before I could move, she turned and ran into the night, and with that, Sandra plastered herself up against me again.

"Come on, big boy," she said, "let's grind a little."

I overslept, and arrived at the studio an hour late. Most of it was Sandra's fault. When the party broke up, she stayed behind and the next thing I knew, she had me in bed and was doing things that even Marsha Wyss would never have dreamed of. We were both pretty drunk, but that didn't ease my conscience as I drove frantically down Santa Monica, unshowered, my clothes plastered to me by sweat and my own and Sandra's frantic juices. I screeched up to the parking lot, dashed into Stage 4 where the first production meeting had been set, and found the entire cast assembled, listening to Jed Roberts read the script. He looked up as I entered, then turned back to the script and continued as if I did not exist. He read well. Roberts had been an actor, both on the stage and in pictures, before he took up directing in the late '40s. The cast of *Chicken Run* was excellent, as I knew before today, and I was ashamed to be late in their presence. Diana and I had the two juvenile leads, as the rebellious kids who try to find on the dangerous drag strip the acceptance they lack at home. Todd Green played my father, and Norma Byron was my mother. Green reached fame during the war in a series of wild comedies that established him as the successor to Harold Lloyd, and now openly admitted his middle age by accepting character roles. Norma Byron once ranked third in popularity polls, topped only by Mary Pickford and Lillian Gish, and had made the changeover from young leading lady to mature actress with grace and wit.

Roberts finished the script, put it down and asked, "Are there any questions? Any sequences that bother you? This is a group enterprise, and I want all of us to be happy in what we do." No one spoke up, so he continued: "All right. Marvin Hopper—Marvin, stand up—Marvin is our assistant director. He has your rough shooting schedules already made out. Marvin will see that you all are given the most reasonable calls we can arrange. If you aren't on camera until after lunch, you won't be asked to be on set in the early morning. But please be on time when you are called. Each hour of unnecessary delay costs the studio more than five thousand dollars in overhead and salaries. This is a business that is also an art. I believe it can be both successfully. But only with your fullest cooperation. May I say also that I am delighted, in every case, with the cast I have been assigned on this film. Together, I believe we will make a film we can all be proud of creating. See Marvin for your schedules, and if you have any problems, come directly to me. Mr. Lewis, would you remain for a few minutes? I'll join you as soon as I finish with Mr. Fleming." Jed Roberts left as most of the cast gathered around the thin, boyish assistant director. I went over and sat beside Diana. She drew back from me a little.

"Gee, honey," I said, "I wish you could have stayed. It was a ball."

"John Calvin Lewis," she said tightly, "unless I am willing to do anything you want, I'll never reproach you for what you do when you find *me* unwilling. But please, stay away from me until you take a shower. I can smell her on you!" She jumped up and went over to Marvin, and I sat there feeling sillier than ever.

A little later, Jed Roberts came back and sat near me. Sandra's perfume didn't seem to bother him. What did was my tardiness.

"Johnny," he said, "let's not begin badly. I admit, I resisted you for this film. But having seen your work in *Paradise Gate,* I believe you will do a splendid job. I know also that you are ordinarily punctual, and I apologize for seeming to make an example of you here today. In truth, that was exactly what I was doing. I know I may never have to worry about you being on time again, but I wanted the rest of the cast to see that this is one point on which I must stand firm. Please forgive me."

"No sweat," I said. "I *was* late, and it was all my own fault, so nobody's mad at you. And in case you're worried, the trouble I had with Newman was a personal matter. It won't happen again in a milion years."

"Good," he said, sticking out his hand. "I'm very glad to be working with you, Johnny."

"Likewise," I said. Then I headed for my dressing room and took a long, hot shower. When I emerged, in clean khaki pants and sport shirt that had been hanging in the closet, I wandered out into the studio and was surprised to find Diana still there.

"Can you give me a lift?" she asked. "Mama brought me here this morning, and she thinks I won't be through until five."

"You're not mad at me?"

"Not really, Johnny. It's partially my fault, as I said. If I wouldn't go to your party, I have no right to be angry because someone else did. Just don't flaunt her at me. Please, Johnny, be kind to me. I need kindness more than anything."

"You also need some lunch," I said. "Do you realize we have a whole afternoon ahead of us before Mama shows up on her fire-breathing dragon?"

"She's not so bad," Diana said. "Not when you know her."

We headed down to the Farmer's Market, on Fairfax and 3rd Street, and stood in line to have tacos and enchilladas at one of the little booths. There wasn't any beer, so we both had iced tea and Diana laughed when I pretended to burn my mouth on the glass.

"Mama's just old-fashioned about so many things," she said. "Most of it is left over from my father, who came over from the old country in 1924 and never really accepted his life here. When I got into pictures, we had to go out a lot. I remember one time when Randolph Scott picked me up for dinner before a premiere. I was only eleven, and Mama and Papa were dressed in their most elegant formals, and we went to the Brown Derby for dinner, and all during that wonderful meal, with Mr. Scott being so charming to all of us, all Papa could do was complain that he wasn't able to get chicken livers the way he wanted them. I don't think he ever got over being a Pine Street tailor. He was happy there, cursing at Brooks for stealing his narrow shoulders. Out here, even with all the money and the servants and all, he was a lost little man. I really believe, Johnny, that Mama hangs onto so many of the old habits just because they were *his,* and by doing that, she's still hanging onto *him.* "

"I'm sorry," I said. "I don't really mean to make fun of her. I guess I want her to like me and it bugs me that she won't."

"She will," Diana said. "Give her time. She may be old-fashioned, but she is very realistic, too. She didn't want me to do this picture, but when she saw how my mind was made up, she submitted gracefully. It's all in how you handle her."

"Well, what shall we do now?" I asked. "Having blown a dollar seventy, I think I am entitled to the rest of your afternoon."

"That seems fair, sir. I am at your command."

We wasted the whole rest of the day, doing nothing. We drove down to Malibu and looked at the water, and stopped in at a Playland and shot pool and pounded on the pinball machines. The sun was warm and the sky was clear, and there was no smog at all. We seemed to be always eating. Hot dogs, ice cream, candied apples. I learned that she did not drink, and so did not want to drink myself. I let her drive the Porsche for one hair-raising mile along the beach road, and decided then and there that she had better stick to her knitting.

It was a warm and glowing day, a day of happiness such as I had not known for years. Our bodies and our souls grew closer together as the hours wore on, and when evening came, we stopped in a cafe and Diana telephoned her mother. The old bat was obviously upset, judging from Diana's side of the conversation, but my girl held out, and we wrangled another few hours together for dinner. I took her to Don the Beachcomber's and we ate until we were unable to move, and in celebration, she had her very first drink of her life, a Mai Tai, while I had a zombie. The rum worked its effect on both of us, and I managed to miss the turnoff into Laurel, and soon we were zooming up into Coldwater Canyon.

"Come on in," I said, "just for a minute."

"I shouldn't," she said. "But I will. I want to see where you live."

She shook her head over the noose. The smartest thing I had ever done, I knew now, was to hire the maid to come in every morning, so the most obvious remnants of the party last night were all gone, the bed was made and the ashtrays near it were empty of lipstick stained butts. Still, the place reeked of cigarette smoke and liquor. I turned on the hi-fi and she sat near me and we twined our fingers together.

"Poor Johnny," she said. "You're really not as awful as they say. You're just a boy, not much older than I am, and you're trying so hard not to let all this go to your head. Why do people have to be so cruel?"

"What people are you referring to?"

"Oh, just—people. Everyone hates success, you know that. Especially people who have tried to make it for so long without succeeding, and then along you come, the golden boy, and reach the top in a matter of weeks. I envy you myself. Not only your achievement, but the way you seem to handle it. Even though I grew up in the business, I find your interviews fascinating and am amazed at how well you handle those writers. They leave me a quivering wreck."

"I don't know," I said, "I just made up my mind not to tell

them anything I didn't want to. It seems to work all right."

"But the way you treat the columnists! Why, Hedda Hopper thinks you're a monster. Is it true that you actually spit in her eye?"

"Of course not. It was Robert Taylor's eye and it was only a photo. And, besides, I wasn't mad at her. One of these days I'll straighten things out there. She didn't understand what I was up to, that's all. You see, I don't know if I can really explain it, but I honestly think that my own personal life is my own, that it should not be merchandised to sell me, and the picture. To me, that's cheating, sending people in to see me because they think I'm some kind of a nut, or because they're fascinated by my childhood, or whatever. After all, it's what I *do,* what they see on the screen, that counts. Or should count, anyway. I agree with Roberts. This may be a business, but it should still be an art. And as an artist, I reserve the right to my privacy, at least, as much of it as I decide I want to keep. What's so new about that? Brando did it."

"And they're saying right now that you copy him."

"That's a lie! Marlon himself said so."

"And I agree, dear. But you have to remember that most people don't know you as well as Marlon does, or as I do. All they see is what you appear to be. And more and more, you appear to be the deliberate rebel, laughing in the faces of the very people who have brought you success. That, plus those jealous ones who would resent you if you were Saint Joseph himself, could mean trouble."

"Hey, pretty girl, stop being so serious, huh?"

"It's only because I like you, Johnny. I don't want to see you hurt. You're so innocent in some ways. You don't know what really goes on out here, do you?"

"I know that all the girls talk and talk and talk, when all I want to do is. . . ."

"No, Johnny. Not there."

250

"You feel so warm and cuddly."

"And you feel so fast and fresh."

"Just for a little while."

"Mmmmm. I shouldn't let you do it. But it's so much fun."

"Move your leg. That's right. Now, don't tense up. I'm not going to hurt you."

"Johnny, be kind to me."

"Diana, I think I love you."

"And I think I love you too, Johnny. But don't be rough, be kind to me, please be kind."

"Hold me there."

"Oh, Johnny. . . ."

"Lift up. Yes . . . yes, like that. . . ."

"Oh, darling, we shouldn't. . . ."

"A little higher . . . don't be afraid. I won't hurt you, don't be afraid. . . ."

"You'll be kind, won't you, Johnny? Johnny? What. . . . What's wrong, dear?"

"Nothing."

"Why did you stop? Why are you hitting yourself? Don't hit yourself, darling, please, it hurts *me,* don't hit yourself. Why are you so angry? Is it me? Did I do something wrong? If I did, please forgive me, I don't know very much yet, but I'll learn for you, darling. Johnny, what's wrong?"

"Nothing," I repeated, cursing my suddenly unwilling flesh. "Come on. I'll take you home."

Much of *Chicken Run* was shot along Ventura Boulevard, where the real drag races often took place late at night. The title referred to a little game the local kids had invented in which two drivers headed right down the center lane, directly at each other at sixty miles an hour, and the one who veered away first was the chicken. Most of these drag strip sequences were shot at night, and since there was no back lot available that matched the real Ventura site closely enough, a monumental traffic jam developed along the boulevard that lasted until the film was finished. The key scene was one in which Diana and I played chicken with one of the hottest drivers from Hollywood High School. Actually, stunt drivers were supposed to fake the shot for us, but when I insisted on doing my own driving, Roberts had to agree, since there were around fifty reporters taking down everything we said. The sequence was a simple one: my car was supposed to head directly for the other one, and at the last minute, he would veer off. I had a talk with the stunt man who would drive the second car, and we made a private agreement to have me cue him with my headlights when he should turn away. There were automatic cameras mounted in each car, two stationary cameras on one side of the road, and a fifth camera in a helicopter that would track along with the vehicles. There would be one take, and one only.

All of the buildup to the chicken run had already been shot at the studio, so all there was for me to do was get into the car, strap myself in, and take off. The sequence was merely to record the action of the cars themselves, and so I was surprised when the other door opened and Diana slipped into my car and began strapping up.

"Get the hell out of here," I yelled. "This is no place for a girl."

"Well it sure isn't any place for *this* girl," she said, "considering that I get sick on a merry-go-round. But unless you get out, I stay."

"What the Christ are you trying to do, blackmail me?"

"No, Johnny," she said. "If you really have to do this yourself, go ahead. But if you do, I have the right to be with you."

"Suppose we crack up?" I asked. "You could ruin your face."

"I suppose yours is made of sheet metal."

"Diana, please get out. I can't do a decent job with you in here. I'd be too busy worrying about you."

"Don't worry about me. I've got the same chance you do. Are we going? They're waving the flags, and here comes the helicopter."

"You little bitch!" I screamed, unsnapping my shoulder harness. "Okay, you win. Get the hell out. I'll let the stunt man take it."

We both crawled out and the stunt driver slipped under the wheel. Time was short, because all cameras were rolling now. "Smart kid," he muttered. "This is rough enough for professionals." I cussed at him a little, and then he was screeching off down Ventura, toward the lighted area where the cameras were waiting. The helicopter wheeled off after the car. Diana and I stood close together, watching, as the straight pipes growled in the night, and as the other car appeared around a distant curve. The two machines got closer and closer to each other, and then both entered camera range, and the helicopter moved closer to my car, the huge camera snout peering down at the road. I could hear the drivers shifting gears as the cars drew nearer to each other, and then in one horrifying second, as they were almost upon each other, I heard brakes scream and both machines started to veer but it was too late and the left fender of each car struck with a shower of sparks and both spun wildly and flipped up and over and turned end over end, down Ventura with a clanging smash of metal against cement. The other car rolled up against a parked truck and as its door was flung open, I could see from the corner of my eye, the driver struggling out. But my stare was full on the other car, the one I should have been driving, and just then it hit a dip in the road and seemed to leap high into the air, and as it fell to earth again there was a whoosh of sound as the gas tank exploded and over the roar of the flames and the crash of metal, I could hear the distant, horrifying, helpless screams of the driver as the car was filled with flaming gasoline.

253

"Oh, dear God," I said, "I forgot to tell him to blink his lights!"

The script writers took advantage of the accident, which had been captured completely by three cameras and partially by the camera of the unburned car. In my own automobile, both camera and film melted.

The final scenes of the picture became a corny hospital sequence, in which the boy—who had miraculously escaped from the flaming car—admitted his wrongs and promised to try and find the answer in his home and church instead of on a drag strip. I did the scenes numbly, unable to forget that the stunt driver had not been so lucky as the fictional character was made to be. And finally, after one tear-filled closeup with Diana clinging to me, Roberts called, "Cut!" and *Chicken Run* was in the can. I sat up and ripped the phony bandages from me and headed for my dressing room, Diana trailing helplessly behind.

Inside, I slammed the door and slid the bolt home, leaving her outside, and when I turned, Corley was standing there.

"You lousy bastard!" I screamed at him. "You *knew* that was going to happen up there on Ventura. You knew it, didn't you?"

He said slowly, "I knew that a stunt man had been killed making one of your pictures, yes."

"Why didn't you tell me? Don't you know that poor guy had a wife and three kids? How the hell could you just lay back and say nothing? You should have heard him scream."

"I did," he said. "But what could I do? It was history. It happened. How could I change it?"

"I don't know," I said. "All I know is I'm sick of the whole goddamned mess."

After a pause, he whispered, "So am I."

There was a knock at the door. I opened it, and Diana came in.

"Are you all right?" she asked.

"Fine," I told her, and we embraced. "Listen, let's go to my place and celebrate, huh?"

"Let's go to the Capri instead," she said.

Since that one night at my pad when I couldn't get it up, she had taken affectionate care not to be alone with me in a bedroom again. Some hot and heavy petting when we were parked had served to excite me, but it still took the inventive administrations of Sandra to bring about the climax after I had taken Diana home. Twice, Diana had almost trapped me by phoning a few minutes after I dropped her off, but I explained that I took long drives at night when I couldn't sleep and it satisfied her while making me feel like a rat.

"Isn't it delicious?" Diana said. "Knowing it's all over? No more six A.M. makeup calls, no more box lunches."

"Until the next one."

"Not right away, darling. I'm going to the Springs and lie by the pool for a week. Then I might bestir myself enough to lift a newspaper and catch up on Orphan Annie."

"Sounds lazy."

"Why don't you come with us, Johnny? We've got plenty of room."

"Just you and me and your mother?"

"Why not?"

"For one thing, you'd get up late one morning and find out she'd fed me down the garbage disposal."

"You've got to get to know her sooner or later, dear."

"I know. But let's make it later. Besides, I want to go down to Tijuana for the fights this Sunday."

"What fights? This is November, darling. The season is over."

"There's a benefit fight for the orphanage. It's the last of the year."

"Wonderful. I'll come with you."

"I'm riding the motorcycle."

"Brrr," she said, hugging me. "I'll wear my woolies." I started to kiss her, and there came a knock at the door. "Yeah?" I yelled.

It opened, and in stepped Jean Billingham. I had forgotten how small she was, and the last time I saw her those flecks of gray certainly hadn't been in her hair. She hesitated, then stuck out her hand to Diana.

"Hello, Miss Cooper," she said. "I'm Jean Billingham. I wrote Johnny's first play."

"Yes, I know," said Diana, and at that moment I regretted having told her the truth about my days in New York. She took Jean's hand coldly, dropped it, and said to me, "I know you two will have a lot to talk about. I'll get Marvin to send me home in a studio car."

"No, please don't go," said Jean, catching on at once. "I only have a minute. I was in town talking to Warner's about my latest book and just had time to say hello to old friends. And now that I have, I must be on my way. Good luck, to both of you." She mashed my hand quickly and flitted out the door.

"So that's the fabulous Jean," Diana said. "How could you, Johnny? She's an old woman!"

"Don't let the gray hair fool you, sweetheart," I said. "Anyway, that was a long time ago. I'm hooked on younger chicks these days."

"You'd better be," she said. This time when she kissed me, she wasn't fooling around. Of course, that had to be when Marvin would come in, a bottle in his hand.

"Just passing out bury-the-hatchet drinks," he said. "But it looks like you don't need one."

CHAPTER
TEN

Early Saturday morning, both saddlebags stuffed with sandwiches and extra sweaters, we piled aboard the Harley and roared up Coldwater Canyon Drive, turned right on Mulholland and snaked our way through the Santa Monica Mountains. We found ourselves on Cahuenga Boulevard West and at the entrance ramp to the Hollywood Freeway and Highway 101, which would take us all the way to San Diego and beyond, to San Ysidro, the gateway to Mexico. It was still early, and there was a nip in the air as it rushed through my hair. Behind me, Diana sat easily on the buddy seat; her years of horseback riding paid off in ease and grace on the Harley. Her hands held my waist loosely. They wore light cotton gloves. "Better than leather," I had told her. "Leather will freeze your fingers off in ten miles unless you have cotton on under them."

Now, on the first Sunday in December of 1954, the California day would warm up as the morning shadows grew shorter, but right now both of us wore windbreakers and plastic goggles. With just over 3,000 miles on the odometer, the bike was nicely broken in, and felt properly free in all moving parts, without being too loose. Now, out of the city streets, I opened up the "snuff–don't snuff" baffles on the mufflers, and the deep song of the engine bounced off the concrete freeway walls and purred in my ear. Passing through Los Angeles, the pointed obelisk of the courthouse to our right, I found myself catching up with a highway patrolman on his own heavily-laden machine, complete with radio antenna and windscreen. I checked my speedometer, saw it was exactly on 60, so let myself creep up alongside him and past. I gave him a wave, and from the corner of my eye, saw him checking our speed, looking for signs of the bandit cycle clubs, and seeing none, wave back casually. We crossed the Los Angeles River, almost dry in its concrete bed, and turned right onto the Santa Ana Freeway. Soon we were in relatively open country, although the blight of the housing projects was starting to spread over the nearby hills.

I let her out to 70 now; that was actually the speed of the traffic flow, and the last thing you want on a bike is to have cars constantly passing you. I had learned a long time ago that the only way to ride a bike safely is to pretend it is a car. The hell with riding the shoulder so cars can get by in the same lane. That's just asking for some joker to brush you off the road with his rear fender. I staked out a claim in the exact middle of the lane, stayed far enough behind the forward car so I'd have time to stop if he jammed on his brakes, and tried to keep the ignorant bastards behind me from tailgating. That could be the most dangerous part of the ride, letting some guy get up close enough so he couldn't stop if you should go down. More guys have been run over after they successfully dumped their machines than have been killed by taking bad falls. My anti-tailgating maneuver was to signal for him to pass; if he didn't, I would slowly ease up on the throttle, until he would by Christ pass or else be going 30 miles an hour.

Soon we sped through Buena Park, home of the Walt Disney studios, and were approaching Anaheim, where the master of Mickey Mouse was building a huge amusement park called Disneyland. Now the sun was higher in the sky and the cars were fewer on the road, and the ride began to settle down into a kind of pleasant monotony. Every so often Diana would pinch my waist to let me know she was still alive, and once, as we roared along between two groves of orange trees, she leaned forward and shouted in my ear, "Oh, this is so wonderful! You miss all the sounds and the smells in a car!"

Past San Juan Capistrano, we turned down the hill toward the beach, past old San Juan Capistrano Mission, just as the bells were tolling the hour into the crisp morning air. The bike backfired several times as I eased up on the throttle and coasted down the hill into Capistrano Beach, and five miles further along the highway I turned off into San Clemente and parked at a diner.

"Let's get a little coffee," I said. "And a word of warning, if you want to wash your hands, this is the place. For the next thirty miles or so, we're inside Camp Pendleton and those Marines don't exactly have facilities for ladies."

"You make a terrific tour director," she said, nuzzling me as we went in. "I'll send all my business to you."

I sat at the counter and ordered coffee and Danish for both of us while she went to the john, and the combination of the beautiful morning and the delight of sharing this ride with her sent little goosebumps of pleasure springing up all over me. She came back and joined me and we sipped coffee and relaxed.

"Oh, Johnny," she said excitedly, "now I understand why

259

you love riding so much. It's so different from being closed up in a car, or even riding in a convertible. You're right in there with the sound and the air and the wonderful odors of the countryside. It's almost like flying."

"That's part of it," I said. "The rest is the riding itself. It's not like a car, where you just shove on the gas and steer. With a bike, you become part of the machine. You steer by leaning your body. You can feel the road through the tires as if they were part of you. A lot of nuts have given riding a bad name because of the cruddy things they do. But I think those same guys would still be cruds if motorcycles had never been invented. They'd be riding cars, or pogo sticks, or something. It isn't the bike's fault, what the nuts do."

We finished our coffee and got back on the road. Riding through Camp Pendleton, we could hear the Marines blowing things up, back in the hills. Soon we were through the military reservation, passing San Luis Rey, and were slowed up by the dozens of little beach towns as we got closer to San Diego. Encinitas, Cardiff-by-the-Sea, Solana Beach, all fell behind and then we were at Torrey Pines where I pulled off to a picnic area that overlooked the Pacific.

"Lunch," I said. Actually, the coffee an hour before had taken off the edge, but in the fresh air and surrounded by the rugged beauty of the sea and of mountains far to the east, we managed to do all right by the sandwiches and the thermos bottle of iced tea. "See?" I pointed, "Up there? That's Palomar Mountain, where the Palomar Observatory is. One of these days I'm going to head up there. They say the ride up the mountain from Rincon Springs is some trip."

"Good heavens," she said. "I think you study the road maps like you do a script."

"You're just about right," I said. "You can't take out a map and look at it while you're riding, so it helps to have most of the routes in your head."

"Do you think I could learn to ride?"

"I don't know why not. A lot of girls do. And you've got better balance and timing than most of them."

We cleaned up our mess and got back on the highway. Now we turned inland and soon were bypassing San Diego, its tall buildings sliding by on the right. We went through National City, past Chula Vista and at almost exactly 1:00 P.M. were creeping through the International Gate. We went across the long bridge over the dry bed of the Tia Juana River in second gear, and now the fetid odors and screeching sounds that swirled up around us were anything but pleasant.

"This isn't really Mexico," I told her. "No border town is worth a damn, and Tijuana is worth a little less than most. See those huts down there? They're made of cardboard and old tires. If a cloudburst ever comes up and fills this riverbed, they'll lose a couple of thousand peons pronto. And nobody will give a damn, that's the truth. The only reason for coming to a place like this is for the fights."

"I hope they're worth it," she said.

We turned left onto the main drag, filled with garish signs offering, "Lawyer," "Marriage and Divorce" and "Sexpot Girl Show." Every doorway was filled with slim, dark Mexican men in colorless sports shirts. They huddled in groups of three and four, and leaped forward to accost passing tourists with whatever specialty they had to offer. "Some of them have dirty pictures," I told Diana. "Some have Spanish Fly, or French Ticklers. All of them can take you to a girl, or set up an exhibition between a guy and a girl, two girls, a girl and a goat, or whatever combination you might want to ask for."

"Ugh," she said. "I didn't know people lived like this."

"You'd be surprised, honey," I said. "This is only what you see at one o'clock in the afternoon in broad daylight. Life is cheap down here."

I didn't tell her how cheap, though. I didn't tell her about the time I was offered a girl for three hundred dollars, a fantastic price in a town where five bucks was a top demand. When I wanted to know why she was so special, the pimp told that I would be allowed to mount the girl as she was strapped on a kind of leaning board over a sunken tub. And that as I signaled that my climax was approaching, she would be lowered, head-first, into the water, and I could complete my orgasm into her twitching body as she drowned in two feet of water. In case I was afraid of being cheated, the pimp went on, I would be allowed to cut her throat to be sure she was truly dead.

I had a brief vision of Diana being tilted down into the filthy bath water, her silken limbs twisting in a final spasm, and it shook me so hard that I almost ran down an old lady with a cardboard box on her head. She leaped out of the way and shouted curses after us as I turned up the hill to the small hotel I usually stayed at. Six blocks from the rickety bull ring, it offered indoor parking which would protect my Harley from the thieving kids who roam the streets day and night.

"Here we are," I said, pulling up outside the Hotel El Presidente. "The boy will unclip the bags and bring them up to our room. Or rooms. Whichever you say."

She looked at me and a little stab of fear passed through her eyes, then she said, "Don't they have a bridal suite, Johnny? With white sheets and a walk-in bathtub and mirrors on the wall?"

I nodded and kissed her as we went up the crumbling steps.

When we were in the room, I moved to hold her, but she pulled away and said, "Not now, dear. Let's go out and do whatever it is that visitors do. Let's buy junk and eat hot things and drink Mexican beer. Let's spend the day like tourists."

So we did. We started out by buying straw hats to keep the sun off; a plain, yellow ten-gallon job for me, and a colorful

262

woven one for her, with little bells strung from the brim, and black and green stitching around the edges. She tied it on with a blue and white drawstring and cinched in her belt another notch, and damn it all if she didn't start looking a little like Delores del Rio!

Since the dollar was better than gold in Tijuana, we didn't bother to change any money, but paid for everything with U.S. bills and coins. We strolled the wide streets, stopping in the doorless shops that lined both sides and examining the onyx chess sets and leather boots and beaten copper jewelry. In one shop, I bought her a little Aztec idol who seemed to be all eyes and mouth. He had a chain coming out of his ears and she hung him around her neck by it.

We stopped at a street corner photographer and had our pictures taken together, standing next to a donkey and with colorful blankets over our shoulders. The pictures were gray and dingy, but I gladly paid a dollar for the two and we carried them by the corners, still slightly damp, as we strolled up the street.

Harsh, jangling music followed us, flooding out of every door and up from every cellar club. Since it was Saturday, and the Navy was in town, the clip joints were in full swing, and standing at every door was one of the brown, mustached men in his colorless sport shirt, saying, "Come on in, senor, the show is just beginning."

"What kind of show is he talking about?" Diana whispered.

"Girl show," I said. "Strip tease. You know."

"I never saw one," she said. "Let's go in."

"You won't like it. It's all pretty crude."

"Well, if I don't, we can leave."

As luck would have it, we were outside the Bum Bum Club at that moment. While all of the joints operate wide open, the Bum Bum has a well-earned reputation for going a little further than most. "Okay," I said, taking her arm and leading her down the winding stone steps, "but remember, you asked for it."

Inside, the music was even louder. Three girls were on the arena stage, surrounded by tiny tables jammed up against its edge. I took a table further back and when the waiter came, ordered two Mexicali Beers.

Watching the girls, who wore G-strings and lace bras, Diana said, "I don't know what you were so worried about. This isn't so bad."

"Just drink your beer, honey," I said, "and hang on."

One music number finished and as two of the babes scampered off, the third began to strut along the edge of the stage, and the sailors in the front row set up a shout of encouragement. She whipped off her bra, and her taut breasts bounced with each step. Although the G-string did a minimum job of covering her pubic area, it disappeared into the crack of her buttocks and back there she might as well have been completely nude. The band struck up a driving tempo and the girl began swishing her behind in swirling circles, just inches above the faces of the men seated at the edge of the platform. They set up a yowl of anticipation, and when her posterior brushed against one swabbie's nose he leaped up screaming, "I'm gonna eat it! I'm gonna bite it to pieces!" His buddies screamed with raucous laughter and pulled him back down in his chair. The girl shook her finger at him over her shoulder, and continued her promenade around the stage, swishing her ass closer and closer to the perspiring faces. Eventually, she returned to the sailor who had shouted, and as the drums took over with a frenetic beat, she wiggled herself down with a screwing motion as if she were settling on a piano stool, lower and lower, closer to the bulging eyes and the dry lips licked by a nervous tongue, until suddenly there was a crescendo of music and she had pressed her bare

264

behind directly on his face. His hands crept around her naked thighs and pulled her closer, and now the music was only a throbbing pulse of the brushes on the snare drum, and I knew suddenly that this was no gag, that that sonofabitch had his tongue right in there and working and you could see it on the girl's face as she tensed her legs and settled down further. I felt a savage anger and I got up and dragged Diana to her feet. Her eyes were wide and fixed on the sight across the room. "Come on," I said, and when she did not seem to hear me, I yanked her after me and headed for the door. "Goddamn it," I yelled, "I said come on. Let's get the hell out of here!"

The sunlight on the street blinded us for a minute and as I waited to be able to see, I could feel my hands trembling. Diana caught my arm and pressed my hand against her burning face. "Why are you so mad, Johnny?"

"I'm not mad," I said. "I just don't like queers."

"Queers? But they weren't the same sex."

"What do you know about it?" I said, too loudly, and as she drew back with hurt on her face, I reached out and caught her hand. "Look, I'm sorry. I just don't like those kind of shows. Let's start back, huh? It's almost seven, and we ought to get cleaned up and have supper."

We got a cab and rode out to the hotel. Without speaking about it, we came to an agreement that happened naturally; I waited in the bar while she showered and changed, and then I went up and she sat on the small balcony while I took a quick shower and got into my clean khaki pants and the extra T-shirt I'd brought along. Somehow she had managed to pack an uncrushable linen dress in the bags, and with her hair down and fresh lipstick, she looked beautiful in the soft light of the sunset.

We ate on the terrace, sticking to simple foods that I hoped wouldn't disagree with us. With the meal, we had a white wine from Chile, and after it a Tia Maria for Diana and a double martini for me.

"Heavens," she said, sipping her liquor. "For a girl who never drank in her life, I'm rapidly becoming a lush."

"If Mama could only see you now," I said. It was the wrong thing to say. She gave me a sharp look and said little for the rest of the time we were at the table. Out by the pool, a string quartet struck up wheezing renditions of popular songs, and we wandered over and sat nearby. I ordered another drink and she had coffee. Twice, we danced, and her warm, full body felt just right in my arms. "I'm sorry," I said. "I didn't mean that crack. I know what it meant for you to come down here with me." She didn't answer, nor did she make any sound, but a hot tear burned its way down between our closely-pressed cheeks.

A little after nine, when we had both passed enough yawns, I got up and held out my hand. She took it, slipped her arm through mine, and we went up to the room. Inside, she clung to me and I could feel her entire body trembling.

"You go out on the balcony," she said, "and don't come in until I call you."

I sat out there, in the chill evening, and listened to the shouting mob going by a few blocks away. The language was foreign, but the drive and the goals were the same as the mob on Sunset Strip. Money and position and someone to scratch the itches of desire. I put my feet up on the railing and half dozed until I heard her voice.

"Now, Johnny. Now."

When I went in, the lights were all out. But enough filtered in from the window to let me see her standing near the bed. Her body was white against the shadowed walls, and I could sense, rather than see, that her two hands were crossed over her breasts. My clothes made an obscenely loud rustle as I slipped out of them and moved slowly to her. Her hands came away from her body and reached for me and then we clutched at each other savagely as our lips pressed together. I let my hands slide down her back and then the globes of her buttocks were caught in my grasping fingers and under the soft flesh the muscles tightened as she pressed up against me.

"Oh, Johnny," she whispered, "I want you so."

"I want you, too, Diana."

"Johnny," she said, "I'm not Diana. I'm Sharon."

"I want you, too, Sharon."

"Yes, that's good. Touch me there. And there. Oh, oh, you know just what to do."

"Lie down here, Sharon. That's it. No, be careful, not too much there! I'm too hot."

"You're so big. Is it possible. How can it ever fit?"

"It will, when you're ready. Maybe not all the way the first time."

"Oh, sweet Johnny, don't worry. I'm not a virgin. Physically, that is. The horses took care of that. There won't be a horrible mess and you can even ease your conscience because how do you know for sure that horseback riding is all I really did? And you're not the only boy I ever petted with, either."

"You're some woman of the world, huh? Did any of your nice boy friends ever try this?"

"What are you doing? Ooooooh!"

"Do you like it?"

"Oh, yes, yes! You make me feel like my body is one long string of nerves, and at the very end of them all, there is this little spot and your finger, rolling it back and forth and causing the spot to grow and swell until it is bigger than the world. Ohhh, yes, darling, yes. Let me do it to you."

"Not yet. First I want you to come. Have you ever come before?"

"I don't know."

"Then you haven't. Lie still, darling."

"Mmmm. It's starting to tingle."

"You're getting juicy. Listen."

"Oh, I'm so embarrassed."

"No you're not. That's the way it's supposed to sound."

"Do you love me, Johnny?"

"You know I do."

"Really? Enough to marry me? Mmmm! Did you hear me, darling?"

"I heard you. How's that?"

"Ummmm. Delicious! Yes, right there. Oh, oh, darling, what's happening? No, no, right there, don't stop. Oh my God, I never felt like this before. What are you doing to me? I can't get my breath, I'm going to faint, help, I'm dying, I'm— Aaaaaah! Oh! Oh . . . I'm scared, darling. Hold me. Is *that* what it is? No wonder people do it all the time. Oh, did I scratch you, dear? I'm sorry. I just went wild. Nothing has ever felt like that. It was wonderful, but it's over now, you can stop . . . Mmmmm. Why don't you . . . oh, Jesus, *here it comes again!*"

In the land of mañana, where clocks run slow and nothing ever happens on time, there is one thing you can set your watch by: four o'clock on a Sunday afternoon in the Plaza de Toros. When the minute hand of the big clock over the arena points at twelve and the little hand at four, you can stake your life on hearing the sharp blare of a trumpet, and the parade of matadors and their entourage will begin into the sand of the bull ring.

Sharon and I sat in the shady fifteen-dollar seats just alongside the presidente of the arena. We had slept late, exhausted by the long sequence of love play and the ultimate lunging of sex. I felt warm and pleased with myself. My old potency had come back in her arms, and there had been enough libido left over for an encore before lunch. As we climbed to the seats in the arena, she pressed close to me and whispered, "You awful man. I'm *raw!* But it feels good." Her fingers dug into the inside of my arm and when I turned to look at her, she gave me a deep, ecstatic smile.

The parade over, the men retired to their respective places and the first bull was released into the arena. He came out fast, and each matador in turn made a series of passes with the large cape. I only knew one of the matadors personally, Gabino Armaderiz, a 26-year-old who was born on the ranch of Piedras Negras, where some of Mexico's finest fighting bulls are calved. He was fighting second on today's corrida.

"Why are they all fighting the bull?" Sharon asked.

"They're not, honey. This is to get some idea of the way he charges, of which horn he favors. You see, until today, this bull has never seen a man on the ground."

"Why not?"

"Because bulls learn too quickly. By the end of the fight, this bull will be so dangerous that it would be sure death to let him recover and fight another matador. You may find it hard to believe, but on some ranches in Spain, it's legal to shoot a novillero if he is spotted on the land."

"What's a novillero?"

"He's a would-be matador. They sneak onto the ranches to get practice in fighting the real bulls. The only thing is, the bull gets practice, too. That's why they make it rough on the novilleros if they get caught."

Now the crowd started booing, and the picadors were riding into the ring on their heavily-padded horses. The bull spotted a nearby horse and charged it. The *pic* aimed his lance and drove it into the ball of muscle atop the shoulders and neck of the bull.

269

"What's he doing?" Sharon shrieked. "He's spearing the bull!"

"They have to weaken those back muscles," I said. "Otherwise, the bull would never get his head down, and the matador couldn't go over the horns with the sword."

The trumpet blared again, and the matador came out to place his own banderillas. "These do the same thing," I told her. "And they help correct against hooking."

"They look like little sticks with feathers on them," she said.

"Feathers—and barbs," I said. The crowd cheered as the matador did a skillful job of jabbing in the miniature spears. "Now comes the last act. See that little red cape? It's called a muleta. It's windy out there today, so he's wet it down to keep it from flapping. Now, every one of those passes he's doing has a name. The closer he works to the bull and the slower he works, the better it is. Notice, the bull is getting tired. And he's getting dangerous. Instead of reacting, he's starting to think. It's up to the matador to know the exact moment to complete his passes and line the bull up for what they call the moment of truth. That's when he goes over the horns with the sword. Now!"

The matador had killed well. The blade drove between the bull's shoulder blades, severing the great artery, and the animal dropped in his tracks. The man strode stiff-legged around the ring, and by petition from the crowd, waving their handkerchiefs, was allowed to cut an ear of the bull.

"The better the fight," I said, "the more they let him have. A really great matador might get both ears and the tail. Not very often, he gets a hoof too. And very, very rarely, they award him the whole bull. That's only happened three times in the whole history of bull fighting."

"Look at the horses, dragging him off," Sharon said. "It's so sad. What do they do with him now?"

270

"He's too tough for steaks," I said. "They generally make dog food out of him."

"And you actually want to *fight* a bull?"

"Right. I think you have to test your courage every so often. That's the entire principle of bullfighting. Courage is everything."

"You've got plenty of courage. Why do you have to prove it?"

"You just do."

None of the fights that day were particularly spectacular. Gabino Armaderiz did well enough with his second bull to cut two ears, and that was fun for us because, spotting us in the crowd, he had dedicated the animal to Sharon by tossing his hat over his shoulder to her. "Now," I whispered, "if you were the kind of girl who usually comes down to these fights, you'd put your hotel room key in the hat when you toss it back to him."

"I'd be delighted," she hissed back, "but where would we put *you,* darling?"

After the fights, we went to La Casita Cafe, on 4th Street and had some of the juicy Mexican abalone and a couple of bottles of beer. When we were almost finished, Gabino entered and the crowd applauded him as he came over and bowed gracefully to Sharon.

"Exquisite," he said to me. "She is a flower of beauty."

He sat down and had a small whisky with us, refusing food.

"My stomach," he explained, pressing it. "After a fight, the muscles are so tight from crawling away from the bull that food is an abomination. Later tonight, I will eat."

"Do you mean you're afraid when you fight?" Sharon asked.

"Always," he admitted. "All fighters are afraid; those who are sane, at any rate. What would it all mean if we were not afraid? It takes no courage to sit on a veranda, and that is why no one pays to watch a man sitting on a veranda. But to gather your bravery up in your hands and throw it into the face of death, yes! That is why men face the horns. That is why your *caballero* here will one day face them, to test his soul."

"I just want to see what it feels like," I mumbled.

Sharon was full of silly questions about bullfighting, and I could tell that he enjoyed answering them. At every opportunity, he shaded meanings so as to put me in the best possible light, and I knew he was going far out of his usual way to be pleasant.

"To see the best fights," he said, "you must come to Mexico City. The ring here in Tijuana is bush league. But in Mexico City, the great fighters come to make their reputations. *There* is a corrida! Still, today's was not so very bad. I have seen some where the picador virtually murdered the bull with his lance to protect a cowardly matador. Forgive me, but your *touristas* do not know the difference. Such a picador would be driven from the arena in Mexico City."

Sharon said, "I'd like to see Mexico City. Who knows? Next year, if things work out."

"Aha," he said, "a honeymoon trip? Then you must be my guests. Johnny knows how to contact me. In the spring, eh? That is a good time for Mexico City."

Sharon looked at me, waiting for me to say something. My lousy friend! He'd really put me under the gun. I took a final swig of my beer and stood up. "Sorry," I said. "Never happen. No honeymoons yet. I'm still a growing boy."

Sharon looked away.

"It's getting late, amigo," I told Gabino. "The lady and I must return to Los Angeles very early in the morning. If you will forgive us?"

"Certainly," he nodded, springing up to draw Sharon's chair out for her. "Will you be here for the celebration of Christmas?"

272

"I don't think so," I said. "I have to go to New York for the premiere of a motion picture. But I'll get in touch with you before the season starts. I haven't forgotten your promise to train me for my novillada."

"Nor have I," he said. "Adios, Senorita."

"Goodbye," she said in a small voice. Outside, we caught a taxi and rode back to the hotel. She didn't want another drink, so we went right up to the suite. "Excuse me," she said and went into the bathroom and shut the door. I turned on the radio and listened to a San Diego station for a little while. Except for the music, the room was ominously quiet. I began to get itchy. Finally I went over and knocked on the bathroom door. There was no answer. I knocked again, and when there was no reply, tried the knob. It was not locked. "Hey, Sharon?" I yelled. Again no answer. I rattled the knob and, with rising panic, pushed against the door with my shoulder. It didn't budge. I drew back and gave it a good kick, smashing the heel of my shoe against the wood as hard as I could. There was a crunching sound and the door sprang open. "Sharon?"

She sat inside on the closed john, staring at me. Maybe she had been crying, but she wasn't now. As I half fell into the room, she made no move. "Sharon's not here," she said. "Not any more. Not to you."

"Look," I said, "I'm sorry. I was worried. You didn't answer me when I knocked. I thought—"

"That I had used your razor?" She shook her head slowly. "Never happen. Isn't that what you say to all your girls? You swordsmen? You cocksmen? You *liars*? Never happen! You aren't going to marry me, are you, Johnny? And you never intended to."

"How the hell do I know?" I said. "Marriage is a big step. Up to now I never figured on taking it. Now I don't know. Honey, I'm doing the best I can. But give me just a little time."

273

Coldly, she said, "No."

Paradise Gate was scheduled to open in New York City at the Astor Theatre on December 16, 1954. The first gala screening would be a benefit for the Performer's Workshop, with tickets going for a hundred bucks a whack. Half the name actors under contract to Argos were going to be on hand to act as ushers, in snappy uniforms with gold-plated flashlights. Fleming had ordered me to come to New York and cooperate with the publicity staff because, as he put it, "This is a New York type picture. Newman's a New York director and damned near every one in it is a New York actor. If you can't deliver New York to the box office, we don't have a prayer in Kansas City."

Although I did not really want to be separated from Diana, her attitude to me since our trip to Mexico had me puzzled and I figured a few days away from Hollywood might help me think. The long flight East was eased by a flask of twelve-year-old-Scotch produced from Ira Winton's briefcase. Ira was a studio press agent, and had been assigned to me for the trip and the premiere. He was a skinny guy in his late twenties, with heavy horn-rimmed glasses, a blonde crew cut, and a bitter sense of humor.

"Just think of it as taking medicine," he advised.

"What? The Scotch?"

"No, the interviews. Bitter medicine, that will make Papa Fleming healthy in the bank book department. Publicity sells tickets, Johnny. Sad but true."

"I don't object to publicity about the picture," I said. "But where the hell do those complete strangers get off asking me personal questions that I wouldn't even answer for a psychiatrist? What business is it of theirs?"

"The public is like that. If you're a nobody, they don't want to see you or hear about you or give you the time of day. But when you're somebody, they eat you alive. They can't get enough. You'll see. It's the price you pay for being a star. They make you a star, and they have a price for it."

"Suppose I won't pay?"

"Who knows? A few have gotten away with it. Not many." He handed me the flask. "Here, have another blast. Now, one thing's going to make you mad, I know that already. But I might as well warn you now. They're going to want to know about you and Diana Cooper."

"Know what?"

"Whether there's anything serious between you. If you're thinking of marrying her."

I sipped the Scotch, and realized that I wanted to talk about her. Ira listened, nodding when indicated, and refraining from comment.

"So, now I'm starting to see how wrong I figured her," I finished. "I feel about her in a way I never felt for any of the others. I don't know what love really is, I guess, but if this is it, I've got a good dose of it. Hell's bells, I miss her so much already that I'm almost tempted to go up and ask the pilot to turn the plane around."

"You could do worse," Ira said. "In this business, there aren't very many good ones around. But she's one of the best."

"Then why don't I jump at the chance to marry her?"

"Because you're scared of the responsibility," he said. "Just like I'm scared, and I'm working on my second time around, and like any man with brains in his head is scared. Marriage changes you, and maybe you're worried about what you might change into. If it was anyone else but Diana, I'd tell you, hell no, kid, you're too young to get hooked up with a full-time female. But I think she'd be good for you. You could sure as hell do a lot worse."

That was all of the conversation about her. Eventually we got on the ground at La Guardia, and there were about a million photographers with blinding flash guns, and reporters with microphones and, sure enough, the second question out of the darkness was whether or not I intended to marry Diana Cooper.

"No comment," I said.

"Does that mean you want the announcement to come from her?" another asked.

"Goddamnit," I yelled, "no comment means no comment."

"Knock off that profanity," said one of the TV guys. "Now we'll have to edit the film to get rid of it."

"Isn't that tough shit?" I said. The radio and TV reporters started hollering at me and Ira grabbed my arm and started to lead me through the crowd. The newspaper writers were angry with the broadcast technicians and there were signs of a free-for-all developing as we pushed our way through the mob. One of the TV reporters grabbed my shoulder and said, "Listen, punk, you'll get yours. We'll be laying for you."

"Take your fucking hand off me," I said, "or you'll be laying on your back."

He jumped back and started to square off, but two of his buddies grabbed him and held him. There was a studio car waiting outside the terminal, and we piled in and headed over the Tri-Boro Bridge into the city. The studio kept a suite at the Plaza, and I was whisked right by the desk without registering. By the time we got to the room, the phone was ringing, and sure enough it was Fleming who ate me out for five minutes. I promised him I'd try to be nicer to the press, but that I wasn't going to answer any questions about Diana.

"Very wise," he said, surprising me. I'd have imagined that any publicity she and I might get could only help *Chicken Run.*

The round of interviews went better during the next three

276

days. At Ira's urging I dropped notes of apology to the TV reporters I'd upset at the airport, and was rewarded by some moderately accurate coverage on the Late News programs. I made the rounds and looked up friends; lunched with Jerry Conklin who was putting on weight and who had a list of projects a foot long that wouldn't conflict with my studio commitments. One was so odd that I had to dig into it further.

"A night club act?" I said, over coffee. "What the hell's that?"

"All we do," he said, "is teach you to sing."

"So who wants to hear an eighty-year-old singer? Because that's how long it will take me to learn."

"Don't be ridiculous," he said. "Singing with a microphone is different. You don't need a voice. What you need is personality. And that you've got."

"So what? Why the hell would I want to sing in a night club?"

"Because that's where the big dough is," he said. "How about twenty-five grand for a week at a joint in Vegas? I'm not kidding, Johnny, that's the way things are going. People are getting money in their pockets again. And a lot of that money is going to be heading for the only gambling action in this country, the only legal action, that is. Night club acts in Vegas are going to be big business any day now, and I want you to be ready. No big rush; we'll talk the next time I'm on the coast. I know a voice coach who'll have you chirping like a bird in six months."

"I think you're nuts," I said. "But what the hell? I'm starting to think the whole *world's* nuts. If I can get twenty-five thousand bucks a week for crooning 'Avalon,' who am I to say no? Just so it doesn't get in the way of my real work."

"Guaranteed," he said. The check came and he handed it

to me. "Believe it or not, he grinned, "it's cheaper for you to pay it yourself. If I do, it'll just come back on your account, marked up forty percent."

I cursed a little, good-naturedly, and paid the bill. There wasn't anything new about this. I was getting used to paying bills. In Hollywood, the waiter just presented them to me automatically, unless there happened to be another, better-known, star at the table, in which case *he* got it. "The price of fame," Mickey Rooney growled at me one night when handed a tab for all the drinks the hangers-on had swilled down before he had joined the group. When I fought him successfully for the check, he looked at me with unconcealed interest and said, "Well I'll be damned. A real person hides behind those specs. You're all right, kid. Just don't let the bastards get you down."

In between interviews and meetings with Conklin, I went to the theater every night. Geraldine Page and Darren McGavin were appearing at the Cort in *The Rainmaker,* directed by Joe Anthony, and I sat in the third row, entranced by the production. Anthony had put together a magnificent supporting cast, including Cameron Prud'Homme as the father and Albert Salmi as the kid brother, but my eyes feasted on the magic Gerry Page brought to the role of the spinster sister. When McGavin put a tin funnel on her head and told her she was beautiful, she became beautiful, as if by magic. I went back after the performance and said hello to the playwright, N. Richard Nash, and then played the game of "Do you know so-and-so" with Gerry. Although we had never worked together, we'd met several times at parties, and I was amazed, as always, to see again how gentle and unaffected she was.

"Oh, Johnny," she said, smoothing off her makeup, "while you're in town, you just *have* to get down to the Theatre de Lys and see *The Threepenny Opera.* It will actually change your life! There has never been anything like it in the world."

278

I promised to go and then, before we went out to have a drink with Darren McGavin, she dug down into her huge purse and pulled out a little booklet. "Look at this," she said, "I'm an *authoress.*"

I looked at the cover, and saw I was holding a copy of *Off Broadway,* and the feature story was "Peanut Butter Sandwiches and Dreams," by Geraldine Page.

"Can I keep this?" I asked.

"Oh, sure," she said. "You'd be surprised, Johnny, how busy the Off-Broadway theater is becoming. And they're doing some really fine work now. But you be sure to see *Threepenny,* promise me."

"Cross my heart," I said. But I never did see it.

On December 15, the day before the premiere, I had lunch at the Theatre Bar with Tony Warden. When I asked how things were going, he said, "Not bad. I'm doing a Kraft next week, and one of the networks is talking to me about going on staff to work on something called 'Playhouse 90.' Have you seen Jerry Newman since you got back?"

"No," I said.

"He's married now, you know. Some photographer, you probably know her, Dee Dee Aldiss. She works for *Life.*"

"I used to know her," I said.

"That's right, she did that series on you when you went out West. And speaking of marriage, what's this I hear about you and that child star, what's her name?"

"Sharon Eisenberg?" I asked

"Who?"

"You know her as Diana Cooper."

"That's the one. The word is that you're pretty serious about each other."

"I guess we are, Tony. It's the first time, for me, anyway, and

279

I've been doing a lot of hesitating. You know the kind of life I've led. It's one thing to screw every cunt in sight, and another to settle down with a nice girl like Diana. I'm afraid, and that bothers me a lot, because I've never been afraid of anything else before. I don't know how to handle her. We went down to Mexico a couple of weeks ago, and it started out to be a wonderful weekend, except I ruined it at the end by not handling her right. Since then, she's been avoiding me. I get her old battle-axe of a mother on the phone and she tells me that Diana is out."

"What makes you think you have to handle her, Johnny? Why not be yourself and let whatever happens happen? That's always worked for you in the past. As for Diana being out, I have a hunch that unless you're willing to lead her to the altar, she'll remain permanently out, to *you* anyway."

"That's the feeling I get too. Jesus, what a mess. What the hell am I supposed to do?"

Tony beckoned for another round of beers and Patsy brought them over. "Do what you want to do," he said. "What else is there?"

"I think I want to marry her."

"Then get the hell back to Beverly Hills and do it before somebody else does. That is not exactly distress merchandise, you know. I bet she has them lined up around the block. I know Fleming was interested, before you showed up."

"Tony, you're a good friend. Why is it that I live in California, but all my friends are in New York?"

"Because you're the forerunner, my boy. Take my word, in five years, we'll all be out there. Live television is on its way out. Film and this new videotape process will take over, and then if you want to work you'll have to do it in California. Don't get lonely. We'll all join you soon enough."

We had a little too much to drink, switching to martinis in the late afternoon, and along about six, when it was already dark outside, we bundled up and strolled up to Broadway to look at my name in foot-high letters on the marquee of the Astor. Tony and I walked along the traffic island separating Broadway from Seventh Avenue, our hands jammed deep into our pockets, slushing through the dirty gray snow.

"How does it feel?" Tony asked, nodding toward the marquee.

"I don't know," I said. "I honestly don't feel a thing."

Then I heard the featherly flick of a camera shutter, just inches away.

"Beautiful," said Dee Dee's voice. "Hold still for one more." The camera clicked again and she came up close to the fence, a stout, middle-aged man with her. "Johnny, this is Harry Fine of the *News*. We've been looking for you all afternoon."

"Nice to see you again, Dee Dee. But aren't you a day early? The premiere isn't until tomorrow."

"Oh, we'll leave that up to the critics," she said. "The story we're on is your reaction to the news."

"What news?" asked Tony.

"You're Tony Warden, I remember you," she said, clicking away as she talked. "What news? Don't either of you read the afternoon papers? Why, the news that Diana Cooper is getting married tomorrow. To B.J. Fleming, head of Argos Films." Her voice was as cold as the shutter click of her camera. "Oh, dear, Johnny, do you mean you didn't *know?* And to think I had to break the news! Hold still, love, for just one more." The Leica clicked again and as I started to stride off, Tony following hesitantly, she called after me, "Better luck next time, darling!"

Weather problems in Chicago delayed my flight for five hours, and now my dawn arrival was getting closer to 10:00

A.M. California time. I had called ahead from Chicago, and hoped that when we touched down in Los Angeles my Sunset Strip friend would have been able to open my garage and get out the Harley. I would have preferred the Porsche, but the extra keys were locked up in the house and I was afraid the cops might prevent any successful break-in.

We landed and during the taxiing to the ramp, I slipped off my seat belt and headed up to the door where the stewardess waited.

"Sir," she said, "you're supposed to remain in your seat—"

"So sue me," I told her.

"Oh, Mr. Lewis. I didn't recognize you."

"Sure, sugar," I said. "I'm in a hurry. I don't suppose you're staying at the Roosevelt tonight?"

"No," she said. "But you could reach me at the Sportsman's Lodge."

"Who would I ask for?"

"Linda Burke."

"Hang loose, Linda," I said. "I just might call you for dinner."

"I already have a tentative date," she said.

"That's your problem," I said, hating myself as the door was pulled open.

The ramp was already in place and as I ran down it I asked myself, what the hell are you doing? Lining up a girl for the night when you've just flown coast to coast to see your real girl, the one you love? *What's wrong with you?*

My friend was waiting for me inside the gate. "The Harley's out front," he said. "In the No Parking zone. There's probably a ticket on it."

"Who the hell cares? Here. Take these baggage checks and when you pick up my stuff, drop it off at the studio. No, wait a minute. Not there. Take a cab and dump the stuff in my garage. Here's twenty bucks. And thanks, kid." He was still babbling his thanks at having been asked to help when I took off down the corridor. A cop was just writing out a ticket when I burst out the door and started to get on the machine.

"Hold on, buddy," he said, "I'm sorry, you overstayed the three minutes parking. I got to give you this ticket."

"I'm in a real hurry," I said, pulling out my wallet. "Let me pay you the fine."

"None of that," he growled, and then looked at me closer. "Say, ain't you Johnny Lewis, the picture star?"

"That's me. Please, officer—"

"Okay, what the hell," he said. "Take off. I read about your girl marrying that big shot. But watch yourself on the freeway. There's been some rain on and off and the pavement's slick, especially in the low parts."

"Thanks," I said, and kicked the starter. The bike roared into life and I booted her into first, shot forward and lifted the kick stand at the same time. I was in third and still accelerating before I reached the turn at the end of the loading ramp.

I got on the San Diego freeway and barreled along at 70, past Culver City and Mar Vista. In West Los Angeles, I turned off onto Santa Monica Boulevard, and headed for Beverly Hills. The sun was out, but there were rain puddles on the road. My travel-stained suit was splattered with mud and water thrown up by the skidding wheels. Twice, I felt the rear wheel going, and barely managed to keep from going into a slide.

I made it all the way to my turnoff at Beverly Drive, which would take me up to Laurel, and then went into the turn too fast for the road. The rear wheel went out from under and I just got my leg up as the machine dumped and screeched across the concrete, with the motor running away. I rode the sliding machine like a carpet for a few yards, then it dug in and flipped and threw me free and I landed on my back and shoulders and

283

rolled into a storm drain. The Harley coughed and died, and some kids came running out of a nearby house yelling, "Hey, mister, are you okay?"

My jacket was torn down the back and I had a good case of road rash on both forearms, but I didn't seem to have any broken bones. I limped over to the bike and grunted as I lifted it up and examined it for damage. One handlebar was bent out of shape, and a footpeg had been doubled up, and all the paint was ground off on the left side of the gas tank, but she seemed to be all right. I kicked her over twice, and she caught then, and seemed to be missing slightly in one cylinder but otherwise all was in order. The kids looked after me as I roared up Beverly Drive, heading for Diana's house. There were cars parked bumper to bumper along both sides of Laurel, and I could see a big tent out on the back lawn. I pulled up near the driveway and sat there for a minute, goosing the engine with the throttle grip. Two photographers came over from a nearby car and started taking pictures of me. I wanted to belt them, but instead managed a smile and asked, "What's the story, fellows?"

"The ceremony's taking place right now," one of them said. The other just kept shooting away with his 4x5 press camera.

I put the bike in neutral and opened her up, *va-rooming* exhaust noises bouncing off the nearby houses with barking echoes. The cameramen had stepped back, fearful that I might run over them. The front door of the house opened and some-one came running across the lawn. It was Marcel. "Here," he said, "you'll have to stop that. We can't hear a word of the . . . oh, Mr. Lewis. We didn't expect you."

"I'll bet," I said. "What's going on in there?"

"The ceremony is almost over," he said, folding both hands piously.

"Swell," I said, and opened the throttle until the engine threatened to come off the mounts. Marcel stepped forward as if to stop me, and I kicked her into first and let off on the clutch and he let out a shriek and took off across the lawn, with me and the big Harley hot in pursuit. His foot slipped and he fell, crying out in terror, and I steered around him, goosing the bike as I went past to give him a faceful of grass and mud thrown from the rear wheel. Then I found myself near the edge of the house, and there was enough room between it and the privacy hedge for me to get through, so I roared into the back yard and crashed through the canvas of the caterer's tent. It ripped easily, and I was brushing along the edge of a row of folding tables that collapsed as the bike hit them, spilling dozens of pretty little Cornish hens and plates of potato salad onto the grass. Ahead of me was the huge, white wedding cake, on a cotton-draped pedestal, and high on its top, two little figurines of a white-gowned candy girl and a man in a top hat. I hit it head on, and cake flew every which way, amidst the shrieks of frightened waiters and the curses of two private policemen who started chasing me as I finished skidding through the mushy remains of the wedding cake. I tried to make a clean exit through the canvas side of the tent, but hit a pole instead and barely managed to stay erect. Then I ripped out into the open, and behind me the big tent quivered and settled slowly onto the ground, flat except where the writhing shapes of trapped waiters could be seen. I skidded around and made out through the gap between the house and the hedge, almost clobbering Marcel who had started into the walkway to see what what was going on in the back yard. He dived into the hedge for safety, and I burst out onto the front lawn which was becoming filled with wedding guests and photographers. I brought the Harley to a stop near the front door and ignored the jabbering questions hurled at me by the reporters. Finally the door opened and Mrs. Eisenberg appeared, regal in her pearl-encrusted black dress.

"My son-in-law, the well-known B.J. Fleming, wanted to

come out and beat you up," she said. "Except my daughter was afraid he might lower his dignity by touching your filthy hide. But unless you leave this instant, we will call the police and prefer charges and *have you put away!*"

"I was just going, old lady," I said. "The hell with all of you, and that goes double for your daughter."

I kicked the machine into gear and headed for Sunset Boulevard. The tears were so hot in my eyes that I could barely see the road.

Naturally, I was suspended from the studio while the lawyers munched their way through my contract to see if there was any legal way they could hang me by my balls over Fleming's overtime clock. But the upshot was that any more publicity might hurt *Chicken Run,* and it all faded away except for a $2,700 tab for damages that I had to pay to the caterer. Fleming was going to make me sit on my ass without working until my contract ran out, but Jerry Conklin put a stop to that, and it worked out that I would probably be used for loan-outs until some contract settlement could be made.

I *did* call little Linda Burke at the Sportsman's Lodge, and we ended up in the sack just as I knew we would, and when I realized my old impotency was back again and tried to get her to perform in the only way I could stay interested she backed into a corner, whimpering, and I finally had to put her in a taxi and send her home.

Christmas came and went and on New Year's Eve, the phone rang. It had been silent recently, as news of Fleming's displeasure had leaked through the film community. Only the rave notices *Paradise Gate* had received kept me from being exiled to that never-never land reserved for fallen angels and out-of-favor stars. I answered the phone, and it was Sandra Vidor.

"We're going to fuck in the New Year," she said. "Why don't you come over?"

"Why not?" I said. Fleming and Diana were off in Hawaii, on their 'honeymoon. I'd had two calls from Jean Billingham, neither of which I returned. My relations with the studio were still strained, since few on salary there wanted to be seen talking with me, and for the holiday season I had been more lonely than ever before in my life. My father called me and asked me out for Christmas, but I begged off, and spent the day lying in bed listening to the radio. Now, the promise of some action was enough to pry me out of my depression.

There was some talk around town that I might be going into Sam Merridith's production of the Pulitzer Prize novel, *Texas,* but outside of vague hints in the columns, there was no confirmation of the rumors. Conklin advised me to lay low and let everything blow over. "After all," he said, "half the big names in Hollywood lost their wedding lunch, thanks to that goddamned machine of yours. You're not too high on the popularity list right now. But wait until the returns start coming in from *Paradise.* You know, Ira Winton got fired on account of your shenanigans back here. So I hired him at two hun a week to handle you on a personal basis. He thinks there's going to be a big teen-age following busting out any day now."

"Teen-agers? What the hell do I care about a bunch of kids!"

"Don't knock it until you've tried it," he said. "It's the teen-agers who are going to the movies these days. If they swing for you, you're in."

I grumbled a little through my new teeth, which were now all freshly capped by the dentist, but agreed to hang loose for a while. Now, at the low point of my loneliness, a New Year's Eve at Sandra's didn't sound too bad. I decided to use the Porsche, in case I would be bringing someone back with me who might not like the idea of straddling a bike in an evening gown, and about nine o'clock I headed over to Sandra's place. The bash was already in progress: the windows were open and bongo noises spilled out into the warm California air.

287

Sandra had used her weird props to turn the apartment into a funeral parlor, complete with coffin and embalming instruments. The beakers were filled with vodka instead of formaldehyde, and the swizzle sticks were contained in a genuine human skull.

It was the usual crowd of minor actors, of over-groomed girls who aspire to film success, of writers hoping to get further than the patch jobs they now did on work created by other men, of exceedingly handsome men who usually turned out to be fags and who discussed the sex lives of prominent actors with the authority of those who had spent most of their waking hours under the beds in question.

I spent much of the evening sitting by myself, talking briefly to those who dropped over to my solitary post near the piano. Luckily no one there could play, so the big Baldwin remained silent. As midnight approached, and as drunkenness had already taken charge of the party, Sandra got up on the piano and stamped her foot for silence.

"Let's get this fucking party under way," she said. "In exactly two minutes, the lights are going to go out. I want everybody in dresses on this side of the room, everybody in pants on the other side."

"Oh, Sandra," squealed one red-headed girl in slacks, "what do *I* do?"

"You stay on the pants side," she was told. "Next time you'll wear a dress. Now, is everybody in place? When the lights go out, they will stay out until dawn, because I'm pulling the fuse and throwing it away. So make sure you get lined up with the one on the other side you want to start the night with, because it's going to be darker than a welldigger's asshole in here in just one minute from now. Get ready, 1955, here we come!"

I had my eye on a big blonde on the other side of the room. She had come in late and had spent much of the evening close by Sandra. I knew without being told that she had probably been invited to be my companion, and as I looked up at her over my glasses, she nodded and pointed toward a vacant corner. I turned my head that way and nodded myself, and just then the party started chanting, "Eleven-Fifty-Nine and 51 seconds . . . 52, 53, 54, 55, 56, 57, 58, 59—"

The radio burst into chiming bells and as a cry went up of, "Happy New Year!" the lights went out. I scuttled over into the corner and in a few seconds sensed movement near me, and sniffed a rich perfume and then the big blonde was in my arms. We clutched at each other, and kissed deeply, and a writhing tongue slipped into my mouth. I felt hard breasts thrusting against my chest, and as the kiss grew more passionate, a hand groped for my crotch and fumbled with my zipper. I stroked my own hand down over the heavy behind, ran it up the short dress, and froze suddenly with shocked surprise.

My big blonde was all boy.

Before I could pull away, a match flared, and Sandra was huddled close up against us. "Naughty, naughty," she said to me. "You weren't supposed to find out so soon. Come on: I reserved the upstairs bedroom for us. You come too, Holly."

Holly was the little redhead in slacks. I followed them up the stairs, still numbed by my discovery. The match flickered out, and a hand reached back and found mine and drew me up the stairs, through an open door which then closed behind us and I heard a lock click. Another match was struck, and a candle was lighted, and soft light rushed out to the corners of the room.

"What the hell are you up to, Sandra?" I said. She handed me a glass and just then a champagne bottle went *pop*, and as I turned my big blonde had opened it and poured some wine into my glass.

"I thought we'd swing the New Year in a new way," she said. "You know Holly. And this is Richard Devine."

"My friends call me Dick," said the big blonde.

"What do you think you're pulling, you mixed-up broad?" I yelled. "You know I don't go that route."

"There's always a first time," Sandra said, giggling into her champagne.

"You've got the name," said Devine. "You might as well have the game." He snickered and stroked his blonde wig. I felt sick to my stomach.

"Unlock the door," I told Sandra. "I'm getting the hell out of here."

"Later, darling," she crooned. "Have some more champagne." She poured some more into my glass from a second bottle. Involuntarily, I drank it down. "Who knows? You may like it."

"I know *I* do," chirped Devine.

I wanted to leave at that very second. But before I moved, I saw, in a haze of alcohol and a strange kind of fascination that clouded my brain, Sandra reach out for the girl, Holly, and in a frantic clutching they were wound up in each other's arms and kissing one another full on the mouth.

"Sit down, sweetie," said Devine, "and watch this. I mean, it really turns you on."

The two women fumbled with their garments and were naked as soon as they could rip the clothes from themselves. "Sandra," breathed the red-head, "let's sixty-nine."

"No good," said Sandra. "Neither one of us can concentrate that way. I'll do you, and then you can do me."

"All right," breathed the girl, "but hurry . . . hurry!"

As I watched, frozen in my voyeuristic fascination, Sandra lowered her head and began to kiss Holly's genitals. The act became more frenzied and deeper, and Holly threw her head

290

back and began to make spastic hissing sounds. Her fingernails clawed at Sandra's shoulders and at her neck, leaving red welts. Sandra slipped her hands under Holly's writhing buttocks and lifted the girl's lower torso into the air as she pushed her own head tighter and deeper into the trembling flesh.

"See what I mean?" said Richard Devine, putting his hand on my knee. I brushed it off, but I could not take my eyes away from the two women. Now Holly was panting and snorting in a frenzy of rutting that reminded me of nothing so much as the sounds the sow back on the farm made when Uncle Ray loosed the boar upon her. Her eyes rolled back in her head and as Sandra worked faster and deeper, with her two hands tightening on Holly's erect nipples, the redheaded girl let out a wail that sounded for all the world like she was dying.

"*That's it!*" she shrieked. "Don't stop. Eat me, chew me, swallow me up!"

"Oh, it makes me so *hot,*" whispered Devine. He had his own hand up his dress and I caught a glimpse of his swollen organ.

"Aaaaaah," gasped Holly and her hands beat against Sandra's head in a wild frenzy. Then there was quiet in the room, except for Holly's rasping breath. Sandra raised her face into view and turned to look at me.

"Doesn't that give you ideas?" she said.

"I'll do you first," said Devine, reaching for my fly.

"I don't know," I whispered. I felt in a daze. I was unable to make any decision, unable to stand up and leave this nightmare of a room. The metallic sound of the zipper jarred against my ears, and then, as if from a very far distance, I heard Devine's husky voice saying, "Look at that. He's all ready for me."

And, as I sank back onto a pillow and inched my way out of my khaki pants, Devine pulled off the blonde wig and I saw that he was completely shaven bald, and now his face had become very old under the garish makeup and behind the red lipstick. "I'll do you," he said, stroking my trembling legs, "and then you do me."

"Yes . . . yes," I said thickly. "I'll do you. . . ."

CHAPTER
ELEVEN

AS JANUARY unwound toward February, I spent more time with Dick Devine and less with my other friends. Indeed, I felt I had no friends any more, only the one-night stands he and I picked up cruising the Strip. We generally tried to go to his apartment near Hancock Park, since whenever our scores recognized me, there were almost invariably veiled requests for "loans" which were never repaid.

Two days after the party, I had turned up at Sandra's to be greeted with a bland look and an announcement that she had gotten "all I wanted out of the experiment. So I'm back to guys again." When I offered my own services, she gave me a wry look and said, "Sorry, Johnny. I don't sleep with fags." I leaped at her and hit the closing door with my forehead and collapsed backward in a blast of pain and shooting stars. When I got on

293

my Harley, I could see her, peeking out past the corner of a curtain. Then another shadow passed across the window and drew her away.

Jean Billingham called twice more, and I didn't return the calls. The studio sent my checks over by messenger, and I endorsed them and mailed them to the bank. Jerry Conklin phoned from New York and said he would be out in early February, and for me to do whatever the studio asked, but not an ounce more, which was fine with me since the studio was not asking anything at all. I saw in the paper where Mr. And Mrs. B. J. Fleming had returned from their honeymoon, and had purchased a large house on Holmby Avenue. I heard nothing from either of them.

One evening my phone was ringing when I got home, and when I picked it up, I heard Hedda Hopper's dry voice.

"Johnny," she said, "it's time you and I had a serious talk. I want you to come over, right away. Don't worry about how you're dressed. This is important."

"Sorry," I told her. "I don't have anything to say to you."

"Do you know where Tropical is? It turns off Benedict Canyon, just above Chevy Chase. I'm at 1708 Tropical. I'll leave the porch light on."

"Sorry, Hedda," I said, the alcohol and weariness fogging my brain. "I just don't see any point in bothering you." I hung up the phone, and crumpled down on the couch with my dirty jeans and T-shirt still on.

A ringing noise awoke me. I tried to force it away, but it continued. I struggled up from sleep and realized someone was leaning on the door bell. I covered my ears, but the sound would not stop, and finally I got up and staggered to the door and opened it to find Jean Billingham standing there. She pushed her way in, sniffed at my appearance and probably my odor.

"I got a call," she said, "from Hedda Hopper. She asked me

to get you over to talk with her, just the way I found you. But I can't inflict you on her the way you are now. Where the hell is your shower?"

I pointed to the stairs and she shoved me up them and into the stall and before I could stop her, turned on the cold water full blast.

"Might as well get out of your clothes," she said, "if you can call them clothes. Look more like old gunny sacks to me."

It got the water adjusted to a more comfortable temperature, and scrubbed myself down good with soap and a rough washcloth, and had to admit that it made me feel better. She had instant coffee waiting when I dried off, and had pulled out some clean clothes. I shrugged into them and sipped the coffee, holding the cup in both hands.

"My car's outside," she said. "I'll take you down. I doubt that you're in any condition to drive."

"I don't want to go," I mumbled.

"Tough," she said, helping me to my feet. A few minutes later, we were turning into Tropical, and I could see the porch light shining through the light fog that had come up in the early morning. "You go on up there and ring that doorbell," Jean told me. "I'll come on back in half an hour and honk the horn for you."

Feeling unsteady on my feet, I limped up the path to the porch, climbed it and touched the doorbell. Inside, chimes tinkled, and the door was flung open, and I recognized Miss Hopper even though the bright lights were behind her.

"Come in, Johnny," she said, and stepped aside to let me enter. She led me right to the kitchen, where a bottle of Scotch and a single glass sat on the table, and where a white enamel pot simmered on the stove. "Soup," she said, "and then Scotch. The soup to settle your stomach, the Scotch if you want it to quiet your nerves. I know you've been through a lot."

I sipped the soup out of a cup. She had some with me. She sat quietly, watching me eat, and when I had finished offered me a drink. I shook my head, and we went into the living room.

"Johnny," she said, "I don't know why you went so far out of your way to try to shock and offend me the first time we met—"

"Wanted to see if anyone in this town had the guts to write the truth," I interrupted. "You did. Admire you for it."

"It doesn't matter any more," she said. "What matters is that you are a bright, vital young talent. They don't come along like you very often. You're too valuable to destroy yourself. That's why I had to talk to you tonight, to tell you what I and your other friends know, and to offer our help. We all know about you and Diana. Good heavens, how could we help but know, after what you did at the wedding? But that's over, Johnny. You have to lead your own life, and it can be a tremendously exciting and fruitful life, if you don't let yourself get sidetracked by your temporary troubles. Now, all of us aren't blind. We know what you've been doing with yourself the last month or so. Hollywood is really such a small town. There are no secrets here. And while we tried to keep our noses out of your business, now that you've made your business *news,* there's no way we can keep your behavior a secret much longer. Unless you change it. Do you know I had a telephone call from Sam Merridith tonight, Johnny? He's worried about trusting you for the role in *Texas.* He asked me if I thought you could be depended on. And I had to tell him, 'Sam, I don't know. But I'll find out and call you back.' That was what I promised to Sam Merridith, who is one of the real gentlemen in this industry, and that's why I had to talk with you tonight. I think the role was made for you. But you can't go on location in Amarillo the way you are now. You must order your life, you *must,* or you're through in this town. You can go on to greatness, or you can wash it all out with liquor and stupidity. Which is it going to be? Take your time and give me your honest answer. Sam is waiting."

My first impulse was to tell her to mind her own business. Instead, I ran my hands through my hair and stared at the floor. Finally, I asked, "Can I have that drink now?"

She got up and made me a very weak Scotch and water. I took it and sipped. The alcohol taste almost made me nauseous.

"Look," I said finally, "I don't know what's happening to me. Everything seems to be out of control all of a sudden. The work used to be the most important thing. Now it's kicks, everything is for kicks."

"It has happened before," she said softly, "and it will again. This town is full of such tragedy. Young Wally Reid, dead of dope. Lupe Velez and Carole Landis, both dead by their own hands. I love this place, Johnny, but it is in many ways a place of insanity, where dreams become real. Making the dreams is your job. But please don't *believe* in them."

"I don't know how to stop," I said.

"We'll all help," she promised. "I talked to Lolly and Sheilah and Jimmy Fiddler, and they're leaning on the rest of the columnists. Up to now, so far as we're concerned, nothing has happened except that you're sad at losing your girl. From here on, it's up to you."

"I don't understand," I mumbled. "Why should you all go out of your way to do this for me? What did I ever do for you except spit in your eye?"

"You brought real talent to our town," she said. "We need more like you. Without more Johnny Lewises, Hollywood will become a factory for television. We can't afford to lose you."

"What if I let you down?"

"Johnny, let's get one thing straight. What you do in strict privacy is your own concern, not mine. *Until* it becomes a public scandal."

"Anything I can't do in public, I'm not going to do!" I said.

"No one's asking you to be an angel," she said. "If you get involved in girl-boy trouble, no one will write it up more gleefully or with less hesitation than I. Because that kind of trouble won't hurt you. It's the other kind that can spoil your life."

"In other words," I said brutally, "you're telling me I'd better stop eating cock."

She winced. "Oh, Johnny, why do you hide behind that wall? Why won't you let us help?"

"Nobody ever helped me before," I said. "Everything I got I got on my own."

"You know that's not true," she said. "Now, I've tried to be patient and understanding. If I'm getting through, it's worth the effort. But if I'm not—"

"Hold it, hold it," I said, lifting my arms over my head. "You win. I surrender. I just talk too much. Okay, I buy what you say. I don't know what's going to happen, but I promise you I'll cool it in public. And as for Sam What's-His-Name, you can call him back and tell him he's got nothing to worry about. I'm so hungry to go back to work I'll even sweep the goddamned studio floor for him. Okay? Does that make you happy?"

Her eyes were cool and intent on me as she answered, "I'd much rather have *you* be happy, Johnny."

Route 66 runs right through Amarillo, Texas, and it is an ugly scar in the desert, lined with filling stations and neon-lighted motels. The heavy, trans-continental trucks barrel through all day and night, their high stacked exhausts belching diesel fumes and slapping backfire echoes against the distant hills. The sun sears down all day and then icicles form on your chin when it drops behind the horizon. Downtown is a kind of modified Jersey City, with dime stores and drug counters and the people seem about the same, except most of the men wear ten-gallon hats and cowboy boots.

The *Texas* company arrived in early March, when angry patches of snow still skittered around as the northerly wind blew down from the Panhandle. By then, Jean Billingham and I had been ensconced in our cosy apartment near the stockyards for more than two weeks, and I'd already created my own claque of town people, guys *and* girls. *Paradise Gate* had played here in January, and the turnout when Jean and I got off the plane from Sun Valley was the first one I'd seen that I knew was real, truly for me and not gimmicked up by the studio publicity department. "Welcome, Johnny," read one sign, and others said "We love Johnny," "Amarillo High Welcomes You," and JOHNNY with a big heart drawn around it. Jean played it cool and stayed in the background while the local newspaper guys gave me the business, and I was courteous and helpful to them which seemed to surprise everybody, including Jean.

"No," I said, "the film people won't be coming for a few weeks. I just came on ahead so I could get to know you folks and the town. I want to feel like I'm part of Amarillo." That went over big, and so did the part when I read from a fan letter I'd gotten from a Amarillo high school girl, asking me to speak to the school assembly. Actually, it was Ira Winton who had forwarded the letter, along with suggestions about handling it, but it was Johnny Lewis who told the reporters, "I can't think of anything I'd rather do than address the student body. After all, it was only a couple of years ago that I was a student myself," and who got the enthusiastic applause from everyone in sight including one photographer who forgot himself.

I was tanned by the snow-reflected sun our two weeks on the slopes at Sun Valley had given me, and the liquor puffiness was gone. I looked good, and I felt good. The two weeks with Jean had gone better than expected. We wore ourselves to a frazzle every day on the ski run, fell into bed exhausted and got up in the morning ready to eat a bear. The little sex there had been was gentle and without intensity, although our last night at the lodge, stimulated by a couple of extra mulled rums, recaptured some of the old magic. Jean never mentioned the past, mine or her own, and I kept my own mouth shut too. Without saying it, both of us knew this was only an interlude, a resting time until I was able to cope by myself again.

Those weeks in Amarillo, we rode a good deal, and I got to know the city inside out. We sat in the little side street saloons, drinking Lone Star Beer and toasting chewing gum on the red-hot pot-bellied stoves, and laughing and joking like kids. I suppose I was like one of the walking wounded, able to get around under my own power but still needing treatment and care. Under Jean's cheerful eye, I felt the old randiness coming back and it was only through severe self-discipline that I kept my claws off the well-developed high school girls who plastered themselves against me at every possible occasion. Once, when I was sure the young lady in question was over the age of consent, since she was an instructor in gym and had been to college, I snared her out of the crowd and in the company of a bottle of Jack Daniels we took off like two rockets for the nearest motel. There weren't any preliminary mushings around: that girl wanted to get screwed by a movie star, and I was only too happy to oblige. Afterwards, she mentioned something about maybe coming to Hollywood some day, and I said to look me up, and she gave me a lift back downtown. When I turned up at the apartment after midnight, Jean was tight-lipped for a while, but that passed without a real argument and it was the closest we came to one until much later.

I kept in touch with Sam Merridith's office, and for a while there it looked like I was going to be teamed up with Joel McCrea and Barbara Stanwyck, but it finally shook down to Tom Fields and Marilyn MacArthur, both big names right then: Tom for his hard-hitting work in a series of adult Westerns and one Oscar nomination for his *Billy The Kid;* Marilyn for three box office hits in a row, playing the dumb blonde in what would have otherwise been a series of tasteless sex comedies. Her presence turned them into delightful satires.

Merridith was producing as well as directing, handling the whole thing through his own S. M. Productions, although his release would probably come through United Artists. Early in the negotiation stage, he'd told me, "Listen, kid, you wouldn't believe what Fleming's holding me up for your loan-out. And you won't see any of it, either, because I bet he's keeping you on your regular salary." When I agreed, he gave me a dig with his elbow. "Tell you what, Johnny, we'll ding that cockney bastard. For every day the picture comes in under schedule, you get a grand in cash, under the table. No one, not even Uncle Sam knows about it."

I shook my head. "I don't have to be bribed to do my best for you, Mr. Merridith. If I can get you in a day ahead, I will."

"Hell, I know that, kid. I wasn't trying to grease you. Okay, don't worry. I'll work something out so you get a few bucks without Fleming raking off his cut. Leave it to me."

One section of Amarillo, over on the far side of the Sante Fe tracks, was close enough to the nineteenth century period of the early part of the film that all it took were a few fixes on the store fronts and a temporary wooden sidewalk over the present-day cement one to turn the clock back more than half a century. The modern sequences could be made in the up-to-date part of town without change.

It's too bad it wasn't as simple for the three of us, Tom, Marilyn and me. We had to age around fifty years over the course of the film, and the studio edict was that the aging had to be glamorous. Instead of shaving off all my hair and sticking on false jowls, as I wanted him to, the makeup man's instructions were to make me 65 years old by touching up my temples with white and lightening my mustache and eyebrows! I hit the roof and refused to play the scene until Sam Merridith came over and laid down the law.

"You have to remember you're a star, not an actor," he said. "Paul Muni changed his appearance so much from picture to picture that to this day, he's never built up a following as big as the one you have right now."

"Muni? For Christ's sake, he's one of the best actors on the screen!" I plucked at my gently grayed temples. "If Muni were doing this part, you'd see the age in every pore. You wouldn't see someone *playing* an old man, you'd have a real one."

"Right you are," Sam said. "And the fans don't want to see a real old man. You put your finger on it. What they want to see is you, playing at being old. You have to remain you. If you change it to any significant degree, to where you're no longer the Johnny Lewis they came to see, they feel cheated and angry. I know it's false and that Muni's way is better art. But this isn't art; it's a commerical film that's costing me three million bucks, and I want to get it back."

"Well, I'll be go to hell," I muttered. But I didn't insist on the makeup. It looked like I was mellowing in spite of myself.

Early in May, Gabino Armaderiz turned up.

"Amigo!" he yelled, springing out at me from behind a camera truck as I left the location one evening. Merridith had decided to do all of *Texas* out of the studio, and instead of sets, we were shooting in real homes and other places rented for the occasion.

"Gabino! What the hell are you doing in Texas?"

302

"I had some business in Juarez. When I heard you were in Amarillo, I decided to come visit you, to see what this of the motion pictures is all about. After all, I may one day become a film star in my own country, when I retire from the bulls. Stranger things have happened."

"Well, boy, I'm glad to see you old buddy. It's duller than stale beer around here. Maybe we can liven it up."

"There is another thing. On July the Fourth, in the arena at Tijuana, there will be a *novillada* for beginners. The competition for the card will be heavy, but I am sure my recommendation would be enough. If you were ready."

"July? Jesus, that's only a couple of months away! How the hell can I be ready? I'll be stuck out here until the end of June."

"Suppose I remained here to work with you?"

"Would you? That's be great. But what about your own schedule?"

"I do not fight again this year."

For the first time, I noticed he was limping. I stopped short and he nodded.

"A bad one, in Monterey," he said. "It will take another operation to correct the muscle, which has shortened. So I will have time enough to stay here in Amarillo."

A bad one, he said, and that was all. Later, I got a copy of *The Bullfighter* and looked up the Monterey fight. Gabino had been badly gored, but finished the fight and was awarded both ears and the tail.

We began to work out, between takes. While I learned the lore of the bull ring, Gabino kept an observing eye on the technique of movie-making. At first, I got some ribbing from the crew and Tom Fields, in particular, as I flicked the cape at the boys we had hired to wheel the horns toward

303

me. But when I got in the corral with a young bull to try the passes on a living creature, their attitude changed.

"Come on in, Tom," I yelled, as the snorting animal's flank brushed against me for the tenth time.

"Never mind, Johnny," he hollered back. "It's all yours. I know when I'm out-classed."

Texas was going well. As the month of May passed and warmer weather came on, we were almost a week ahead of schedule, and Sam Merridith became expansive in his attitude toward the cast.

"Those studio bastards said we couldn't do it," he crowed. "Shoot a three-hour film in color and Cinemascope, completely on location? Impossible! Well, we'll show them what impossible is. And it's all thanks to you kids. I couldn't have done it without you and I'm grateful."

Since the film was in color, the dailies took two days to get back from Hollywood, so twice a week we would gather and look at two or three days' work all together. To do so, we had to rent one of the local theaters after their regular program, so we found ourselves staggering out of the movie house at one in the morning, blind with exhaustion and scheduled to go on camera at eight o'clock at least twice a week.

As I grew more involved with the film, and with the instructions from Gabino, I saw less and less of Jean. Oh, she was there, although she had sat out of the way on the location all afternoon, but I would realize that I had not spoken two words to her. Marilyn MacArthur and I began to play grab-ass, as we got a clearer reading on each other and liked what we saw, and one day when our love scene played longer than it needed—in fact, several minutes after Sam yelled, "Cut!"—Jean grabbed me when I returned to my trailer dressing room and gave me a wicked smash across the cheek.

"Hey," I yelled, grabbing both her wrists. "Don't bruise the merchandise. If you have to hit me, do it where the camera can't see."

"I'd like to bruise your balls," she said. "And I will if you don't stop rubbing up against that blonde."

"What's eating you? You act like we're married or something. Look, Jeannie, I know better than anybody how much you've helped me, and I'm grateful as hell, but—"

"Who wants your gratitude? I just want you to realize there are other things worth having besides a big pair of tits."

"Honey, I think you're just about the best goddamned dame in the world, and I always have. But you know what I'm like, so why don't you just accept it and take me the way I am?"

"If I'd just accepted it," she said grimly, "you'd still be blowing high school kids on Sunset Strip, you lousy little queer!"

So now it had come full circle. I had passed through the valley of my own despair, been dragged out of its dismal wastes by the love and care of my dear Jeannie, and—having reached the safety of sanity again— we were back to where it had all ended so long ago in Philadelphia when a drunken tramp excited Jean's jealousy.

She apologized for her "queer" remark before the night was over, and after we had made love and she slept in my arms, I lay there in the night and knew that things would never be the same between us again. The poison which had been expelled from my own mind had planted a tiny seedling in hers.

It was a long night.

The following morning we were scheduled to do a scene in downtown Amarillo. I got on the set early, and sat in my canvas chair and sipped coffee out of a paper cup. Even though it was June, the morning was still chilly and I wiggled my toes in my cowboy boots to get them warm, and tucked my neckerchief inside my shirt to keep in the body heat.

Someone sat down beside me, and of course, it was the spook.

"How about some coffee?" I asked. "Seeing as how no one else will offer you any?"

"I'd like some," Corley said. "It's chilly this morning."

I got him a cup and we sat there watching the gaffer direct the grips as they moved the lights around. "It's silly as hell," I said. "A film unit takes all the trouble to go on location, and then they waste days, and thousands of dollars moving things around and re-lighting the great outdoors so it'll look as if it were filmed in a studio."

"That'll change," he said. "One day they'll be out on location with hand-held cameras, and battery-operated tape recorders, and no lights at all."

"Too bad I won't live to see it, huh?" I said. He didn't answer. "So how are things with the Great American movie script?"

"Moving," he said. "Only it runs around six hours long, and I don't have the slightest idea where to start cutting."

"My heart bleeds for you," I said. "But I guess that's not enough, is it? You've got to hang around and wait for the real blood. That'll be what it takes to finish up your script in style, right? Where do I get it, Corley? In the bull ring? You know I'm scheduled to fight in Tijuana on the Fourth of July? There? Or in the Porsche, blowing a right front at eighty and rolling off the road? Or how about the cycle? Everybody says they're dangerous. Or maybe some six-foot rattler'll nail me out here on location. If so, maybe they'll keep the cameras rolling and get it all on film like they did with that poor bastard in *Chicken Run.* How about it, amigo?"

He sipped his coffee and said nothing.

"Goddamn it," I yelled, "you're just like a woman! It's pulling teeth to get a straight answer out of you!"

306

"Johnny, you don't want a straight answer."

"How the hell do you know?"

"Look," he said, "I'm sorry it's wearing thin for you. But it's almost over. The script is practically finished."

"And just what does that mean for me? That I'm practically finished, too?"

He didn't answer. I rammed my face up close to his.

"Well, you hear this good, old buddy. I think you're full of it, do you know what I mean? I don't think you know everything that's going to happen. I don't believe that everything is carved in stone, impossible to change. If you knew everything, you wouldn't have to sit around like some big-assed bird, croaking out your goddamned silly questions. I don't know why I ever let you spook me. And from now on I won't, no more, my friend. You have worn out your welcome around here. Don't let me see you again, do you understand? You got your nose busted back here once, how would you like to try for a punctured liver?"

The assistant director came over and said, "Hey, Johnny, we're ready for the barroom sequence."

"Be right with you," I said. I turned to give the spook another couple of shots, but of course he was gone.

Texas finished shooting on the morning of July 2nd. That was the morning my father turned up on the set.

"Hello, John Calvin," he said.

"Hi," I said. "What brings you here?" We were about ready to wrap, with only one long shot of me riding a carriage down the street left to do.

"I don't know," he said. "I just felt like I ought to see you. Don't ask me why. I don't know any reason, except I *am* your father."

"Excuse me," I said, as Hank waved me out into the street.

307

We did the scene and although it went perfectly the first time, we did a second take for safety, and then Sam Merridith began firing an ancient six-shooter into the air and the film was finished.

"Amazing," said my father. "Is there always so much noise?"

"No," I said, "this is special. That was the last shot of the film. It's like, oh, a celebration. We've been tied up to this bastard for the past four months. It's the same as getting out of prison."

"I didn't understand," he said. "There's so much work to making a picture. I guess I never thought about it enough."

"Come on," I said. "I'll buy you a drink."

"I'll buy *you* one," he said.

We headed down to the Silver Saddle, a joint I liked because no one in there had ever passed a word about my being in the movies. I had my own bottle there, with my name on it, Texas style, because in that state you can't buy a drink over the bar. My father and I had a couple and the tension eased a little.

"John," he said after a while, "when I get back to California, I'd like to see more of you. If it won't upset you."

"It won't upset me," I said. "I've been thinking the same thing myself. But what do you mean, when you get back? Where are you going?"

"To the Mayo Clinic," he said.

"Up in Minnesota? What the hell are you going way up there for? What's wrong?"

He took another swallow of his drink before answering. "I've got this tumor," he said. "My doctor figured the docs at Mayo ought to have a look at it."

I hit my hand on the table and broke the glass in my fingers. "Goddamn!" I said. "Goddamn it all to hell!"

He held out his handkerchief and I wrapped my fingers in it.

The blood came slowly; the cut was a slight one. Something nudged at my brain. Where had this happened before? When?

"Don't go on like that, son," he said. "I've got a long time yet. You'll see."

"Why the hell did we both wait so long?" I asked, choking on a lump in my throat. "What was more important? Oh, shit! Do you need any money or anything? Anything?"

"Nothing that I ain't got now," he said. "I'm glad you took time to see me, boy. You'll see. Everything will work out."

"Yeah," I said. "It has to. For Christ's sake, they owe it to us."

We had a couple more drinks, and then I drove him to the airport for the next plane out. He stood on the ramp and waved back and I waved too and felt the hot tears flood my eyes as the C-47 taxied down the runway on the first lap of my father's journey to Rochester, Minnesota.

I went back to the apartment to pack, and knew instantly as I entered that Jeannie had already gone. The rooms had an empty, hollow quality and in spite of the July heat, they were cold and dismal. The note was on the pillow and said simply, "Johnny, dear: Don't follow me. I am glad that you were able to see things as they really are, and now it's my time to try. But you can't help me in this battle. It's my own, and I've been putting it off since I left Cedartown. God bless you, you little monster. I'll never forget you." It was sighed with a slashing "J."

Picking up the phone, I called Marilyn MacArthur.

"Honey, it's lonely over here," I said. "Why don't you come on over and we'll have a ball."

"Gee, honey, I'd like to," she said, "but Sam and I are flying to Dallas tonight. You won't say anything, will you? He doesn't want his wife to know."

"No, baby," I said. "I won't say anything. Have a good time."

On the early morning flight to Los Angeles, I tried to be excited about the fight tomorrow in Tijuana. It was all set: Gabino's recommendation had counted for me in the assignments to the fighting card. I was to fight third on a card of seven newcomers. Gabino would be at my side everywhere except in the ring.

I'd phoned ahead, and the Harley would be waiting at the airport. Three hours down to Mexico, a leisurely evening with Gabino, some last-minute practice in the morning, and then, at four in the afternoon, the moment of truth. Would I fight well? Would I let my fear get the better of me? Would I find the courage and strength to use this defiance of horned death to shape my own life into a more sensible pattern?

Hank had shipped my baggage back to the studio. With me I had only my recently fitted torero's costume and a change of underwear, all crammed into a leather saddlebag. It rested under my seat, near my heel.

The stewardess was another one with the black bangs and large, staring eyes. We made the usual double-meaning conversation, and she got all agog when I told her I was going down to Mexico to fight a bull. Naturally, she agreed to fly down on Western Airlines in the morning, using her free courtesy card, to watch me in the ring.

"Check into the El Presidente," I told her. "I'll see you after the fight."

"It'll be late," she said. "I guess I'd better figure on staying over."

"Guess you might as well," I said, grinning up at her. She smiled back, and we landed, and I was halfway out of the terminal before I realized that I had not even bothered to get this one's name.

I shrugged and said to myself, "What the hell?" If she came, I'd know her name soon enough. And if she didn't . . . well, Gabino would know where the action in Tijuana was.

I went out to the bar and ordered a beer. Things were going to work out all right after all. I *knew*. We were on the track at last. When I got to the hotel, I would call my father in Minnesota. If there was anything money could do, he would have it. I would call Uncle Ray, too, and see if I could bring Dad home for a long visit, and the three of us would stalk the broom grass in the fields and try to scare up a quail or two for Miss Mary to cook. As for the rest of it, the films and everything, what the hell? It would come out one way or the other. Either way, I wasn't worried.

As I stood, a hand caught my arm and pulled me back onto the stool. It was the spook.

"Some other time, man," I said. "I'm in a hurry."

"No you're not," Corley said. "Have a martini."

"Not now. I've got to ride. I don't need one of those things on an empty stomach."

"You might as well drink it," he said. "You're not riding anywhere."

"Like hell I'm not. I'm due in Tijuana tonight. See you around."

"Okay," he said. "But I think you're going to have a hell of a time starting your bike."

"What's that supposed to mean?"

He held up his hand. "Ever see one of these before?"

I looked at the piece of metal in his hand. "That looks like a magneto rotor."

"It is. That's the rotor out of your Harley." He dropped it to the floor and ground it under his heel.

"What are you doing?"

"You're not hitting the road today, Johnny. Not on that Harley, anyway."

"Why not?"

Corley sighed. "You got me off the fence. What you said in Texas sank in. Maybe things aren't cast in stone. I don't know. But I've got to try."

"Thanks," I said. "Look, I really mean that. But I'm not worried any more. Jesus, man, what a crazy time these past few years have been, with you looking over my shoulder every time I turned around. It all happened too fast, you know what I mean? But I'm on the track now, and if you want to come along, you'd better move, because I'm on my way."

He followed me out to the parking lot. "Listen to me," he said, "I disabled your bike because I had to stop you from riding it down the coast. If you had, that would have been it. Today was the day, Johnny."

"What day?"

"The day you ran head-on into a bridge abutment at a Palm City exit of the freeway, down near San Diego. So now all that's changed. I don't know what will happen next. My knowledge ends right here. Maybe when I wake up, there won't even be any *Johnny Lewis Story* to be filmed because Johnny Lewis is an old fart of forty who's too busy chasing teeny-boppers to take time out to authorize a screen biography. Who knows? But one thing's for sure—you're not riding any Harleys today."

We were at my bike now. I opened one of the saddle bags and took out the parts kit. The spare rotor was next to the extra plugs. I put it in the magneto, snapped the top shut, and straddled the machine.

"Johnny!" Corley yelled. "You can't."

I leaned forward and said softly, "You've been telling me that maybe things can be changed. Well, they *are* changed. And I'm going to Tijuana now. Do you want to come along?"

He hesitated, and I laughed. "What's the matter, spook? Chicken? You dish it out all right, but you're afraid to take it?"

312

The Harley settled under his weight. "What the hell?" he said. "I guess we were always headed for this moment."

"Hang on," I said, and let out the clutch. The big bike burned rubber and we headed for the freeway.

The flight had tired me, but I still felt good. As the cycle unwound the miles down the coast, I was almost dozing and the world was warm and happy. I didn't push it. There was plenty of time. After hurrying so long and so far, I suddenly realized how much time there was after all.

Just outside Disneyland, a truck cut me off. I almost slammed into him as I braked. We skittered down the freeway, cut inside on the shoulder and ran on the dirt for a few hundred yards, then I was past him and wound up the throttle again and listened to the exhaust pinging off the flat buildings that lined the road. I glanced over my shoulder. The spook was trying to look unconcerned, but his face was white. The wind ripped at his hair, and brought tears to his eyes.

When we passed Capistrano, where the swallows had been and gone, I pulled over by the side of the road.

"Let's stretch," I said. Down below the ocean was calm and blue and went on so far that it hurt my eyes.

"You know," I told Corley, "I'm going to call Diana. I mean, Sharon. And Fleming, too. I'm not mad any more. It was better the way it finally worked out. I was all wrong for her."

"Maybe you were," he said slowly. "But you might be right for her now."

I shrugged. "Shit, buddy, there's another Sharon somewhere else, just waiting. I mean, there *has* to be."

We got on the bike and I wound it up again. At sixty, the engine's song thrummed in my ears. I wondered if the stewardess I'd met on the flight would be waiting. I hoped not.

The hours passed in the hazy afternoon. When the mountains were close on my left, and the blue sea was almost directly under my right hand, gauntletted and tight on the throttle handle, Corley tapped my shoulder.

"Slow down," he said.

I did and glanced at him questioningly. He pointed to a green and white sign ahead.

NEXT 3 EXITS, PALM CITY, it read.

We crept along at thirty, past the three Palm City exits. Then they were behind us. I felt Corley shift his weight, and thought I heard him give a heavy sigh.

"Okay," he said. "Everything's okay."

I let the red needle move up toward the peg again. Then, just as I turned half around to yell, "How's your ass holding out?" a big Greyhound bus came around a curve on the wrong side of the road, air horn blasting as it tried to avoid a little Volkswagen that was peddling along at around twenty. I jinked a little to miss them both, and I did, and then I came into the slipstream of the bus, and even that might have been all right but I hit a big patch of oil and the bike skidded. A bridge abutment was coming up fast and I was running out of road and brakes, and everything was in slow motion so I had plenty of time to read the big green and white sign that said:

PALM CITY—TEMPORARY EXIT.

I laid down the Harley and tried to ride it like a carpet, but it got away from me and there was a tremendous, blinding flash inside my head, and I thought, *What a lousy shame,* and there came a puff of flame, and that was all.

.

EPILOGUE

THERE was a curious smell of burning oil in my nostrils as I awoke in my hotel room and found the mattress aflame. I grabbed the phone and yelled, "There's a fire up here!" and then filled the waste basket in the shower and dumped it on the smouldering mattress, refilled it and dumped again.

A pass key turned in the lock and two men rushed in with a fire extinguisher. They sprayed it all over the mattress.

I looked out the window. The sun was up and my watch said it was a little after eight. While the men were dragging the mattress out into the hall, I got into my clothes. I said, "I don't know what happened. I must have gone to sleep with a cigarette burning. I'm sorry. Put it on my bill." And I went down in the elevator and walked along the wide sidewalk of Central Park South.

People were hurrying to work. The day was bright and clear

and it seemed as if the fog and the miseries of early Spring were finally over.

I knew *mine* were. The events of the past weeks had faded, just as an untreated proof photograph, sharp and clear at first, will recede and vanish. I even whistled as I strode along the path by the lake. The ending of the screenplay was firmly in my mind. I knew I would finish the job today. The uncertainty that had gripped me so often was gone.

Johnny was gone too, I knew. I would never see him—or dream of him—again. I had reached the place where "The End" fades up over the scene. Now the cult would be born, the Johnny Lewis legend would grow until I would find myself examining his life and wondering what was truth and what was fantasy.

The scavengers would pillage his grave, as they were intended to do. Small life masks of Johnny would sell for $30 or even $50 each, to wind up on some tearful teenager's bed table. And when that teenager became thirty years old? The mask would go into the attic limbo, to be rediscovered by younger sisters who would start the cycle again. Bits of metal from the flaming motorcycle would be sold in such quantity that the Harley-Davidson would have had to have been as large as a Boeing 707.

Although, in his will, Johnny requested burial in the little country cemetery beside his mother, his wishes were ignored and the Centerville main cemetery would be his final shrine, and even there, souvenir ghouls would sneak in under cover of darkness and chip away at his tombstone for bits of marble to be sealed in plastic and sold at inflated prices.

Naturally, Johnny's inconvenient death caused some problems for the studios. Just as in the case of Rudolph Valentino's death in 1926, with *Son of the Sheik* still unreleased, B.J. Fleming and Sam Merridith had to face the unpleasant fact that their star was dead and the chances were good that his last two pictures would be also unless something was done to keep the public's interest alive.

Johnny's father would have nothing to do with plans for a circus funeral, and so John Calvin Lewis was quietly interred in the Centerville Cemetery on July 9, 1955. B.J. Fleming was present; Mrs. Fleming was not. Mrs. Jerome Newman was present; Mr. Newman was not. Gabino Armaderiz did not attend the funeral, but arrived after the crowd had gone and, kneeling, draped a small red muleta over the marble stone. Bert Klen and Tony Warden were both at the funeral and then went downtown and got distressingly drunk, but the police were understanding and took them home in a squad car. Jerry Conklin was too busy to attend, but sent a magnificent flower spray.

Sandra Vidor immediately established contact with the dead actor and, two months after his death, her *Conversations with John Calvin Lewis* hit the paperback bestseller list. Her book was billed, "as told to Ira Winton," and the press agent must have taken his share and gone to Tibet, because since then no one has ever heard a word from him, including his second wife.

On Christmas of 1955, Maggie McBride made a trip out to Iowa and visited Johnny's grave, joining the thousands who still make the pilgrimage, although no "lady in black" has yet come forth as did for Valentino.

Between the drumbeating and the honest affection of the movie fans for the Johnny they knew, both films were released and made money. In fact, they are still making money. The recent Schaefer Award Theater screening of *Paradise Gate* in New York City outdrew all the competing shows, including a New York TV premiere of a recent Marlon Brando film. Fan mail, most of it addressed to B. J. Fleming's Argos Studios, still runs a thousand letters a month, and requests for autographed pictures come in every day.

In 1956, Johnny was nominated for a posthumous Academy Award, and in 1957, again. In both cases, the Academy of Motion Picture Arts and Sciences withheld the award, perhaps feeling that studio manipulations were behind the nominations. But in 1956, France awarded him the French Film Academy's highest honor, the Crystal Star, and in 1958 the Hollywood Foreign Press Association voted him "The World's Favorite Film Actor." This was three years after his death.

So it was no wonder now that Ned Barker felt there was money to be made with Johnny's film biography. Although the frantic teen-agers who had adored him were now solid citizens in their thirties, each and every year new rebels come along, new kids to discover Johnny for the first time. And Ned Barker knew that their discovery would add up to nice jingling sounds at the box office.

Maybe that was good, maybe it was bad. Perhaps the world isn't supposed to turn just so the Ned Barkers can make a quick buck. But anyway, for better or for worse, he would soon have his script.

I hated myself a little as I walked there in the park, enjoying the first real sunshine of the year. I had invaded the world of John Calvin Lewis more deeply than I had any right. No one can survive the kind of scrutiny I had given him.

But he was still my hero; slightly tarnished, perhaps, yet uniquely, unforgettably special in a world that is accustomed to second best. Hedda Hopper was right when she said his kind come along so seldom that we cannot afford to lose them. In the years since Johnny died, his replacement has yet to arrive, and it may be that he never will.

I stopped at the coffee shop in the bottom of the General Motors building and ordered Danish and coffee. When it came,

I fished in my pockets and tossed the only coin I found there onto the counter.

"That's a silver dollar, mister," said the waitress.

I looked at it. She was right. It was an uncirculated Morgan one dollar piece with the date 1879 embossed on its edge. What, I wondered, was I doing with a silver dollar? You don't see them much anymore.

"Don't you want to keep it?" she asked.

I didn't want to break a ten, so I said, "That's all right. I don't really want it. It's not important, anyway."

By the time I finished my breakfast the day was warmer, and I slipped out of my jacket as I started back to the hotel. I knew it would take only about two pages to finish up and then I could call up Dick Fowler and we would get blasted on martinis, because one way or the other, April had run out its allotted time and the story of John Calvin Lewis was finally over.